STALIN VERSUS ME

DONALD JACK

The Bandy Papers

Three Cheers For Me
That's Me in the Middle
It's Me Again
(containing *It's Me Again* and *Me Among the Ruins*)
Me Bandy, You Cissie
Me Too
This One's On Me
Me So Far
Hitler Versus Me
Stalin Versus Me

First published 2005 by Sybertooth Inc.
59 Salem Street
Sackville, NB
E4L 4J6
Canada

This book is printed on acid-free paper.
ISBN-10: 0-9688024-7-8 / ISBN-13: 978-0-9688024-7-2

Library and Archives Canada Cataloguing in Publication

Jack, Donald, 1924-2003
Stalin versus me / Donald Jack.

(The Bandy papers ; v. 9)
ISBN 0-9688024-7-8

I. Title. II. Series.

PS8519.A3S72 2005 C813'.54 C2005-904733-X

STALIN VERSUS ME

Being the Ninth and Final Volume of the Bandy Papers

DONALD JACK

SYBERTOOTH INC
SACKVILLE, NEW BRUNSWICK

Litteris Elegantis Madefimus

Publisher's Foreword

MORE THAN FORTY YEARS HAVE PASSED since Bandy was first unleashed upon the world, in 1962. The real veterans of the Great War have now dwindled in number until only a handful remain. As they go, knowledge of that war passes out of living memory. And yet Bandy, and his misadventures in and between the First and Second World Wars, remain as compelling today as when Donald Jack first imagined them decades ago. The Bandy of fiction was, of course, loved only by a few friends, and loathed or dismissed by practically everyone else. In this Bandy shares a fate with many of his fellow Canadians who, because they have perversely chosen to reject the establishment, receive the worst of all insults — they are ignored by their countrymen, and forced to seek recognition abroad. To an extent, the Bandy series has had a similar experience, at least from the eighties onward, and Donald Jack himself received "shameful treatment", as theatre critic Nathan Cohen put it, from the Canadian theatrical community, which never gave his plays the respect they deserved, despite their success. Perhaps the Canadian literary establishment has never acknowledged humour as a legitimate art; orthodoxy always despises laughter, after all. Like so many other insular, committee-minded cliques, it may simply lack a sense of humour. It certainly disregards what it doesn't understand, and re-forges words to cast itself as "literary" while all others are relegated to "genre" status. Possibly Bandy is just too likeable a hero for a time that adores the powerful and the sentimental, while looking only at its heroes' clay feet. Whatever the reason, it's certainly the case that Donald Jack has received less than his due by way of acclaim. Even *Bandy* received a knighthood, after all.

In *Stalin vs. Me* we see an older, lonelier Bandy. Time has robbed him of friends, fortunes, wives, and family. His country has become a foreign place that he has had occasion to flee from and to, but which neither welcomes him, nor offers him any opportunities. The world of the mid-1940s was a more populist, but also a more brutal one than that of 1916. There were no more knights of the air; instead there were V-2 ballistic missiles, and fleets of bombers that could lay waste to entire cities. And worse, there were atrocities more horrific than even the wholesale slaughter of the Great War trenches. Contentment, as we have seen over the previous eight volumes of the series, has been something Bandy only fleetingly achieved in a lifetime of war, struggle, and disappointment, so he can perhaps be forgiven for surrendering to despair and self-pity at times. But Bandy needs only great adversaries to shake him out of his funks, his lifelong philosophy being *if I can't please myself, I can at least displease my enemies*.

At the time of Donald Jack's death in 2003, the manuscript of *Stalin vs. Me*, while a complete draft, was still being edited and revised, and so readers should perhaps bear in mind that Jack would no doubt have continued to re-write and improve the book had he had the chance. They will notice that, in addition to Jack's footnotes, there are also some by our editor, as well as an editorial afterword. In a curious way, this hearkens back to the original Bandy book, *Three Cheers for Me* (before it was revised in 1973) since in the 1962 version Jack pretended, more explicitly, to having discovered and edited the "journals". The editorial intrusions in later versions and volumes consisted only of the occasional footnote, but in that first version's introduction there are details of the history of the journals, along with a little biographical information on the hero himself, which subsequently changed: Bandy, then, was said to have died with his wife in an air accident in 1934, his papers only re-emerging in 1956, after which Donald Jack somehow obtained and edited them. Sadly, the loss of Donald Jack has made it necessary for someone else to take up the task of editing his final Bandy manuscript. A discussion of the process by which this version of the book emerged can be found in the editor's afterword. Also, after the afterword, you can find a glossary of military slang, medals, foreign words, acronyms, and persons mentioned in *Stalin vs. Me*.

And now, for everyone who loves Bandy, one last adventure.

Chris Paul
July 2005

STALIN VERSUS ME

PART ONE

BACK IN HOSPITAL

I EXPERIENCED SEVERAL UNSETTLING DREAMS while I was in hospital in England in 1944, recovering from a trip to France, when the Gestapo became a tad irritated by my reluctance to tell them the date of the D-day landings.* The worst nightmare was the one involving George Garanine and Serge Ossipov. I had first met Garanine in Moscow way back in 1919 while I was on parole as a prisoner of war. Formerly one of Trotsky's aides, George was supposed to keep his eye on me at all times, but a mixture of excessive tolerance and even more excessive indolence made him rather an incompetent watchdog. He was so warm-hearted and sympathetic a fellow I could never decide whether I loved or detested him, or whether I was just jealous of his wonderfully good looks.

Anyway, I dreamed that I was back in Moscow with the blighter and his relatives in the requisitioned house off the Petrovska Ulitsa. One moment I was being roasted on a spit by his ghastly family, one of whom turned into the Petrograd spy, Ossipov, who kept prodding me with a toasting fork to see if I was done. The next moment a deeply concerned George Garanine was offering me platefuls of pirozhki, and assuring me of his undying affection and respect, whilst treating me to an unending supply of typical Russians proverbs such as, *He who is unwilling to take risks is not advised to leap into the Mikhail Pazelski gorge*, or *A fly cannot land on the ceiling the right way up*. In my dreams, even the proverbs were terrible.

Actually, there was much more reason for Ossipov to figure in the nightmares, for his story had dominated much of my life. He was a former Tsarist agent whose outfit, the Okhranka, had been taken over by its successor, the Cheka. One day, skunk drunk, he let me into the world's greatest secret: the fact that up to the October Revolution, Josef Stalin had collaborated with the Okhranka for his own ends; for instance, he had got rid of a Bolshevik rival or two by denouncing them to the Tsarist police. Ossipov clamed to have proof of this in the form

* As related in *Hitler vs. Me*, *The Bandy Papers* Vol. VIII. — Ed.

of a few pages snitched from an Okhranka dossier. Suspecting that Ossipov — and I — knew this explosive secret, Stalin had Ossipov liquidated. Fortunately, I was out of reach in Canada by then, though still in a modicum of danger. Giving in to his paranoia, as he invariably did even if it took twenty years, Stalin sent George Garanine to Canada with orders to liquidate me, assuming that I hadn't already been taken care of by the Prime Minister, Mr. Mackenzie King, who had his own reasons to hate me, but was short of gulags and firing squads. But George, whose gentleness and decency were in direct proportion to his indolence, could not bring himself to harm me, even though a failure to do so would probably doom his entire family. The last time I saw George was in Ottawa, when he confessed the purpose of his mission to Canada, but announced that he had decided not to kill me after all. He would go back to the USSR and sacrifice himself on behalf of his relatives. I had pointed out that, knowing the Bolshies, his relatives were probably doomed anyway. Nevertheless he affirmed his determination to sacrifice himself. This was typical of George, the stupid bastard.*

Anyway, here I was, all these years later, dreaming about the blighter. Why? No doubt convalescence had something to do with it. In the Kent hospital, it was hard to decide which was worse, the behaviour of the doctors in their appalling indifference to the grave injury to my foot, which would take days to recover, or the unbearable cruelty of the nurses in their determination to keep me clean and tidy, inside and out. In addition, I was under emotional and physical pressure, from Guinevere Plumley and the bed I was lying in. The latter discomfort, brought about by a threatened visit from some bigwig or other — who never actually turned up — was particularly effective that morning. The bed was treating me as if it had joined the Gestapo. The spotless top sheet that pinioned my arms had been turned down the regulation fourteen inches and tucked in so firmly that it was only by stiffening a few sinews and summoning up some blood that I managed to force one shoulder free of the hospital corners and other clamps, though I was pretty dishevelled by the time I had escaped the linen stronghold to limp panting to the window, to keep watch so I'd know when Guinevere arrived.

As a senior officer I'd been awarded a whole window to myself, through which, squinching my eyes against the July sun, I was just in time to see Guinevere's second-hand Wolseley shudder to a halt at the

* See *Me Too*, Volume V of *The Bandy Papers*. — Ed.

front portico of the hospital. Only it was not she who was the first to emerge from the car but another piece of bad news in the form of Air Vice-Marshal Oliver Chistelow, AFC — the man who had presided over the court of enquiry into my theft of a de Havilland Mosquito fighter-bomber. I hoped they weren't both coming to see me. Guinevere was bad enough, but putting up with Chistelow as well .... Maybe he was bringing the results of the enquiry. Probably. He would enjoy delivering it, the bastard.

However, I had more immediate worries on my mind: Miss Guinevere Plumley, a dedicated employee of the British security services, and even more dedicated sex-maniac, on one of her dreaded visits. There she was now, swivelling just a little ungracefully out of the driver's seat, showing off her garters in the process. Normally one would not have minded viewing that stretch of limb. Her legs, like the rest of her figure, were quite perfect; almost perfect enough to make up for her marvellous, dreadful face, which she had borrowed from one of the Gorgon sisters, or all three of them.

Leaving the car parked at a slight angle and nearly two feet from the curb at the main entrance, she linked arms with the air vice-marshal, and the two of them disappeared under the grey granite portico of the hospital.

Uttering a moan that was far from yearning, I stood jittering at the window on one foot, staring out with haunted eyes, trying to decide what to do. Damn her. She'd probably brought me a present. She was always bringing me presents. Like the new watch I was wearing, to replace the one lost a few weeks ago in Normandy, just before the D-day landings. And these ivory pyjamas I was wearing — they were a gift from Gwinny as well. *And* this white dressing gown, which looked like it was owned by a pernickity pathologist. Into which I was now struggling, whilst lurching about as if one of my legs was shorter than the other — which was probably the case, after the surgeons had finished teasing out all the redundant muscle tissue.

As if things weren't bad enough, now Nurse Killy was entering the private room — barging the door open with a mighty, sashaying hip, her Hibernian mitts burdened with a stainless steel tray laden with unguents, swabs, fresh bandages, and steel dishes filled with hospital smells. She laid the tray aside and placed her hands on her hips.

"And whhhere d'you think you're going?" she said, with what she probably thought of as mock-severity, but which to me was as genuine as her biceps. "Get back into bed this minute, young man." Anyone under the age of eighty was likely to be addressed by her as 'young man'.

"Tchk, and just look what you've done to my hospital corners! Come on, in you get, so I can repair the damage before matron sees it. Where d'you think you're going anyway?"

"It's Miss Plumley," I gibbered. "She's just arrived. Saw her out the window."

"And desperate you are to welcome her with open arms is it?" said Nurse Killy, who knew perfectly well that I had come to dread Gwinny's visits. "Very understandable, Group Captain. All the same, this will never do, with matron due at any minute. So you get back in there, or oy won't be bringing you your jelly and custard, begorrah."

For a moment I forgot to be terrified. "Begorrah? Do the Irish really say that?"

"Not really. I picked it up in the English music halls. Come on, now — in you get."

"Listen, you gotta help me, Killy. She's trying to take over my entire life," I whined, backing away. "When she finds out I'm being discharged tomorrow, she may try to take me home," I whimpered. "You haven't seen her home, Killy, it's fully of secret passages and all the floors slope at forty-five degrees. Come on, be a pal and hide me somewhere 'til she's gone. No need to worry, Killy, I'll be safely back in bed by the time matron sobers up," I wheedled, sweating in the summer heat. "Come on, where can I hide?"

The prodigious nurse was not unsympathetic — Guinevere tended to treat her as if she were socially on a level with a bedpan. She informed me severely that she would be back in a while, and if I wasn't in bed by then there would be hell to pay from 'the au'torities'. However, she seemed to be hinting that 'a while' might be long enough to give me a chance to find a good hidey-hole, so as soon as she withdrew I withdrew, too, into the hospital corridor, which boasted linoleum polished to a fine skiddy sheen and skirting boards that were parting from the walls under the pressure of all the stuff collecting behind them: dust, fluff, dead skin, toenail clippings, and toffee wrappers. Passing a couple of airmen in their convalescent red and bright blue gear, I limped toward the elevator, intending to skulk in one of the bathrooms on another floor. There was an anxious wait — "Come on, come on!" – – before the palsied apparatus arrived, and the door reluctantly rattled aside.

But by the time I had entered and was being carried, shuddering, toward the bathrooms on the second floor, I had second thoughts. Dammit, at my age, fifty years old at last count, surely I had enough guts to tell Gwinny that it was all over between us; that my feeling for her had boiled away like spit on a hot stove. It wasn't my fault that her feeling for me had gotten out of hand to the point where she was now hinting that one day all this could be mine if I was prepared to marry her; 'all this' amounting to a vegetable garden, a decrepit manor house, two sharp scythes, and an old Wolseley.

No, it was time I faced up to her. Darn it, I was a man, wasn't I, not a horse to be ridden into the sunset by the wheedling spurs of her devotion. By George, I would do it! I would tell her it was all over between us. I would have it out with her. Today. Right now. Definitely.

The elevator had also come to a similar decision. Reaching the second floor, it had wondered whether to open the doors or not. After a while, it decided. The doors parted, to reveal an anxious-looking chap in a white cap and gown.

"Ah, there you are at last," he exclaimed. And then, looking uncertainly at my white gown, "It is Mr ...?"

"Bandy," I supplied.

"Ah, yes ... I think that was the name ..."

"It's definitely the name," I said. "Bandy."

"Ah. We were getting quite, uh ... I'm Willing, by the way."

"Uh, willing to do what?"

"We've been waiting for you, for ... Do hurry, old man. She's all prepped and ready."

"Uh," I said again, as he took my arm and hurried me along a pure white corridor. A change from the usual green walls, I thought, as we proceeded into another white room gleaming with stainless steel thingamyjigs. I thought for a moment that it was kitchen, when he led me worriedly to a sink.

"I'll have to start again, now," he was muttering, as he turned on the tap with his elbow. Then, noting a certain hesitation in my demeanour: "Do hurry up, Mr ... Bandy, was it? Someone could come along at any moment."

He seemed to want me to scrub my hands, even though they were perfectly clean. I'd washed them that very morning. Still, I went along with his fussy hygiene, while continuing to look around wonderingly. There was a large window in one wall. Through the window I could see a table. Stretched out on the table was a form, covered in white cloth.

So. Not a kitchen after all. Hospital mortuary, was it? Were they so short of staff they were getting the patients to help out? Somebody must have told them that I had medical experience. But that was quite a while ago, at the University of Toronto in 1915. The war must really have taken a turn for the worse, eh?

"It's a post?" I asked.

"What?"

"You want me to help? A PM?"

"PM? No, right away. This morning."

"What?"

"Look, do hurry, old man. You know the situation. We only have a few minutes," Mr. Willing said. For by then I had guessed that Willing was his name rather than an indication of his helpfulness. Though he seemed to me a bit disoriented, the way he kept looking at the clock on the wall, almost as if he feared it were connected to a time bomb.

Or was it I who was disoriented, after my decision to face up to Guinevere? Yes, I suppose I was a trifle disoriented, possibly through a case of mistaken identity. Which had happened quite a few times in my life, strangely enough not always on purpose, either. All the same, I hoped they weren't *really* expecting me to do the cutting, especially that first slash from breast to groin. When I was a medical student that first cut had always made me wince and twist as if it were my breast and groin.

But if this was a mortuary, why were they applying a surgical mask? For now, following an irritated gesture from Mr. Willing, a nurse with grey hair escaping from her cap was tying a surgical mask to my face. But you didn't usually wear masks in the mortuary, did you — unless for some mysterious reason they didn't want you to be recognized. Maybe that was it. They didn't want me to be recognized. Which was fine with me. I didn't want to be recognized either, specially by Guinevere, not to mention Air Vice-Marshal Chistelow.

Now the nurse with the tufts of grey hair was leading the way into the room beyond the glass window where the body was laid out. The room was more like an operating theatre than your typical mortuary .... At which point, rather belatedly, perhaps, I decided I had better make the position abundantly clear: that I had not done any cutting since those few months at the Moscow University way back there in the, when was it, the nineteen-twenties, was it?*

So I turned determinedly toward Mr. Willing, and was just about to explain that I might just possibly be a bit rusty in the thorax and entrails department, and besides I was a patient, and was he sure he hadn't mistaken me for someone else, when I stopped dead at the sight of the cadaver. It wasn't one at all. It was a woman. Not that women couldn't be cadavers, but this one was alive. A very pretty girl, actually, and not

---

* See *Me Bandy, You Cissie*, Vol. IV of *The Bandy Papers*. — Ed.

only not dead but wide awake, and with her private parts gone public. Lying there, shamelessly exposing herself for all to see.

Even as I stared, open-mouthed beneath the mask, the nurse proceeded to adjust the girl's limbs in stirrups in the classic position for a pelvic examination. And now she was readjusting the disposable cloths so as to expose a little less of her pubic region — the girl's, that is, not hers, the nurse's, if you follow me. Not being of a peeping-tom disposition, I turned away to look at the nearby surgical tray. It held scissors, sterile gauze, speculum, graduated cylinders and the like. I finally understood what was going on. It appeared that I had been mistaken not for the surgeon or the pathologist, but for the anaesthesiologist. I realized this because Mr. Willing was now urging me, nay, positively pushing me northward so to speak, toward the other end of the patient, where the anaesthetic paraphernalia had been rather hurriedly laid out.

In the process of taking up this position, I received a frightened stare from a pair of baby-blue eyes. Perhaps my grown-up deep brown equivalents looked equally apprehensive, for on locking horns with them so to speak, the girl looked more frightened than ever, especially when I picked up the semi-circular mesh thingamy through which the ether was to be poured. Except that it was labelled as chloroform.

"You're using chloroform?" I asked disapprovingly.

"Yes, yes," Mr. Willing said distractedly.

"Tchk," I said. "I thought that nowadays they used ether rather than chloroform. Assuming, of course that they used either or ether, or do I mean ether or either?"

They were still looking at me when another white-gowned figure peered into the operating room and said jauntily, "Sorry I'm late, chaps. Had to fob off old Allington. Thinks I'm off to clean the cystoscopes."

He stopped as he saw me at the head of the table, holding a bottle of chloroform. "Hello," he said.

"Hello."

He stared a moment longer before turning to Mr. Willing, who had already positioned himself at the far end of the patient. He said, "You're the surgeon are you? Mr. Willing, isn't it?"

"Uh," Willing began, stopped, then started again. "Well, yes. Who are you?" he asked.

"Who am I?"

"Yes, who are you?"

"Look here, are you trying to fob me off?"

"Fob you off?"

"I was told there was a little discreet work for an anaesthetist down here. You haven't got someone else to do the job, have you? Just because I'm a minute late?"

The new arrival took a moment off to glare at me, then turned back to the surgeon, lowered his voice, and said darkly, "You still have to pay me, you know. I've taken enough risks over this."

Mr. Willing gazed at him blankly. I thought I could see his face reddening through the mask. At which point I spoke up. "Look here," I said in my most authoritative voice, recently learned at the senior officers' school, "there seems to be some confusion here. However, to save embarrassment," I said, turning to the newcomer, "if you were the first choice to do the anaesthesia, of course you must go right ahead," I said, making for the exit. "I'm quite content to move out of the picture," I concluded. And, with the surgeon staring at me over his pink-tinged mask and the new man also staring, and the lady with the tufts, I sidled out of the picture, and limped heavily along the corridor. I arrived back at the elevator completely unharmed, confident that Willing was not likely to pursue the matter. He would probably not wish to publicise the fact that he was performing a clandestine abortion. Especially in a military hospital.

LOOKING HAUNTED

HOPING THAT BY NOW GUINEVERE would have given up waiting for me and gone back to London to continue the work of safeguarding the nation's interests by pouncing on potential spies and other malcontents, reading people's letters, tapping their telephones, and hectoring honest, sincere, dignified and utterly patriotic aviators despite the sufferings such flying gentlemen might have undergone, as symbolized by their well-deserved wound stripes, and despite the dazzling awards and badges on faultless blue uniforms drenched in stars, bars, crowns, and chevrons, and various other jewelled insignia, not to mention hosts of wings, rings, and ribbons, that could compete even with the most recently outfitted military conscript in the U.S. Army — hectoring and bullying, I say, even glorious and distinguished pilots about whom not the slightest doubt as to their patriotism, reliability, and moral and political steadfastness could ever be entertained despite any misunderstandings that might have arisen following absurd suspicions in regard to any treasons, stratagems, and spoils, that might have ....

Where was I? Oh, yes, I was ascending to the third floor, and stepping out of the lift/hoist/elevator on my way back to my room; which was where I caught sight of Air Vice-Marshal Oliver Chistelow. He was just emerging from my room, and, worse still, looking in my direction.

By then, of course, I had removed the surgical mask, so he recognized me straight away. Assuming he had come specially to give me the bad news, I went forward to meet him with a brave smile and a heavy limp, hoping that this would simultaneously melt his heart and permanently alter the findings of the court of enquiry.

"Ah, there you are, Bandy," he said, approaching with his rolling gait. He walked as if aboard a listing steamer. Judging by his tone, though, his heart was in a totally unmelted condition. "Your friend, Major Plumley, has been looking all over for you."

"She's a major today, is she?" I began, but Chistelow was too busy explaining that Guinevere, whose family were near neighbours in his part of Buckinghamshire, had been kind enough to offer him a lift to the hospital in her motor car.

"So thought I would take this opportunity," he said, gazing around at everything of interest in the vicinity except me, "to call on you and see how you were. And, I'm afraid, to prepare you for the worst." So saying, he took a deep breath, perhaps hoping the resultant chest expansion would contrive to exaggerate the number of medals ribbons below his wings. It really annoyed him that I had more medals than he had.

Together with the thoracic expansion he was also attempting equalize our respective altitudes. This took even more of an effort, there being so much of him to draw up, for he was a decidedly plump cove. A plump, hostile cove. "Prepare you for the worst," he repeated grimly.

He had been detesting me steadily for twenty years, now. It had started when he was a flight lieutenant at 59 Training Depot Station in Huntingdon, back in '24. At the time, I was organizing an air force on behalf of an Indian maharajah.* The Air Ministry, alerted by an alarmed Foreign Office that this activity was not even remotely in the national interest, had attempted to block my purchase of sixty fighter aircraft from the RAF, but I had managed to outmanoeuvre them all, and ship the aircraft out of the country before the establishment realized what was going on. Oliver Chistelow was one of those (Prime Minister Ramsay Macdonald among them) whose careers had been affected by my sterling endeavours, and he had never forgiven me for it. For once, that was a matter of some regret as far as I was concerned. I had been getting on with him quite well, until I stole his entire supply of Sopwith Snipes. I admired him, even. He had been a noted mountain climber in his day, having led an RAF expedition up more than one Himalayan slope. He was also one of the air force's pioneer bomber pilots. He had quite liked me when he was a fine-looking junior officer with a low fat content and an appreciative humour. But unlike me, promotion and advancement had not been good for him. Success had applied too many layers of self-satisfaction and cholesterol to his Hermann Goering-type face.

No, I fear there was not much fun left in his eyes — certainly not when they were pointing in my direction.

"It's not good, I'm afraid," he now confided.

"What isn't? You mean the enquiry?"

"Of course I mean the enquiry!" he snapped, not appreciating, I

---

* As thrillingly described in *This One's On Me* and *Me So Far*, Vols. VI and VII of *The Bandy Papers*.

suppose, my failure to address him as sir, though he was not quite pompous enough to insist on it.

"So what's the verdict?"

He opened his mouth to reply, just as we became aware of a deep, rumbling sound. It grew rapidly louder.

Both of us tensed. We knew what it was.

The deep growl of the V-1 grew louder still, increasing in volume to a shattering roar that made the entire hospital vibrate. We stood there rigidly, each of us hoping that the other would set a good example by diving under the nearest matron, or at least descend with careful insouciance into a shelter, just in case the doodlebug decided to cut its rocket motor and dive straight down onto us with its ton of high explosive.

Please God, let it continue on to London and clobber somebody else, I thought.

Luckily the heavy, blasting uproar died away naturally as the doodlebug sped onward over the Kentish countryside.

We both shifted about for a moment, busily avoiding each other's gaze, until I cleared my throat.

"So what's the verdict?" I asked.

"It's not actually official yet," Chistelow said, lowering his voice as a couple of patients wandered past. He actually started to move away without telling me a thing.

"Half a mo," I said, perhaps just a shade peremptorily. The truth was, I couldn't see that I'd done anything wrong. After all, the Mosquito I was accused of destroying had been a write-off anyway. All I had done was to get the wing staff to render it airworthy again. It wasn't my fault that it had been written off for a second time.

I mean, damn it all, they ought to have been grateful to me for giving it another lease of life before pranging it again, and I had said so. But somehow they hadn't quite seen it my way.

Besides, as I had informed Air Vice-Marshal Chistelow, it wasn't I who had actually cartwheeled the Mossie all over the Normandy countryside. "It was my son, Flying Officer Bandy, who pranged it," I'd told him.

"What?"

"It's my son you ought to be charging," I'd explained in reasonable tones. "He's to blame; it was all his fault."

"Your son?"

"Yes, it's his fault. He's the one you should be charging, not me," I said stoutly.

Chistelow's lip had curled in utter disdain, and he had thought even worse of me ever since, not appreciating my clever tactic in blaming somebody who was fireproof. By then, my son Bart had been honourably discharged from the air force, and was therefore home free.

Funnily enough, BW, as I always called him, hadn't appreciated it much, either, when I told him. In fact he seemed quite annoyed when I explained how I had tried to put all the blame on him. "But don't you see, lad, I could safely blame you," I cried, "because you were safely invalided out of the air force." And when he continued to glare: "I mean, why should you care?" I'd said, quite hurt by his reaction. "I really don't know why you're looking so peevish, son." But BW had continued to growl like Etna for quite some time afterwards.

"Well, what is it?" Chistelow said now, halting in the hospital corridor and looking impatiently at his watch.

"Whajamean, what is it? Aren't you going to tell me the result of the enquiry?"

"You'll get it in due course," Chistelow said, trying not to look too satisfied. "I only came this morning to prepare you for the worst." And he turned and marched off, plainly determined to keep me in a healthy state of anxiety for a while longer.

He was barely out sight when Guinevere's feet sounded from the other direction. I whirled, and confirmed that I had not mistaken her heavy tread. At the sight of her, my craven heart bounced wildly on the trampoline of its ligaments. Urged on by the instincts that had preserved me in aerial dogfights in two world wars, I headed for the nearest mop cupboard. Before I could scuttle into it she saw me and started waving.

I waved back, smiling heartily, rehearsing what I was going to say to her. Yes, that was it. I would inform her in a kindly but utterly firm fashion that it was all over between us. Gently I would take her hand, give it a pat or two, and tell her I wanted nothing more to do with her; that her recent efforts in Quebec City to have me executed for treason had, oh, I don't know, had rather *diminished* the former feelings I'd had for her.

So, with heart flushed and face pounding, I limped — pitifully — toward her, affixed an ingratiating smile to my equine countenance, and exclaimed, "Why hello, Gwinny, this is a surprise, fancy meeting you here."

I had hardly cravened out the words before she had seized my arm and hurled me into my room like a rocket from a Typhoon. And then she was kissing me, rather more intimately than I was in the mood for, especially as it brought her interesting face so frighteningly close.

Frightening and interesting indeed, with that chin jutting like a bulldozer blade, competing hopelessly with the curved beak of her nose, which had been borrowed without so much as a thank-you from some motherly golden eagle, and her eyes, inset in the sockets of an Afghan warrior, even closer, were that possible, which it weren't.

The astonishing thing about Gwinny was that the portions south of her ferocious mien were so utterly perfect, from dimpled knees to Venusian knockers. I remember, as clearly as if it were only four years ago, the shock to my optics when, after running amuck northward over her glorious form, my eyes first arrived at her face. For a moment I thought I'd encountered a transvestite admiral in a skirt and a bad mood. Dizzy from roaming over her gloamings and plumbing her voluptuous S-bends, the effect was like reaching Valhalla and finding that the gods were all on crutches, dribbling like mad. The culmination of the face with its ferocious beak and the eyebrows bristling like wart-hogs caused me to recoil as if illustrating terror in an actors' studio.

"Darling, where on earth have you been?" she was now breathing into my earhole, creating a number of epileptic frissons. "I've been waiting for ages."

Our relationship had been travelling a rocky road without shock absorbers even since 1940 when we first met — in a field latrine, actually. After the initial shock I had come to appreciate what a magnificent sort of face it was. It wasn't every day that you encountered something so unique, a face perfect for conducting human sacrifices during the full moon. All she needed was a helmet of writhing snakes to earn her a place in *The Dictionary of Classical Iniquities*. By the time I came to be sharing a pillow with it, it had become a face that I was proud to be seen with, perhaps not least because it was as splendidly different as my own.

Ultimately, though, I had begun to have doubts about her, not least when she very nearly got me hanged for treason. Admittedly she had merely been doing her job as a member of the security services. Still, I had been rather shocked by her readiness to sacrifice me merely in the name of national security.

I became aware that we were sitting on the hospital bed. I didn't remember even feinting in that direction, let alone steeling myself for seduction, which was now taking the form of being pressed close, and having sweet nothings whispered in my lug hole.

"Eh?"

"Bart, do you think ...?"

"What?"

"Do you — you know — feel like it?"

She was smoothing the bed with her hand in what seemed to be a distinctly lascivious fashion, and smirking.

"You're not seriously ... ?"

"We could put that cabinet against the door."

"For God's sake ... A half ton cabinet wouldn't stop Nurse Killy."

"I wouldn't mind her watching," said Guinevere, breathlessly. "It's something I've always wanted to do myself — watch somebody at it." She moved closer still. I had not thought that was possible. "It would make it all the more exciting, don't you think?"

"Listen, Guinevere, there's something I have to say," I said, twitching a bit, not least because she was groping into my silk jammies. "No, stop, look, listen, Gwinny, this is important — "

Her hand certainly wasn't listening. It was too busy appreciating the silken material.

"Well, if you haven't got the guts at this moment, you might at least regularize the position, Bartholomew," she whispered.

Far as I could make out, it was already regularized: her on top. "To conserve your strength," as she once explained.

"You know, what I was talking about," she went on. "The possibility of your becoming — well, shall we say a permanent feature of the Buckingham landscape?"

"Like a folly, you mean? Anyway, you were the only one talking about it, Gwinny, not me. I've never said a thing about settling down in —"

"After all, my darling, what have you got to lose? You're still poverty-stricken after losing all your money in the Depression, and you've no real prospects. I mean, all you know is flying, and you can't go on doing that for ever. Whereas ... Well, when father dies, I'll inherit everything, you know," she said, coyly driving a carefully honed elbow into my serratus magnus. "They say he won't last much longer. Though mind you, they've been saying that for years," she added, trying to be fair about it.

Suddenly brightening, she added, "But I'm sure he won't last much longer, once we're married and he has to look at you over the breakfast kipper."

To give myself time to collect a few vicious thoughts together I placed my hand over hers in a friendly, preoccupied sort of way while saying to myself, "Go on then, for God's sake, man, go on! Now's the time to tell her!" Apart from anything else, she was becoming much too demanding, groinwise. Not that I was entirely unresponsive in such matters. I mean, I was a reasonably vigorous chap when not preoccupied, distracted, worried, or in hospital.

Yes, but, trouble was, she'd heard the call of the wild rather late in life. Her face had held a previous supply of swains at bay for thirty-five years until I came along and was overcome by the sheer power of her physiognomical aggression. I was the bowler who helped her break her duck, if I might use a cricketing term without knowing what it meant. I was overly intrigued by the uniqueness of her countenance. Moreover, when we were together, people hardly glanced in my direction. Which was fine by me. I was heartily sick of being notable, not least by being mistaken for a horse and offered metaphorical oats. But, even before her treatment of me in Quebec, I'd begun to hae me doots as they say in Wales or somewhere; while on her part, at the age of forty, she found she couldn't get enough of me.

Well, things had to be straightened out right now. In preparation for the showdown I unclamped her hand from my thigh; or, rather, attempted to do so. She was too strong for me. I found myself caught up in a variation of arm-wrestling, with me trying for force her larcenous fingers away from my jewellery box and her resisting with equal and opposite force. And she was actually winning.

Of course, this was because I was not at my best, having been in hospital for a while, and also because of the digital activity. Damned sex — always getting in the way of rational argument. I mean, how can you concentrate your resources properly if a soft hand is slowly enclosing your decision-making process?

So of course nothing had been sorted out by the time she unjammed the door a few minutes later, leaving me feeling furious with myself, and needing a shower, and despising myself all the way there. What a contemptible coward I was. It was not as if I'd had the excuse that she was some vulnerable girl unable to withstand the shock of being turned down by a colonial parvenu. Her sensibilities had been carefully anesthetized as part of her training as an intelligence agent. I would not have had to suffer floods of tears from her. The worst I could have faced was a sharp blow to the Adam's apple with the heel of her hand. Damned, craven, yeller-bellied, dunderheaded ninnyhammer that I was.

But as I stood towelling myself in front of the mirror in the bacteria-riddled hospital showers, and stared at my reflection, my jaw turned positively orthognathous with renewed determination. I would definitely tell her next time that it was all over between us. I would be as hard as a cricket ball, unyielding as an umpire, resolute as a fast bowler, decided as a pair of bails, firm as a set of stumps, upright as — but enough cricketing similes. The point was that I was utterly determined to end the affair. I would — the very next time I failed to avoid her. Definitely.

Of course, it wasn't just Guinevere who was making me somewhat discontented. I was also feeling really annoyed at the illogical attitude of the authorities in blaming me for wrecking an aircraft that had already been written off before I'd had it repaired. So, on my way back to bed cuddling a damp towel, and espying Air Vice-Marshal Chistelow in one of the private rooms, I determined to have it out with him, even if he was busy talking to another patient, or rather, was holding her hand in a comforting sort of way.

I would get it over with. I had failed to sort out Gwinny, but I would not let Chistelow off the hook as well. I would insist that he come clean on exactly what they were going to do with me.

So I hobbled straight into the room. "Sorry to bother you, sir," I began, addressing him respectfully in the hope that it would put him in a more receptive mood, "but I really would like some idea of what the decision is likely to be, sir," I said, actually throwing in a free sir. "You know, get it all straightened out and cleared up, if you don't mind, Air Vice-Marshal, so I'll know where I stand ..."

I seemed to have taken him entirely by surprise, for he jumped quite violently. He had been holding the patient's hand in both of his when I entered. Now he let go so hurriedly as to cause her mitt to rap against the metal bed frame in what must have been quite a painful fashion, while Chistelow himself started back against the bedside table, almost upsetting it.

This sort of reaction was not entirely unfamiliar to me. Many's the time people had recoiled somewhat either at the sound of my voice, or the sight of my face, or both, so I suppose it was understandable. But they did not usually turn pale, as Chistelow did now. His obese mush took on the colour and texture of the whitewashed coal I'd seen at one RAF station.

Which made me falter a bit, as I continued rather less forthrightly, "Couldn't you just let me know the decision? You know, so I could make plans?"

"Yes," he said quickly, his lineaments fluttering like cabbagewhite butterflies. Good Lord, he was sounding quite accommodating. "Yes, of course, Bandy, of course I can let you know. Not that there's much to tell really," he babbled, "as it's not yet promulgated, but what there is, well, not very good, I'm afraid. It's likely to be a reprimand."

"Oh."

"Which won't look very good on your records, of course," he mumbled, almost — Good Lord, again — apologetically.

"M'm."

"Quite," he replied. For some reason he was standing with his back to the patient.

His tone so far had been so sympathetic that I wondered if I had been wrong all these years about him being a bit of stuffed shirt who had forgotten what it was like to be a fundamentally young, joyous, intrepid birdman like me.

I shifted slightly to see if the lady in the bed was listening and might serve as a witness, but he made a similar sort of movement as well, as if initiating a folk dance — *Dashing White Sergeant*, perhaps, unless he was class-conscious enough to think of it a *Dashing White Air Vice-Marshal.*

"Look, if you wouldn't mind, Bandy," he said quickly, "I'm sure you have lots to attend to elsewhere, eh, what?" — concluding with a fluttery sort of gesture not generally to be found among the senior ranks.

At that point I took a quick folk-dance step around the obese barricade, and met a not entirely unfamiliar bright blue gaze.

"Hello," I said, in some surprise.

"Yes, well, off you go," said the AVM said curtly.

"Why, this is the girl who was having the operation down below," I breathed.

"There's no need to be vulgar, Bandy."

"I'm not talking about that," I said faintly, still busily goggling. "By 'down below' I meant down on the second floor — or was it the ground floor?"

"Yes, well — sorry you have to leave, Bandy," said the Air Vice-Marshal through gritted teeth, continuing the dance with sidesteps and shooing motions.

At which point I began to smirk, a facial inlay greatly to be deplored in other people. "Oh, now I get it," I said, looking at him in a winking sort of tone, and lowering my voice conspiratorially. "Your *petite amie*, eh?" I said. "And it's you who got her into difficulties, eh?"

But his only response was to flutter his nostrils like sphincters, and convert the shade of his plump, jowly face into damson jam.

"But hold on, thar," I said wonderingly. "You're married to the lovely Jane Maelona, née Rainer-Cloudburste, aren't you, sir? The society hostess and patron of the Vivisection Society? The one in the *Field*?"

"Field, field?"

"You know — the magazine? For posh people?"

"Look, Bandy. Will you get out of here? Please?" the air vice-marshal said, in distinctly shaky tones.

So all I said was, "Well, well," once again peering around him for another look at the pretty girl with the huge blue peepers. And as I caught his evasive eye my heart grew as light as an iridescent bubble from a clay pipe. Gossamer wings of an unheard-of perfection in the way of airfoil section sprouted, on which I flew to Valhalla by way of Mount Olympus, New Jerusalem, Eden, and Arcadia, designing in the air en route gold vapour trails straight from the exquisite patterns of the Pleiades and the Hyades, while my celestial feet danced Sarabandes, Scottisches, and Schuplatters.

And amazingly, he, too, grew all calm and tranquil. It was as if all cares and worries had suddenly been lifted from his brow and buried in St. Middens Cemetery with full military honours. He took my arm almost gently. Murmuring to the patient that he would be back in a moment, he drew me as far from the bed as possible. To be exact, right out of the private ward and into the corridor.

The corridor was empty. "All right," he said. "I'll do what I can to soften the enquiry. All right?"

"And I'd like to be demoted, sir."

"Promoted, you mean. Well, that won't be too easy, Bandy. After all, you haven't been a group captain all that long."

"No, no, sir. I meant —"

"If I could manage it, presumably you'd be satisfied with the rank of air commodore? For a while, anyway?"

"No, no, I was thinking of demotion."

"Demotion?"

"Yes."

"You're not asking for promotion?"

"No."

"What's wrong with being an air commodore?"

"I couldn't do any more flying," I said.

He stared. He stared and stared, and finally, "Well, I'll see what I can do about reducing you in rank," he said faintly, starting to turn away. And turned back, just long enough to say, "Blackmailing scoundrel that you are!"

THE PICTURE OF DERRING-DON'T

IT WAS RAINING the day I flew into landing strip B-2 in the Normandy beachhead that August of 1944, to assume command of my new TAF squadron. I made such an impression on my pilots that they immediately started preparations for departure. I was appalled to see them gathering all their personal possessions together and packing them into the nooks and crannies of the squadron's dozen or so Spitfires, and assumed it was a reaction to my face, with its horse lineaments pickled in nearly thirty years of adrenaline, or to the fact that their new CO was perched like a giant budgie on a silver-topped cane. Unless it was because their new leader was an old man, or at least Godamned middle-aged, which was the same to them. In summary, a lame, horse-faced, ancient, sashaying CO who had come mincing out of the supply Anson under a pink umbrella (the only brolly I could find in the time available, there being a shortage of umbrellas in Great Britain, as well as a scarcity of everything else, from food and clothing to theatre tickets and sunshine).

It was relief when I realized that they were fleeing the scene because of a movement order. This turned out to be just another snafu, and the order was almost immediately cancelled. Nevertheless, the Canadian veterans, who had been fighting so recently on the Italian front that their knees were still brown, found it hard to accept that this odd-looking person — who looked old enough to play Polonius behind the arras, and seemed to be on the point of death (a hangover cringed under my pink umbrella) — that *this* was to be their new commanding officer, their leader, their inspiration.

Their worst moment was still to come, when I limped, grimacing through the rain, into the dark mess tent and felt my way toward the bar, a trestle table held down with beer bottles. The climax came when I removed my cap, exposing a noble but scantily-clad pate, with the five hairs so carefully arranged across the scalp, as if to suggest a musical stave waiting for a leitmotif.

"Oh, my God," someone said, "It's Robertson Hare."

"Come on, somebody at Wing's playing a joke, right?" said Kit Corner, B Flight's commander, as he loomed out of the gloom. About five foot nine, the perfect height for a pilot, he was a tall, blond lad with a prominent nose and steady blue eyes. He turned these on me hopefully. "You're with the Crazy Gang, right?"

I had been told that morale in the squadron was low, partly caused by the nightly bombing of the beachhead, and partly by the activities of an enemy Deadeye Dick, a German ace named Willy Strand, who had despatched several members of the squadron despite their skill and experience.

Still, I thought I'd better make a start at the old sinew-stiffening and blood-summoning humbuggery. "Gentlemen," quoth I hoarsely, closing my eyes against what little light seeped into the tent. "Gentlemen," I began again, raising my voice over the pluvial uproar — the rain was positively thundering on the canvas — "judging by your faces you don't seem to realize how incredibly fortunate you are in your choice of CO."

"We had a choice?" someone called out.

I ploughed on regardless. "To start with," I ploughed, "I'm astonished that you don't know who I am, amazed that my name isn't known the length and breadth of this entire tent. I can only assume that the RAF tradition of not publicising its aerial heroes has spread like green bean rust or potato blight to the Royal Canadian Air Force as well. But let me tell you that I'm not just your common or garden commanding officer, you know. For a start — just take a look at these." And with all the pride and aplomb of a raincoated flasher, I opened wide the glistening groundsheet I was wearing, to reveal the five and a quarter rows of medal ribbons that had been awarded me over the years by various grateful, and sometime rather ungrateful, governments: KCSI, CBE, MC, DFC, Croix de Guerre, Legion of Decency — no, Legion of Honour, I mean — except I'd forgotten that I was wearing a new battledress onto which I had not had the opportunity to affix even the wings, let alone the gongs.

"Jesus Christ," Brad Solving, the A Flight leader, said. "It's not even a friggin' pilot."

Somehow I had a feeling that I'd have my work cut out to make an impression on these rude vets, many of whom were barely out of their teens.

Still, after a while, at least one of the pilots proved friendly enough. This was Pilot Officer Oakley, who said to me quite sympathetically, "I guess you're just putting in time here until your pension comes through, eh?"

John Oakley was a tallish, weedy lad with mouse brown hair and terribly sincere blue eyes, which made his tactlessness all the more wounding. That same day I heard him telling Corporal David Carp, one of the mechanics, that he really should shower more often. "I'm only telling you this for your own good, Dave," he said, "so you'll understand what it means when the other guys start throwing your underwear out of the tent."

Oakley had been an apprentice tailor in Montreal before joining up. Boy, I could just hear him trying to make his clients feel comfortable. "Yes, it's a reasonably good fit, sir, considering your arms aren't the same length."

My self- appointed task of improving morale was not made easier by the nightly bombing. The Germans, aware that they had very little time left before a breakout became inevitable, were making desperate efforts to destroy the mountains of supplies piled high in the bridgehead, but we had such complete command of the air that they were having to make do with upsetting the neighbourhood at night.

There were so few enemy aircraft to be spotted in daylight that the boys spent most of the time beating up ground targets, particularly the buzz bomb ramps. I wasn't too crazy about having to carry explosives on almost every trip. Dammit, the Spitfire was a fighter, not just another Typhoon or Mosquito. Still, the Hun on the ground had to be kept busy, I guess, so that they didn't get into any mischief, like counterattacking.

At least I soon proved that whatever my short and longcomings as a creaking CO, I could actually fly the magnificent Spitfire, which was better and faster than ever, after four years developing its muscles. As soon as the rain stopped I squeezed into the cockpit of the latest cannon version with the new gyroscopic gunsight, and took off down the metal runway, marvelling at the power and responsiveness of this sleek machine. So much better than the Mark I version I'd flown back in 1940.

The larger ration of power was much needed, as I discovered as we lifted off from the runway grid laid over the grass and mud. Usually, when you took off, you could rely on the way being clear of obstructions such as electric pylons or the odd chimney for at least a few hundred yards. But here in the beachhead you actually had to climb steeply to clear the war material that crowded in on the airstrip from all sides: lines of trucks, great tank parks, fuel dumps, infantry and hospital encampments, smoking cookhouses, and engineering and supply yards and depots — vast compounds of war equipment piled up right to the perimeter of the airfield and almost joining us on the runway.

Still, I managed to evade it all, and to level out without incident. It was thrilling to be flying again after mooning about on the ground for so many months, once more to be teasing stick and rudder, and feeling again the unique responsiveness of this marvellous, compact fighter. I was yodeling by the time I reached 5000 feet. Until it occurred to me that the tra-la-ing might be the effect of poisoning rather than light-heartedness. There were fumes in the cockpit, from the engine and perhaps the starter cartridge. Hastily I clamped the oxygen mask to my face.

There weren't likely to be any hostile aircraft in daylight, unless you counted Yankee fighters, which had been known to attack unfamiliar aircraft first and recognize them as friendly afterwards. Still, thirty years experience could not be snubbed all that readily, so automatically I kept a careful lookout as I heeled toward Arromanches. Its crippled houses appeared in a minute or two, surrounded by Allied camps. As we swept onward over the beach I was careful to behave in a non-threatening way, with tranquil movements of the controls. I circled several times, staring down at the prefabricated harbour which had been towed in sections all the way across the stormy Channel. Only now did I get a proper idea of what an achievement that had been, this Mulberry Harbour, indeed this entire Normandy adventure. Of the fleets of ships involved in the D-day attack, there were still literally hundreds of them down there, scattered all over the briny, or queuing up to offload still more supplies onto the metal pier; yet more flail tanks and their carriers, trucks, bowsers, tankers, troop carriers, low-loaders, and dozens of other types of specialized transport.

Even as I gazed down, British and American cruisers and battleships commenced firing way out to sea. Still being careful to fly as unaggressively as possible, and relying on the uniquely recognizable elliptical wings of the Spit to soothe the nerves of even the most truculent ship's padre, I flew out to sea a few miles, keeping my distance while I watched the great gouts of flame and smoke billowing from the guns as they flung shells the size of automobiles into the German lines twenty miles inland over the tangled Normandy countryside.

What an amazing sight. There were so many ships scattered over the silver sea that you felt you could have used them as stepping stones all the way back to Blighty.

★

After that first solitary flight I settled down as a member of a regular patrol; except that most of them were highly irregular. You flew in response to clamorous calls for the elimination of such obstacles as veteran Jerries in ruined farms, and such calls came in thick and fast, and in all daylight hours. Most flights were rhubarbs. I was never too keen on beating up ground targets, especially with today's hideously accurate 37 mm ack-ack. Luckily, most of the targets hereabouts were easy if you were quick enough: transports of various sorts cringing in the woodland, or, with luck, a Jerry officer risking a quick dash from HQ to VW or al fresco crap in a ditch. There was little aerial opposition, and what there was had to be shared out among the hundreds of Allied aircraft that were constantly ranging over the puny fields and narrow, sheltered roads of Normandy. Nevertheless, we were suffering steady casualties from ground fire. In one month the squadron had lost five COs, though two of them turned up a few days or weeks later, which is why, once the boys had gotten over the shock of Granddad Bandy, they consoled themselves with the thought that I would be gone before the end of the month — or by Sunday brunch.

I was particularly unhappy at the way the Allies seemed to have swept the Luftwaffe from the skies, during daylight hours, at least. There was just one Staffel to be feared, it seemed: a pack of Focke Wulf 190s from Dreux — the Luftwaffe outfit to which the German ace Willy Strand belonged.

"I thought you guys said it was quite rare to encounter Jerry aircraft," I said as we lined up outside the open air cookhouse for the evening meal.

Kit Corner, who was just ahead of me in the queue, turned round and said, "It is."

"So how does this fellow Strand keep adding to his score?"

"He's shithot at using cloud cover."

"Ah. And he's really good, is he?"

Brad Solving joined in. "You don't want to tangle with him, Squadron Leader," he said in a hard voice which matched his anvil of a face. "He has reflexes."

As the cook whacked dollops of moist powdered spuds and canned stew into my mess tin and added just a soupçon of rotting algae, I ran a hand over my airy pate and nodded, letting the inference wash over me that, given my elderly reflexes, I wouldn't stand an earthly against someone like Willy Strand.

Actually, I suspected that at my age I probably wouldn't do all that well against the Hun equivalent of Pilot Officer Prune, either, compared with whipper-snappers like Brad Solving. He was the most aggressive pilot in the squadron. In a time when dogfights were becoming quite rare, he had gained a DFC and several victories in North Africa and Italy. Unlike me, he was utterly fearless. He positively enjoyed roaming at 2000 feet over the formidable German ack-ack, clobbering everything that moved down there, especially locomotives, because they emitted such satisfying gouts of steam when hit. Personally, that sort of work, involving hate flying up at you from four barrel flak guns and the like, made me wince like listening to squeaky chalk. It had been bad enough four years ago, but now the radar-guided flak guns were almost infallible. I was beginning to suspect that I was no longer appropriately typecast for the Derring-do role. Somebody had recently replaced my nerves with old fuse wire. If I'd known how dangerous it had become, I might have thought twice about signing up for another tour. But I was stuck with the part, now, and would have to conceal the fact that the balls of fire coming up from the ground were causing me to twitch like an epileptic yak.

It greatly annoyed me that the flak didn't seem to bother either of the flight leaders, Brad Solving or Kit Corner. Their attitude was that if they were going to be hit they were going to be hit, and there was nothing they could do about it, so why worry?

"Quite right," I said. "No point in worrying, absolutely no point at all," I said, insouciantly nibbling the Daily Routine Orders with my teeth.

Mind you, the bombing didn't help, either. Even the MO noticed the rapid deterioration in the intrepid birdman act, the pretence that I didn't mind a bit about the balls of fire.

"You're already developing a bit of a tic or spasm," he pointed out one night, after observing my reaction to a 2000-pound bomb as it exploded a few inches away.

He and I shared a tent, and on this occasion, during a particularly heavy air raid, we shared a nice, waterlogged trench as well. "In fact," he continued, examining a dent in his tin hat, "I'm surprised they still let you fly at all, after being in enemy hands."

"I volunteered," I bellowed over the din.

"At your age you should have known better."

"I never seem to know better," I shouted over the uproar of bombs and anti-aircraft fire from the surrounding batteries. To make matters worse, the water in the trench was sopping Guinevere's nice new pyjamas.

"You can still get out, if you really want."

"Too late. I bullied them too much to get me here, now I'm stuck –– in this here mud," I added quickly. I hadn't liked his remark about tics and spasms. "And on top of everything else my jimjams are wet."

"Yes, of course. Quite understandable," the MO shouted back.

"What, what?"

"Wetting yourself, I mean. In moments of fear and peril one tends to lose control over one's bladder."

I raised my head so that I could glare at him. "You're not by any chance related to Pilot Officer Oakley, are you?" I enquired.

"Christ, no. You want to be careful of him, Squadron Leader. He has no tact."

"Anyway, I don't mean I've wet myself that way," I snapped, flapping the pyjama material irritably, then ducking down again to avoid another cascade from the bombilating heavens. "I was referring to this wet trench."

"As for volunteering for another tour," said the doctor, "it's obvious you should never have done it. It's your death wish, obviously."

"Death wish? I don't have a death wish. Whajamean, death wish?"

"It would certainly solve your problems," he went on, obliviously.

"Damn it, don't have any problems!"

"For instance, it would enable you to escape the clutches of that lady friend of yours. The one you're always on about — what's her name again? Judging by the way you keep talking about her, you have a good reason for killing yourself right there."

The conversation languished for a while as a bomb headed straight for me, and in a hurry, too, judging by the way it was rushing.

Fortunately it changed course and landed some distance away on a field hospital.

Perceiving a way of turning the conversation to my advantage, I gripped his forearm in an encouraging way. "I guess what you're really saying," I shouted, "is that I shouldn't demean myself by flying too close to the ack-ack guns. You are recommending that I cut out all the low-level flying, aren't you?"

"Am I? I don't know. It's hard to think with all this noise, and the way you're cutting the blood supply to my arm."

"It's the low-level work that occasionally causes me to twitch, you see — or rather, causes me to wince — ever so slightly."

"How's that again?"

"I was saying," I screamed, "that it's your opinion, Doctor, that I should concentrate on what I do best, i.e. fly as high as possible, to ensure that I have 'slipped the silly bonds of earth, and danced the skies on ...' uh, how does it go again?"

"What, the poem? Something about laughable wings, isn't it? But I don't think it's the silly bonds of earth, is it?"

"Course it is," I said frigidly, to match the ditchwater.

"I don't think so."

"Yes, it is. That's exactly what I was talking about, the silly bonds of earth."

"No, I don't think it's the silly bonds of earth."

"How would you know, anyway?" quoth I, scornfully. "You can't even remember the medical term for malingering."

"There isn't one — is there?"

"So let's have no more talk of wincing, Doctor, if you don't mind," I said haughtily.

"Wincing was your word, not mine," the MO said defiantly. "Mine was tic-ing and spasming. Yours was wincing."

"Anyway, the point is that much as I want to go on flying low over deadly accurate thirty-seven millimetre flak guns," I said, "and other lethal sorts of ordnance, the twitch, as you call it, is a possible sign that a chap should be advised to restrict his flying to more enjoyable tasks, like attacking enemy fighters, or censoring the mail. Right?"

As I spoke I raised my head cautiously above ground level to find out where the huge bonfire was coming from. A great yellow conflagration, it was busily burning half the horizon. A fuel dump on the beach, perhaps.

"Personally," replied the doctor, "I'm sure that what you have there is a flinch, rather than a twitch. As Squadron Medical Officer I might have to take it seriously if you were twitching. But flinching is another matter entire."

"Surely a flinch is as good as a twitch?"

"Oh, no," said the MO authoritatively. "According to Osler, a twitch is worse than a flinch any day."

"'tisn't."

"'fraid so."

"It isn't," I said loudly — even louder than the bombs. "I know Osler, so I know it isn't."

"Yes, it is. I distinctly remember it says in the *Theory and Practice* that a twitch takes precedence over a flinch any day, in traumatic terms and degree of seriousness."

"Well, I studied medicine before you did," I shouted, ducking lower than ever, "and I distinctly remember —"

"You studied medicine, Bart? Where?"

"Toronto."

"Did you really?" he asked, suddenly looking quite respectful. "Then perhaps you can help me, sir. I've been trying to remember a certain medical term. One of the fellows came to me the other day, a wireless operator, and he said he couldn't hear properly over his headphones. I diagnosed ear wax, but I couldn't just say that, could I? It sounds so — what's that French term meaning you're behaving in an undignified way? Lees something?"

"Lèse-Majesté?"

"That's it. It would be lèse-majesté to tell a patient merely that he had an ear wax problem."

"Cerumen impaction."

"What? What's that?"

"Means you have ear — "

"What, what?"

"You have ear wax, Doctor."

"I do not. I could hear you quite clearly if it wasn't for this racket."

"I was explaining," I explained patiently, "that that's what we medical men call it when you have ear wax problems: cerumen impaction."

"Ah, I see. That's very good. I must remember that. What was the term again?"

"I think, Doctor," I said heavily, "that one of us definitely needs a respite from the strains of war. And it's not me, so there."

A few days later, I was basking in the first decent spot of sunshine we'd had so far that August, sunning myself near the admin tent, pretending to work on the bumph that my clerk, LAC Burley, was always dumping on me, when there came the familiar sound of Merlin engines: A Flight returning from the morning patrol. Except that only two of the four machines that had set out a couple of hours ago entered the circuit.

One of them circled widely over the field. The other was already lining up for a landing. I adjusted the field glasses, and watched as it side-slipped.

I turned to the nearest man, Flight Lieutenant Corner, and said, "Hit the crash button."

"Eh?"

"Crash alarm. Quick."

The alert wailed out across the field. Emergency crews sprinted to their vehicles.

The tattered Spit managed to land safely. But it remained on the steel grid, the propeller turning quietly. It was making no effort to taxi clear.

When we got there we found the pilot slumped over the controls.

The cockpit stank of hot metal, high explosive, and blood.

As he was hauled out, his entrails started to spill. How the boy had managed to land the plane I don't know. The cockpit instruments were so thoroughly painted in red they were unreadable. The pilot was still alive, though only just, when the MO and I finally got him out.

After a quick shower and a change into a fresh shirt and trousers, I walked over to the debriefing tent where the intelligence officer was questioning the only uninjured pilot of Brad Solving's flight. His name was Baynes, a flight lieutenant who had been instructing in New Brunswick for three years, until a few months ago. He had been sent on ops when they started to run down the air training program in Canada.

He was shakily describing how the flight had been bounced by a pack of Huns over toward Dreux.

"The 190s came out of nowhere," Baynes was saying. "Brad went down right away. Got hit from underneath. Blown to bits. Never knew what hit him."

"What's that about Brad?" someone asked.

"Gone for a Burton."

"Jesus."

"I think I got one of the FWs," Baynes told the squadron spy. "It should show up on film, though I had to get out of there in a hurry, eh? The 190 that got Brad, it had red and white checks on the fuselage."

"You were Brad's wingman, weren't you?"

"Yes. This red and white job came from underneath and stood on its tail to pump shell into Brad's kite. It was all over in two seconds."

"Willy Strand, you think?" asked the I/O.

"I guess so. He nearly got me, too," Baynes said with a laugh that sounded as if somebody had driven a fist into his midriff. The pupils of his eyes were huge. Adrenaline was still titrating onto his nerves. "You've seen my kite. Didn't think I'd get back."

"They say he has a thirty mil cannon," said John Oakley.

"Who says?"

"Willy Strand has? Where'd you hear that?"

"I dunno. I just heard it."

"Thirty mil? Christ, you'd only need one shell up your ass."

The mood in the mess that evening was a bit fraught. I guess they were trying not to conclude that if someone as good as Brad could get the chop, what chance had any of them?

To cheer everybody up I made a special effort to ensure that a plentiful supply of booze arrived in the supply Anson, along with the mail and other supplies.

"That's a hell of a lot of Scotch you've ordered," Kit Corner said. Wearing only a pair of gym shorts, I was inspecting the morale-boosting cargo, a case of Wee Sleekit Cowrin' Tim'rous Beastie Highland Cream.

"M'm," I said, wrenching the case open right there and then, to make sure that none of the bottles had been filched by the Anson crew. It was necessary that I make sure. They looked like alcoholics to me, the Anson crew. Flew like it, too.

"Well, the boys really need this, Kitty," I said, with my usual authority.

"Oh, yeah?"

"To calm their nerves," I added, caressing the label of one of the bottles.

"But sir," Kit said innocently, "hardly any of the guy drink Scotch. Most of them are well-brought-up country boys from Ontario or the Prairies who don't drink at all."

"That's nonsense, Kitty. If nobody drinks this fine liquor, then how come I need to keep ordering fresh supplies? Answer me that."

"Yeah," Kit mused. "It's a real mystery how we manage to get through so much of the stuff, when you're the one who depreciates it most."

"You mean appreciate, Kitty, not depreciate. Your grammar, vocabulary, et cetera, needs looking into, Kit. But wait a minute. By jiminy, you're right! Somebody must be illegally disposing of our liquor, possibly for cash or other favours to be negotiated in shady *estaminets*. I think perhaps I'd better move this case of whisky to my tent for safe keeping."

"That's a good idea, Squadron Leader. So that if the bottles are subsequently found to have sprung a leak we'll know who to blame."

"You mean the MO with whom I share a tent? H'm, maybe you're right, Kitty, I'll keep an eye on him," I said, and turned away to confer with the Anson pilot, who was standing beside his twin-engined greenhouse, moaning and complaining.

"Hurry it up will you?" he was saying. "I want to get away before the VIP gets here. You know how they like to clear the airspace for the really big cheeses."

"VIP?" I asked. "What VIP? I don't know anything about a VIP."

"You must have got a signal about it."

"Signal? I don't know anything about a signal."

Our intelligence officer spoke up. He had such a speech impediment that for a few days I thought he was called Inclair Mith. Actually, it was Sinclair Smith.

The squadron spy asserted indignantly that he had definitely informed me of the imminent arrival of a VIP, who had not been identified, for security reasons. "I 'owed you the 'ignal," he said.

"You didn't."

"Did."

"You did not. I'd 've noticed!"

"It was probably one of the bits of paper you sign without bothering to read it," put in my clerk, LAC Burley, who was six foot six inches tall, and almost as thin as the excuses he was always treating me to.

"Ah, then it's all your fault, Burley," I said sternly. "It's up to you to tell me when I'm signing anything important."

"Anyway, in case it's Monty," said the Anson pilot, glancing at his watch, "I'm getting the hell out. You know what he's like if he doesn't get respect — and you guys don't look too respectful to me," he added, looking pointedly at my bareish torso with its variety of punctures derived from a lifetime of being shot at.

"You think it might be Field Marshal Montgomery?" I asked in alarm.

"It's certainly somebody high up."

In further alarm I grabbed Len Burley's emaciated arm, dragged him over to the admin tent, and ordered him to help me look through the signals file. We were still rummaging through the bumph when three things happened in alarmingly quick succession. First, the supply Anson took off at an unseemly speed. Second, some army bigwigs including a lieutenant-colonel, assorted military coppers, and no less a brasshat than a major-general in full combat gear, came grinding onto the landing ground in a couple of APCs. And third, a twin-engine Dakota droned onto final, one mile away.

Presumably this was the machine that a few minutes previously had been circling the airstrip to make sure that all the bumps had been ironed out of it.

Now the camouflaged Dak with the black and white invasion stripes was touching down on the mesh runway — and we still hadn't found the signal, and the major-general was demanding the officer commanding the squadron be summoned forthwith. Having failed to find him so far, he was beginning to look agitated, and to raise his voice.

When we recovered the signal from the latrine about a week later it was found to contain the usual admonition that for security reasons no undue fuss should be made of the visitor. This would surely have warned us that the VIP was more than usually important, so that even more fuss than usual should be made.

As it turned out, the admonition was being taken all too literally. Up to the last moment no fuss whatsoever was being made. Nearly naked mechanics, riggers, and fitters were sunning themselves all over the landscape, or snoozing under the Spitfires' wings. A group of sergeant pilots and NCOs were playing ball with an apple — though I'll concede they did manage a glance at the general. Other members of the squadron were larking about around a shower made out of fuel cans and tomato juice tins, spraying anyone who was stuffy enough to be wearing any clothing. At the cookhouse lean-to, a chef in a filthy blue shirt was indulging his hobby of moulding old porridge into the shape of an outsized phallus, complete with bollocks. Elsewhere, an enterprising army type, or brown job, as we called them, had rigged a hammock between a Bofors gun and a heap of ammo boxes, and was swinging in it gently, snoring with his mouth open. And over by the hedge, two LACs and a corporal were rehearsing for our evening concert, using a descant recorder, a Jew's harp, and a sheet of corrugated iron.

As the Dakota's engines wheezed to a stop not far from where I was running in circles, waving my arms and ordering people to look respectable, I suddenly realized that this might just possibly apply to me as well; I was still attired only in gym shorts, and, worse, wearing ridiculous clodhopping boots because both my gym shoes and the nice slippers Gwinny had given me were still drying out after the rainy season. And I hadn't shaved for two or three days.

As the rear door of the Dak opened, I scuttled out of sight behind a water bowser, miming frantically at my clerk to bring me my uniform and a shaving brush filled with foam. Burley failed to understand, but then, I suppose uniforms and foam were not all that easy to mime.

Damn it all, if this had been a British outfit, my batman would have had me looking spruce and respectable in no time at all. But Canadian officers, blast it, didn't have servants, and had to do their own chores. Disgusting, I thought.

Now, from behind the bowser, I could hear the army general demanding to know where the guard of honour was. And now I was wincing as I heard Corporal Carp, our most unwashed colleague, telling the general that we didn't have one.

"But dammit, he'll be here any minute now!" the red tab was

hissing through panicky teeth. And I was wincing again when I heard one of my men say, "We don't know nothin' about it, sir. Anyways, Mr. Bandy, our CO, don't go in much for bullshit."

Blast! Why did they have to give away my name like that!

By now, tanned and sweat-gleaming members of the squadron, in various stages of déshabillé, were wandering up, curious to find out what the Dakota wanted. Half-concealed, I waved frantically at the men, urging them to get away and for God's sake look busy or something; but all I attracted were some curious glances as I hunched, very untypically people later said, close to the water wagon.

Of course, I soon pulled myself together. After a while, realizing that I was demeaning the dignity of my office, I straightened up, pretended that I had merely been inspecting this particular vehicle. And I risked a quick look at what was going on in the vicinity of the Dak.

What was going on was that a slight, khaki-clad figure drenched in almost as many stars, medals, sashes, tabs, shiny buttons, and insignia as I had on my best uniform, was waiting patiently in the doorway of the Dak. Patiently because no steps had been provided to lead him onto terra firma.

I moaned harder than ever as I recognized the visitor. It was the bloody Emperor of India, Defender of the Faith. Christ, the King!

Quickly abandoning any intention of emerging into the open, and keeping the bowser between me and the seething brass hats and members of the King's entourage — for of course it was it was His Royal Highness King George VI out there — I scuttled toward the sleeping quarters. As luck would have it, mine was near the end of the line of tents, about as far away as it could be. By the time I had shaved with skin-slashing speed and hauled my best battledress out of the valise — badly creased but it would have to do — floundered into it and returned to the scene of the crime, His Majesty had departed in the general's APC, and all that was left was one furious civilian in striped trousers who informed me that I was a disgrace to the Air Force and that I ought to be incarcerated in the Tower for treating the Sovereign with such disregard, with such casual incivility.

"Disgraceful!" he fumed.

"Sorry," I said.

Shortly before sunset the APC reappeared, and drove back to the Dak — and to the maintenance ladder that Flight Sergeant Baker had managed to provide. As the civvy in the striped pants had made it plain that he hoped never to see me again, I remained in the background.

Otherwise, our now very smartly turned-out officers and other ranks were in their best air force khakis,* and were drawn up in extremely neat ranks. Actually, I looked quite smart, too, as I'd managed to get some of the creases out of my uniform, and had removed most of the tiny pieces of toilet paper from my face, except where removing them would have caused fresh bleeding.

From this safe distance I watched as the King climbed out of the APC and stood there for a moment, chatting to the major-general, while his entourage and the Dakota crew stood by, ready for boarding. They were all obviously taken by surprised when the general, in response to something the King had said, looked around and beckoned to the nearest air force officer; who happened to be Inclair Mith, the squadron spy.

I turned cold. I swear my blood temperature sank thirty degrees as Smith, complete with speech defect, which grew even worse when its owner was nervous, marched up to the King and saluted so enthusiastically that his cap slid to one side.

"Oh, God," I whispered, starting forward involuntarily. Even Kit Corner, who had been tittering steadily all afternoon, looked a bit worried.

Unfortunately, my involuntary reaction had taken me closer to the bigwigs so I could hear what was being said — or worse, not being said. The King, who both stuttered and lisped slightly, was saying, "I understand that B ... B ... Andy is the Squadwon Weader here."

To which Inclair Mith was replying, "As wite erect, or mahes," bowing out of sheer nervousness, with his cap on one side.

"I b ... beg pardon?" said the King.

"I os agreen or maahes. He is mere, your aye, aye, ayeness."

His Majesty looked helplessly at the major-general, who turned to the I/O and said briskly, "Pull yourself together, man. No need to be nervous in the presence of His Royal Highness, His Majesty King George the Sixth. Speak up!"

"I was meaking up," Mith said, resentfully but slightly more intelligibly.

"What's that?" said the general sharply, suspecting that our squadron spy was being Impertinent.

"I was meaking up. I was agreeing that Mandy was our commanding officer."

---

* Khaki battledress was issued for the Italian and African campaigns, at least by the RAF. — Ed.

"Who the devil's Mandy?"

"Mandy, Mandy," the I/O persisted, despite his difficulty in pronouncing the letter b — not to mention fifteen or sixteen other letters of the alphabet.

I moaned again, realizing I would have to come to his aid. After all, he was one of my officers. I was responsible for him. So to clear matters up, I stepped forward.

"It's all right, General," I said. "I'll explain."

"And who the devil are you?"

"I'm the Mandy in question. Or, Bandy, rather." And turning to the King I said, "Hello, sir."

There was an intake of breath from Striped Pants. Some breach of protocol or other. But the King didn't look too breached. "Ah, B ... Bandy," he said, smiling. "I was told you were h ... here. In fact I was huh-hoping to see you."

"Really, sir? Why?"

In reply he offered his hand, and, after a brief shake, he took my arm and led me aside, apparently for a quiet word, for he lowered his voice and moved even closer. "I've been looking you up, Bandy."

"Oh-oh."

"I think I know quite a bit about your caweer, Bandy," he continued, lowering his voice even further, as if he didn't want anyone else to hear the ghastly news.

"Look, sir," I said, "I think I can explain to your satisfaction about how I came to be demote —"

"Yes, yes," he interrupted. "I only have a minute, Bandy. The point is, you've met various members of my family over the years, especially my dear father. He mentioned you more than once. In fact, so often that we —" Something in his memory bank caused him to pause and twitch slightly before hurriedly continuing, "Anyway, what I wanted to ask you, Buh-Bandy was — are you a twue fwiend of ours – – of the Woyal Family, that is?"

"Well, I — I think so, sir," I said, feeling as bewildered as the rest of them were very plainly looking.

"Actually, you're the reason I insisted on visiting the bridgehead," he went on, looking as if he was counting the pieces of toilet papers stuck to my face. "I just wanted a general idea at this stage as to whether you would be pwepared to carry out an ewand for us sometime in the future?"

"Ewand, Your Majesty?"

He paused to clear some grit from his eyes. It was quite dusty in

Normandy. "I think you're ju-just the man for the job, you know," he said, drawing still closer. "As a Canadian you're not like the usual types I ...." He gestured covertly at the group of brasshats and striped pants. "Anyway, I need a chap like you, with a mind of his own. You know, an outsider."

"Sure thing, sir," I said stoutly, without a clue as to what he was on about. "Any time. Bandy is willing, yes siree bob. Call on my any time you like, Your Maj."

He touched my arm shyly, and smiled. "Thank you vewy much, my dear Bandy," he said. "It may not be possible, but it is good to know ... You don't speak German, by any chance?"

"Oh, I'm afraid not, sir. But I know one or two songs in German," I added helpfully.

"Oh, w ... well, it may not be needed," he said, almost to himself, and with another confidential sort of smile, he turned back to the others. After a final salute from the general, he climbed back into the Dakota, urged on with flapping motions by S. Trousers, who obviously considered the King's visit to the battlefield a really bad show, and a mistake that almost certainly had something to do with me.

Whether it had or not, I'd no idea. I remained as mystified as the rest of them as to what the sovereign had wanted from me. Still, I felt that the visit had been worthwhile: it must surely have impressed the men with my august connections that August. I'm sure it did my prestige no end of good. From then on, even LAC Burley would occasionally give me a glance which was almost definitely tinged with respect.

THAT'S GUINEVERE THERE

A FEW DAYS BEFORE THE GREAT BREAKTHROUGH, on the day I had decided to take a day off, the supply Anson disgorged the usual loads of food parcels from Canada, some heating oil (now that the temperature was up in the nineties), a packet of charge forms, urgently required Spitfire components, another two replacement pilots from OTU, and Guinevere.

The ground crew greatly appreciated her visit, especially when, in climbing down from the twin-engined machine, she showed off her sublime legs and a flash of knickers, Khaki type, women, for the use of. Last time I saw her she was a WREN depth charger. Today she was a brown job with Catering Corps flashes.

I enjoyed the heedless garterscape as well, until I remembered that I was through with lust, and utterly resolved to have done with her in particular, once and for all, definitely. Even the grandeur of her magnificently ferocious face must no longer be allowed to influence me. This time I must be as unbending as your typical magistrate faced with a exhibitionist.

"Oh, hulloa," quoth I with a blemished smile. Before I could express my astonishment to find her here she rushed up and started to stick kisses to my face like Patagonian stamps into an old album.

"Darling," she breathed, rustling the hairs in my ear holes, "it's lovely to see you again. I've missed you so much."

"Yeah, but howja get here?" I enquired in a feeble sort of way, though I knew she had more than enough influence to get her into the war zone. She was acquainted with all sorts of important people. Even so, it was surprising. Hell, my close friend and confidante, His Royal Highness and Majesty the sextuple George, had had difficulty in persuading *les grands fromages* to allow him into the Normandy bridgehead — and here was a mere intelligence agent sashaying into the war zone like it was Ascot on a race day.

Meanwhile, the rest of the squadron had come running up to enjoy the sight of their rigid-face commandant being amorously pursued by a female brown job, though they recoiled somewhat, when they hauled up their eyeballs from her garter to her kisser.

"Wow," as Kit Corner said, "what a dame. No wonder you took

one look at her and fell."

"What?"

"Fell for her, I mean. You've been going with her four years, I hear. You're really smitten, eh?"

"How could he look at her and not be smitten?" said Sergeant Rod Childer. He, too, was trying really hard to keep his face in line.

"Yeah, well," I said.

In fact, I often wondered how I had come to be attracted initially to someone who, like me, was so spectacularly different in the lineaments department. I guess it was because I had always been interested in people who were different or eccentric or unusual, or simply because they'd had the misfortune to take a fancy to yours truly. Or, who knows, maybe it was just a matter of pride, because I was the one who had sprung Gwinny from the jail of her virginity — she being thirty-five before she discovered that sex was, as she put it, jolly good for the complexion.

For a while, the affair with her had been quite stimulating in a way, but it had begun to go wrong last year in Quebec City when I was accused of espionage — just because I happened to learn the invasion plans for D-day — and I discovered how ruthless she could be on behalf of MI5, or whichever secret organization she belonged to. I hadn't particularly minded that she was a ruthless sort of person until it was directed at me. By the time I was cleared of suspicion my feelings for her had cooled like soup in an igloo. Unfortunately her own affections, which had been put in abeyance while she was checking me out, veered in inverse proportion, to the point where she was now utterly convinced that she was head over garters in love with me.

As affirmed now in the middle of a Normandy field, whilst looking around for an empty tent for us to snog in. "You've grown on me more and more, Bartholomew," she said, as if talking about a beauty spot, or wart. "I can no longer sleep late each morning for thinking about you, or eat like a horse the way I used to. Why, every time I scoff a plate of oysters I think of you, and immediately my heart starts to beat. You remember that time you held me at bay with my own pistol?" she murmured, huddling closer to hide her blushes. "I even found myself kissing the handle of the gun, because your hand had been wrapped around my butt."

"Huh?"

Now, as she smothered me with smooches — Christ, it was like being attacked by a lamprey — she was whispering again on the subject of spare tents. It was all terribly embarrassing. After all my efforts to impress the men with my sophistication and my range of choice acquaintances, like George the Sixth, here was I being loved up to scrumps by a mere ATS lieutenant.

"Darling, I need to talk to you in private," she murmured, looking at me in what she probably though of as a seductively tender fashion. "Isn't there somewhere where we can ... you know? What about your tent?"

Quickly I informed her that this was impossible, as I shared the tent with the MO.

"A hotel, then?"

"Good Lord, Gwinny, this is a battlefield. And incidentally, just how did you manage to —"

"What about Bayeux? We could go there and ... look at the tapestry," she giggled.

"Darn, I'm afraid I have an appointment," I laughed regretfully, looking at my watch. It was well worth looking at, even if it had stopped from the moment Gwinny emerged from the Anson. It was made of steel so bright you could see your reflection in it, if you had a very small face.

"An appointment?" she said, smoothing out a wrinkle in my khaki shorts.

"M'm. A Flight has orders to attack a suspected V-1 site." I said, and started to explain everything in detail except the fact that my name wasn't down for that particular sortie.

"But I only have a few hours," she wailed. "I have to be back in London first thing tomorrow."

"Gee, I'm really sorry, Gwin, but there you are. I'm so busy these days, you know. Quite apart from flying duties, I'm, you know, really busy, for instance there's this important Type 4657 business, and then there's Conjoint RV I have to attend to over in 2TAF HQ, and — well, the fact is I'll be AWOL practically the whole PM, and besides there's no spare tent for you to stay in and as I say I've already explained about me sleeping with the MO, and there's also the new ATOL-9Y arriving on the Handley Page 0/400 which I have to see to, as well as the talk I have to give the other ranks, a lecture on how to find, or rather, avoid, the shocking number of brothels to be found dotted around the country. And then there's —" But I made the mistake of pausing at this point when it occurred to me that I'd made a mistake. That Handley Page I mentioned, that was hardly likely to appear as it was a WWI bomber. The rest of my speech would have died of suffocation anyway, as Guinevere had dragged me behind the medical tent where we kept the arsenic for the gonorrhoea cases, and now she was lampreying herself once more to my kisser, and once again talking about a permanent arrangement between the two of us. Marriage? Was the woman CRAZY?

Obviously it was high time I set her straight, that there was not the slightest chance of our relationship burgeoning into wedded bliss she was trying to drift me towards. No, the high time had definitely arrived. Nothing if not doughty and resolute, I spoke up again. "No, but look, really, we have to face up to it, Gwinny," I told her, taking her hand, and cuddling it, protectively, in case it turned into a fist. Speaking with several catches in my voice, I continued, "Much as I would love to proceed into — whatever was being, um — considered, it would never work. For one thing, your butler would never give his consent," I said, trying like mad to lighten the occasion. Though it was true enough that Davis the Butler was not a minor impediment. He had taken a scunner to me ever since I'd soiled his sparkling new driveway with foul engine oil, as described in *Hitler Versus Me*. "Besides," I added, with another light laugh to indicate that coming up was yet another amusing touch, "let's face it, your family doesn't have the wherewithal to keep me in the style to which I am accustomed."

Her family manor house was undoubtedly in an acute state of disrepair, but I was just making another little joke, you see, namely, that if I had to live in a stately home it ought at least to look stately, and not resemble an Elizabethan barn with the bovine staggers.

But another smooch, disguised as a wrestling hold, strangled my excuses at birth. Nowadays she seemed to think that kisses, or exchanges of hot spit, solved everything. On this occasion it was becoming clear that the only way I could get away from her was by insisting that I was booked for flying duty.

Luckily, the ground staff didn't look too surprised when I shouted for my machine to be wheeled out pronto. I suspect they had long since decided, somehow, that I was a slightly unusual sort of chap; but then, what air force CO wasn't a bit mad, eh?

As I wrenched free and staggered first into my tent and then into my distinctive flying gear — air force blue overalls, yellow silk scarf to protect my neck from the abrasions caused by constantly revolving my head through 359 degrees — she began to look a tad resentful. "I still don't see why you can't take the day off and spend just a few hours with me," she sulked. "I went to a lot of trouble to organize this trip."

"Gosh, really sorry, Gwin," I said. I seemed to be saying sorry quite a bit, these days.

"After all, you're in charge here. Besides, you look as if you need a rest. When's the last time you had time off?"

"Oh, Good Lord," I said, with a merry gesture shaped like last weekend. But once again she sidled close enough to flatten her chest against mine, and murmured in babyish tones, "I could be your next furlough, darling. You know?"

"M'm, yes, but as I say, oh darn it, duty calls, Gwin," I said, flapping my flying helmet in the breeze as if it needed airing. Then I was looking around vaguely, as if I might have forgotten some trivial item. Oh, yes. Parachute.

She went off like a flare. "I might just as well go home right now," she said, glaring like anything. "Then you'll be sorry. Missing such an opportunity!"

A moment later, though, she was doing her ear-nibbling act. "We could do it in a field, or something," she whispered, making me twitch as her hot breath parted the hairs in my ears. "I've always wondered what it would be like, a spot of al fresco dalliance, what?"

"No, I've really got to go," I said, writhing as if the latrine was my destination rather than that Spitfire over there, the one surrounded by a crew hurriedly assembled by Flight Sergeant Selkirk. "Duty calls, Gwinny, duty calls, eh?" I said in what, after thirty years trying, I still believed to be an English accent. "Rather. Definitely. What, what?"

She emitted a furious snort, turned, and marched out of the tent toward the Anson, which had finished loading for the return journey to Manston. Luckily the crew had waited for her, though I suspected that she had been hoping to miss it so I'd 've been forced to put her up for the night.

I had intended hopping out of the Spit as soon as she was out of sight, but the field controller took so long giving the Anson permission to take off — no doubt waiting for the CO to make up his bloody mind — that I was forced to signal the crew to juice me up from the cart. The rest of the flight, with Bill Baynes as Yellow Leader, were already airborne and climbing in the distance. Normally they were led by Kit Corner, but it was his day off.

This was piss-poor leadership. How they must despise me. I should have told her exactly where I stood, as distinct from where I was standing, in a metaphorical sewage farm. Now, because she was still watching from the doorway of the Anson I was having to continue priming, pumping, wiggling controls, nudging levers, right up to the point of furiously gesturing for the chocks to be yanked aside, as if I really meant to fly on my day off. My day off? They should all be my days off. I was not compelled to fly, I was perfectly entitled to goof off, perfectly. What was I doing, what was I doing?

For a moment as I saw her looking at me from the Anson I felt sorry for her. A middle-aged spinster, it was understandable, her falling for a splendid bloke like me. No, it wasn't bloody understandable! It was stupid, she ought to have more sense than to fall for another middle-aged crock. Suddenly the fury rekindled itself with the black coal of guilt. Which, of course, I instantly dismissed. It was her bleeding fault. Why didn't she pull herself together. "Go on, go off, bugger off back to London!" But she was still watching. No, wait. At last. She was climbing aboard. Oh, thank Christ. She was off. No, wait again. Now she was staring at me through all that bloody Perspex.

I couldn't just sit here, engine idling. It was growing almost as hot as I was. And now the bastards were signalling me to take off before the Anson. Thoroughly basted with sweat in the hot cockpit, I started to taxi, viciously swinging the nose of the plane from side to side with violent bursts of throttle, travelling too fast over the now sun-hardened grass, feet treading on the pedals as if I was producing a shroud for myself on a Singer, as if I was actually intent on flying! It was all her fault. Why hadn't I told her it was all over between us bar the whimpering, why, why?

I was still hoping that by the time I reached the top of the runway and started slowly along the grid I would be out of sight and I could hide, let's say behind those Bailey bridge sections, over there in this far corner of a foreign field that was forever. But the Anson still had me in sight. So I had to go. I would have to go NOW, or prang the kite before I'd even unstuck from the grid. Then they'd really have cause to snort in Sniggersville. I hadn't even flipped the magneto switches or adjusted the radiator regulator in the billowing warmth. I hadn't even connected up the oxygen and the radio.

As my old pal Oliver Hardy used to say, way back there in my filum days, another nice mess I'd gotten myself into. But who would care? Not even me. So I'd prang the kite. So what? So what?

Taking a last few breaths of oily air, I made an angry check of the various switches and levers, and shoved the throttle forward into my first day off since I took on this job. It was a sortie I'd particularly wished to avoid, too. It was to be an attack on a buzz bomb ramp. It would be heavily defended, whether it was real or a dummy. The Jerries had built quite a few phoney ramps to divert us from the ones that really did fling buzz bombs into England. There were becoming pretty good at it, camouflaging the dummy sites with their usual skill but with just enough clumsiness to make the structures sufficiently real-looking so as to lure us into the range of their deadly 88s.

It was not that I was a yeller-bellied fraidy cat. Certainly not, not in the least. It was just that I was already doing more operational flying than many other COs. And to no purpose. I hadn't even seen an enemy aircraft, let alone shot at one. Though of course, squadron commanders had many other responsibilities to attend to, you know, other than flying. Vital things like, well, like signing well-deserved leave applications, making sure the field latrines were properly disinfected — very important that for the wellbeing of the men, you know. And ... What else? Oh, yes, putting erks on jankers. Vital things like that. I mean, let's face it, there was no need, no requirement, no formal obligation on a squadron commander to do any war flying at all unless he was desperate for flying pay.

Anyway, it just wasn't fair, making me risk my life this way, an old chap like me with half a century's wear and tear on his poor old nerves. How dare they force a man who was practically a pensioner, force him to go out there day after day, risking his gluteus maximus, when he ought really to be settling down by hearth and hob, with no other obligations than to pull on his pipe and smoke his slippers, safe at last from life's baleful hazards. I mean. Apart from anything else, couldn't they see that I was far too valuable to lose on some paltry operation? Oh, the waste, the waste!

Thinking about it later, I think it was at this point that I was starting to have a nervous breakdown, whatever that was — I'd never come across such a thing during my medical training. Or perhaps it was just age. Operational flying at my age had been ridiculous enough four years ago, now it was plain stupid, especially with the pilot pools swimming with eager beavers at this downward stage of the war. Many of them would never even get on ops. And here was I, a half-century-old crock — oh, forget it, forget it, get on with it, now you're here. But, oh, the depression.

I was falling further behind the other aircraft, and had to buster to catch up. I managed to join them a few minutes later as they gained height over 'Crotch on Sea', as we called the tiny town of St. Croix-sur-Mer.

The voice of Kit's deputy, Bill Baynes, rasped over the intercom. "Hello, Yellow One," he said.

"Who you calling yellow?" I responded. "I don't have to be here, you know!"

There was a surprised pause, then: "Aren't you taking over, Yellow Leader?"

"Hah? Oh. Yes. No. You carry on, Bill," I said, and attached myself, sweating more than ever despite the chill.

By the time we had punched through the clouds and levelled out at 10,000 feet just west of Le Havre, I had started to calm down. You couldn't feel irritated for long in a machine like this. The Spitfire was such an enormous pleasure to fly, the most responsive to the controls of any of the dozens of machines I'd flown in my lifetime, and one of the least temperamental. A marvellous airplane, even after years of modifications and refinements, still sleek and powerful as a killer whale, a truly beautiful fighter.

Gradually the nasty feeling drained out of my sump, and when our sector controller, Kenway, rang up to cancel the attack on the ramp and alert us to a formation of 190s in the direction of Dreux, suddenly the day was full of sunlight and good cheer at the prospect of a scrap, and the opportunity to take it out on somebody.

Flight Lieutenant Baynes, leading, immediately ordered a change of course and a climb on full power. For the first time since reaching Normandy I clamped oxygen to my face. Until now we had been operating almost exclusively at fairly low level. I felt toned-up by a feeling that we were going to see some action, a distinct sensation of something impending — a funny feeling, a hunch, a sixth sense, an inexplicable anticipation — except that I was explaining it as a throbbing in the great adductor or possibly the gastroenemius, a hallucino-entropical southwest Melanesian dyspnea, a distinct sensation of beggar's blanket, Aaron's rod, lady's foxglove or donkey's ears, a definite impression of pedimental entablature, or, to put it another way, a machicolation of mixed corbels or brackets projecting from some mysterious parapet from which missiles or boiling oil might be launched at various aggressors; a twinge, in other words, of excitement, or call it what you will, but it was there: the imminence of battle. Since D-day, the Allied air forces had bleached the Luftwaffe so thoroughly from the blue skies that formations of enemy machines had almost entirely disappeared. It looked like they were coming back.

I was feeling so much better so suddenly that even when the supercharger punched in with a bang at 20,000, I hardly twitched.

But then, anticlimax: we failed to get there in time. Some American Lightnings had rushed to the scene ahead of us, and scattered the enemy force, though I gathered that they didn't get any.

Disappointed, we wandered about above a mountain range of clouds for another twenty minutes or so before Baynes turned west again. We'd had nothing to report. He was heading back. The alarums and excursions seemed to have ended. And we were not far from home, having dropped already through the cloud base, when we were bounced by at least a dozen Fw.190s.

They seemed to come out of nowhere. In seconds one of our kites went spinning down out of control.

As supernumerary, out-on-a-limb, tail-end-type Charlie, I should have gone, too, had not that old, worn instinct nudged me knowingly in the ribs. Because my neck was becoming stiffer these days I usually avoided twisting it around unnecessarily, even though I knew that looking back over my shoulder had saved my life a good many time in the past. Lately I tended to rely on the rear view mirror, despite its shortcomings. But luck, though I no longer deserved it, was still hanging around, however disconsolately. For once I cranked my leather-clad cranium around to make sure there was nothing back there but oxygen, nitrogen, and a few trace elements. Jesus Christ! Somebody sure was! Enemy. Focke Wulf. Levelling out less than two hundred yards away.

Bellowing an RT warning to the others, I slammed the Spitfire into one of its famous turns, simultaneously switching on the sights, hauling back on the throttle so as to confuse the enemy by reducing speed. No time to adjust the seat to its lowest position, but every other action instinctive, fright-free, and somehow providing me with at least one extra arm for the sudden rush, a spare humerus, radius, and hand complete with recently bitten-down nails.

Otherwise, no time for twitch or flinch. I came out of the turn to such centrifugal effect as to plaster my brains hard against the inside of my cranium, leaving nothing in the centre of my head but a black hole and some oxtail soup.

Supercharger power on again, and as the turn turned out, it brought me behind one of the dozen or so German fighters that had gotten ahead. It wasn't one of Hitler's surviving veterans, judging by his amateurish efforts, which were as creaky as my joints usually were after a night on the palliase. A quick look behind. Clear for at least a second. Him in front I steadied between the bars of the advanced gyro sight. The poor sap went climbing as gently as if on his way to deliver plover eggs to the Herr General. He would be going down when the gyro sight settled. My thumb was on cannon's tit. I took a quick look back. Good job I did. The FW was back on my tail.

This one was a vet. I knew it right away. I was not going to throw him off easily.

This was confirmed less than two minutes later. I simply could not get rid of him. And from then on, not the most violent and unexpected manoeuvres were the slightest use. He hung on as if I owed him money.

No time to feel scared. Once again, adrenaline came to the rescue, speeding up the old, worn reflexes, accelerating the thinking power. But as it turned out ....

At first I was confident enough. All those years of flying had helped accumulate a substantial credit of defensive experience. I was certainly drawing on the account now, going through every manoeuvre, trick, and villainy in the ledger. It was only when I got to the last bit of aerial knavery that I began to worry, for beyond it I had nothing more to offer. The last manoeuvre entailed slamming the machine into a vertical bank, jamming down the right pedal, then almost immediately a centring of the rudder in a frame-wrenching jolt so as to avoid a complete cartwheel. Even that stunt didn't do a bit of good. The Hun was still behind me. Heavy cannon fire soon confirmed it. Smoky tracer was feathering past, literally inches from the canopy.

I was right, I should never have gone on ops again, never. He was far much too much for me, and the jolting was beginning to disorient me badly. I couldn't take splitarsing the way I used to. Even four years ago, in 1940, I'd usually felt sodden as wet knickers after a fight. It was much worse now. As I tried to claw my way out of the web of tracer I could feel my throat filling up with the bitter yellow stuff.

He was still there, hours or seconds later. Now I was starting to feel dangerously anxious as well as sick and disoriented. I'd thought it was ground-strafing that would finally get me. Not for one moment had I ever believed that I might be bested in a dogfight.

I believed it now.

In desperation I slammed the machine into a hurtling, vertical dive, pouring on so much power that no Hun in his right mind would follow. Surely. But the mirror said he was still there, right there, right behind. Presumably by then he had reckoned that he was dealing with more than a novice, and was feeling all the better for it, rejoicing in the challenge, as I had rejoiced in the past at defeating a skilled opponent. Anyway, he was hanging on. In fact, this guy seemed prepared to accompany me right down to the cretaceous level of the Mesozoic era. In his formidable Focke Wulf he was even closing the wavering gap between us. Settling down for the kill.

I gave up the descent then, and pulled out, so sharply that for a couple of seconds my sight did a fade and dissolve, and I was staring down the dark tunnel that led to oblivion. Now the Spitfire was totally on the automatic pilot of reflex rather than skill. God knows how the plane was putting up with this sort of treatment. As for the automatic pilot, it needed another spell at OTU. When I twisted back to the horizontal for a split second and looked back, wide-eyed, the pervert of a Focke Wulf was still clamped to my ass. And at last his shells were starting to hit home.

The fuselage was shuddering under the impact; I felt the armoured seat beating me unmercifully. It was one hell of a shaking up. What was he using, a howitzer?

Obviously he'd had even more practice than me in this business. It was time to order the women, the children, and me into the lifeboat. Successful fighter pilots were the ones who knew when to quit. I was already planning on bailing out. If I resisted the temptation for a few seconds it was only because I'd have to fly straight and level for a couple of seconds to manage it, and that was all the time he would need.

No. Forget it. I kicked the Spit into a spin.

Borrowing much more luck than I could afford to repay, I let the control column flail about in the cockpit to its heart's content — until I saw that the quilt of the earth below, of yellow and brown patches, was very much closer than I'd thought. Good Lord — the whirling, violent jerking, spinning fields were only about 2000 feet down. We'd fought down nearly twenty thousand feet.

I started to reduce power from this mad speed, though as inconspicuously as possible so as not to encourage him to keep up — mustn't make it too obvious that the plane was still under control — if it was under control — I wasn't too sure about that. But the ground was certainly coming up too fast. I couldn't hold the dive a second longer — if it was a dive and not a decline and fall. I grabbed the lashing stick in both hands, and hauled. It refused to be hauled.

Obviously I was still alive, for I panicked, thinking my Jerry friend had damaged the elevator controls with his cannon shells. But controls going on strike in this fashion was a phenomenon I'd heard about from another desperate pilot, of how contradictorily the controls could behave at very high diving speeds — almost as if they wanted you to disobey all the rules and shove in the opposite direction.

It was a temptation I resisted. Fanning the last embers of strength, throttle lever right back, shoulder muscles bunched as if trying out for a weight-lifting competition, I hauled so hard on the stick I could feel the muscles crackling. The entire Spitfire was shuddering and rattling, the wings surely bending far out of true. And the ground was coming up to welcome me in maybe seven seconds. I'd never make it, never, hopeless.

Maybe, maybe. My weight was quadrupling. The Spit's nose was coming up. But so was the ground. Stubbled fields rushing underneath, faster and faster, lonely trees whipping by. Farm cart on a road seemingly just inches down, and a moment later one mile behind. And then the aircraft nose starting sniff freedom.

Brute strength had managed to haul the shuddering machine level, my guts no longer rolling in the dust on the cockpit floor. We were actually pulling up from an altitude of five feet, maybe.

I looked back. The Hun machine had already pulled out.

Which — thank you so much, God, I'll never swear, blaspheme, and make fun of your beautiful world again — was the other pilot's mistake. His one sole, blessed mistake. Having decided not to follow my example and embed himself in a hayfield, he had pulled out a few hundred feet above, and was still travelling in the same direction, but upward, now.

Thus the Spitfire, wings bending like a lumberjack's saw, in coming out of the near-supersonic dive, and hurtling skyward again, found itself on an intersect course. The 190 was neatly orienting itself between the adjustable bars of the gyro sight.

With the last foot-pound of mental and physical energy left, keeping him firmly in place in the red sights, I inverted the Spit while climbing upside down at a shallow angle. From this attitude, with the stick forward, nearly on full power again, Sutton harness biting into my shoulders, dust from the cockpit floor swirling around, I presented him with a good half my store of cannon shells. Red flashes danced over the underside of his nose and continued erratically into the wing root.

To avoid a collision, for I was going upward faster than he was travelling horizontally, I turned away with a quarter roll and a vertical turn that almost shoved my bulging eyes through the bald patch at the top of my head. And I continued to splitarse, just in case he's somehow managed to recover and take his proper place behind me again. There was no need to worry. When the FW swept into view again he was going down, trailing smoke, prop windmilling.

In case there was another deadly Heinie in the neighbourhood I racked my head around, then turned back to watch as the Focke Wulf neared the ground. It flattened out at the last moment, leaped a boundary or two of *bocage*, then whacked down into a yellow field.

The hayfield had been mowed and the slippery stubble sent him skidding along for quite a distance. He must have smacked down at a pretty high speed. Finally he came to a lurching stop with the nose deep in one of your typical Normandy hedges. A great cloud of thrashed leaves and branches flew into the air. A moment later white and black smoke lazily coiled and billowed around.

Feeling as if I were in there with him, I circled, throttling back. I rather hoped he'd get out in time. Just when I thought he'd had it, a figure emerged groggily from the smoke and staggered clear.

He was just in time. The machine exploded, sending up a fresh gout of black smoke, and now, yellow flame to match the field stubble. Covering his head with both arms, the pilot lurched onward for another hundred feet or so, then collapsed, though still protecting his head from possible chunks of debris.

As I flew over for the third time with the canopy open for some fresh air, he waved, albeit without a great deal of enthusiasm.

CAMP SCENES

WHEN I PARKED THE SPITFIRE in one of the sandbagged bays and climbed out and looked it over, I was surprised to find that the kite had been hit more often than I'd thought. The boys would have to repair two large holes in the wings, including a chunk of port aileron. A cannon shell had even fractured the canopy. I kept fingering my helmet, wondering where the hole was, but it seemed that once again I'd been lucky. Surely this sort of thing couldn't continue. I was happy enough with dissoluteness, but dissolution was another matter, and was long overdue.

The erks were going to be busy, patching things up. When Flight Sergeant Baker wandered up to inspect the kite, he inspected me as well. "Godamn it," he said, "I thought I could at least rely on you to bring the equipment back in good shape."

Limping over to the operations tent for debriefing, I felt old, shaky, and itchy with dried sweat. Sinclair Smith, the intelligence officer, agreed that I wasn't looking too good, but then, after all, I was getting on a bit, wasn't I? Suddenly realizing that I hadn't seen a single pilot since I had slammed so awkwardly onto the mesh landing strip, I had this crazy thought that I had lost the whole of A Flight. Smith reassured me. Only one of the guys had gone for a Burton, though Sergeant Hemming had ground-looped on landing. So it wasn't so bad. Assuming the gun camera footage came out, or I could provide the co-ordinates for where my 190 had gone in, the squadron could claim two e.a. destroyed.

I had been late getting back, and by now the rest of the boys had repaired to the "mar", as Smith put it. Presumably he meant the bar. After the fight I had flown around for a bit, to give myself time to recover from the encounter with that Jerry, whoever he was. He was a shithot pilot, that was for sure, and I was glad he had survived. We were informed later that he had been picked up and taken to the temporary POW camp on the coast. In the Great War I'd probably have invited him to the mess for a thoroughgoing binge, but not these days.

Otherwise I was still pretty dismayed at the way we had been taken by surprise — an experienced leader like me. Mind you, I hadn't actually been leading. All the same, I was the boss and it had not been a good show. Probably the boys would again be lamenting their ill-luck in having been saddled with a horse-faced CO who should have been put out to pasture long ago.

The ground staff were probably thinking the same thing, judging by the way they kept staring at me as I made for my tent: clerks, cooks, riggers, fitters, wireless ops, and met men, all seemed to be nudging each other and twitching their eyebrows as I limped and lurched over the worn, yellowing grass, the parachute appropriately spanking my bum. It was plain they knew all about the flight that had been taken by surprise.

I felt like skulking in my tent, but duty called, at least in the form of duty-free booze. So after a quick wash in the ablutions lean-to, and after carefully combing and rearranging the hairs over my exhibitionist pate, I collected the walking stick and made for the mess tent.

Sinclair Smith was already there, having completed all the details for Comic Cuts, the intelligence reports. He probably felt he needed a drink, too, after debriefing me. If I hadn't been so shaky and decrepit I would have felt quite indignant about the way he had kept staring at me during the debriefing. After all, I hadn't been leading the flight. And downing a 190 was not exactly a minor achievement these days.

Outside the mess tent I hesitated, aware of the racket within. They were all talking loudly, explosively, or was it angrily? However, after taking a few deep breaths of fading fumes, hot rubber and engine oil, and ghastly cookhouse smells, I braced myself with the guy ropes of defiance, pushed through the tent flaps, and entered.

Just as I expected, they all turned, and fell utterly silent. They were staring as hard as had the ground staff. If I'd entered singing and dancing and farting the refrain from "Jack was Every Inch a Sailor" they couldn't have goggled more intently.

I stared back defiantly. "Wot?" I said after a moment, into the hush.

They remained silent, staring as if they'd never seen me before, except for Sinclair Smith, who had a hand to his face, perhaps to conceal his hare lip with a self-conscious fist. I leaned more heavily on my cane, partly because the support was still sometimes necessary, but mainly in the hopes of arousing a bit of sympathy from the others. After all, I'd had a hard time.

At which point Kit Corner came forward and said almost shyly, "Can I get you a drink, boss? You look like you need it."

"Damn right." Without waiting for him I rolled over to the trestle table. They made way for me as if I were openly festering; though Corporal Carp, serving at the bar, offered me a glass of beer in a kindly enough way.

"Better make it a whisky," Kit said. "A double."

They all watched as I downed most of it in one go.

"Boy, that was some flying," a member of A Flight said, sounding as hushed as if he were in Bayeux cathedral.

"What was? "

"You, knocking down that chequered bastard, eh?"

"Oh, yes," I said abstractedly.

Flight Lieutenant Baynes pushed forward. He looked flushed and red-eyed, as if he'd been talking explosively for hours. "Yeah, that was quite a show, boss."

"Eh? Oh, yes. Any Scotch left?"

There was a bit of scramble to fill up my glass. "Here you are, sir," said the winner, almost respectfully.

"I can hardly believe we're finally rid of him," Kit Corner said.

For a ghastly moment I thought they were referring to me. However, now slightly fortified, I pretended to misunderstand. "H'm?" quoth I. "Who?"

"Strand, of course. Willy Strand."

I must have continued to look blank, for after a moment someone said, "The guy you shot down."

"Oh. Is that who it was?"

"You mean you didn't know?" a pilot exclaimed, and another said, "You didn't see those red and white marking on his kite?"

"How could I? He was behind me most of the time," I said, and was busily gazing around more blankly than ever when, as if a dam had burst, they all started to laugh, and writhe, and fall about in a most disorderly fashion, slapping each other on the back, and howling as if something screamingly funny had happened; possibly my expression, which may have suggested blank incomprehension, which it often did, unless it was only dyspepsia and ruination. Whichever, the laughter went on an on, becoming almost a hysteria of the sort one would expect to find among a pack of hyenas who had come across a wildebeest with a gammy leg.

Even my most vapid remarks were sending them into bellows of laughter — positive paroxysm. "I got one of their aces, eh?" I asked. "So that's why he was so difficult." That really broke them up.

"I got one as well," Baynes said, his face swollen with excitement; and he went on to describe how he'd accomplished it. But he must have been telling the story ever since he landed, for he was losing his audience. Most of them continued to cluster around me, asking questions or just staring as if seeing me for the first time.

"I mean, hell," said Sergeant Childer, who was trespassing in the officer's mess, "you're old enough to be my grandfather."

And Kit Corner was saying wonderingly, "They claimed you used to be a shithot pilot, but we just couldn't see it. I mean, Jesus, you had one foot and half your ass in the grave, practically."

"I say, steady on," I riposted, on my third drink and in my best brasshat accent, which caused even more of a commotion if that were possible, and it weren't.

The celebrations went on all evening, many of the fellows not even breaking off for supper. In fact the racket continued well into the dusk, and even the MO contributed to the party in a particularly handsome way, i.e., by bringing out several of the bottles of whisky he had been trying to keep from me, out of concern, he said, for my red hot liver, which was very unfair because I'd been doing a lot less drinking lately, hardly more than a bottle a day, and then only when all flying had ceased. Though after I'd started on a second bottle that evening the MO hid the balance of Scotch all over again. But I didn't mind, I was having such a good time by then, enjoying the awe and respect that the boys were finally showing me, as I described for the third or ninth time the brilliant manoeuvre that had vanquished the Heinie, while not thinking it worth mentioning that the manoeuvre had been purely fortuitous. No, it was my sublime experience that had done it, an exquisite splitarsing that had overcome the great German ace who had been tormenting the squadron since Tobruk, Benghazi, and Mersa Matruh.

My land, but it was good to be appreciated again, to be looked upon with such drooling respect. And high time, too.

"Now I believe everything they said about you," said Kit. "Even some of the good things."

"Yes, well, let's have a little more sense of proportion in future, laddie," I said. "But please, don't let me interrupt the proceedings. Carry on with the well-deserved praise, if you wish. Don't worry, gentlemen, I can take it."

"Lying down," someone put in; and indeed, I was flat on the grass at that particular moment.

"Right, so let's have a toast to Bartholomew W. Bandy," Kit shouted, raising his beer glass. "Who has finally rid us of our Oberstleutnant Strand, or whatever his title or tittle. Our bugaboo and bugbear, our scourge and affliction, our burden, our cross, the thorn in our flesh since Africa, and the bane of our life. To Bandy!"

"To Bandy," they bellowed, and sloshed back the pale ale with a will and a testament. "Speech, speech!"

"Well, I kept telling you I was the greatest," I said, when the racket had died down. "Over and over didn't I kept telling you? But no: you wouldn't believe me. Oh, you're all so typical of a sceptical generation. I mean, look. How d'you think I managed to earn these?" I said, placing a buckling finger on the part of my battledress where five rows of ribbons were supposed to adhere.

"What?" asked Hartley Huntington owlishly, "them soup stains?"

I peered owlishly down at my chest. "Oh, yes," I said. "I'd forgotten that my breastful of colourful orders, awards, decorations, and things blaze and brag only on my proper tunic, not this khaki charlatan, this battle impostor dress. Because nobody in the entire, whole, complete squadron has offered to sew one single ribbon onto my nice khaki tunic. I mean, I couldn't do it myself, could I? After all, I've lost my batman, for the simple reason that, unlike Brit officers, Canadians don't have servants, poor devils, and also because I've lost my housewife or hussif as she is called, namely the little sewing kit that the air force issues to its lucky entrants."

"My, isn't he eloquent," someone said, which, though it was not the least funny, created the most merriment of the entire evening.

Even my clerk, Len Burley, whose job it was every day to bring me something to read, eat, wear, or sign, was nice to me that night, even though he wasn't supposed to be in the mess.

"Don't you worry, sir," he said, wagging an ink-stained finger at me, "I'll look after the admin from now on. I know how you hate signing things, in case it's a confession and might be used in evidence. But don't you worry, sir, you just have a good time beating up buzz bomb sites. I can handle it all. I usually do all the work anyway."

Stewed as I was by then, I wasn't going to let him get away with that. Taking the risk that my head would split open and disgorge its riches like some munificent cornucopia, I arose again from the dead grass in the tent and said forthrightly, "Whatjamean, you do everything? I spend hours and hours poring over various paper — things."

"Sure, and then I have to pour it all back," said Len. "Sort it all out again. But that's okay, that's what I'm here for."

"Oh, bugger off, Burley."

"Well! If that's all the thanks I get," he said, but was drowned out by a fresh burst of whooping and hollering as Kit Corner failed to balance a glass of beer on his head as he danced the gavotte or malagueña or danse macabre, or possibly all three.

"It just goes to show," I said, after I'd again described how I'd lured the German ace into a sense of false security by positioning him right on my tail so he could pump cannon shells up my ass, "that the tactics of the Great War still apply just as much as they did in the first war."

"Oh, God, he's not on about that again."

"Laddie, we have much to learn from World War One," I said. "No jus shibaltry, ribaldry, and tic, but —"

"No just what, sir?"

"Not just chivalry, reverie, and tictacs, but — not just them but this!" I cried, gesturing grandly, and rapping my knuckles painfully against the tent pole. "The traditional binge, I mean. Makes me feel really at home at last," I said, feeling so sentimental that there was a great danger of a tear forming in my eye. "But as I am saying, in the Great War we always had these great parties in the mess on every conceivable occasion, an' an' plenty of inconceivable ones. And here we are, carrying on this glorious tradition of destructive inebriation. Except here we don't have furniture to smash up like we used to."

"Smashing up furniture was part of the fun?" said Kitty Corner. "Quick, Sam, rush out and get some furniture for old Bandy to smash."

In a quieter moment, breathing beer fumes into my face and holding onto me, Kit said, "Boy, have we ever under — under —" His face went blank.

"Underwear?"

"No, no, no, no. Under — under —"

"Underpants? Undergrowth?"

"No, no, no, no, no."

"Uunderfoot? Uunderhung, underhand?"

"Shut up. How can I think when you're being so helpful. Underestimated! Tha's it. Tha's the word for you — and it's not even obscene." He was remaining upright only by hanging on to my sleeve. As a result the sleeve was starting to look all puffy and misshapen, and if there was anything I hated it was misshapen sleeves.

"Leggo, you cad," I said. "You're drunk."

"That's true. That's perfectly true, old boy, old boy. But thank goodness there's at least one person is sober enough to make sure the rest of us don't come to any harm."

"Thank you, Kitty. I'll do my best."

"Not you. Certainly not talking about you. I mean, look at you."

"How can I look at me? I haven't got a looking glass."

"Right. Sam, while you're out looking for furniture for Bandy to smash," Kit shouted, "get Mr. Bandy a mirror!"

Somebody had been trying to attract my attention for some time. I turned and gazed at him very intelligently.

"Air Vice-Marshal Chistelow!" hissed my informant.

"No, no, old boy, you've got me all wrong. I'm slim and slender Squadron Leader Bandy, don't you know. Air Marshal Chistelow is the one with the paunch."

For some reason, my informant, whoever he was, was screwing up his face and shaking his head with infinitesimal twitches. Fortunately, these movements got through to me in good time, chiefly because I suddenly caught sight of AVM Chistelow. He was only a few feet away, surrounded by a diminishing hubbub.

"Oh, Christ," I said into what was now a thunderous silence. However, nothing if not quick-witted, I continued as if I hadn't yet espied *le grand fromage*. In tones smooth as the finest emery I said, "Who'd you say it was, our new replacements, is it, Chiseler and Lowe? Flying Officer Chiseler, you mean, an' - an' Cuthbert Lowe, the replacement pilots, is it?" Then, pretending I'd just that moment noticed our distinguished visitor, I started back in so thoroughly convincing a fashion as to cause several beer glasses to clash together on the trestle table as if they too, were offering a toast. "Why, it's our own 'stinguished Tattycul Air Force commander. Snot Pilot Officers Chiseler and Lowe after all," I said, rounding accusingly on the sleeve plucker, whatever his name was, and saying to him severely, "Why didn't you tell me our 'stinguished officer commanding was paying us a visit? That's very 'miss of you, you know. Very 'miss."

"Sorry, sir," quoth the offender, sounding distinctly strangled.

I turned back to the AVM. I even shifted towards him, slightly sideways. Confident that no harm had been done, I continued loudly, "Well, well, well! Welcome, Air Vice-Marshal, welcome to our mess, however humble." And I bowed, quite gracefully, I thought.

"Good evening, Bandy," he said, in a way suggesting that it was neither a good evening nor that no harm had been done. "I'd been intending to call in and see how you were getting on," he said, looking as if he had been expecting the worst. "They tell me that congratulations are in order."

"Ah. Ah," I said.

Removing his eyes from me without much of an effort, he turned to the rest of the swaying company in general, and said, "I believe you all put up quite a good show. It certainly won't do the Luftwaffe morale much good, eh?"

"No, sir," somebody said politely, just as there came an almighty crash. This was because the drinks table had collapsed, as some oaf who'd had far too much to drink in far too short a time, considering the state of his emotions, his fears and apprehension, his age, and his fatigue, fell backward onto the trestle in a shower of shards and froth.

STAGGERING ADVANCES

BY NOW, THE GERMAN ARMY WAS RETREATING at such a pace that we could hardly keep up with them. While General Patton and his Third Army were speeding towards Paris and would be there by August 25, on our front the Jerries were still being encircled in the fifty miles square of countryside that would become known as the Falaise Gap. We were having to move to new landing fields about every half hour, or so it seemed. We were on ops almost continuously, shooting up everything that moved, until darkness cloaked the chaos on the roads. For once the ack-ack was bearable, especially as there was hardly any of it — Jerry was in such a hurry to depart that usually he didn't have time to set up the guns. Actually, the hornets were worse than the ack-ack. The French versions were particularly vicious, perhaps because they'd had so many tasty corpses to work on lately. Around the open air cookhouse at the airstrip, the insects were so omnipresently confident in the heat of August that they felt fully entitled to grab the food before we did. You had to hold your filthy hanky over the mess tin and stick the mush in your gob at lightning speed, and even then the hornets often got there first with stings aimed at your tonsils.

By the end of August we'd packed and unpacked so many times that my valise, anticipating a move, was starting to spring over every time I entered the tent. Half the time we hardly knew the name of the nearest village, though somehow we always knew how far we were from Paris. Personally, I hadn't visited the capital since retreating from Spain in 1939. I looked forward eagerly to receiving a share of the Parisian plaudits, though as it turned out, I ended up in an entirely different location. I was to get shot up again, and worse, shot down.

It happened quite early in the morning. We had been filling Comic Cuts with volumes of braggadocio based on our casualty reports as we trounced the fleeing Hun. By now they had become easy targets. The survivors of formerly huge Wehrmacht units were jamming the roads with their armoured vehicles and carts in the full scale rout that had followed the Allied breakthrough after the closure of the Falaise Gap. So many targets were available that to keep the pilots as busy as they wished to be, I had reorganized them into pairs so that one pilot could guard the other's back while he blasted the fleeing enemy, and then reversed the arrangement to give the guardian his share of the action. Not that they seemed to need this protection. There was almost no ack-ack, no pink balls of fire being flung up by the multi-barrelled guns, and thanks to the plenitude of targets on the roads under the sunlit sky, there were oodles of interesting murders to commit, and bags of flying. We were going out as many as six times a day, to create almost unbelievable damage on the enemy vehicles and ground troops. So what with the lack of opposition, it was particularly annoying to get shot down by mere potshots from the few infantrymen who were not too demoralized to shoot back.

Imagine being brought down by field-grey sharpshooters with just rifles. One moment my Spit was whizzing along at 300 mph above a road flaming with burning vehicles of all sorts, exploding gun carriages, half-tracks, little VWs that looked as if they had been can-opened, and upended tanks including even a Tiger here and there, with my cannon and machine-guns thudding dementedly, their smoke streaming over the fuselage as well as the wings, and causing the cockpit to fill with fumes. Then to find that something critical had been hit.

Which, God damn it — God bleeding screaming with rage damn it — is what happened, and it was enough to bring down the plane. Within seconds of a tinkling hit, the engine was misbehaving badly enough to make me try for more height so I could observe a possible landing site. It was evident that the kite was in trouble, and worse, the only available space in the rolling wooded countryside was one unruly field, not nearly spacious enough for a landing. A landing was definitely required, though.

Worst of all was the realization that John Oakley, my companion flyer, was not being clobbered at all. He was not to receive a single bullet hole in his kite.

I had taken him along as wingman to see how he fared, so that I could have him transferred to another outfit if it became evident that he was as incompetent as he looked. Unfortunately he had performed pretty well so far, sticking dedicatedly to my tail except when it was his turn to shoot. I was in danger of finding little to complain about except an excess of RT — though I thought rather meanly that that might supply the grounds for grounding him. He was using the RT to discomfit me — like keeping on and on about my being so brilliant a pilot that any normal person overhearing the chatter would immediately assume that it was I who was the incompetent one and he was there just to make sure I didn't get lost.

Suddenly, the smoke in the cockpit was not just incidental to the guns but potentially lethal. The Merlin had started to screech. Rather late in the day it obeyed a New Year Resolution to not only quit smoking but functioning. I had time only to bank slightly toward the field while I still had any control, and slap down the flaps before the machine whacked down so hard that I bit my tongue. The fighter thrashed over the straggly ground, slowed only slightly by the flaps, before smashing into a stand of trees. Luckily they were dense enough to bring it to a halt quite smartly.

I sat there for a few seconds, clicking switches in case anything caught fire — apart from me, that is. Oh, the shame of it, the shame! I had not even been brought down by a 37 mil gun with its brilliant barrels, but probably just an infantry rifle. Or maybe a Kraut in his impotent rage had just thrown a rock at me — there had been a rattling sound from the engine. And I was sure that Oakley had something to do with it, too. He hadn't even noticed that I'd gone down. And it was his fault that I had bitten my tongue, too, not to mention the way I had banged my left knee on the landing light control.

However, it was time to get away before the Jerries got me. They would undoubtedly be in a mood to kill, after what we'd been doing to them. I started to heave out of the cockpit, wincing over my knee, still feeling really annoyed at the way Oakley had bitten my tongue. Caused me to bite it, I mean, but all the same ....

Climbing over the coaming gave me a better view. Too good a view. The spindly trees I had run into bordered a path that led up a hill into deeper woodland, but in the other direction led straight to the vehicular shambles on the main road, and enemy soldiers were already heading toward the crashed aircraft, hoping no doubt that the pilot was still just alive enough to be butchered. I'd heard of pilots being killed.

There was not the slightest hope of escape. The maddened soldiers were just seconds away, a few who had managed to survive the terrible air attacks which had been going on from dawn to merciful dusk for days on end. I knew how they would behave. I'd been strafed myself. I knew the rage, I knew the feeling. As I climbed out and slid to the ground I released my chute, and raised my hands. Not that it would help, after all the appalling carnage down on the road. For a second I was tempted to run, and get it over with quickly. Better to receive a swift end with a bullet in the back, rather than face the inevitable savagery they were sure to mete out to a hated aviator. One could hardly blame them, after the slaughter of the days since the Falaise encirclement. And the Germans weren't noted for genuflecting to the Geneva Convention.

A few infantrymen, emerging from the smoke and fire on the road, were struggling towards the splintered fighter. I couldn't help feeling frissons of fear as they lurched forward, their eyes seemingly embedded in blinkless hatred. Some staggered as they reached splintered fragments of a hawthorn tree, that had been chewed up by the Spit. As there was nothing to do but wait for the worst, I leaned against the shattered fuselage, now with folded arms. It would have made a great shot for *Picture Post*: the sight of a beautifully posed airman standing directly in front of the roundel from which the red and blue had been so deliberately faded that almost no colour was left, and next to it, a grubby white letter, K. Together with the air force roundel it seemed to spell OK, if you ignored a fuselage festooned in arborial rubbish and the prop curled like spaghetti, not to mention the failure that the crash represented. Still, the black and white invasion stripes were unmarked and in defiant view, as was the courageous airman standing there, trying to look as if he was just waiting for a lift to the nearest three-course dinner, rather than already being in the first course, the soup, waiting to be eviscerated by enraged troops. The tension was not eased in the slightest when another pair of Spitfires blasted past, a hundred yards to the east, neither of them noticing my crashed aircraft. Instead, the two machines hurtled onward, streaming smoke from their chattering guns, sending yet more death and dismemberment into the packed convoy.

I unfolded my arms as the Germans, presumably ordered to check out the crashed Allied aircraft, stopped a few feet away, swaying and glaring. At the front was a man in a torn and filthy uniform. Not an officer, I didn't think. Possibly only a corporal, with quite modest insignia, except for the red and black ribbon peeking from his uniform. Iron Cross, first class. He was a stalwart chap who might once have had a feeling of pride about him. He was missing a helmet, and his entire head was so dirty and dishevelled that the sweat was dyeing his fair hair dark grey, to match the uniform.

He gestured savagely towards his men, two of whom grabbed me and started wrenching at me. One of them struck me with the butt of his rifle, hard enough to send me staggering back against the fuselage. Then they were all over me; checking for weapons, I supposed, though it must have been obvious that, not expecting any trouble or high altitude work, I was wearing little but overalls and a sweaty vest, the Mae West at my feet. One of them had wrenched off my leather helmet, taking a quantity of hair with it that I could ill-afford to lose. He threw the helmet aside, and again struck me with his rifle.

"You are English officer?" the corporal asked, loudly and hoarsely over the thump of exploding armaments and crackle of guns. The question had caused him to cough wretchedly, and bend over. "Your rank?"

"Well, you'd be a bit rank, too, if you were in these sweaty overalls."

"*Bitte?*"

"Oh, you mean ... Well, if it matters, I'm a squadron leader," I said, somewhat short of breath. That last rifle blow had really hurt.

The leader, who emanated a surprising authority considering his rank, seemed to be trying to save ammunition by drilling me to death with his eyes. I actually had difficulty in not looking away, even though he had the dead same expression as his men. Their gaze, from deep inside their skulls, was unwavering, unblinking, inhuman. I couldn't understand why they had not already beaten me to the ground and finished me off. Or were they just too tired for the moment?

"You are old," the corporal said tonelessly.

"What?" I faltered, staring back, momentarily nonplussed, wondering what my age had to do with it. When he merely continued to drill me with his mad, vacant eyes, I said, "Well, it's hardly surprising. I've been fighting you since nineteen-sixteen."

"*Ach, so,*" he muttered indifferently, as one of his men said something and gestured toward me in a definitely unfriendly fashion. The corporal just stood there. For a moment I thought he was giving permission for the prisoner to be disembowelled without further ado. Instead, he turned back, and said, "You have authority?"

"Authority? Well, naturally," I said, forcing myself upright again, and hoping he hadn't heard from Pilot Officer Oakley.

The corporal suddenly swayed, and half-fell against one of his men, who himself was not in a particularly stable condition, judging by the slowness of his own reactions as he helped his colleague upright. It was only then that I realized that the company, far from comprising a bunch of the usual fit, efficient Teutons, were men at the end of their tether. Some looked as if they'd been recruited from an old people's home. Their demeanour would not have merited much praise from their sergeant-major, I can tell you. Apart from the one who had had the strength to club me, they were far from being enraged. Their eyes, though bright, were like those of automatons, fixed, almost unseeing. They seemed unable to blink, after the savage beating they had taken for days, possibly weeks. And for the first time I realized that most of them were physically wounded as well; they weren't just terminally exhausted.

Recovering his balance and forcing some strength back into his tones, the corporal said, "You have killed thousands of our men with your bombs and rockets."

"*Ja,*" I said, using one of the few German words I was familiar with, the others being *Arbeitschlosenunterstutsungsgeld*, and *Schadenfreude*.

He seemed to have lost track of what he was saying. He lowered his hand to his pistol, and for a moment I thought he was going to take lethal action personally. Instead, he rested his hand on the muddy holster for only a second before letting it flop listlessly away. Instead, he turned to his men, who seemed to have increased in number, and started to talk to them.

For a moment they appeared galvanized out of their stupor. One of them protested, even heatedly, the one shortest in stature but the most dehumanized in appearance. He hoisted his rifle and started to point me out with it. Had the corporal decided to eliminate me, but was too tired to do it himself? I hoped the rest were all as punchy as the corporal was. It was possible. All two dozen of the men, except for the short, brutal one, were starting to reel like bigtop clowns. Many seemed unable to concentrate, perhaps more than half deafened by near misses, or distracted by their injuries. Those that had rifles — not all of them had — seemed too feeble even to lift the weapons.

For a moment the corporal's voice sharpened, and he even managed to straighten up. After some minutes the protests died away so that we could all hear the gunfire as fresh Spitfires, and now, rocket-firing Typhoons, joined in the good work further up the road. Now the corporal was unsnapping his mud-smeared holster. He was taking out a remarkably clean Luger pistol. He was glaring at me. He was pointing the pistol at me. This was it, then. I straightened up, trying my best to look like Gary Cooper, and wondering if I could delay the execution a bit by asking for a blindfold. A clean blindfold. Gary Cooper would not have accepted one, but I would. I would insist on it, so long as it was a scrupulously clean handkerchief or something similar, as befitted an absolutely top-of-the-range junior officer like me.

Except that the corporal was jiggling the Luger in the direction of the pathway bordered by my splintered trees, the path that led to the carnage on the road down there; except that he was flicking the barrel in the opposite direction, jerking the gun up the gently rising ground into the woodland.

And he was speaking to me again. "We are now democrats," he said. "For us the war is over. We have decided to surrender to you." And so saying, he handed the pistol, butt foremost, to me.

On the following morning and doctor and I were having a nice lie-in, tentwise, he because he'd been up late the previous evening treating a possible case of gonorrhoea — his own —while I was making up for lost sleep, and also taking advantage of the lull in the war work caused by a bout of bad weather. I had managed a glorious half morning of snores and slumber before Pilot Officer Oakley ducked in out of the rain, crunching an apple, tracking mud onto the MO's groundsheet, and shaking water over me. In spite of which, I was determined to remain sound asleep, until he shook me and also tapped me on the head with the unmunched part of the apple, and announced that the boys were impatient to hear an account of how I had single-handedly captured a thousand Jerry prisoners. The foreign correspondents had been calling up about it.

When I returned to the squadron the previous evening, most of the fellows had been out on a sightseeing tour — cathedrals, brothels and the like — and I was full of pills and sound asleep by the time they returned. This morning I was not in the best of moods even after several hours buckshee sleep, but Oakley distracted me before I could remember the bayonet I had been sharpening especially for him.

"They've been waiting hours in the mess," he said, loudly crunching another segment of pomme.

"Who has, our boys or the correspondents?"

"Oh, the correspondents were only phoning, sir. The squadron is quite keen to hear all about it, though. They asked me to come and wake you, so you could give your side of it, even though I told them that I was on my way to my own pit. I'm not feeling too well this morning," he continued, sitting on my canvas cot, sneezing toward my pillow, and going on for a good two minutes about his symptoms, until he finally explained why he'd been deputized to wake me. "Trouble is," he said, flinging aside the apple core so he could feel his pulse, "none of the chaps wanted to come in here and risk it with the doctor's syphilis."

Now it was the MO's turn to wake. "What the hell d'you mean, syphilis?" he shouted, leaning up. "It's not syphilis as all, it's —" He stopped himself just in time, and turned away, to rearrange himself roughly north-west in his cot, with his legs tucked up and his head more deeply embedded in his very own pillow, a present from a hefty village girl. But then he rose on an elbow again, and shouted even more loudly, "And get the hell out of the tent, you god-damn milk pudding-faced god-damn lump! It's bad enough seeing you on parade, Oakley, without you sopping into my tent! Just get out!"

I had gone to bed the previous evening feeling as if an ancient Egyptian had drawn out my brain with a hook in preparation for a sojourn in a pyramid. However, after a long hot shower, a shampoo, a shave, and other shushing activities, I felt ready to face yet another occasion in the mess, a celebration of my capture of four or five score Hun. Incidentally, while the prisoner business would be extensively reported in the papers, resulting in a promotion, for some reason the vanquishing of the great German air ace would not be detailed for a good many weeks. But, scurrying from the ablutions to the mess tent under the drenching rain, it was Oakley I was thinking about, trying to decide whether or not the MO had been unfair in describing Oakley as being a milk pudding-faced lump. I soon concluded that the estimation had not been overly unjust. After all, the lad did have a pale, expressionless sort of face, made worse by a pair of appallingly sincere eyes which looked like spills of dolly-blue bleach that had been accidentally mixed with a package of blancmange. Mind you, to be perfectly fair and honest, as I could always be relied on to be, I thought that the doc had gone just a little overboard with his milk pudding remark, which could have been considered unfair to milk puddings. Personally, I loved milk puddings. I would have rejoiced if such a dessert had been served up in the tent, but the cookhouse staff had not had any milk for weeks, not even the powdered variety. But otherwise, when you got right down to it, I was much too modest a person to quarrel with the informed characterizations of our esteemed medical officer, re Oakley.

Even en route through rain I was being questioned. The met officer shouted something like, what the hell had I been up to the previous day. The scuttlebutt had been coming in since last night about an air force officer with not all that much hair but with a helluva lot of captured Jerries in tow. The met type was so interested that he actually abandoned an urgent visit to the latrines and followed me into the tent. I learned later that he was developing dysentery, which made his detour even more impressive, though mind you he didn't stay for long. Also, a couple of the sergeant pilots looked so interested that I couldn't help but invite them in, out of the rain.

The moment I got inside there was a barrage of questions, starting with Huntley Hartington's enquiring, "Hey, skipper, what's this crap about you taking five hundred prisoners yesterday?" with a sceptical twist to the lips.

"It wasn't nearly that many," I said, looking around for a certain trestle table. "There were only a couple dozen at first. Though mind you, we seemed to pick up quite a number of others on the way back."

They all fell silent, until Flying Officer Billing said faintly, "Jesus, it's all crap. You were so pissed off with the Germans that you landed in their territory and took hundreds of them prisoner? That can't be right."

"Single-handed?" somebody else breathed. "I mean, Jesus, we've heard some screwy stuff about Bandy, but this is crazy."

"I told you," I said, still looking for the booze. The sun must surely be over the yardarm by now, even if it was skulking above the rain clouds. "There were only a few Huns to start with. It's just that some others decided to be taken prisoner as well, you see."

"You mean they just joined up behind you?"

Kit Corner shouldered his way forward. "Lemmee get this straight," he said. "You landed on purpose in some field —"

"Hell, no. I was hit."

"Okay, they got you. But where do the prisoners come in?"

"They came into the field, of course. By the way, hasn't anybody opened the bar yet?"

"Never mind the bar," Kit said impatiently. "Why didn't they just grab you?"

"I think they were too tired from all the hard travelling. Fleeing from the enemy is very tiring, you know. As for getting them to follow me, I guess I just brought to bear my impeccable logic and persuaded them to give themselves up instead," I fibbed. "Look, guys, what's happened to the bar? Surely it's after twelve by now?"

"Hold on thar, Sir Bandy," said H. Hartington. "Have I really got this straight — that you corralled a bunch of their soldiers and got them to follow you? All the way back to our lines from the road we were beating-up yesterday?"

"M'm," I muttered, hoping that Hartington was joking with his "Sir Bandy" reference, and that he was not aware that I really did have a knighthood. It had been earned in India — not one of top quality, of course, like the companions in the bath, but quite good, and with a beautiful ribbon and insignia and so forth. Knowing how Canadians felt about them sorts of honours I'd been keeping it secret, eh?

Anyway, as they seemed interested, I thought I might as well fill in the details, starting with me at the head of an initial two dozen Heinies as we trudged up the hill away from the road choked with death and destruction. The path had led gently up into woodland, the density of which provided us with excellent cover for a while, until we finally emerged into the open country south of Amiens.

By then the band of stragglers had grown remarkedly, augmented by quite a number of other Wehrmachters who had fled earlier into the woods. All in all, I gained a very strange retinue. Many were old, even older than me; some real codgers of the sort who had been so eager to support old Adolf out of their conviction that they had not lost the last war but had been betrayed. Mixed in with them were some sixteen-year-old Hitler Youth types. Fortunately, they had lost their drive and arrogance, and had turned mindless with fatigue. There were even some foreign troops among my bulging Bund, though they were in German uniform; Romanians, I think. They were quite grateful to be captured, as if I were saving them from something even worse than a POW camp.

Anyway, by the time we had broken into the dangerously open countryside, the reeling rabble behind me had grown by dribs and drabs into a staggering company that must have numbered over a hundred. Mind you, the number was sorely reduced when a force of Typhoons blasted us with broadsides of rockets; this in spite of the fact that we were not taken by surprise. The attackers did not snarl into view at low level like our Spitfires, but from a couple of thousand feet in bright air. By the time two of them had peeled off and winged-over to attack, somebody had had the good sense — I think it was me — to issue enough yells and gestures to lower many of the old men and boys into the ditch. Even so, many of them did not reappear.

Because of a sudden headache, it was some time afterwards before the absurdity of the situation struck me almost as hard as the clump of earth that one of the Typhoons had flung up: that I'd actually been warning the enemy to take cover from my own side.

It took quite a while for the somewhat diminished band to reach — wherever it was — a village south of Amiens. I had kept a lookout for some sort of support from the local inhabitants, but though we had passed a few scattered houses they seemed deserted, or at least nobody emerged to stare at the limping, lurching levy of volunteers for incarceration. By then it was afternoon, I think, and the Teutonic procession behind me had reached a sum total of exhaustion, hunger, and some physical but mostly nervous damage from the vicious aerial browbeating from the enemy. From their enemy, that is; from our friendly flyers, I should say. By now I was turning somewhat lightheaded after the staggering, wary walk in the late August heat, or perhaps the goofiness was delayed shock, or simply the result of being clobbered with hard mud by the swine up there in the cerulean blue. Swine? What on earth was I talking about? The Typhoons had been part of my own beloved air force, I needed to get that straight. They were my friends, I had to remember that, the chaps whose tactic against this exhausted band was usually to sneak up at an exceptionally high speed and low altitude and clobber ziss defenceless Bund mittout varning, though luckily, so far, I had handled zuh fellows quite vell. Yah vole, ve had been extraordinarily lucky, as the brutes up there in the Tiffies had been flying higher than usual when they spotted my men. Did I say brutes? Course not. My men were not brutal but fine, wholesome Canadian lads who loved their mothers and hated any sort of controversy. Where was I? Oh, yes, feeling lightheaded. I was even starting to stagger as much as Corporal Wassistdas. That's what I called him, Wassistdas. The clump of mud had clobbered the noggin as well as whacked the port patella. Also, I was faint with hunger, or so I believe, though I may be wrong about that. Still, I was pretty sure that I hadn't had breakfast. The countryside we were staggering through — I mean, where were all the Normandy apples we'd been told about? Or was this Brittany? Or Belgium?

So far, we disorganized soldiers had not come across the slightest sign of the enemy — no, no, surely I mean sign of the Allies — apart from the dull, threatening thunder of distant aircraft. But my guard remained unlowered. They were likely to start biffing us again at any moment. It seemed to me that it was important .... Important to do what? Ah, yes, to get in touch with the en- with our side. Not their side, of course, these Jerry stragglers, but the British side. Right?

Suddenly I came across a road sign. Amiens, that way. Whatdoyouknow, my old railhead. From thirty years ago. What was it doing here? The UK had scrubbed the names of towns from their signposts from as far back as 1940 so as to cause an invading force even more confusion than the Brits themselves enjoyed, but the French countryside was positively lavish with helpful directions. I looked again at the sign. It was pointing to the bottom of a hill. Hornoy. I fell to wondering how the pilots would pronounce that name. They would probably pronounce it as Horny, except for Flying Officer Asselin, our sole French-Canadian representative, who was called Assline. He would probably pronounce it Hornoy, I surmised.

From up here, the town seemed to have a remarkable number of roads leading into it, or out of it. Perhaps the inhabitants might tell us which way to go, to reach ... wherever we were going. God, this sun was hot. I was sweating cobs under the overalls, but I couldn't take them off as I wasn't wearing much underneath. I wouldn't want to embarrass my men. I'd already discarded the parachute. I was certain I had started out with it. Mind you, that was just when you were flying. At the moment I wasn't flying, so that was all right, then. What wasn't all right, though, was that I had long since lost the flying helmet as well, exposing a tinder-dry pate to the sun's embers. I raised a listless mitt to the lump already established as hiding in the scanty hair. It was about the size of an undersized hen's egg, but though the hen might have been undersized, the bump certainly wasn't. How the hell did I get that? In the crash I'd felt only the blow to the knee. To prove that at least one of my injuries was genuine I started limping again.

One of my men drew my attention to another sight. Ah, *enfin*: finally a few French peasants. They were walking up the hill towards us. But they suddenly turned back at the sight of about a hundred men in German helmets. Or seventy-five in helmets, twenty-five without, give or take a helmet and a spot of arithmetic.

Two or three of the chaps now came up to me, among them Corporal Wassistdas. "There will be English soldiers soon?" he asked, sagging onto a grassy bank.

"Soon ...."

"The French down there, they will be hostile," he went on, shielding his bloodshot eyes from the sun. Raising his arm again with an effort, he indicated the town at the bottom of the hill. "Civilians are always worse. Also, we are in the open. If more aircraft come ...."

"Yes, that's right," I said, watching as my men started to hunker down into the ditch, some to remove their helmets if they still had them, and lie back, grey forearms exhaustedly shielding their faces, others just standing there by the side of the road, as if willpower had melted in the heat. They were weaving about unsteadily, faces turned from the sun. They were disinclined to worship the sun just at that moment.

"You are sensible?" Wassistdas asked.

"Huh?"

"You are not going to faint, and desert us?"

"Oh. No ...."

"How long is it before your soldiers come?" Wassistdas added, staring down into the roasted grass.

"How should I know?" I nearly said. I had not the slightest idea where we were, except that we were slightly south-west of wherever we had started from. Feeling as if I were in a warm, soporific soup which might be poisoned by high explosive from aircraft at any moment, I muttered, "You have a lot of old men in your company."

"*Bitte?*"

"I bet they're sorry now they didn't accept the truth in nineteen-eighteen, and get on with their lives .... As for us, we got on with it too well."

He looked at me with a morphic expression, but after an hour or a few seconds he replied tonelessly, "*Ja*, you are describing my father."

Not many minutes or hours later I caught the flick-flash of reflected light, possibly from field glasses. Then followed an awareness of brown men with funny tin hats. They were still quite distant, but scuttling ever closer, from the far edge of one of the fields. Also a troop carrier was just visible down the road, moving slowly, followed by the jittery movements of infantry. I got up slowly, as if getting ready to be introduced to somebody of no great importance, feeling even more detached from reality.

"Tell everybody to throw down their rifles ..." I began, as if I had not the slightest sense of danger, no fear whatsoever of the stealthy infantry.

"*Bitte?*" Wassistdas mumbled, before raising his head with enormous effort and finally discerning what I was seeing.

"Tell them to stand up, arms up," I said, and for some reason nodded encouragingly three times before stepping out onto the road, demonstrating by raising my own arms, and starting to walk down the road, slowly, towards the troop carrier.

"And that's it? That's the whole story?" Kit Corner asked, this day later, as he finally fished a bottle of beer from the case and held it out to me.

"Remember that colonel who was with the King that time?" I asked. "The one in the personnel carrier? Well, he was in command of the company making its way through Hornoy, and there he was again in his APC. He told me he was tempted to shoot me for the way I was weaving down the road in my overalls."

"Shooting you? H'm — quite understandable, really," said Huntley Hartington thoughtfully.

Kit Corner was still shaking his head. "I don't find anything understandable," he ventured. "He prangs his kite, bumps his knee slightly, but to make up for all the pain and suffering he has to endure, he brings in a few hundred enemy prisoners single-handed."

"There's no need to exaggerate, Mr. Corner," quoth I. "There were only about four score of them in the end."

John Oakley, who for some reason was wearing a glistening groundsheet, came in at this point with his usual calm certainty. "It's not right, the way you're all laughing at our squadron leader," he said.

"You talk as if his amazing achievement was quite natural. I must point out that his is a pretty terrific story, and I don't think you should treat our Mr. Bandy so disparagingly."

"For crysake," Kit muttered, sounding a little fed up.

"Let's face it, our squadron leader is a great man," John said admonishingly.

"Well, thank you, John," I said, "but —"

"And I believe everything he says," John determinedly asserted. "Just because we haven't received any real confirmation of anything, is there any reason for you to harbour these shameful doubts?"

"What shameful doubts? We haven't any," someone asserted almost as strongly.

"Hell, no, none at all," someone else said. "At least ...."

"Yeah," someone else put in. "Admittedly, it does sound kind of, you know ...?"

"Dubious?"

"Yeah, that's the word. At least ...."

There was a confused silence. "Yeah, well ..." someone else muttered discontentedly, and after a moment people began to drift away, from an account that had now quite plainly been utterly discredited.

★

A couple of days later, near the end of the squadron's sojourn in France, I was thrilled to hear that Oakley was sick. "Oh, dear," I said when I visited his pit, "not feeling too good, eh, John?"

"They say it's dysentery," he replied wanly.

"Oh, dear."

"It's all the discomforts," he continued. "Like having to sleep on the damp ground, and wearing the same clothes for days on end, and not having enough hot meals."

"Yes, I know."

"Not much fun, you know, dysentery."

"No, I guess not. Actually, quite a few of the boys have it. It's the —"

"I'll be so busy dashing to the latrines I won't be able to help everybody make the move to the next airfield, that's what bothers me."

"Won't you?"

"I'll be in no condition to help with the heavy lifting."

"You won't?"

"The belts, the ammo, the engine spares, the stuff in the radio van, the 1054s and the 1055s."

"No, I suppose —"

"Especially the really heavy stuff, the boxes, the met easels, the aerial poles and all the rest of the gear, and the fuel, the oil, the boxes of ammo —"

"Yes, there is quite a lot of stuff to —"

"— the I/O's files, the cookhouse hardware, the engine starter, the heavy lifting gear."

"Of course, some of the boys are still managing to —"

"The charge files, the fitters' tools, the paint pots for your aircraft insignia, the cleaner for all the mud gumming up the radiator when it rains, the spare parts for the engine, and the ..." and he continued so extensively with his list of things he couldn't help with that I had time to despatch a hornet. It had been darting over his bed and over his own little bedside table which his mother had given him as a going-away present, along with a little medical chest containing pink pills for pale people, and a packet of French letters sneaked into his pharmacopoeia, apparently by a malevolent cousin.

After I'd done Oakley the favour of swatting the wasp, I got even more interested in the family Vespidae when three or four hornet pals actually gathered round the corpse and decapitated it. It's true, honest to God. I actually witnessed it myself, the way the quartet, working together, removed its head. It took all four of them to accomplish this, though only one of them actually carried it off.

I was just visualizing the head being mounted over some tiny little mantelpiece, when John interrupted his list of things he wouldn't have to carry, with "But at least you've been spared my affliction, Squadron Leader," he was saying. "And that's the main thing. I'm so happy to have spared you the same suffering, sir."

Shortly afterwards a dysenteric assault had him dashing to the nearest latrine at a remarkable velocity considering that his knees were locked together. Meanwhile I was just as busy, preparing a recommendation to Group that Pilot Officer Oakley be court-martialled for gross glossopharyngeal malpractice, i.e., excessive use of the tongue and pharynx in listing his reasons for goofing off work. If other pilots could restrain themselves latrinewise while helping the move to the new airstrip, then so could he, right? After all, he wasn't the only one to have developed the shits from the bowser.

It was only after I'd settled at our penultimate base in Normandy, B-44, that it occurred to me that a substantial change was taking place in my life. Until now it had reeked of conflict with superior officers, earning for me substantial quantities of ire. I had been making enemies of bigger and bigger cheeses ever since 1916, starting with that infantry colonel in the WWI trenches, the one whom I clobbered with a tin hat –– purely by accident, of course. Funnily enough, it happened in this very region, near Amiens. Then there was the general who came to hate me so much that he volunteered me for a test on a very dangerous parachute, with the result that I had ended up as an innocent quarry in a filthy one. Soon I was earning the hostility not just of splenetic brasshats or paltry politicians, but of the leaders of entire countries, for instance, Russia, and even, believe it or not, of my very own Canada — the Prime Minister of which actually threw me out of the country, believe it or not! Me, who had never done anyone one iota of harm — or at least not on purpose, or very rarely so. Boy I could tell you a few things about Mackenzie King that — but never mind that. The point is, I seemed to have spent my entire life making enemies of people who otherwise would have helped my career to no end. Oh yes, and there was that billionaire American publisher Chaffington. He really hated me, just because I had blown him up in Ottawa — entirely by mistake, of course. No, I mean, the way he treated me was absolutely disgraceful, especially when I threatened to become part of the family after falling in love with his daughter, Cissie. Oh yes, and let's not forget the Viceroy of India. Now *there* was someone who might have been really useful in my career. And what was happening now? John Oakley, that's what was happening now. Him and me.

It was rather a shock to realize that I was thinking of doing the sort of things to PO Oakley that others had done to me over the centuries. Suddenly I was quite overcome with shame. Why, I was now in the same company as all those people who had attempted to do me down all my life: brasshats and government ministers, and all those rulers and nabobs, all those billionaires and generals and remorseless dictators like Stalin. Now I was actually proposing to fell Oakley as determinedly, as dementedly as my superiors had always attempted to grind me into the dust.

Mind you, the situation was not entirely similar. After all, not one of the fiends who had tried to demolish me in the past, not even Stalin himself, was as deserving of demolition as John Oakley. I mean, one had to be objective, you know, and clear-headed about the true situation. Pilot Officer Oakley was worse than any of them. So that was all right, then. I was going to get him, one way or another, one of these days. And the decision to pursue him to the end became firmer still after some swine commented that Oakley looked as smooth, bland, and imperturbable as I had looked when I was young.

BRUSSELS '44

BY THE BEGINNING OF SEPTEMBER the speed of the German retreat was astounding everybody, even we who had helped to speed it up with slavering guns, and had seen for ourselves the thousands of Wehrmacht vehicles and tanks brushed aside from the roads, and the stinking dead in the ditches. In four days our armies had swept so far eastward that northern France, just about all of Belgium, and even most of the Netherlands was back in decent, democratic, hard-working, honest-to-God hands; this despite the beastly enemy attempts to open the taps of the dykes that held the sea back from turning much of Holland into a cranberry farm. By then the Jerries were in such a mad rush for home that we simply couldn't keep up with them. So we went to the movies instead.

As well as the picture palaces, we rejoiced in the other glories of Brussels: the fifteenth-century Gothic-style hall, nearly as fine as our town hall in Toronto, and the Rue Neuve, which was almost as interesting as our Sparks Street in Ottawa, and the Josaphat Park, St. Joost-Ten Node, which was almost as spacious as High Park. There were also some glorious nude shows, phenomena quite unknown in North America but terribly welcome nonetheless, really inspiring and educational, especially the one I visited where this gorgeous girl could pick up various small items of merchandise with her .... But I digress from the main point, which was that we were out of canvas at last, and into decent accommodation, surrounded by real bricks, electric lights, et cetera. I had not exactly relished the Boy Scout life, with stinky toilets and having to wash your own dinner pans under canvas pregnant with rain or done to a turn under the August sun. All this, and having to sleep with the MO, as well. And earwigs, deafening bangs in the night, and French peasants looking as if their liberation from the Nazi tyranny was only slightly more interesting than Père Philippe's calf, the one with the extra leg.

Paris had been liberated on August 25th, but it had been bagged by General Patton, so we collared Brussels, otherwise known as Brussel, or Bruxelles. In the first week of September our ground staff set off in trucks, while the pilots packed their smalls into smaller cockpits, and flew joyfully to Evere, Belgium's principal airport, close to the capital. So, apart from the grass field, the alfresco life was behind us now, and my squadron had the pick of the accommodation, because we were there first. I even nabbed the Sabena general manager's former suite for a while, until AVM Chistelow claimed it for himself. So I had to make do with a room in the former German officer's annexe, and found it perfectly satisfactory, at least until I discovered that John Oakley, now with the rank of Flying Officer, had moved next door. Once again, he seemed to be cosying up to me. But that was all right. I was not there very often anyway, as I was busy meeting the new love of my life.

When the first British and Canadian units had swept into Brussels in clouds of diesel fumes that September, the city had went quite mad with joy. They wreathed the wary guns of the liberators with flowers, and the grimy faces of the chin-strapped tank commanders with kisses. The humblest private soldier or aircraftsman was treated like a hero, and doused with beer and kirsch. For days the city was as gay and feverish as a Rio carnival. You only had to pause at a street intersection to receive an invitation to dinner, or at least a drink of grenadine beer in the nearest bar, or cognac in a private residence.

To be an Allied soldier or airman in Belgium in 1944 was an unforgettable experience; we took full advantage of the gratitude and adulation. It was positively disgusting the way we swanked and skirmished among the citizenry, and it lasted for weeks. And it was all free, too. For quite a while, we glorious liberators paid for little except, later, our excesses. Rides on the streetcars, admission to cinemas, galleries, night clubs, and best of all, admission to girls — everything was free.

Naturally my pilots were as eager as anybody to dive into the dives and drink to their kidneys' content. They even seemed quite eager for their ancient commander to join them. Things had certainly changed since I first limped and wheezed onto the field. They were still just as disrespectful, but now there almost seemed to be affection in their attitude. I suspected, though, that this was because they expected me to go west fairly soon, and not by the compass. Since that aerial engagement I'd been looking worse than ever, and they thought they'd better make the poor old soul's last few days a little easier.

Bill Baynes even asked me to come downtown with them.

"Got work to do," I said, busily tamping tobacco. A Belgian tobacconist had rushed out of his shop one day to offer me a brand new pipe and a tobacco pouch, so I'd been forced to take up smoking again.

There was a chorus of protest. "Hey, come on, boss, you can finish the crossword tomorrow," was one of the typically impertinent comments.

"Aw, shucks, you young fellers don't really want a middle-aged old coot like me along with you guys," I said with a little jerk of my shoulders, in the way I'd seen my friend Groucho Marx do it.

"Sure we do. So you can drive us downtown in that stolen car of yours," Sergeant Childer said, referring to the small German car I had liberated. Made of tin and ersatz rubber, it had been left behind by the enemy so hurriedly that they hadn't had time to booby trap or demolish it.

So we all piled into the little tin car and headed for town via the Avenue Leopold and the Boulevard Auguste Reyers. Even days after the Liberation, the thoroughfares were still packed with revelling Belgians, and it was quite late in the sunlit evening before we reached the central boulevard leading to the Parc du Cinquantenaire. We could barely creep the overloaded vehicle through the celebrating crowds. The populace was so pressing with the plaudits and the invitations that the casualty rate in my small car alone was frightful. One by one our pilots were carried off, struggling, by pretty girls and importunate matrons, like an up-to-date Rape of the Sabines. Only the senior member of the party ultimate survived to drive back to base, his only injury being sustained by his pride.

Anyway, now that I had been freshly promoted, following the collaring of the Krauts, I had more responsibility than ever. Why, only yesterday I had to supervise the DROs, put four fellows on jankers, and issue contradictory orders to the SWO, as well as seeing if the MO had any rejuvenating tablets to spare.

It was a while before I managed to get downtown again. "You're missing all the fun," they told me one evening, as they prepared for the usual rush downtown, following an uneventful patrol.

"Yeah, come on, boss," they said as they scrambled into their best blue. "You ain't been up to mischief all week."

"They've opened a swank officers club near the Metropole," Kit said encouragingly, as if he thought that the prospect of a deep club armchair — say next to old Colonel Blenkinsopp of the 2nd Battalion, Senile Rangers — might appeal to me.

"We've been telling everybody about you," someone else said.

"Really? Was that wise?"

"Funnily enough, some people seemed to know your name already," Kit said thoughtfully. "Like, somebody said you were an army general once, fighting the filthy commie bastards until they became our noble Russian Allies."*

"That was a long time ago, when I was twenty-six or so."

"You mean you really were a general?"

"Only a major-general," I said, gazing modestly at the ceiling and sucking judiciously at my new pipe with the Congolese tobacco. "Though it proved to be very useful. The temporary rank earned me a good payoff when I got demobbed in Ottawa."

"I'll be damned," Kit said faintly.

After a moment he went on, "Even one of the ladies there had heard about you."

"What ladies where?"

"In this new club downtown. Fact, she said she wanted to meet you."

"Yeah, that's right," Flying Officer Billing — or Late Billing, as we called him — said excitedly. "The dame that old Chistelow was busy entertaining."

"Jesus, it wasn't Guinevere Plumley, was it?" I asked in alarm.

"Hell, no, this was a great-looking broad."

"And she wanted to meet me?"

"Soon as she heard your name she started asking questions."

"Like she knew you."

"Yeah, that's right," Kit said, eyeing me with the unwavering look of your typical fighter pilot.

"But I don't know anyone in Belgium."

"Well, she was real keen on meeting you, boss."

"Somebody said she was a baroness," said John Oakley. "Boy!"

"No," I said, very, very thoughtfully. "I'm pretty sure I'm not acquainted with any baronesses — in *Brussels*," I mused, in a tone suggesting that baronesses were not all that high up in the scale of aristocrats with whom I was acquainted.

"Maybe the squadron leader would prefer to go to the all-Schoenberg concert at the Palais des Beaux Arts," said Huntley Hartington, our poshest pilot, who was from some suspiciously rich Montreal family.

"Gee, that sure is a tough choice to make," I said, stroking my chin. "Drinks in a swinging new club with a beautiful baroness, or an entire evening of twelve-tone music."

"They're playing several of his quartets," Hartington said encour-

---

* As told in *It's Me Again*, vol. III of *The Bandy Papers*. — Ed.

agingly.

"Good Lord, Hunt, you're making it so hard for me to decide ...."

I managed to get there a few seconds later, but the baroness wasn't in the club that evening, so I made do with a quiet chat with Kit Corner. Quiet, that is, whenever there was a lull in the noisy swing from a Belgian band that hadn't quite got the hang of Glen Miller, or even Paul Whiteman.

After a drink or two, Kit started asking questions about my past, and explained why there had been so much discontent in the squadron. "We were so busy griping about getting a has-been for a CO, we obviously didn't make enough effort to get to know you," he said, scowling, "and appreciate what we had. Some of us aren't too happy about the way you were treated, Bart."

"Hell, Kit, you were right," I said. "At my age I was crazy to get involved, even in nineteen-forty. Anyway, it's all over now. I've been told to act responsible from now on."

"That'll be the day."

"Chisters has told me I'm practically grounded."

"Yeah? Yeah, I guess, now you're a wingco," Kit muttered, not sounding sufficiently dismayed for my liking. "All the same, it's been a duff show, Bart. For a guy who was a journalist, I should've been more clued up for a good story."

"What paper were you on, Kit?"

"Toronto Daily Stare — as we called it. Mind you, I wasn't on it very long. They made me a travel writer, but I hated going places. So I often just made it all up. They fired me when someone wrote in to say he believed the Parthenon was actually a ruin, not the beautiful perfect building I'd described. I'd failed to spot the words, 'Artist's reconstruction' in the reference book I used."

"So to avoid travel you joined the air force, eh?"

"Yeah. The recruiting office promised faithfully I wouldn't have to travel, and first thing they did was post me to New Brunswick. To guard a fish-canning factory. So you see, you're not the only one who's led a colourful life."

He resumed massaging his eyeballs with thumb and forefinger on either side of his prominent nose. "Anyways, I just wanted to say we kind of appreciate you now, that's all I wanted to say. Okay?" he concluded aggressively, as if I was likely to argue about it.

Before I could reassure him, a club functionary came up, bowed, and asked if one of us gentlemen was a Commandant Bandy.

Holding an envelope, he proceeded to explain, in the English that many Belgians seemed to have a better grasp of than Canadians, that the letter had been left for me at the desk earlier that day.

I took it, and looked at it suspiciously, but it was for me, all right, being addressed to a 'Commandant B. Bandy, RAF.' It contained a letter, written on parchment stout enough to wedge open a meat locker, inviting me to a small party to be held at five o'clock on the following day, a Friday, at an address just off the Boulevard de Waterloo.

The exquisitely penned note hoped that I would be able to come. I must feel free to bring a couple of friends or colleagues if I wished. It was signed Clemence d'Aspremont de Forget.

"That's your baroness," said Kit Corner.

The baroness' joint turned out to be a neglected but still handsome mansion right in the centre of the city. Inside, it was wonderfully spacious, though the rooms needed redecorating. They had obviously not had a lick of paint since Leopold the Second.

For protection, in case the baroness had rude designs on me, I'd brought Kit Corner and Rod Childer. They were extremely impressed by the lounge, into which we were shown by an old crone doubling as a lady's maid. The lounge ceilings were so high that cumulus was starting to gather. The huge room was as exquisitely plastered as I was hoping to be by the end of the evening.

I hadn't seen such luxury since the Hermitage in Leningrad. Underfoot was acres of parquetry and marquetry equally well-worn, and the walls were covered in yellow silk that was mostly concealed by baleful portraits of fellows in fancy uniforms, mostly diplomatic, judging by the pessimistic expressions. In fact, much of the interior was decorated in shades of yellow, including the formerly white trim of the windows and skirting boards.

There were thirty or so people present, most of them servants of the Belgian state in beautiful, formal uniform, and their wives who had been too old or too important to be carted away to serve in German factories. There was just a sprinkling of Allied personnel. Among the latter, oh, hell, was Air Vice-Marshal Chistelow, who seemed to have been struck all of a heap by one lady, judging by the way he kept following her around wearing a smile nourished by ripe plums. It became equally obvious that the lady was the baroness, because she was giving instructions to a servant who seemed to be having trouble balancing a tray of conical glasses.

"It is so long since we have a party that Albert is quite out of practice at this sort of thing," she was saying, with a laugh that sounded like a casketful of the finest brandy and got me right here. And down there, as well.

As she came over to greet us, my heart gave a trilling laugh of its own. She was quite lovely, albeit rather thin. But I wasn't dismayed. She was a lady of about my age, but decades younger; a slender, smiling creature so lovely, gracious, and charming that I too would have followed her around, if Chistelow hadn't pulled rank and elbowed me out of the way with his face.

Oh, Lord, it was happening again: love and all that rubbish. For a heart-bludgeoning moment I thought I'd made a bad impression, for she barely glanced at me before turning to my companions and greeting them as if they were recent but likeable acquaintances. She put Sergeant Childer so quickly at ease that it quite reinforced my feeling that this was the woman I'd been looking for all my life. Honestly. All my life, except for Katherine and Sigridur.

Damn. The feeling was confirmed when she finally turned to me with her shining grey eyes, her long, slim hand outstretched, and said, "And you are surely Commandant Bandy. I have heard so much about you, Mr. Bandy."

"Why, what have you heard?" I asked worriedly; but she just laughed, as if she thought I was joking.

Oliver Chistelow, who had been flapping over her like a voluminous cloak and simpering like Oliver Hardy — I half-expected him to start twiddling his black air force tie — didn't share her amusement. He frowned. "Don't be ridiculous, Bandy, for once in your life," he said, and tried to interpose his bulk between me and my new love.

He interposed in vain, though. The baroness continued to smile delightedly, almost as if she had been expecting such a response. "I have heard nothing but good, Commandant, I assure you," she said, in a voice that sounded a lot more rich and mature than her bonny, bony frame seemed to warrant. And two or three seconds loitered by before she let go of my outsized paw.

Oh, boy. She had fallen for me, too. Yes, this terribly thin but radiant creature in the simple black dress and king's ransom of diamonds might just possibly be my next wife.

From then on, none of the other guests made much of an impression; except perhaps for the intense lady with the beads who asked if I had any soap to spare. "I would exchange two of my children for a bar of scented soap," she said nostalgically. Apparently there was a terrible shortage of the stuff in Belgium.

I asked her if there happened to be a baron to match our hostess, and if so, was there a nice park nearby where I could challenge him to a duel. However, I was informed that our hostess had been on her own throughout the war. She had separated from her husband sometime in the 'thirties, my interviewee seemed to recall.

"What are you gloating about?" Kit asked, seizing another two cocktails from a tray and handing one of them to Rod Childer, who had been too overawed to abandon Kit and strike out on his own.

Rod observed rather shyly that the baroness seemed very nice. At which we all turned to look at her. Just in time, goddamn it, to observe Chistelow hovering around the lady like an oversized moth, smirking all over his fat face. He was actually touching her. Patting her hand. I felt most indignant, especially when he held it for a moment between both of his, as if he were making a ham sandwich.

Thinking I wouldn't notice, Kit Corner winked at Rod and nudged his head in my direction, as if to say, Hullo, what's up with the CO?

I was merely deep in thought. To whit: Who the hell did he think he was, the AVM, trying to smarm in that way with my future wife. He had no right. Immoral sod. Just because he had known the Forget family since before the war — according to the lady who needed the soap.

"Our great leader has stopped smiling," Rod said.

"Why, I believe you're right, Sergeant," Kit said.

No, but I mean. Chistelow already had that girl from the hospital. The fair, baby-blue-eyed bit of skirt. He had her tucked into his past. Not to mention a wife to boot. Who was actually said to resemble a boot. And here he was, attempting another seduction, hoovering up yet more fluff.

I don't know. What is it with some men, that they have this ability to charm the women out of the shoetrees, despite their often quite gross appearance? I mean, Chistelow was no Adonis. Mind you, neither was I. But still, I don't know.

I wasn't going to stand for it. Excusing myself from my smirking confrères I put myself into nonchalant gear and sauntered over to Chistelow and the lady.

"Ah, Air Vice-Marshal," I said.

"Ah, Bandy," he said. "Again."

We regarded each other like two stray tomcats over a fish head. Chistelow was faster in the quick think department. "Well, my dear," he said, turning to the baroness, "now you've met Wing Commander Bandy, what do you think? I know you'll find this hard to believe, but he's one of our more successful flyers, despite the obvious ravages of age. And I do mean ravages," he said, and laughed heartily, as if he were just joking.

I couldn't help noticing his stomach. Somehow it didn't seem as girth-like as heretofore. There was a good hole to spare in his blue belt.

"I say, Air Vice-Marshal," I said, using my poshest English-type tones to impress the baroness, "have you been on a slimming course?"

"What?"

"You're not as circumferential as you were. Revised your girth, sir, since last we met, eh?"

I'd observed before that short Anglo-Saxon or Middle English words often had a hackle-raising effect on people to whom they were applied. Old Oliver was no exception. "What the hell d'you mean, girth?" he demanded, expanding his chest, and thus his medal ribbons, in an attempt to overawe me.

"You know, sir, girth. As in rotundity, bulk, corpulence —"

"Yes, yes, I know the word —"

"— obesity, pudginess, adiposity —"

"Look, Bandy, I don't need any grammar lessons, especially not from a Canadian —"

"You did ask what I meant, sir, re girth, you know, as in plumpness, paunchiness, tubbiness —"

"Will you shut up, you — blasted agitator!" he spat, flushing like mad. By now he had produced a hush and a small, interested crowd. Aware that two other air force types were among the listeners, he bit his tongue in the interests of discipline, and tried to turn, but I seemed to be in the way.

"I was just praising you sir — pointing out that you've lost weight, that's all," I said, circumnavigating his bulk. "I mean, look, there's an entire spare hole in your belt. See," I said, pointing. And it was quite true: he had one hole to go before the belt slipped down to his ankles.

"Be quiet, Bandy, and that's an order!" he hissed, aware of how deep an interest the people in the vicinity were taking in his beltness.

"I don't know why you're not pleased," I said, and turned to Kit. "Don't you think the air vice-marshal has lost quite a bit of weight, Flight Lieutenant?" I said. "I mean, that's good, isn't it? Everybody likes to lose a spot of excessive girth, surely?" But nobody seemed inclined to express an opinion on this subject, even Sergeant Childer, who had developed an intense interest in a nearby example of Belgian furniture, a walnut dresser of indifferent quality that he was actually stroking as if he expected it to sit up and purr.

"I didn't think that was funny," Kit said later, over the canapés and other tasty snacks at the long side table.

"No?"

"No," he said coldly. "Making a fool of the man that way, in front of all these people."

Actually, I wasn't too amused either. The AVM wasn't an enemy, the way, for example, that other brasshats had been, way back there in comeuppance country. In fact, I was feeling just a bit ashamed at having once again given way to the etymological ruffianism that had blighted my relationships over the oppugnant decades.

"I know he's pompous sometimes, but ..." Corner went on, "what brought that on, anyway?"

When I just looked down and shuffled my metatarsals, Childer added, "They said you could be a real bastard, sometimes." He arranged two olives and a stick of celery suggestively on a plate whilst adding quickly, "Not that I agree with them, of course. Though I must say you've got some nerve, sir, I will say that for you. I mean, cheeking an AVM. Now you'll never get to the top of the profession."

"Don't want to anyway," I mumbled defiantly.

The pilots weren't the only ones I was in trouble with. Clemence would not speak to me for ages; at least, not until after the AVM had left.

"I say, I haven't offended you, have I?" I enquired, uttering a light laugh.

"Yes, Mr. Bandy, you have," was the rejoinder which reduced my height even lower than my sergeant had taken me.

"You were impolite to one of my honoured guests," she added, looking almost as chilly as Kit.

"Um, sorry."

"So you should be, Commandant, so you should be," she scolded, adding in a softer tone, "Perhaps he is a little fat, but that is nothing. Like many men of his form, he can be very nimble and graceful," she said, instantly creating a picture in my overheated imagination of Chistelow being nimble in her bedroom. I almost moaned aloud.

"I have heard you are a mischievous person," she went on with a subsiding frown that nevertheless stapped me vitals. "But Oliver was my guest. And, you know, he is very nice when you get to know him."

"Perhaps if he didn't use his rank on people ..." I said sulkily.

"My goodness, Mr. Bandy, what else is rank good for? I myself use my rank, such as it is, whenever possible, especially on shopkeepers when they are too slow — or when I don't have the money necessary to pay them."

As she moved, a breeze of exquisitely subtle perfume wafted over me, borne on the warmth of her slender body under that simple black dress which so lasciviously groped the perfect teeter-totter of her bottom and its balancing bosom.

Thinking about which threatened to produce another moan. But only after I'd asked her to have dinner with me the following night.

She almost rocked back on her heels, staring at me.

"I'll call for you at eight o'clock, okay?"

She continued to stare for the duration of a tumescent salute. Slowly the look converted to one of wonder.

"It really is true what they say," she said, her lips parting to reveal a set of white teeth that were quite evenly matched, considering the state of European dentistry. "You are utterly impervious."

"Perhaps you could recommend a good noshery, or eating place," I said.

After another long moment: "I might know one," she faltered.

"And while you're at it, book us a table, eh? Okay? Okay?"

At which, after some more discontinuity, she started to laugh.

IN A BIT OF A RUSH

IN OCTOBER, EVEN MY CLERK, Len Burley, noticed that I was carrying out only the occasional patrol or sortie. "If you want to get out into the wild blue yonder and do your duty," he said one day, as I settled cosily into my office in the Sabena administration block, "it'll be okay with me, you know. As I said, I can handle most of the bumph."

I didn't like that bit about doing my duty, but, being a high flyer, I decided to rise above it. "No, Burley," said I, gravely, "there are some things only a CO can attend to. I've been badly neglecting the administration of late, in my eagerness to get at the enemy."

"Air Vice-Marshal Chisel, you mean?"

"No, no, the Germans, man. The point is, however tempting it is, to, you know, get out there and give the Jerries what for," I explained, illustrating the Bandy dedication to duty by giving the air a friendly punch with my fist, "my responsibility toward the squadron as a whole takes precedence. Besides, it's raining."

"Anyway, if you want a change, sir, from staring dreamily out the window, it'll be okay with me."

I glared at every inch of the six and a half foot clerk. "Impertinent remarks like that may earn you a spot of jankers — like I had to impose on LAC Dobbs," I said. "Furthermore, Burley, I won't have you referring to our esteemed commander, Air Vice-Marshal Chistelow, as a chisel."

"That's what you call him."

"Don't change the subject. And another thing: I will not have you writing your novel on the office typewriter. You'll wear it out with your clichés. Anyway, it's settled: I've decided to take the admin more responsibly from now on," I said, faltering only slightly as I attempted to meet his sceptical eye.

To tell the truth, I really was starting to chicken out of the aerial coop. That confrontation with Strand — who was maybe related to a fellow I'd known pretty well in India, actually* — had sucked most of the juice out of me, leaving only scraps of desiccated rind. Call it what you will: drive, ambition, determination, utter dedication to duty, re-

---

* See Volume VII, *Me So Far*. — Ed.

sourcefulness, guts, stamina, loyalty, courage — whatever it was, it had gone. Obviously it was Clemence's fault.

In the past I had loved quite a few frails. I'd had an affection even for Dasha, for a while anyway. And maybe Anne as well, and possibly Emmy, Maria, and Mila, Margaret, Felicity, and Calanthe, not to mention Gershom, Sybil, Dorinda, and, oh, just one or two others. But apart from Katherine and Sigridur, I had not hitherto experienced the intensity of feeling and the sentiment that crowded in on me now.

I wasn't too pleased about it. I'd bloody-well hoped I had gotten over that sort of thing. After Guinevere, I thought I'd managed to pull myself together. But no: it looked as if I'd have to go through it all again, with Clemence. Even as a lad in the Ottawa Valley, and at medical school (where one is supposed to be most susceptible to crushes and infatuations), I had rarely felt anything like this soppy. Even a few bars of the music the baroness and I danced to in the Terre Neuve or that new place on the Rue des Tanneurs could produce this special feeling. Even worse was this reverence and respect for her person that forbade even a moment's lustful attention, because of her feelings for her lost husband (more about that bugger in good time). I don't know how I was able to stand it. When I clamped the barnacles of my eyes to her hull, or optically tickled the ivories of her contours while dreaming of sipping the nectar of her every single dingle and dabbling dell, all hell broke loose in my every square inch of constitution.

Which was why I was becoming reconciled to the Air Ministry order that my combat days had to end. The chop was finally imposed in late October, when I was ordered to report to Supreme Headquarters. Here, Air Vice-Marshal Chistelow had his lair, and it was he who was given the job of imparting the sad news of my downfall. He was so upset at losing his shy, modest fighter ace — who had actually managed only one aerial victory in three years, and that by pure luck — that he kept me waiting for only ten minutes before calling me into his portly office on the fifth floor of the SHAEF building.

"Ah, Bandy," he said, pushing aside the paperwork on his desk to make room for his forearms. For a moment he sat there, frowning at my threadbarish uniform with the two grubby rings on the sleeve enclosing the bright new replacement ring.

"Well, let's get down to business," he continued, in tones of finality, as if we'd just concluded a long, friendly discussion about the weather, the V2 rocket bombardment of London, General MacArthur's return to the Philippines, the British landing in Greece, and the Russian irruption into Czechoslovakia. "The word has come through from our masters," he said, "that they've had enough of you. They've decided that after your latest escapades, the downing of this chap Willy Strand — who none of us have ever heard of, as a matter of fact, but there you are — and your leading to safety of a handful of decrepit Jerries —"

"Eight-five of them at last count," I put in helpfully.

He locked his plump fingers together as if they deserved to be locked up. "So I gathered. Though I understand that the Huns were either underaged types or fellows left over from the last war who were utterly shagged-out. Still, as a result of such activities, it seems we have to consider you an asset, worthy of being spared the horrors of war."

"M'm."

"Though it's my own opinion that the word describing you as an asset has two superfluous letters in it," he said, smiling in a twistedly cordial sort of way, and opening his mouth to join in what he hoped would be a spot of laughter.

"Two too many letters in the word asset, eh?" I responded. "Leaving just the word 'set', you mean? But 'set' suggests an entity of more than one; for instance, a set or collection of gold coins or precious vases. But you must admit I'm not a set of anything. There's definitely only one of me."

"Thank Christ," said the AVM almost under his breath. Irritably drawing the pile of papers toward him, he started tidying them all over again. "Anyway, it seems the buggers at the — I mean our superiors at the Air Ministry — they really mean it this time, that your operational days are over. Or in your case, your operational bi-centennial."

Strangely enough, he now raised his eyes to me almost pleadingly, as if hoping that this might whet my appetite for some sort of dissent, like a heated assertion that I was determined to go on biffing the Nazis. But my integrity remained uncompromised.

"Well, though devastated at the thought of giving up war flying and sheer joy of being bracketed by the enemy's deadly eighty-eights," I said, adopting a hangdog look, "I realize I must genuflect to the inevitable, sir." I paused to give him a moment to admire my command of English. I even treated him to a posh French word as well. "*Neanmoins*, Air Vice-Marshal, it's my duty to accommodate the understandable concern and anxiety of the authorities for my safety, however hard it is for me to give up the cut and thrust of aerial combat that I have always —"

I realized that I'd gone too far when he put in quickly, "Of course, it's still possible for me to request that a special exception be made in your case, Bandy. I —"

"No, no, sir. I must bow to the inevitable," I said hurriedly. "It's too late to stop them. The ministry is plainly determined that I refrain from doing any more good work in the cause of democracy."

"Yes, well," the AVM said. Now it was his turn to look hangdog – – though he was still barking. "Anyway, for the time being they've left me to decide what to do with you." He hesitated, giving me that look again. "I ... I don't suppose you'd consider a posting to the Far East?" he added hopefully. "No, I suppose not ...." He shuffled his papers all over again, before continuing with, "Best I can think of just now is a job with the admin branch, here at SHAEF. Later on we'll find something rather more suitable to your ..." There was a faint grinding sound — from either his chair or his teeth. "... suitable to your talents," he concluded. "How does that strike you?"

"Very well, sir. Will I get that spacious office just along the corridor from you?"

"No!" he said, very loudly indeed; at such volume, in fact, that for a few seconds he actually looked a trifle embarrassed by his own reaction. "No," he went on more softly. "The one I have in mind is several floors up — or down. Ask Gibbons in the other office there, when you leave. He'll point you in the right direction."

Only now was it beginning to dawn on me that the downing of Willy Strand, together with the infantry caper, had made me more celebrated than at any other time in my career; this despite the fact that I'd only added one air victory to my score since the end of 1941, and that nobody had actually heard of the 'famous German ace' I'd shot down, until it became politic for the Ministry of Information to let the public know a little about him. The fame had started with a couple of interviews by war correspondents, and the resultant magazine and newspaper articles were now filling my latest scrap album to the brim.* In the very week that I moved into a shared office on the second floor at the back of Supreme Headquarters, Allied Expeditionary Force, I found myself featured in one of those shiny London magazines, the sort filled with pictures of swank ladies, country houses, army generals, and pieces of porcelain. I had a full shiny page to myself. Personally, I thought I looked wonderful in the photograph, though I heard that LAC Dobbs was using it as a dartboard. Otherwise I was so pleased that I sent away for two dozen copies and offered them to whomever showed

* *See Bandy Archive, University of Alberta,*** *Vol 164-IIc.*

** Does our hero mean to suggest an archival rivalry with the Donald Jack archive at University of Calgary? We don't know. -Ed.

the slightest interest.

Unfortunately, the interested parties did not include my new office mate, Harriet K. Hullborne. She was a forty-year-old US Army major, and definitely not the most eager of recipients. "From some crap magazine, is it?" she snorted — literally — there was a slight problem with her nasal storehouses. "Yeah, well, Jackson will appreciate it. Stick it in his in-tray." Jackson was Hullborne's white bulldog. The in-tray was its dog basket, under her desk.

My first sight of Hullborne reminded me of the medical article that my MO in Normandy had attempted to sell to *The Reader's Digest*. His medical article stated that by the time he dies the average American male has accumulated an average of five pounds of undigested meat in his gut. Hullborne seemed a female equivalent who could have illustrated the item quite satisfactorily if my medical friend had managed to flog it. She was quite handsome though somewhat exaggeratedly hourglass overall. Thatching a distinctly olive complexion was some determinedly neat brown hair that was defying good discipline by curling wantonly at the ends. Her eyes were black, and quite penetrating, unless that was the magnifying effect of her cheapish military spectacles.

As for what she was doing in Brussels, she was to be an administrator of a new educational scheme. Now that the end was in sight, the army was to train a number of PFCs as education instructors, a sort of forerunner or dummy run for the GI Bill of Rights which would entitle all members of the armed forces to a free college education after the war. Her other problem was that she was anti-British. I soon discovered that she was not too crazy about Canadians, either, though it was not until later that I learned the reason for her distaste for Canucks. Apparently one of her forebears, General Hull, had been forced to surrender Detroit to the Canadian militia in the War of 1812. She had still not forgiven Canada for shaming the family.

For the time being I was supposed to be some sort of contact officer between the RAF and the US army, but Hullborne could not be bothered with this liaison crap. While waiting for the new educational system to be set up, she was busy writing a biography of her military forbear. As there was little for me to do, increasingly I found myself mooching between my comfy pit at Evere and Clemence's mansion on the tree-lined turnoff from the Boulevard de Waterloo.

Naturally, Clemmy was one of the first to receive a copy of the glossy magazine. To make sure she didn't miss the best part, I folded the mag in such a way as to make it spring open at my full page photograph.

"It's you?" she asked, looking at the photograph with tremendous admiration. "But you look so young."

"The artist took great pains with it."

"Yes, I can see that. I didn't recognize you at first," she said, as I manoeuvred her into her ground floor lounge, and then veered her to the one with all the portraits.

"My picture will look very nice in here," I said, gesturing around grandly. "How about right there, next to the one of your Great-Uncle, the Count Ghislain de Leiderkerke Savonet? What do you think?"

"But, Bart'olomew, don't you think a page torn from a magazine will look just a little out of place next to an eight-foot portrait?"

"Oh, Clemence, my dear, naturally I expect you to mount my picture in a nice gold frame first," quoth I, looking at her indulgently.

"Gee whillickers, Clem, you're beautiful," I husked, as my knees gave way. Fortunately this failure occurred just above the more comfortable of the big room's two yellow sofas.

"Why, thank you, darling," she said, reverently placing the magazine into a wrought-iron container on the long table nearby. The bucket was quite handsome, actually — cleverly designed to display ladies' magazines and a slender copy of *World Famous Belgians*.

After pressing a bell push on the far wall, she returned to join me on a sofa. Unfortunately, it was the other yellow sofa.

"I am glad you have called, Bart'olomew," she said. "I was talking to some Air Force people about you."

"Ah."

"Is it true that you are familiar —" she began, before pausing to pass instructions to the servant who had been summoned by the bell.

"Oh, I wouldn't dream of behaving that way with you, Baroness," I said.

"Pardon?"

"Being familiar. Unless, of course," I added with an inviting smirk, "a smidgeon of familiarity would not come amiss, h'm?"

"I was asking about Russia," she said, frowning slightly. "Your familiarity with it. You have been there, yes?"

"M'oh, yes," I said quickly, but very seriously. "Russia. Yes. Years ago, of course. Met all sorts of Russians. Served in Moscow Hospital. Also in Peter and Paul. Fortress, you know. Learned to speak a spot of the lingo. Tend to forget most of it, naturally."

I must have blethered onward for longer than these words suggest, though it seemed only seconds before the servant reappeared bearing a tray containing spoons, cream, sugar, and an interlinked pair of exceptionally heavy coffee receptacles of some sort of weighty metal, the top item acting as percolator, and the base part for receiving the coffee that dripped through from the top compartment of the contraption.

As the servant placed a small table between us, and set the heavy equipment upon it discretely before departing, Clemence went on, "It is why I have shown such interest in you, Bart'olomew. You really know the Soviet Union?"

"Par'n me?"

"Oh, if only there was a way ..." she sighed.

"A way what?" I was starting to feel a little disoriented.

"I myself have tried to get to Russia," she said, her shoulders suddenly sagging. "To find out. But with no luck. Have I told you about my husband, Bart'olomew?"

"Bartholomew? Gosh, he had the same name as me, eh?" I said, wondering if this was highly significant — her interest in a chap with the same name as her deceased spouse.

She was now looking at me even more uncertainly. "I do not understand .... Who has the same name?" she enquired.

"Bartholomew. Your husband?"

"My husband's name is Gay-org. Surely I have mentioned that *precedement*, Bart'olomew?"

As there appeared to have been some sort of misunderstanding I contented myself with just a h'm, or possibly a hum.

"Gay-orgi," she sighed. "It is so long, Bart'olomew."

I cleared my throat and raised my port finger toward my upper lip, perhaps to draw attention to its stiffness. "But he's been missing for years?" I said haltingly. "Surely it's time ... you know?" Time you forgot the dead bugger and concentrated a bit more on somebody alive, like me, I was thinking.

"Perhaps," she murmured, but obviously not listening. "Please help yourself, Commandant," she murmured, looking down at the hands in her lap, which, unfortunately, were not mine. The distance between us was too great.

Obediently, if somewhat perplexed by the conversation so far, particularly my own part in it, I turned to the fancy table which the servant had placed between us, and reached over to grasp the coffee apparatus, preparatory to loading the bottom component, which would serve as a cup, with three or four spoonfuls of sugar, though, not wishing to upset my digestion with overindulgence, intending to add no more than an inch or two of rich cream, a foodstuff which seemed much more abundant in Belgium than bars of soap. It was then I discovered that the weighty metal was even hotter than my brow. The crash as I dropped the equipment on the tray with a hiss like a rattlesnake was about as loud and awful as the clash of the gong near the end of Tchaikovsky's sixth symphony.

"It's all right, Bart'olomew," Clemence said in quite a kindly way, though from a safe distance. "Albert will clear it all up when you've gone."

★

A few days later I still had a few of the magazines with my picture in them, so I decided to offer a copy to the mess committee at Evere one wet morning. However, the committee claimed that the paper was too slippery and shiny for the purpose they had in mind. What purpose? I enquired; to which the response was a certain shiftiness before they changed the subject.

I didn't press them, as I was there principally for the delightful task of passing on the latest time-ex postings to the squadron. The first attempt, though, was not greeted with joy. When I threw off my old raincoat and cap and strode into the mess to give him the good news, Kit Corner's joy was definitely not unconfined. I found him seated, hunched, by the mess window, sipping coffee, presumably watching for a break in the weather. He withdrew his generous beak from the coffee mug and treated me to a look of lowering hostility.

"What?" he said.

"For you zuh war ist over, Kitty," quoth I, ever so heartily, positively beaming with pleasure.

He didn't look the least grateful. In fact, his light blue eyes turned to arctic ice.

"What the hell you talking about?" he demanded. "I'm nowhere near tour-expired."

"Close enough, Kit, close enough, mon vieux. I looked at your records. You've done enough. My God, over two years continuously on ops. I don't know how you've stuck it out."

"What is this?" he said, so loudly and aggressively that people, scenting a row, started to edge toward us. "You trying to get rid of me? You think I'm through, do you?"

"Course not, old bean —"

"Well, for your information, *old bean*, I'm staying on ops. So screw you."

"But Kit —"

"I'm not giving up, like you think. So bugger off, Bandy."

"Come on, Kitty —"

"You think I've turned yellow, don't you, because I turned back from Arnheim that time. Well, for your information, Wing Commander, I had a godamn good reason. But apparently not good enough for you."

"Kitty, what's wrong with you? I'm just passing on some great news," I said, astounded at the crumpling of his pallid features.

"And quit calling me Kitty. Anyways, forget it," he said, his face flushed, his eyes moist with rage. "I'm staying."

"I'm just trying to tell you that you've more than done your bit, Kit," I protested; and I continued to reason with him, though I started getting somewhere only when I mentioned that Rod Childer was going home as well.

"You're sending Rod back as well?"

"Yes. He's also definitely tour-ex."

He lowered his conk into the mug again, but he was starting to protest a little less vehemently. "It's crazy. I mean, it's so near the end," he muttered. "We'll be in Germany soon."

"All the more reason to go home, Kit, if it's nearly over."

When he next looked straight at me, his eyes were filled with a relief he couldn't hide.

"Well," he mumbled. "Well, if Rod's going too ...? But Jesus, Bart, if anyone should go home, it's you. You look worse than Rod does. I mean, you never did look great, but now, Jesus ..."

"Hell, things couldn't be better for me. I'm glad to be out of ops."

"Yeah? Is that true? You're really ...?"

"Course it's true. Why d'you think I'm looking dejected as a moggy at an open birdcage?"

After a moment, Kit turned away, possibly to hide a bit of manly concern, and to say, "And saving yourself for the baroness, eh?"

"M'm. But listen, what's this about Arnheim? I haven't heard anything, except it was an army screw-up. You were involved, were you?"

"Yeah. I got mud in the radiator, and had to turn back, that's all there is to it." His face turned sour again. "Anyways, what's this crap about not hearing anything? You must have heard. Oakley said you were blaming me."

It was gaping time again. "Oakley said what?" I faltered. "Wait a minute, let's get this straight. You're talking abut our John Oakley —?"

"Said you were looking into how come I'd turned tail without reaching the target, but he thought he had managed to calm you down. So when you turn up here after quite a few days and tell me I'm going home, I assume that's what it's about — that you're still dumping on me."

"I don't believe it ..." I said faintly.

"So now you're calling me a liar?"

After a moment I turned to the other pilots, who had been shuffling steadily closer, and said, "Where's Oakley?"

After a moment, the new CO, Tom Girling, who had been promoted from another squadron, murmured respectfully, "If he's the one with the custard face, sir, he's just gone out for a leak."

"What's up?" asked Rod Childer, also coming forward, accompanied by the medical officer. The MO looked his usual self. His collar was twisted. But Rod looked quite smart in his new uniform. I had insisted on promoting him to flight lieutenant, to ensure that he got a decent settlement when he left the service. The government was not known for superabundant largesse when demobbing sergeants.

"I've just heard, Rod," Kit said. "You and me's going home."

Shortly afterwards the morning's operation was cancelled owing to bad weather. Somebody suggested we open the bar, but for once I was more interested in having a little talk with John Oakley.

"Funny, he was here a moment ago," said the MO, looking around vaguely. "By the way, how are you this morning, Bart?" Sidling closer, he proffered his hand. I assumed he wanted to shake mine. Instead, he felt for my pulse.

"Quit tickling my wrist," I said. "What is this?"

"Just trying to find your whatsaname. You know, pulse. But listen, Bart — you still getting these bouts, are you?"

"Bouts? What bouts?"

"The ones sending your blood pressure sky-high. Like it's doing now."

"What the hell are you talking about, Doc?"

"Your morning sickness, of course. John is quite right. It's affecting your eyesight as well. I don't think I've ever seen you glare so much before. My God — now your breathing is affected. Oakley said you might show symptoms of ... something or other — I've forgotten the technical term just at the moment. Dyspnea, is it? But look, let's take a trip down to sick quarters, okay, Bart? I think I have something that might, you know, help that livid stare ...."

I went looking for Oakley, but I had to give up by nightfall because Clemence and I were going to a concert that evening. It was to take place at the handsome Beaux Arts building, where I was introduced to some of her friends, most of whom seemed to be musicians.

Clemence loved music and attended the concerts at the Beaux Arts about twice a week. She seemed to know many of the famous artists who were starting to reappear on the Belgian platforms, now that the war looked to have receded. One of the artists was the composer Francis Poulenc from Paris, who was visiting his friend, Marcel Cuvelier. Clemence introduced me during the intermission of the Alban Berg concert.

Unfortunately I was not quite up to my usual high standards that evening. I was still a mite disoriented, not so much on account of alcohol, though that helped, but because of John Oakley and his lying trickery. I was trying to work out why he was doing this to me.

"Will you stop going on and on about your nice Mr. Oakley," Clemence said exasperatedly, "and come and meet Monsieur Poulenc."

So I decided to forget all about Oakley, that streak of gnat's piss.

"It's a real pleasure to meet you, Monsieur Pew-lank," I said, bowing, and recovering my balance quite quickly. "I used to perform your music on the pianoforte, you know."

"Ah," he said "I did not know that. Thank you, M'sieur."

"Though some people with no taste complained, I'm afraid."

Passing a puzzled glance to Clemence, the stalwart, beautifully-dressed composer replied, "They complained because they had no taste, Monsieur?"

"No, no, about your music," I explained. "But don't worry, Monsieur Pew-lank, I stuck up for you."

"*Merci.*"

"I stoutly defended you, don't you worry," I went on. "Bunch of Philistines, I thought. Civil servants from Ottawa, of course. Imagine failing to appreciate your music, eh? Even after I'd taken the trouble to explain your eccentric shifts in rhythm and the odd melodic divergencies in your work."

The composer, who had been looking around for someone less challenging to talk to, slowly turned back to me.

"That is," I added comfortingly, "until they in their turn explained that it wasn't your music they were objecting to, it was my playing."

To Clemence, Poulenc asked softly, "The name is ... Bandy, did you say?"

"I don't know," she said, letting go of my arm. "He's not with me. I've never seen him before, *hein*?"

Turning back to me, the great man gave the matter some thought before saying, "In this anecdote of yours, M'sieur Bandy, I am not at all sure who has come off worst, me or you."

Even before the second half of the Alban Berg concert, Clemence seemed determined to steer me away from the bar. But it was too late. I was already there.

"Come on, Bart'olomew," she said, touching my arm. "The concert is starting again."

"No it's not," I said. "They're still tuning up."

"No, that is the music. Come on."

At last we were in the auditorium. During one particularly nerve-shredding passage I leaned over and murmured seductively, "We adore each other, Clemence. Don't you think it's time we did something about it, eh?"

"Shhh."

"Whatjamean, shhh. I'm pouring my heart out."

"Well, pour it back, Bart'olomew. This is not the time."

"Well, when is the time?" I hissed into her ear-hole. "I've tried to tell you how much I love you. But, I dunno, the moment, the moment I start, suddenly we're surrounded by people."

This was true. We never seemed to have a moment to ourselves. Whenever there was the slightest danger of intimacy, somebody else appeared: in this case the Belgian National Orchestra.

"Sometimes I almost think you're trying to ensure we're never alone," I said, not believing this for a second, but hoping to stimulate some positive response.

"Shhh," somebody behind us said, in French. Or possibly in Flemish.

I was silence for a while, toying moodily with my walking stick, the one with the silver handle in the shape of a Borzoi. Then I murmured, "One of your friends said you're still faithful to your husband, but I don't believe that for a second. It's too absurd, after all this time. After all, he must surely be —"

"Shhh, shhh!"

"Hell, he abandoned you years and years ago," I said, nodding emphatically, to encourage her to set up, despite the music, a harmonic assent.

This time, about fifty people in the vicinity glared at me and said, "Shhh," in several languages.

Huh. You'd think they really cared about the music. You'd think they were actually enjoying it, instead of just sitting there pretending to appreciate all that twelvetone stuff.

At the end of the concert, as we were trooping out, Clemence took my hand in hers. At the tender contact, joy rose in my heart. It was obvious she could no longer contain her own love.

Except it turned out that she had taken my hand merely in order to give me a Chinese burn.

"Ow."

"Well, you are such a terrible man," she whispered. But then, to make amends for the grievous bodily harm she had caused me, she smiled and patted the same hand, but not before she had also used it to draw me out of auditorium and into the men's toilet, or quite close to it. Out of sight of her friends, anyway. "All the same, you really are terrible," she said.

I knew we were near the above mentioned toilet because I'd already been in there this very evening, though I had scuttled out again when I saw a grey-haired woman within. I thought I'd gone into the wrong one. I had then re-examined the sign outside. It had definitely said Messieurs. Accordingly, I had bravely re-entered, though I had to stand at the urinal for a little longer than usual, nervously glancing at the lady, who was seated only a couple of feet away, reading a newspaper. In fact, she was so close that a modicum of moisture was starting to appear in the newsprint.

By now, of course, I was much too well-travelled a Canadian sophisticate to be shocked at finding a female employed in man's lavatory; it was not an uncommon phenomenon in uncivilized parts of Europe. Believe it or not, I had actually seen shameless Frenchmen relieving themselves at those fancy metal pissoirs that dot the Parisian boulevards, doing so *whilst still arm-in-arm with their lady friends*! Even if the ladies were genuinely admiring the night sky at the time.

On this follow-up occasion, though I remained outside the toilet, talking disconsolately and muttering, "I'm positively dying —"

"For a piss? Go ahead, Bart'olomew."

"No, no — dying for love of you, Clemence."

"Nonsense. You must not say that," she said, edging behind a pillar when she caught sight of someone she knew — someone she didn't like, obviously. "You know I am a married woman."

"But dammit, your Gay-org is bound to have gone kerblooey by now. You know what it's like, Russia."

For some reason, Clemence looked sceptical when she replied, "Do you really know Russia, Bart'olomew? I mean, really?"

"Well, of course, nobody really knows Russia. Not even Russians. But —"

"You know, that was why I was so interested in meeting you at first, Bart'olomew. You were supposed to know Russia. You spoke the language."

"Well ..."

"But it's true what John said, *hein*? That you are such a fibber, *cheri*. About your experiences of Russia." She made a valiant effort to smile. "And I believed you."

"Admittedly I was only there for a couple of years," I said, looking in some surprise at her sceptical demeanour, "but —"

I stopped dead. "What did you say?" My voice was turning falsetto. "John, did you say? Are you talking about John Oakley — a tall drink of water with a face like a blancmange?"

"He was saying some quite nice things about you."

"What's he been saying, what's he been saying?" I cried. "What?"

"After all, *cheri*, you must admit you do exaggerate a little. Just a little, I'm sure?" she said placatingly, before her own disappointment resurfaced. "All the same, I really believed that you knew Russia, and might help. Somehow," she added, gesturing hopelessly.

"The bastard," I swore, managing to squeeze the word between a couple of pants. "He's even got to you. The bastard," I said again, failing to heed Clemmy's feelings or doubts about me. All I could think of now, was how to assault him — Flying Officer Oakley, as he now was, despite my efforts to have him demoted to stores clerk in Liverpool. Better still would be dealing with him in the ancient Roman fashion by promoting him to the sharp end of a ten-foot pole. You know, the way the good old Romans used to treat their treacherous enemies?

God, yes, I really enjoyed imagining his dying struggles. With any luck he would last long enough for the point of the pole to work its way from his rectum to the quadrate muscle of his lying lower lip. Yeah.

HEAD NOT QUITE IN THE PICTURE

I'D SPENT MOST OF THE PREVIOUS DAY trying to find the bastard — you know who I'm talking about — without success. On the following morning I located him. Unfortunately it turned out that he'd been admitted to sick quarters. Not that I minded that he was at death's door. I just wanted to be sure that it was true. But when I drove my tin jalopy to the Red Cross building on the far side of the airfield and strode inside, they said that Flying Officer Oakley was not to be disturbed.

"We'll see about that," quoth I. "What ailment is he telling lies about now, anyway?"

The cynical-looking LAC at the reception said that he would try again and find out, and picked up the phone.

"So? What's his excuse this time?" I snapped, when he finally put the phone down.

"They said he's been admitted because it's extremely contagious," said the LAC. "But it's all right, sir, they said you can go through."

"Well, I ... Why, what's he got? Exactly what is this contagion?"

"They didn't say, sir," said the erk, "except it's real infectious, they said. You just go down that way, sir. Straight along the corridor and turn right." But by then I was leaving the building.

However, I slowed down when it occurred to me that Oakley wouldn't be in sick quarters if he was seriously ill. He would be in a proper hospital. So I turned and marched straight back into the building, and, upon receiving directions from an LAC who seemed determined not to look me straight in the eye, I strode through to the small ward at the back of the building.

There I halted at the entrance, and took a deep breath — but not too deep, just in case Oakley really was contagious. Nevertheless, it was a determined breath, for I was feeling definitely suspicious about his condition. The LAC's phone conversation with whoever had passed him the word that the patient was at death's door ... I don't know, it seemed to me that the conversation had been a little too casual and evasive, to my way of thinking. So, straightening my shoulders, I walked into the two-bed ward, utterly determined to nail the bastard before he had time to hide under the bed, or jump out of the widow. It seemed to me that his condition was too much of a coincidence. Also, I was suspicious of the LAC at reception, the way he had been trying ever so hard not to meet my deteminedly imperious gaze, as well as the way he had been executing some sort of delaying tactic before telling me to go through.

However, so sick did John look as he lay in the right-hand bed just behind the door, that my shameful doubts scattered like rats from a Vimy corpse. He looked terrible, lying there staring at the spotless ceiling from a frightening white, powdery face.

Instead of taking the determined pace to the bed and upbraiding him for his previous lies and inventions, I recoiled, colliding with the door through which I had just entered, causing it to slam shut and trap me in the sick quarters.

"Ah, Oakley," I said, taking out my handkerchief and using it to wiggle my nose to give the impression that I'd felt a sniffle coming on. "We meet again."

His head turned slowly in my direction, though it took his eyes a moment to follow suit. "Oh, hello, Wing Commander," he said, his speech so feeble that for a moment I thought it was a death rattle.

"Now look here, Oakley," I began, feeling behind me for the door handle of the ward, just in case I was called away in an emergency. "This is rather sudden, isn't it? One moment you're .... And the next moment you look ...."

"Apparently it's not completely fatal," the poor boy whispered, turning away hopelessly. "Provided ...." His voice faded, as if he hadn't the strength to continue. Though with an obvious effort he summoned just enough strength to complete the sentence. "Provided I'm left alone for a ... a while."

"Right. Quite right. Right, John. I won't disturb you a moment longer, then," I said, my hand gripping the hygienic aluminum door handle harder than ever. "So I'll probably see you sometime in the you know, future, when you're more ..."

"I just want to say, sir," John said, rising onto one elbow with a supreme effort, "that I've tried real hard to live up to your high standards." He shook his head hopelessly. "To be just like you, sir, and ... and emulate your sublime reputation as a famous birdman and aerographic emperor and explorer of the cerulian vaults of heaven ...." At which point his voice failed completely — delirium, obviously — and his face sank back in the pillow and turned away.

"Yes, well, better not to talk too much, old chap," I said, holding the hanky to my face more firmly, whilst trying to open the door behind me; except that my damned heels kept getting in the way.

I soon learned that I had been had, when the squadron packed up that very day and was in the process of moving further east so as to keep up with the retreating enemy. The orderly room people believed that Oakley was among those who had already departed for the new airfield, somewhere close to the Dutch border, they thought.

Apparently, he was in sick quarters that morning, but only to receive the ATT and TABC jabs that all ranks were supposed to take, to safeguard them from tetanus and the like. It seems he had persuaded an orderly to allow him the use of a bed so that he could carry out yet another of his filthy jokes.

I seriously considered getting in touch with his new CO and requesting that the boy receive forty or fifty lashes from a length of throttle cable. Failing that, I would drive to the new airfield and put him on a few trumped-up charges for bringing his superiors into disrepute. Maybe ten years in the glasshouse would restore him to some semblance of civilized behaviour. However, even if I was one of the greatest and most forgiving wing commanders the world has ever seen, when I learned that the feeble and maladroit gawkhammer had actually *fainted* on receiving a couple of piddling injections and was being kept back for observation at Evere for a day or so, my opinion of him sank even lower, and I determined that the best course of action on my part was to get my own back on the bastard.

The idea occurred to me while I was strolling up a steepish street off the Rue du Midi. After my morning visit to Major Hullborne and receipt of one of her curt nods giving me permission to goof off for the day, I was indulging in one of my educational tours of the city. On this occasion I was concentrating on the bookshops in order to expand still further the literary material that skulked in a corner of my valise. With nothing more to contribute to the war I was having to resort to reading. The last bookshop I visited on this occasion was by far the friendliest. The proprietor was most affable as he brought out various works for my consideration, including a rare work from China. It featured twenty or so handsome reproductions in full colour. At first I thought it was a child's colouring book, until I looked again and perceived that it was certainly not for children, as the plates featured works of purest pornography.

After careful scrutiny of the material lasting hardly any time at all, I suddenly had the idea of putting the quarto volume to good use. I would plant it on John! I could secrete it among his personal effects, then denounce him to the SP. Tee-hee!

The only problem was a shortage of cash. In general, I favoured candy over pornography, and I couldn't afford the book unless I was to give up the Belgian chocolates I had set my stomach on. Anyway, the artwork was too good to waste on Oakley, the elastic activities and manoeuvres being beautifully delineated, more artistic than many a picture I'd seen in provincial galleries. No siree bob, the watercolours of sexual callisthenics and boudoir dallying, delineated in lovely pastel shades, were much too good for the likes of Oakley.

Besides, only a minute after leaving the bookshop I found the perfect material for getting him into difficulties. Just a few paces further along the narrow street there was a used clothing store, whose proprietor, a woman, was almost as friendly as the art fellow. Moreover, the lady remained quite affable even after she realized that I was interested in buying samples of second-hand women's clothing.

Normally I might have displayed just a touch of embarrassment at not only pawing through ladies' thingamies but actually purchasing an armful of the secondhand — as it were — underwear: drawers, woolies smalls, undies, shifts, and panties; but so determined was I to subject John to the same embarrassment that he had imposed on me, that I persisted with the transaction, if not with aplomb, at least with the proper stonefaced disregard for her curiosity. After all, the price was right. It would leave quite enough money for the Belgian choccies.

The only trouble was that, though she managed to find me a sufficiently capacious brown-paper sack with which to transport the items, I became quite self-conscious, fearing that I looked like a Chinese laundryman bowed under a bulky delivery. There was a danger that I was attracting attention, and if there was one thing I was determined never to do, it was attract attention in public.

Blast. Why hadn't I gone shopping in the car, especially now that it was starting to rain. But the tin Volkswagen was half a mile away on the SHAEF parking lot.

Increasingly redfaced rather than stonefaced, I scuttled through the streets as fast as the bulky package would permit, becoming even more concerned as the downpour increased. That was another thing: I'd come out without a raincoat. By the time I reached headquarters I would be sodden — and I still had to heft the bulky undies all the way out to John's kip at Evere.

Another problem: even if I reached Evere, how was I to get past hundreds of military eyes whilst bearing such a large, misshapen package as this? Now, unlike the Chinese in the watercolours who didn't mind being promiscuous in daylight, I would have to wait until dark.

But by then Oakley might be on the way to his new station in Holland or somewhere. Maybe it had not been such a good idea after all, trying to frame the bastard.

A hundred yards from HQ I faced up to it: I was now becoming so dank under the precipitation that the moisture was actually washing out the joys of imagination, the anticipation of hiding the underwear in John's room, and then confiding my suspicions to the SPs that Flying Officer Oakley was carrying illicit merchandise in his kit, then ordering them to search his living quarters.

Damnation. Had I purchased all this underwear for nothing, leaving me almost penniless — with days and days to go before payday? Just because I was a wing commander didn't mean that I was made of money, you know. And now another painful thought: I'd left the canvas top of my little tin car open to the elements. By now the VW would be as soaked as I was.

There was only one thing for it. I would have to leave the parcel in my office at SHAEF until everything had dried out: me, the car, my reputation, and the bulky undies. I just hoped that I could get the incriminating material to John before they moved him on. Preferably into a specially active sector. The vicious fighting in front of Aachen would suit him quite well, I thought. Or there were still a few opportunities left in air combat. If he was lucky he might even meet one of the new Jerry jet fighters, a Me.262.

But the hell with him. As I snuck round to the rear of the headquarters building, I suddenly felt beaten, buggered, and befuddled, as well as praying that I didn't meet so much as an off-duty wireless operator with bad eyesight. In this frame of mind I made my bedraggled and all too appropriate way through the back passage of the building — only to find that there was no other way up to the office except through the polished entrance hall — which naturally would be thronged with friends who would turn into contemptuous foes, and foes would turn into archenemies. Luckily the office was only two floors up, but that was no guarantee that I wouldn't run into packs of privates or brasshats. Including my air vice-marshal? Oh, my God! If I encountered him .... My imagination wasn't drowned enough to wash out the dialogue that might ensue. "Hello, what's this, Bandy? Having to deal with your own soiled underwear, are you? Too ashamed to let the laundry people see the disgusting state of your undies, eh?" Or else he'd say, "I think perhaps it's time you went back to your old job in Canada, Bandy. Laundry man, was it?"

As weighed down as Atlas but with a burden of wet women's wear rather than a symbolic globe, I peered around a corner, waiting for the last vestige of authority to clear out of the entrance hall so I could scuttle undetected to the stairway, I realized that I should never have thought of paying Oakley back on his terms. Just because he derived pleasure from his tricks was no reason for me to emulate him, even if his japery seemed vindictive. I'd come across such basically hostile attitudes on more than one occasion, and I fear I had often demeaned myself by responding in a like manner. Now I realized that it was really time I grew up. It was about bloody time, anyway. After all, I was half a century old, for God's sake.

Yes, I was definitely going to grow up. And right now, now that the entrance hall was empty. So, squaring my shoulders as much as was possible under the increasingly dank habiliments, I started across the marble floor — just as Air Chief Marshal Tedder, second-in-command to the supreme commander, General Eisenhower, entered the building, accompanied by half a dozen other cheeses, including my very own air vice-marshal, Oliver Chistelow.

But the situation wasn't as bad as it seemed; in fact, I was extraordinarily lucky to remain almost unobserved, and not just because I was not all that visible under the weight of sodden garmenture, my own and that of several unknown ladies. For one thing, both Arthur Tedder and Oliver Chistelow were so intent on their conversation as they strode purposefully toward the elevators that the deputy chief of the Allied forces spared me not even a glance, and even old Chisters did not seem to appreciate my presence immediately. He was too busy nodding respectfully and with deadly serious mien to whatever points the handsome and charming second-in-command was elucidating.

Even the elevator was awed. Just as they reached it, the door slid back, and was good enough to admit not only the leaders but two other big cheeses with armfuls of broad rings on blue sleeves, until only a couple of army brasshats were left in the foyer — and Flying Officer Oakley.

"Oh, hello, sir," he said offhandedly. "Just the man I wanted to see. Are you going up to your office? Can I give you a hand with that bundle, sir?"

"Yes ... No. It's ... What, tum, are you doing here, Oakley?" faltered I.

Just happened to be around when their plane landed at Evere, sir. Uncle Arthur offered me a lift into town. We're related, you know. My sister is married to one of his cousins — forget which one, at the moment. Are you sure I can't take that parcel off you, sir? You look kind of weighted down, or something."

"No, I ..."

"I'm down here specially to apologize to you, Wing Commander," he said, wearing a formal expression rather than smothering me in the usual blandness. He'd even come to attention. I hadn't seen that before. "Excuse me, sir, but could we talk a little more privately? In fact, could I offer you a drink?"

"No, I'm, I'm not thirsty ..."

"In one of the bars nearby?"

"I was on my way up to ..."

"Your office, sir? Well, we could talk there, if you prefer. You see, I realize I've not been doing too well as far as you're concerned, sir. You see ..." And he went on at some length to explain something that I completely failed to listen to. I was too busy lurching upstairs under the heavy burden of frillies, still too disoriented after running into the brasshat band, and then finding Flying Officer Nemesis at the tail end, on snare drum or triangle.

The office was temporarily vacant when we reached the second floor, with Oakley still droning on and on in his drab voice, presumably to the effect that he had not been doing too well as far as I was concerned. Entering the office on the upper floor and dumping the soggy parcel on the floor, I was relieved to find it unoccupied — the office, that is. Major Hullborne must have gone out for a few moment, leaving her trusty Underwood on duty.

Finally I was starting to pay a little attention to what Oakley was saying as he stood there in his smart blue uniform. "Look, exactly what is it you want?" I asked peevishly, breathing hard as I kicked the parcel and sidled my ass onto the spare chair. Actually I was curious to learn how he could possibly explain away his sojourn in sick quarters .... Though maybe it would be better if he didn't explain it, considering that my own part in the sojourn, a spunkless withdrawal, was not to my credit.

"You see, the trouble is, boss, that I took an instant dislike to your face, and I just assumed that you really were as staid, pompous, unfeeling, and hypocritical as you looked," said the custard-faced Montrealer, still without any real sign of sincerity in his demeanour.

"I'm supposed to feel better, now you've said that, Oakley?"

"I just didn't appreciate you properly, that's all I meant," he replied, seating himself at Harriet's desk. "I realized that you were not really like your face at all: frozen, supercilious, and so forth. You know

— strange."

"What the hell d'you mean, strange?"

"You know, really eccentric — in the best possible way, of course," he added, as if he really thought he was putting me at my ease with his confessions, or setting straight a record which — he seemed to imply — needed to be looked into by a large group of service psychologists, if not a specialist team of psychiatrists as well. "You see, I just didn't realize how much you'd done."

"Whatjamean, done? I haven't done anything. You're the one who's been doing things — telling all kinds of fibs about me."

"No, no, I'm talking about how much you've accomplished in your life. It wasn't until I read all the stuff in the papers, about you being such a great, you know, hero —"

"And another thing," I interrupted. "You have the utter impertinence to call me supercilious? That really inspires in me feelings of utter disdain, you know — disdain for you, and contempt, and considerable despisement, you know."

"Anyway, the point is I was totally wrong about you, sir," the lanky but otherwise spotless flying officer said, learning over contritely to read the page fluttering in Hullborne's Underwood. "Realizing that in many ways you're a great man — or," he went on, peering more closely at the typescript, "at least a great warrior — somebody without an iota of bullshit about you, in spite of your rank."

"Yes, well," I muttered, not terribly mollified. I was still somewhat suspicious that one of his slanders disguised as a paean of praise would soon follow. I mean, look at him now. He was sniggering at Hullborne's biography. How could you trust somebody like that? I mean. I guessed that now it would be Harriet Hullborne's turn — or Harry Hullborne, as her friends called her — to be so callously slandered.

Who appeared at that very moment, glaring as usual, and carrying a mug of coffee.

As Harry entered her combined office, den, study, and bolthole, my nerves tightened with alarm; I saw Oakley's expression revert to its usual lard-like look of respect. As the major marched in, he slid from her chair and stood to attention, in so respectful a fashion that I feared the worst. It was soon forthcoming. Looking suspicious, the major paused in the doorway before grunting and marching stiffly to her desk. There she stood and glared at me, obviously expecting an explanation as to what on earth had brought me to the office for the second time in a week. It was very unusual. I was supposed to skedaddle after signing in, so to speak, by sticking my head in and out at eight ack-emma.

Quickly and guiltily I introduced John, explaining that he was one of my old pilots and that he would be leaving in a moment, as would I. "Major Hullborne is my liason officer with the US forces," I told John in a respectful aside.

"I do hope you'll soon be better, Major," said Oakley.

Hullborne looked at him suspiciously. "What?" she barked.

"Recovered from the bout of dysentery, Major," Oakley said, ever so sympathetically. "I nearly had it myself, when I had to live in a tent."

"What?" barked the major again, her eyebrows smouldering under the reflected heat from her eyes.

"It takes awhile, I know. But don't worry, maje, you'll look okay when you've finally gotten over it."

"What is this crap he's talkin'?" Hullborne demanded, looking accusingly, for some reason, at me rather than at the custard-faced pilot. "I don't have dysentery."

"Oh, I thought — it's just that somebody intimated," said Oakley, glancing in my direction and then looking away guiltily, as if the movement had been an involuntary betrayal. "It's just the way your face is all flushed, Major."

"What the hell are you talkin' about, soldier?" Hullborne bawled, except she was again turning to me, as if I were solely responsible for the callow youth. "Look, Bandy, get him out of here, will ya? I got work to do. And don't you got business elsewhere? Well ...?" And she made repelling motions with both hands before slamming her capacious rear down in front of the machine, and starting to proofread its shivering page of typescript, her expression suggesting that it was almost as unsatisfactory as the office mate she'd been saddled with.

At which point, AVM Chistelow rapped noisily at the door, opened it, and stuck his head in. "Excuse me, I don't suppose Bandy is —" he began, addressing the glaring army major, who was angrily wrenching out the typescript and torturing it further in her giant fist. "Oh, sorry, Major, I see he's in. Afternoon, Bandy. So you've actually turned up for work, have you? What's the matter, bars not open yet?"

No doubt he would have continued with another sarcastic remark or two had he not been distracted by the flurry he had caused. Flustered by a tension inspired by the parcel, by fear of what John Oakley would say next, by Chistelow's unexpected appearance, and not least by Hullborne's aggressive manner (despite her inferior rank and status as a foreign brown job), I found myself gibbering hurried excuses to the effect that I had to go now; I couldn't stay because I was just leaving; it was nearly lunchtime and I'd heard that the *Petite Ours* restaurant was offering a particularly good *Viande de Cheval Fameux aux Herbes* that day. To illustrate my point and convert the gibberings into coherent action, I snatched up the parcel of guilty goodies, and made ready to scamper out of the office before Oakley thought up some excuse to create a dangerous curiosity regarding the contents of the parcel. That would have been so typical of him — hoping to create some catastrophe, say, by idly prodding the bulky goods with his polished black shoe. Yes, that would have been so typical of Oakley, and I knew that if he did so, the brown paper would expose itself like an exhibitionist at the top of a Simpson's escalator, to reveal a pair of knickers to the vulgar gaze. With Oakley there was bound to be some such consequence of a nudging toecap.

In fact, it was far worse. In my guilty anxiety I picked up the parcel too abruptly, not realizing the extent to which it had been subjected to Brussels precipitation. As they say, it came apart in my hands. The paper tore, not rippingly but quite soundlessly, given its saturated condition, though the result was as bad as if the paper had slashed itself wide open with a sound like one of Mr. Whittle's jet machines. The parcel dumped its entire contents all over the floor.

The absence of sound with which the brown paper had so shamelessly exposed itself was matched by the silence in the room as Air Vice-Marshal Chistelow, AFC, Major Harriet Hullborne with her eight rows of ribbons and fourteen or fifty gold or silver badges, and finally Flying Officer John Oakley, looked down upon the dampish shreds of brown paper mixed through a surprisingly rich and comprehensive assortment of young, middle-aged, and elderly ladies' underwear: one chemise, one pair bloomers, slips, a shift, three petticoats, step-ins, step-outs, camisole, cami-knickers, and no fewer than three bras, one of them capacious enough to fling some quite hefty medieval war missile.

And then all three of them turned and looked at me.

BUSY SKULKING

FOR A WHILE AFTER THE PARCEL INCIDENT I refrained from visiting the office for even the customary booking-in visit. However, one day in November, while I was busy moving into a flat downtown that had been requisitioned for me — it had been occupied by a collaborator — I was informed that a quantity of mail awaited me. I skulked for half an hour until the major, arms swinging, eyes glaring, marched away on some errand or other. Then I slithered in, intending to snaffle the correspondence and dash out even faster. But ultimately, I was trapped as thoroughly as was P.G. Wodehouse, who, having not realized that a broadcast or two for the Nazis might just possibly cause a frown to furrow the British brow, had just been arrested in Paris. Major Hullborne returned unexpectedly to find me still gathering up my Canadian mail, the most interesting item of which was an ad from Parkers, Inc., offering me ten years' subscription to *The Algonquin Provincial Park Monthly Newsletter*.

Though Chistelow had continued to look a trifle askance at me after that humiliating scene when my undies were spread all over the floor and I was exposed as a filthy transvestite favouring a prodigality of bust and a snakiness of hip (judging by the scattered exhibits), there appeared to be a diminution of disdain from Major Hullborne. Even her dog Jackson was a shade less apathetic. It approached and sniffed one of my shoes.

"No need to rush off, Bandy," quoth the lady major. "It's your office as much as mine, or so they tell me."

"Oh. Ah. Yes. M'm. Kew."

"What are you again? Lieutenant-colonel, is it? Anyways, listen, a couple of fellows from *Stars and Stripes*, a PFC and a sergeant photographer, have been trying to reach you for days — say they want to interview you. Something about you capturing a company a' Fritzes single-handed, some crap like that. Where the hell do you go after you skitter out of here, anyways?"

"Oh, ah — moving into an apartment over near Leopold Park — with a splendid view of the Solvay institute, actually. Uh ... about that large parcel, Major. The one that, you know, fell to bits. I just wanted to explain —"

"They seem to think you're something special," she interrupted, with a glare from her black eyes suggesting that the something special was not to my advantage. "You saved India. That so?"

"Uh?"

"Not that that kind of stuff impresses me, of course. We Americans don't go for empires. Still, musta bin an achievement, as you got a knighthood out of it. Sir Bandy, right?"

"Sir Bartholomew. I don't use the title, actually."

"Quite right. Lotta crap, titles. Still, better than a kick in the nuts, right?" she said, quite shocking me with her language and surprising me with her diminished hostility as she went on to question me about my sojourn in the good old US of A. She was almost friendly by the time I mentioned knowing a few prominent American citizens. At that point she very nearly forgave me for being a Canadian, though she continued to look at me sideways as if not quite able to withstand a full frontal view.

"They say you were acquainted with that great American patriot, Cyrus Chaffington?" she said.

"God, yes."

"A great man, Mr. Chaffington. One of my heroes," she said sententiously.

"M'm. Look, Major — about that parcel —"

"Forget it, Sir Bandy. We all got something to hide in our lives, right?"

"I just wanted to say that they weren't my garments, Major Hullborne," I said, and started to explain that I'd simply meant to teach one of my men a lesson. He was a particularly troublesome junior officer and gossip monger, and it had been my intention to frame him and ruin his bad reputation; for his own good, of course.

"Yeah, sure," the lady Hullborne growled sceptically, though with a faint glimmer of comradeship in her eye. "By the way, you can call me Harry — if that's not too democratic for a goddam knight. A knight of the ream," she added, in case I'd forgotten which knight it was.

I assumed she'd got the word wrong. Actually, she herself was fast becoming a knight of the ream, judging by the quantity of paper clicking through her typewriter — unless she was referring to my history of reaming opponents. (Jeez, what a rich language English was.)

"No, no, not at all, Major — Harriet — Harry," I said, plucking at my lower lip as if it were a little moist guitar. "Uh, but about that parcel, sir — I mean, ma'am. Admittedly I was found in possession of an unconventional sort of kit, but as I say, I definitely had a reason for —"

"Look, forget it," she said sharply, though she softened the tone almost immediately. "Hey, I'm not one to look down on a guy just because he's got a li'l weakness. Hell, I myself —" She stopped, cleared her throat quite daintily, and concluded with, "Anyways, I don't hold it against you, even if you are from the north woods."

From then on I was able to check in at the office nearly ever day, and sometimes for as long as half an hour, to chat in a somewhat stilted but not unfriendly manner to the burly but ample major with the big shiny face and the voice like an unlubricated Massey-Harris chaff-cutter or root-pulper.

Meanwhile, though Guinevere was now thoroughly out of the picture, I did meet a colleague of hers, who was in France and Belgium on some espionage skulduggery, my part in which would make perfect sense, once I understood it. Unfortunately that took some months, and the sorting-out process came dangerously late.

This was Mr. Philby of the SIS, the foreign intelligence outfit. I had first met Kim Philby round about 1941 during my heavy drinking period, and I had come to the conclusion that he was even more confused than I was at the time. Even now, years later, he still seemed unsure as to whether I was as loyal as all get out, or a thoroughgoing Red under true Blue covers who needed to be watched carefully. To begin with at least, he didn't seem entirely sure of me, credentialswise. Maybe I was only pretending to be utterly trustworthy, but was actually slavonically discoloured; though of course I might simply have been tainted by the public view that after their successes on the Eastern Front the Russians could do no wrong. Or had I been idealogically turned? But which way? Maybe I was only pretending to thoroughly hate the Reds. Though mind you, it had to be borne in mind that I had done important work for the Russian medical service in Moscow during the last war, taking pulses, emptying bedpans, and the like. Which was suspicious, right? Or was it? Also, don't forget I had been friends for a time with a noted commissar, Rodominov. On the other hand, Rodominov had ultimately been liquidated — unless Rodominov had been a figment of my imagination, and had never really existed, except in England, which was full of figments?

I tell you, it was a real mystery, or, as my friend Winston Churchill would say, a puzzle wrapped in an enigma and boiled dry over a hot stove. Or perhaps none of the above. I mean, when you got right down to it, maybe Philby was just thinking of using me on behalf of his organization for unknown purposes on that ominous day he approached me in Brussels in late November, 1944.

Anyway, here he was at the Brussels restaurant where Clemence and I had once partaken of cream cakes. I was busily woolgathering at the time, and knitting it into a letter to my son in the United States,* when the spy chief, attired in a civvy suit, bowler, and umbrella — presumably in hopes of passing undetected as a British spy among the Belgians — plonked himself at my table as casually as if we'd arranged the appointment for this very hour, three years previously.

However, after he had talked mysteriously for a while and established, apparently to his satisfaction, that my political sympathies had not changed one whit over the intervening years, which was true enough, he suggested that I get to know Russia even better. Well, that seemed innocuous enough; just polite conversation, followed by some trivial chat about the next three-power conference which was to take place somewhere or other, between Stalin, Roosevelt, and Churchill. Though confessing that he couldn't yet say exactly where it was to be held, his twitching eye informed me that it might be somewhere in the east, probably in February. I pretty much missed the proposition concerning my insinuation into the Allied delegation.

"Insinuate?" I said, accepting his kind offer of yet another cognac. "I never insinuate. If I have something to say I come right out with a knowing wink."

My latest exploit, he went on, would be a great help. Did I realize how famous I had become? Even in the Soviet Union they knew all about me. I would be warmly welcomed, and my knowledge of Russian would be a considerable advantage. The Foreign Office was rather short of linguists, he explained, since familiarity with foreign customs and languages was rather frowned upon at the FO. Still, a smattering of the language could turn out to be quite useful on occasion, like during a bombing raid or a lull in conversation about beastly foreigners.

"Of course, my Russian is a bit rusty by now," I said, with a smile that was meant to look modest and assured. To prove it, I illustrated the rest of the sentence with a hand gesture, which was very assured and becomingly modest. Meanwhile, Philby was going on and on about the value of having an outsider like me as part of ... some delegation or other. I would be especially valuable because I was either sympathetic or possibly not entirely unsympathetic to the regime, was how he put it;

* "B.W.", grandson of the aforementioned Cyrus Chaffington; the appearance of a second Bartholomew W. Bandy caused much consternation in *Hitler versus Me*. — Ed.

or possibly he didn't and I wasn't.

At which point my thoughts, lubricated with cognac, drifted back to Clemence. I sank into romantic depression, and became too confused to absorb anything whatsoever beyond the delicious coffee with sloshes of brandy and oodles of cream in it. I hadn't had such deliciously shiny cream for at least five years. Also, bananas. I hadn't had a banana for, oh, five years, at least. Which reminded me that I had better be careful about what I agreed to. I wasn't entirely certain that Philby could be relied upon. The last time we'd met hadn't been too trust-enhancing. Of course, there was a good excuse for that. I'd been a trifle intoxicated, besotted, and besoused, and had ended up tippling, toppling, and pissed as a newt. So today I must be on my guard.

Somehow pulling myself together, I mumbled, "I mean, what could I do at a political conference anyway?"

"Apart from your duties as a translator, Bandy," Philby said, leaning over, "my Service thinks you could be quite a useful observer. Reporting, for instance, on harmless background stuff — personalities, attitudes, confidences, tactics, that sort of thing. Or," he added, leaning even closer, in what seemed to be a strangely personal way, "anything else you think might be of use."

"Ah."

"Exactly," he said, pleased with the quickness and subtlety of my response. "By the way, old man, congratulations. The German ace you demolished? He was one of Hitler's prize fighters, you know."

"He was a boxer too?" I slurred.

"And as I mentioned, your exploits have attracted interest in Russia, and that could be very useful."

"Really, Mr ... Mr ...?" God, now I'd forgotten his name.

"And there should be a promotion in it for you," Philby said — that was it, Philby — as he glanced at his watch. "But don't worry, we'll take care of it."

"Take care of what?" I slurred, but he was already rising to his feet and adjusting his bowler. "After all, you definitely have it coming to you, old chap," he concluded, with a wonderfully warm and cosy smile that should have caused me to recollect my cogitations on the metaphysics of trustworthiness. But I was not in a recollecting mood just then.

By December I was really starting to miss flying — proper flying, that is, not just stooging about to keep up the flying hours. Still, I managed to keep myself occupied, mainly by moving into the apartment on

Maelbeek, next to Leopold Park. After a couple of days or so of dedicatedly lugging my valise from Evere, dusting a lamp, chatting up a girl in the Natural History Museum, and generally admiring the fine views from my new quarters, I reported once again to SHAEF to see if they'd missed me. To my surprise, they had. I was confronted by a choleric group captain who was in such a furious state that I feared for his blood pressure.

The moment I came in through the unimposing main entrance to the headquarters building he rushed up to me without even an introduction and shouted, "You were supposed to 've been here two days ago, days ago! Where the hell have you been?"

I was somewhat taken aback. They must have known that I had a couple of days off, and here I was, returning at a reasonable enough hour. It wasn't even ten a.m. Yet this fellow with the sandblasted face seemed to think that I'd committed a sin worse than buggery, skulduggery, or overeating.

Still, I was prepared to be polite. "Sorry, old chap," I said.

"Sorry? Sorry? That's the best you can do, that's the best you can manage? You should have been here yesterday! Yesterday!"

"Why? What happened?"

"What happened? What happened?" he bellowed, at a volume that rattled the windows of the entrance hall. "Just who the hell do you think you are, Wing Commander, disobeying orders, flouting orders as if, as if you were Tedder's nephew or somebody? Turning up hours late — days late, practically!"

He seemed to have a habit of repeating himself. "And smelling of booze, too — at ten in the morning! Ten in the morning!"

"Five to ten, actually."

"Shut up. You just — shut up and tell me, just where the bloody hell have you been?" he shouted, and actually repeated some of that, too.

"Well, let me see. First I purchased a pencil in the Rue Rogier van der Weyden," I said, shaking the rain off my blue raincoat before folding it neatly over my important-looking briefcase which today contained, along with some togs, two precious bananas obtained at the market adjoining the Hotel de Ville. (Incidentally, how the devil had Belgium managed to import bananas when Great Britain hadn't managed it for five years?)

"Be silent! You just — be silent!" bellowed the group captain. "And look here, I want an answer. Just, just who d'you think you are, turning up this way, a day late for an important appointment, an important appointment of vital, vital importance," he said, sweating like mad, this despite the fact that it was really quite chilly that morning. Chilly and wet.

It was only after a further repetition of words and queries in a similarly horrisonant fashion (*Roget's Thesaurus*, see "Stridor" — note how assiduously I am working on my vocabulary if not my hair), that I finally understood why he was making such a fuss. Apparently an OP signal had come in from London two days ago, requesting my presence at Buckingham Palace at 1400 hours this very day.

I reckoned that I was in for another gong. They must have discovered I didn't already have it. I hoped it was to be the Datura Cross from our new Peruvian ally. The award not only included an attractive medal, but the gift of a home-grown plant often to be found on South American dunghills, but nonetheless very useful, apparently, for countering convulsions and tic doloureux.

The weather wasn't good enough for a Spitfire jaunt across the Channel, so I had to make do with the duty flight from Evere to Norholt. While I was waiting at the draughty reception hall, which was still adorned with Nazi emblems and a wide, realistic wall painting of a thousand healthy German girls stretching and bending, who should I meet but Air Vice-Marshal Chistelow. I was just too late to dodge into the toilets. Anyway, he was with a group drenched in Allied uniforms.

Even so, he ambled over as soon as he saw me. "Good God," he said. "You've lost even more hair."

Blast, I usually managed to hide it by keeping my cap firmly in place. I'd only taken it off for a few seconds to tuck in a hank or two. On top of the hirsute famine, I needed a haircut.

"Retirement from ops seems to have done you some good, I see," he went on, looking unusually cheerful as he surveyed me from follicle to footwear.

"Thank you, sir."

"But what's all this about you being given a better job than the one you have at present?" Chisters enquired.

"You mean even better than the job of telling foreign officers where to find the local whorehouses, sir?"

"You would know where to find them, would you?" replied the air vice-marshal, looking pleased with himself at being one up with his put-down.

The best I could riposte with was, "M'm."

"You've somebody to cultivate in London?" he enquired, his amusing rejoinder further brightening his big, fat face. "Or is this just a trip to moan about being taken off ops?"

"Actually, it's to see the King," I said offhandedly.

"Yes, very amusing, Bandy. Oh, by the way," he went on, his tone ever so casual and matter-of-fact, "you'll be losing me soon."

"Oh, dear. High blood pressure, is it?"

Apparently it wasn't, though the new tint to his complexion suggested that it could be a problem soon. "I'm listed for the Three Power Conference," he said coldly. "Soon as they've decided who's to be my deputy." And with a nod so curt as to cause his jowls to swing like a cow's udder, he turned and resumed his nationally important toddle to his own warm, handsomely-appointed transport instead of to the cold, draughty, common-or-garden Dak with the butt-freezing canvas seats that awaited me.

Still, I had the silver canteen for company, fully loaded with booze, the one that Sigga had given me half a dozen years ago, just before we set out for Spain. Even before I had struggled into the straps of the Dakota's canvas seat I had made inroads on its store of Scotch. As a result I was in high spirits throughout the trip, despite my uncertainty as to its purpose.

By the time the cab deposited me that afternoon within nonchalant strolling distance of the Entrée — the Ambassadors' Entrance to Buckingham Palace, no less — I had come to the conclusion, aided by another few sips from my luggage, that the King had decided to make me Governor-General of Canada. After all, I was a great man, now. All the papers said so, firmly establishing to my satisfaction that, regardless of what my father used to say, I really was a success: a personage sought after by spy chiefs and ... and Belgian aristocrats alike, as soon as they'd pulled themselves together.

This was to be the third time I had met the King. On this occasion it took place in the private apartments to the rear of the palace. I was a touch surprised at that. Investitures usually took place toward the front of the palace. I felt quite honoured to be at the back.

I was shown into the Guard Room, as they called it, and gosh, only a few minutes elapsed before a servant arrived to escort me to a secretary, who in turn led me personally into the presence of a Principal Secretary who, chatting amiably, deposited me in what was officially called the Green Drawing Room. The King appeared only five minutes later, wearing a general's uniform. My goodness, it was beautiful — the room, that is, not the uniform, though that was nice enough with its crossed swords insignia, and sporting more unearned ribbons than even I was wearing. The room was a glorious saloon over fifty feet in length, all dazzling gold and crystal. So this was where I was to receive my new appointment, eh?

No, it wasn't. There was no sign of the usual bunch to be found on such occasions: courtiers, hangers-on, and so forth. In fact, there was nobody here at all, just me and His Majesty together, all ready to chit-chat and exchange pleasantries in our modest and unassuming ways.

"P- p- please feel completely at home, Bandy," quoth His Majesty, adding so smoothly that he must have been rehearsing the little speech for the last few minutes, "though not quite as much at home as you seemed the last time you were here, when you parachuted into the garden and flirted with my daughters." He pointed to said garden through the room's high windows, which were criss-crossed with rather grimy anti-blast tape.

We both essayed a couple of laughs, one laugh apiece. "Yes, Your Majesty," I said, ever so respectfully. "And how are the princesses these days?"

"Fine, thank you," said the King, coughing gently behind his fist. "Now, to get down to business. I have been following your career with a good deal of interest, Wing Commander, " he went on, "not to mention disbelief on occasion ...." He paused to allow a brief smile to flit across his features. "... and have been giving the matter a lot of thought." At this point he gestured at a comfortable armchair with a slightly awkward sweep of his hand. As he was not making it entirely clear as to whether I should sit in the comfy chair, move it, dust it, or just admire its handsome green and gold upholstery, I settled the matter by plonking into it. Actually, I very nearly missed it by half a buttock. I made a quick memo to myself to the effect that I should not sip quite so much Scotch on my way back to Brussels.

"That's good, Mr. Bandy. Make yourself comfortable," quoth the sovereign doubtfully. "Now, the fact is, I have talked over the situation at considerable length with certain uh- uh- uh-"

He was having such difficulty with the word that I thought I should help him. "Certain uhfficials?" I prompted.

Disinclined to favour the suggestion, he said curtly, "Discussed it with certain members of my family. Not all of them are convinced as to the rightness of the decision I finally arrived at. However, because I have followed your career with uh- uh-"

"Admiration, sir? Reverence? Astonish-"

"Allow me to finish, Bandy, if you don't mind," he snapped. He was beginning to sound so irritated that I thought I had better abandon any more helpful suggestions, even if we were comfortable old friends dating way back to 1940.

After a moment he continued, "As I was saying, I have followed your career with fascination, not to say amazement, and frequently sheer disbelief." He stopped suddenly, as if taken aback by his own words. When he resumed the speech he sounded considerably less certain about whatever it was he was he was being unsure about. "However, I am thoroughly convinced that —" He faltered again, before slightly amending the speech to, "I am really convinced —" And then he stopped once again, with another look at me, and an even more uncertain expression before continuing, "I am fairly sure that you are a man of action as well as discretion, Wing Commander."

"Well, as a matter of fact, Your Majesty, I —"

"Don't interrupt, Bandy, if you don't mind. I'm finding it increasingly diwicult to .. to ..." a frustrated gesture completed the sentence — probably caused by his awareness that he had lapsed into a tendency to lisp. "Anyway, I believe," he continued doubtfully, "that you're just the sort of fellow who would not be overawed by authority, or overly affected by opposition. Hence I have a commission for you, Wing Commander —"

"Yes, I've been waiting for it to come through," I replied, with a forgiving sort of smile.

"But I haven't said what it is, yet."

"My commission?" I prompted. "I presume you mean my promotion to group captain," I said, crossing one leg over the other and leaning back in the comfy chair.

"That's not what I was talking about," he said, really cross now. "I was referring to the job of your undertaking a small tut-task for me. To take place the moment the war is over."

"Oh, sure, Your Majesty," I responded. "Course I will. Yes, siree bob!"

"But I haven't said what it is yet!"

"Oh, sorry."

"Incidentally, all this is huh-highly confidential," he said in his slow and increasingly agitated delivery.

"Yes, of course, sir," I whispered, leaning closer, and adopting an expression jam full of intrigue.

"It is not dangerous —"

"Oh, that's all right, Your Majesty, I don't mind!"

"But it would spare us a certain amount of embarrassment —"

"Yes, of course, sir!"

"A slight involvement —"

"Say no more, sir, don't worry, there's nobody more trustworthy than —"

"Allow me to continue, Mr. Bandy!" he said, beginning to look really desperate. Which told me that the job, or commission, would require every ounce of discretion on my part.

"Of course. Course. Go ahead, Your Royal Highness, I'm all ears."

"As I was saying, before you —"

"Yes, I quite understand, Your Royal Highness. You don't need to —"

"Shut up, man, for God's sake!" he shouted. He actually shouted at me! The King actually shouted at me. "And listen! I'm tut-tut-trying to explain. All I'm asking of you is a discreet enquiry and investigation, to take place at the end of the war, concerning certain written material ..."

He stopped, to struggle for a moment over the next word. The King had a tendency to stutter a bit. Nothing if not observant, I'd noticed it on previous occasions. Or stammer, was it? I must look up both words.

He went on haltingly to explain that before the war his brother, the Duke of Windsor, had expressed certain, er, opinions in his discussions with the Germans; had made outspoken remarks which, if allowed into the public prints, might cause some discomfiture in certain quarters and circles.

I don't know, but it seemed to me that the more he talked the less confident he seemed, the less sure of himself. It was as if he were mentally reviewing the situation in the light of some development or other. In fact, he suddenly stopped dead, turned back to me, and said, "Look, Bandy, I wonder if we should perhaps .... Perhaps review the situation?"

"What situation, sir?"

"This situation."

"Ah. This situation. You mean, review it, sir?"

"Yes. Perhaps change our minds about the whole thing."

"You mean about going into the German Foreign Office archives and abstracting the abstracts wherein the Duke of Windsor had uttered some exceedingly ill-advised remarks?"

"I'm sure they were not all that damaging, when you get right down to it. Not as damaging as all that when you get right down to it, Bandy."

"Do you really think so, Your Majesty?"

"Yes, I believe I really think that suddenly it doesn't seem such a terribly good idea, Bandy."

"But sir, if the beastly Huns have gone and summarized the Duke's comments, it could be terribly embarrassing for your family."

"Oh, I don't think that's too likely, Bandy. I'm sure they won't. After all, we'd be dealing with diplomats, even if they are German."

"I guess the trouble is, some beastly British journalists might see the stuff —"

"I'm sure that won't happen, Bandy."

"As you say, it could be awfully embarrassing, Your Maj."

"Yes, well, as I say, Bandy, I think we should think it over."

"Are you sure, George?" I asked sympathetically. "I mean, it's a member of your own family being terribly, terribly indiscreet, right?"

"Yes, well, I think we should definitely think it over, Wing Commander."

"Are you absolutely sure, sir?"

"Yes, I've definitely decided, Bandy," said the sovereign, quite curtly, now. "We'll forget the whole thing. All right?"

"Well, if you're quite sure ... I mean, it's your family ..."

"Yes, let's forget it, Bandy," the King said, with surprising asperity. "The subject is now closed, understand?" He raised his arm to look at his wrist watch. "Well, now, if there's nothing else, Wing Commander ...?"

And thus I left the palace, empty handed, feeling a shade despondent after the failure of His Majesty to get down to business. Though mind you, it was definitely not the sort of commission I would have gone for anyway. Not even for His Majesty the King, so there.

LOOKING BORED

BY NOW, THOUGH COMFORTABLY ENSCONCED in a fine apartment off the Boulevard Anspach, I was getting pretty browned off with mooching around Brussels with almost nothing to do. As far as the authorities went, the poor things had no idea what to do with me other than to have me act as a messenger for passing on SHAEF bumph to the growing number of Allies who were joining in the war now that victory seemed to be in sight. As late as a couple of years ago I might have been sent on a braggadoccio course to the United States at RAF expense, but now they were busy producing their own aces, and were no longer interested in Stanford Tucks or Johnny Johnsons. Apparently the best I could do now for the war effort was to treat foreign air force representatives to posh dinners, assuming that the splendidly accoutred officers really were in town on business and not just in for a snog with some beauteous Belgian bint. I'd profoundly irritated old Chistelow many weeks ago by turning down his offer of a desk job in Ottawa. I was beginning to think I should have taken it up, especially now that I had so few friends at the aerial front lines because of the attrition of war or time-ex postings.

I still continued to flounce to the fighter squadrons whenever possible, and gain extra flight pay, for instance by trying out unfamiliar aircraft, such as the redoubtable Hawker Tempest (in which I lost a tooth filling, shaken out when I failed to brake the undercarriage before the wheels retracted and thumped home). The flight pay on top of the normal remuneration was a useful $1.25 a day.

"They don't pay you flyers much, do they," said Harriet Hullborne. We were sitting in the office one wet and foggy day in the middle of December, both of us, I think, feeling pleasantly idle in the run-up to Christmas. "All these stories of Indian princes and other rich people you used to hang around with, I thought you must be rich."

"I never did that well after the 1929 crash," I responded, leaning back in the spare chair. "Sometimes, Sigga and I were practically impoverished."

"Yeah, those were tough times," she muttered. "I was lucky to be getting paid in the army, I guess."

Harriet had become decreasingly unfriendly over the last few weeks. It had even slipped her memory on occasion that she detested Canadians. Lately she seemed to be so keen on finding out as much as possible about me that I suspected an intention to become a blackmailer or, worse still, a biographer.

Her own life was certainly worth listening to, though she seemed convinced, without actually admitting it, that it was of little interest. The only girl in a brood of boys, she had managed to escape a poor farming community through an unnatural interest in education, which ultimately gained her a degree from a midwestern college; this in turn got her a commission in the new Women's Army Corps.

"Naturally," she said, addressing her bulldog which, as usual, was flopped under the desk, twitching and sighing, "with my degree in applied mathematics they put me straight into the Godamn cookhouse."

Presumably not as a cook — I'd tasted the home-made cake she brought me one morning.

After that she had gone to work as a classroom instructor and was posted to the European theatre of operations, whereupon she had developed a tremor in her right hand — "Because of the God-damn British weather," she claimed. Not knowing what else to do with her now that her blackboard diagrams were making her look like a modern artist, the brass had designated her a corps liason officer, and given her an Underwood. The typewriter, she told me, had come in quite useful when she was not being forced to liase with Godamn Limeys, as she had been intending to write a defence of her ancestor, General Hull, for quite a few years.

My occasional reference to past incidents in my own life seemed to interest her enough that I usually ended up telling her more than was wise. Like, for instance, the way I had volunteered to fight in the Spanish Civil War in 1938 on the wrong side.

"You were still flying fifteen years after your adventures in India?" she asked. "You couldn't get a decent job?"

I had already told her too much about how I had returned from India with a small fortune. It had turned into a large fortune through reckless investment, despite a profligate expenditure on champagne and the restoration of the Bandy Gander, Mark II, the monoplane I had designed in the early 'twenties but lost while fleeing from Prime Minister Mackenzie King. I had the Gander replicated at the Glenn Martin works in the States, and persisted in trying to sell it to Canadian flyers, the US Army, or whoever else showed the slightest interest in the peacetime future of aviation. The plane was right for its time, I told Harriet, being capable of carrying four passengers and landing on grass or water. What it couldn't do was land on a sea of indifference. By the onslaught of the Great Depression it had gotten nowhere, and after 1930 its now-impoverished designer discovered that it was too out-of-date even if he'd had the money to pour into a new version.

"So what did I do?" I repeated. "I bought Sigridur one last fur coat and tried to make a living flying prospectors, Mounties, surveyors and so forth, in the far north."

That is, until the Mark II Gander cracked up in Tuktoyuktuk, or Port Brabant, as the Hudson's Bay Company officially called it then, and we finally headed south to pursue a flying job offered by a friend.

"By the way, how old are you now, Bandy?" Harriet asked suddenly with a coy growl, after straightening up in order to tighten a light brown shirt over her redoubtable bust.

"Fifty-one," I said truthfully, for once. "Though I deduct a year for good behaviour. So I just tell people I'm fifty."

She looked at me a little distrustfully. My remarks, especially the ironical jabs, often confused her. "Well, go on," she said, turning away to kick her dog. She didn't mind it snoring, but she wasn't too keen on it farting as well. "So you went to work for this pal, and that lasted until you went to fly in Spain? And Sigga went with you?"

"M'm," I finished, unwilling to talk too much about my beloved Sigga for fear of devaluing the memory; though I had already shown Major Harriet too many of the album pictures that featured Sigridur too prominently, i.e., in swimsuits.

"Hell, Bandy, you've sure had a crazy sort of life, ain't you?" she said.

"Well, it's all over now, eh?" I muttered. "Nothing left for me now but to collect a pension or two and huddle against the radiator in winter."

"That baroness would be crazy to dump you," said Harriet, looking at me with an expression which I took to be one of disgust inspired either by me or Clemence, or possibly just a farting bulldog.

The heavy but interestingly-shaped major with the rough voice was just starting to ask for more details about my courtship of Sigridur in Iceland, an account which had already brought forth a guffaw or two from her, when there was a knock at the office door, and a lad in a wet blue raincoat looked in.

"Wing Commander Bandy, is it?" he enquired. "I'm from your old squadron, sir, and —"

"Come in, come in," I cried, welcoming a change of conversation. "Who are you? And take off that moist apparel, lad."

"Flying Officer Piper, sir, Pete to my friends," he said, and went on to explain that he was here because John Oakley had suggested a visit to a former squadron leader. "He said you were a great man, sir, but you would badly need cheering up, sir," said the lad.

On hearing that his flight commander was behind the visit, I had turned into an overwound alarm clock, its tension not lessened or slackened when Pete Piper confessed to a great admiration for Oakley.

"Ah, yes, Oakley," I said, trying to look as if I barely remembered him. Welcoming yet another conversational change whilst hiding my apprehension behind a jolly welcoming tone, I asked Piper if he had ever picked a peck of pickled pepper.

"Sir?"

"You know. Picked a peck of pickled pepper?" I coaxed. "Peter Piper ...?"

"Yes, sir — that's my name."

"Funny you should mention pepper, sir, though actually we never grew pepper at our place off Sherbourne Avenue," the lad went on. "Though we did grow quite a lot of stuff."

"Oh, did you?"

"Yes, sir, lettuces and stuff. Even though we only have a small garden."

"Ah."

"With one elm tree in it. Though they tell me that it's starting to rot, now."

"M'm. Pity about that," I mumbled, after a suspicious glance at his boyish face to see if he had inherited some of his bad habits from Oakley. He was, of course, from Toronto.

"By the way, Pete," I went on, "why should I need cheering up?"

"Sir?"

"You said Oakley said I would need cheering up."

"Oh, yes, sir. Well, because of you being robbed. Robbed in the ..." Pete glanced at Major Hullborne, coughed into his hand embarrassedly, and added quietly, "... in the house of ill-repute, sir."

Major Harriet had returned to her typing job on General Hull. She looked up.

For the third time, I felt that a change of subject was called for. "Well, now, Pete, what do you think of the big news, eh?" I called out loudly.

I was referring to the German onslaught through the Ardennes. It had begun just the previous day, but was already causing fear and anxiety among the Belgians. Some were even fleeing the city. The totally unexpected attack by two dozen divisions, some of them elite SS units, many of them armoured, had already driven deep into American lines. It looked not unlikely that the Germans might totally disrupt the Allied strategy for ending the war. The British and Canadian offensive through Holland was already affected. At the very least, the German attack, whether successful or not, was likely to extend the war by months.

"I know," agreed the young pilot. "And this weather won't help," he added, gesturing out the window at the drenched city. "The weather's grounded the whole of the Allied air force. I'll have trouble getting back. Not that there'll be any flying anyway ..."

"Do you have a place to stay? There should be a room available at Evere," I suggested.

"Just so long as you don't spend it with Bandy," Harriet chortled. "He dresses up in women's —" She stopped dead, realizing she was speaking out of turn. Suddenly she looked quite embarrassed.

"How's that again, Ma'am?" the boy asked. "Dresses up?"

"Forget it, Lieutenant," said Harry — Harriet — Hullborne. Unfortunately, Pete's attention was only temporarily diverted from his scrutiny of the wing commander with the inscrutable face and the brand new twitch.

Actually, the twitch owed more to thoughts of Oakley than anything else, especially after I asked how Oakley was getting on. Surely by now he had fallen foul of his new CO, and was about to be shipped home, or better still — for his ultimate wellbeing, of course — had crashed and lost a few limbs?

"Flight Lieutenant Oakley?" said Pepper. "Oh, he's fine, sir. He got another Focke Wulf the other day."

"Did you say flight lieutenant?" I asked, in a voice remarkably imitative of a factory hooter. "You can't be talking about John Oakley? You mustn't!"

"Yes, sir, Flight Lieutenant Oakley. He was put in command of my flight just the other day."

"And what's this about *another* Focke Wulf? How many does he have?" I asked, only just reining in a piercing scream.

"I don't know exactly. But he got his DFC. Just the other day."

"Jesus Christ," I said, and had to sit down and get my face in order — get in lined up properly on the parade ground of my stupefaction and with the correct arm's length from the nearest shoulder of comprehension. Oakley a flight louie? And already with the five victories he would need to earn a DFC? No, no, tell me it wasn't true!

It sure made me think, when I'd finally calmed down, not only about Oakley, but worse, about me. I, who over the years, had created so very many broken blood vessels in the faces of foes and opponents, from crimsoning colonels to the toppest brass, from prime ministers to great viceroys of India whose throbbing dreams of glory must have involved hurling me into the Black Hole of Calcutta. Now I was beginning to discern the same qualities in Oakley that others had seen in me. Oh, the horror of it. Worse still, I was beginning to respond to him in the way that so many of my superiors had reacted to me, from maddened frustration to outbreaks of impotent fury. Only now the roles were reversed: I was the dreaded superior rather than the innocent victim. I was the cad, the bounder, heaping shovelfuls of injustice on the poor, innocent, unsuper dupe, John Oakley. Oh, the irony of it, the irony! And even worse: Oakley was not only behaving like the past me — he even looked a bit like me! Oh God, no! It was intolerable, unbearable. Even allowing for the age difference there was little doubt about that. He was the same height. His voice often whined, the way mine was said to sound like that of W.C. Fields in his "My little chickadee" era. Unless — a further thought struck me. Oh no! Was Oakley also trying to imitate my voice? Surely not. But still, the rest of the picture was becoming frighteningly clear. His face, smooth, bland, and utterly expressionless, was like mine had been before a hideous combination of age, foolish pride, and follicle scarcity, had overlaid the former condition with ....

I'm sorry. I'm in no shape to discuss it any further.

RUE MONTOVER

ONE MISTY SUNDAY AFTERNOON, a Sunday of chill damp air and watery sunshine, I was strolling with the baroness along Rue Archimede, on our way for morning coffee at *Le Derriere*, when Clemence said almost hopefully, "These feelings of yours for me, Bart'olomew, surely it is just infatuation, *hein*?"

"'s not. I'm mad about you Clemmy. It's hard to sleep, thinking about you, holding you in my arms, and so forth."

As we stopped to cross the boulevard she said suddenly, "Will it at least satisfy you if we make love together?"

"Duh?"

"Will it help?"

"You mean right here?"

"Of course not right here, you idiot!"

"No, I didn't think you meant right here," I faltered, my heart beating like a tramp steamer. "They say it might snow. Quick, let's get back to your house."

"No, not at my place. And certainly not in your *caserne*." She shivered, and turned up the collar of her fur coat.

"A hotel, then?"

"But I might be recognized." She hesitated, before continuing with strangely diminishing enthusiasm, "There is an apartment in the Quartier Leopold ..."

"Perfect! Come on, hurry!"

"Not right now! My God, Bart'olomew! Some evening when the apartment is available and I have no other engagements."

I subsided, swishing my Borzoi walking stick through the dead leaves. "Is that all it would be?" I asked, speaking so forlornly it was quite heartbreaking. "Just another engagement?"

"I told you, darling. I also love Gay-orgi."

"Who?" I asked, pretending not to know she was referring to her long-long husband.

She cuddled my arm gently. "And the truth is, Bart'olomew, I am not particularly mad about the physical side of it. You understand? I know you will be disappointed."

"Never, Clemence, never — even if you just laid there and thought of Belgium."

"I am more likely to be thinking of my next hair appointment."

A convoy of military vehicles came speeding along the boulevard, travelling fast. It was led by a jeep containing a red-tabbed army officer. He was gazing upward as if the sky contained something interesting, but there was nothing to see except overhanging, dripping branches and grey cloud.

"Well," she sighed, "perhaps then you will understand, that there is nothing to me but bones and longing."

I ignored the sense of this in my eagerness to convince her that my love for her was as undying as an Icelandic geyser. "No, no, you are lovely, the most shining creature I've ever met, Clemence," I husked. "You light up everything around you in a citron glow, like an old gas standard."

She stopped and frowned up at me, pretending to be sorely offended, but unable to subdue the humour in her eyes. "Like what?" she asked.

"I mean, you know. Radiant," I said, looking away. I felt a little disappointed by her attitude. She seemed to think that all my love amounted to was the need for light pneumatic relief.

Good Lord, as if she thought sex was all I was after, I thought, as, rubbing my hands, I whipped out my notebook and said briskly, "Right, give me the address, location, telephone number if there is one, precise directions to this rendezvous, and an exact time according to the twenty-four hour clock so that there cannot be the slightest risk of my missing the appointment because of an adherence to the old-fashioned am and pip emma system to which we Anglo-Saxons are so understandably devoted, eh, what-what?" I said, filled with confidence that, once allowed a trial run, I would have no difficulty in overcoming the deleterious effect of her love for this fellow Gay-orgi and her years of self-denial, the trouble being that she had devoted herself to celibacy ever since the fool had so cruelly deserted her so many years ago.

Either her engagement book was overfilled, or her reserve needed a spot of lubrication, but it was days before the longed for moment arrived. We were taking coffee in her favourite cafe, Maggots, on the Rue Neuve — Clemmy loved the oodles of fattening cream that Brussels restaurants were so laden with. We who hadn't seen real cream cakes since Ivor Novello's *The Dancing Years* were struck dumb by the oleaginous display, which, however much she gorged, never made the slightest difference to Clemence's figure.

Anyway, on the great day — when, as usual, I was trying to convince her that I was not suffering from infatuation but that my love for her was entirely rational — she suddenly announced that one of the properties she owned in Brussels was available. It was in an apartment block near the Parc Leopold.

"What about it?"

"It's available," she said offhandedly.

"What for?"

"What do you think?" she said, almost crossly. "You've been talking about it often enough."

"You mean?" I said, leaning half way across the surviving cakes on our table.

"If you want, we can go there this afternoon," she said, still sounding a bit cross.

"If I want?" I said at approximately 113 decibels, causing a waitress to drop a hundredweight of cutlery into a soup tureen — of the 'rat-tailed' design, I believe. Then, rather more sedately, as I plucked cream buns off my sleeves, "If I want?" And gently I took her hand, which was quivering almost as much as mine, cuddled and kissed it.

"If it doesn't matter to you," she said, "that I still exfatulate the humanitarian exogamy of intransigent and gilded adoration summited by extended affectation, despite the arabesques of merrymaking with pistil of carpels, andoecium of stamens, calyx of sepals, all intertwined in perianthal ecstasy?" she enquired. But somehow I wasn't listening to a word of it, I was so excited, so busily dribbling onto her knuckles.

The next three hours were among the hardest ever borne. The arrangement was that I meet her in the Leopold Park, below a statue of a stone bloke in a cocked hat. While she was nearly half an hour late, I was forty-eight minutes early, which gave me plenty of time to flick a couple of motes of dust from my best blue uniform and newly dry-cleaned greatcoat. Oh yes, and time to polish the walking stick, which I was still using for swank purposes, though my limb was almost mended by now.

When she finally arrived she swept past me, and I fell into step beside her, babbling, "Darling Clemence," and some variations on same.

We proceeded though the park, walking side by side but not touching, with me ecstatic as a skylark and relieved that at least I'd had time to spruce myself up with fresh underwear and toothpaste, and some expensive deodorant in case the hot shower had failed in its duty, not to mention the cold shower that followed, to render the old *em-pressment* a little more manageable.

A short rapturous walk brought us to an apartment building on the Rue Montover. I half expected a fairy tale castle with rodomontade turrets bragging from slow silver rotundas, shading quicksilver pavilions. It was actually Belgian ramroddy in appearance, of three or four stories, understandably a bit run-down after years of wartime neglect. No matter. It would no doubt be adequately staffed with beds.

The concierge, a little man in a celluloid collar who practically folded, stapled, and mutilated himself in his eagerness to serve the baroness, led us to a third floor apartment. With many a reverent look at Clemence, laid the keys beside a bust of a Belgian somebody or other, possibly a King. Even as the concierge backed out, gibbering in Flemish, he was still bent almost double.

"Well, this is nice," I said, looking round the living room, fearing that the chill would require us to make love crushed under heavy layers of linen, wool, and duck feathers. However, the place made an effort to heat up when some coughing radiators augmented my own central heating. "Well, this is nice," I said again, admiring the heavy brown furniture, the brown carpet, brown wallpaper, and a ceiling stained by a century of so of continental tobacco fumes. The only ornaments in the place were ash trays.

"We'll just let the rooms warm up a little, first, shall we?" I said briskly. Hoping that abstinence had made her heart grow fonder, I moved happily toward my glorious love with the intention of transposing a few spare calories; but she was too busy looking around the tiny kitchen, though there was not much to see, as it was tiny.

Nearly half an hour later we had still not reached the bedroom, which, oh Christ, had a picture of Mary Magdalene above the bed. I suppose the cold was putting her off, unless it was the tea she was taking so long to brew in the tiny kitchen. Of course, it was understandable that she would feel the cold keenly. The poor darling was thin as a poor excuse (an expression I've used before, but then I was a pioneer at recycling useful material), so naturally she needed time to warm up. For some reason she was reluctant even to remove her fur coat, purchased, she informed me, in Halifax, Nova Scotia, of all places.

"Good Lord," I exclaimed.

Moving about constantly and talking rapidly, glorious grey eyes luminous with interest in her story, she treated me to a wealth of detail as to where, when, how, and why the purchase had been made and by whom: Gay-orgi, naturally. I knew quite a bit about that fur coat by the time I hinted us into the bedroom. There I set a good example by plumping up the surprising number of pillows on the bed, and smoothing the sheets, which were somewhat damp, but would soon warm up, I thought.

"Right!" I said, clapping my hands together. "I think we're cosy enough now, eh?" I know I was. "Tell you want, Clemmy — I'll pop into bed and warm it up for you, eh? How about that, eh?"

Which I did, after carrying out some extremely rapid disrobing in the bathroom, which was five or ten times the size of the kitchen, and had mouldy tiles. Scuttling back to the bedroom, I flung the various mismatched pillows against the headboard and jumped into the giant bedstead, arranging the linenware so that I was decently covered from the waist down. I then settled back to obtain a fine view of Clemence, who had finally removed her coat.

I watched with keen, scientific interest as she folded it with the silken side out, and carefully draped it over a chair. That was good; she looked after her things.

She was now revealed in a lovely green dress decorated with gold curlicues and things at the neckline. Below the hem appeared a pair of black stockings, which made me more eager than ever for the next episode in this exciting Saturday afternoon serial. Did I mention it was a Saturday in December? Well, it was, a lovely winter afternoon, though cold, drab, damp, and overcast.

There was an almost immediately development with the green gown. It was most interesting. I didn't notice the slightest unbuttoning activity, or hear the faintest hiss of some hidden zip. The dress just seemed to fall apart of its own accord without any help from her, as if it were as eager as I was for the fray, even if its delectable contents were behaving perhaps just a tad casually. Otherwise no shyness or coy behaviour was evident as she disrobed. I was pleased about that. My previous lover, her with the face, had been excruciatingly bashful about exposing her epidermis; though admittedly as time leered by a distinct wantonness had finally flown the coop of her English upbringing.

Any moment now. Seeing her half-undressed was almost as good as soloing for the first time. Imagination scrambled ahead of the disrobing. Boy oh boy oh boy. Though she had been loitering from the moment we set off for this unsharp flat, she didn't appear to mind how frankly I ogled, now that she seemed committed.

It was even better when she leaned over to peel off her stockings. Though doing my best not to think of parcels ever again (and though

Chistelow kept glancing at me speculatively whenever our paths crossed), here was a stylish collection, exquisitely personalized. Oh, those long black stockings and that pale green slip and those overdone underpinnings. Her shape was even more stirring than I'd imagined. The wartime scarcity of fat was still evident in her frame, a few bones stuck out here and there, but overall the proportions were sublime, the legs, though a little subdued calf-wise, had otherwise been turned by a fair to middling craftsman, and the breasts, delicate as sherry trifles, were middle-aged amazing, better than even the most dedicated bosom fancier could hope for.

In no time at all, except for a few minutes in the bathroom, she was susurrating into bed, smelling a lot better than the sliver of soap in the bathroom sniffed by me. Perhaps she carried her own soap around, in contrast to the party lady who couldn't get any. Talking about which, the detumescing delay would surely be worth it, especially when she slid beside me and with loving gentleness, put her thin arms around me.

I was quite choked up by the glorious spontaneity of the embrace. "Gee, I love you," I managed.

She held me tighter than ever. "I know," she said. "I wish you didn't."

"Why not? We're both free."

"I am not free, Bart'olomew. I will never be free of Gay-orgi."

I made the mistake of muttering, "How?"

"I love him as much today as I did the very first time I met him," Clemence murmured, making things more difficult than ever by drawing closer. "Can I tell you about him, Bart'olomew?"

"Please don't."

But the answer must have got lost in the blankets. "As I told you, like so many Russians at that time, he was a taxi driver in Paris until we married and he changed his name to mine." She snuffled into my shoulder. "He loved it when people thought he was a baron. Dear Gay-orgi, he was so innocent ..."

"I knew a Gay-orgi like that," I began, hoping to lead the way, somehow, into a more profitable channel.

"I rescued him, of course; saved him from a life of, what d'you call it, igno-money? It was also I who was the cause of — don't do that, Bart'olomew — I must tell you about it, first. You see, I was the cause of the disaster. I got him a job with the French Civil Service."

"Yes, I can see that would lead to his downfall."

"The SDECE[*]. Their foreign espionage service. They persuaded him to return to the Soviet Union for just one mission." She sighed. "The trouble was, there were too many communist sympathizers in France before the war. Perhaps he was betrayed."

"Oh, dear," I said, cupping a hand round her starboard buttock, as if to guess its weight.

"Or perhaps he gave himself away. I know he was anxious to find out what had happened to his relatives."

"How many did he have?" I murmured, drawing her closer still, idly thinking of my friend George Garanine's ten ghastly sisters in the Petrovka Ulitsa.

"Ten, I believe," she said. "Anyway, I have not heard of him since. And yet I am certain he is alive."

I felt myself subsiding. "What makes you think so?" I asked, raising my head so I could see her face.

"I just know it, Bart'olomew, I just know it. We loved each other so much. Sometimes I can feel he is thinking of me. He is just not the sort of man who would die in one of their labour camps."

This made me more than ever uneasy. If it was possible to work your way into a cushy billet in a Soviet gulag, Garanine was the man who could do it. And the name Gay-orgi? Surely she couldn't mean my George.

No, no, it was ridiculous. Garanine had left Ottawa for Russia as long ago as the 'twenties.

I cleared my throat a couple of times and said, "Your husband went missing in the 'thirties? He must be — gone — by now, Clemence."

"The ministry keeps saying so. All the same ... I just know ..." She faltered, and a moment later she shuddered, and my shoulder under her face started to feel wet. Which signalled the end of today's little adventure.

Especially when we heard the rattle of a key. Some fool was trying to insert their key into the wrong door. Except that the door was opening. The lock had stopped clicking and the apartment door was opening. And voices were sounding from the living room.

I lay there, rigid in all the wrong ways, listening to the sound of a man and a woman in muffled conversation.

Now even Clemence had converted herself into an obtuse angle. And the horror grew, as I recognized not just one of the voices, but

---

[*] An anachronism. The SDECE was only formed at the end of WWII. -Ed.

both of them.

He was saying, "She owns property all over the place, and when I mentioned that you were thinking of popping over, she said you could stay here. It's very obliging of her, hm? The hotels are pretty full at the moment."

"Oh, I say," said a hideously, coy, giggly voice in return, "she didn't think you were establishing a little love nest here, did she? You and me?"

"Good God, no," said the Air Officer Commanding 2nd Tactical Air Force with rather ungentlemanly haste. Though he quickly moderated his tones. "I told the truth, that you were just an old friend of the family, what?"

The giggle expired. "It smells a bit," said the woman rather curtly.

"Hasn't been used for a while, I suppose. Anyway, this is the living room. And through there the kitchen. The bathroom ..."

As the voices faded slightly I lay there itching all over with fright, feeling as if assorted tsetse flies and bluebottles were wading through the sweat on my body, in increasing danger of drowning. First the parcel of undies, half-convincing the Air Vice-Marshall that I was even kinkier than he'd thought, and now this. Clemence and I were staring wildly at one another, first with noses inches apart, and then aiming them almost simultaneously at the closed bedroom door. Her head was tilted, listening. She was holding her breath.

It was just amazing, how long she could hold her breath, almost as long as me. Then she was whispering.

I was too frightened to listen. Tsetse flies and bluebottles were drowning by the million, while I remained paralysed.

Clemence was proving rather more active. Her breathing restored, she thrashed the damp top sheet aside and hurled herself out of bed, whispering, "I just knew something like this would happen, with you," as she gathered her clothes. They were in an amazingly neat pile on the chair near the window. Better still, they had been divested in perfect, chronological order, so to speak. She was hopping back into an abbreviation of garments as perfectly as if laying out the cards for a nice hand of whist. And in an amazingly short period of time, too.

As for me, I knew I'd never get my clothes on in time. In my haste I'd scattered them like birdseed.

I lay there, entirely balanced on one elbow, helpless, hopeless. What was the use of trying, struggling through life? Better just to give up. So I just laid there supported by my quivering *capsula articularis cubiti*, suffering from sin and syncope, cerebral ischemia, lockjaw, and an assortment of muscular spasms and seizures. In other words, it was happening again. At my age.

As Clemence drew on her slip and her dress without bothering with certain items of underwear, my eyes flicked around wildly above the prematurely sodden sheets. Window curtain with blackout material. Too skimpy. Bathroom door. Nowhere in there for concealment. Wardrobe. Door partially open. Damaged hinge. Possible. Nowhere else.

But of course there was no point in hiding, absolutely no point, no point whatsoever. I'd be caught, as usual. It had happened so often in the past. Like when I was affianced to Katherine Lewis and Mrs. Cary's bosom turned up in the hotel room accompanied by Mrs. Cary herself, who was convinced I fancied her and who went on disrobing despite my protests. It was then the exceedingly censorious Mrs. Auchinflint also came visiting, and just in time Mrs. Cary hid in the bathroom, but then Katherine was heard, and Mrs. Auchinflint hid in a cupboard not unlike that one over there, just as her husband turned up, Major Auchinflint, my most dedicated enemy at the War Office who immediately became suspicious, and tried to get in, and — or no, it was Rodominov, wasn't it? That Russian spy, wasn't it? Or — anyway, it all went dreadfully wrong when at the end I whispered hoarsely to Katherine that she could come out now ("You can come out now"), and so she came out of hiding. And so did Rodominov. And Mrs. Auchinflint. And Mrs. Cary.

And then there was the dreadful occasion in 1924 when I was an MP in the government of Mr. Mackenzie King, Prime Minister of Canada, who was a spiritualist and indulged in séances, and one night he trapped me behind the curtains in Laurier House as a certain Madam Bite was organizing a séance for him, and I was forced to join in with a few 'responsive raps' of my own from beyond the grave. This was purely in self-defence, you understand, because the spirit they were summoning up was communicating some very damaging information about me, so, rapping on the panelling behind me, I spelled out a few corrective appraisals of myself to the effect that I was a splendid and unjustly censured sort of chap, utterly blameless on every conceivable occasion and some inconceivable ones. And of course there was that time when —

No, but by now I had learned my lesson. I had almost always got caught, and been exposed. It was better by far that this time I be a man and face the firing squad with courage and resolution, and take it on the chin, and get it over with, and besides, surely the worst was over as the Baroness de Forget was nearly dressed by now, and looked quite decent even if she wasn't wearing her knickers, and appeared amazingly calm, considering the — on the other hand, I hadn't always been caught out, if I remembered correctly. And that was when I leaped out of bed, and hid under it.

A second later, just as a pair of sensible brown shoes appeared dead ahead, I realized that my best blue uniform and various other items of service apparel were scattered on the floor in full view.

From the sensible shoes came a gasp of surprise. "Oh, sorry," they tongued. "Sorry. I do beg your pardon," the shoes said, and shuffled backward — to be brought up sharp by some highly polished pumps. Not proper issue at all, those pumps. Someone ought to have had a word with Air Vice-Marshal Chistelow about his footgear, I thought.

Now he too was apologizing, first to Gwinny for trampling on her as she backed up, and then to the baroness, who, though somewhat flushed of face, was nevertheless quite calmly stuffing spare items of underwear into the pockets of her fur coat as casually as if she was merely tidying up the joint before the visitors arrived.

"Clemence? My dear, I'm terribly sorry. I didn't realize you were using the flat," said the pumps.

"How d'you do, Oliver," came the cool response. Her voice was amazingly cool and steady, considering. What self-control these aristocrats had. "If you'll wait in the other room, I shall be with you in a moment," she said.

"Yes, of course," said the polished pumps as they backed out, followed, rather confusedly, by the sensible footwear.

The door closed. The next moment there was a hissing whisper of "Get dressed!"

Sensible fellow, I needed no encouraging. I rolled out from under the bed, attired, because of the perspiration, in balls of fluff, and started to plunge into my scattered apparel.

A minute later, with no further communication, she walked into the living room, carefully closing the door behind her.

Soon I heard Chistelow being polite. "Oh, Baroness, this is the lady I was telling you about. Guinevere Plumley. You remember —"

"Yes, of course, Oliver," came Clemence's cool voice. "How d'you do, Miss Plumley. I hope you'll be comfortable here. Don't worry about me, I'm in something of a rush. I'm just leaving."

And by Christ, I heard the entrance door opening and closing. She was indeed leaving. And now she had left — me in the lurch.

While my feelings can be imagined — or, if the reader has no imagination, I'll spell them out as being those of fear, outrage, and betrayal — those of the other two were of mystification. "That was rather sudden, wasn't it?" Guinevere was saying.

"Was, rather. I didn't get it wrong, did I? Admittedly it was a while ago when she told me you could use this flat, but ..."

"She seemed to have been sleeping here."

"Yes. I noticed."

"I thought you said she had a castle. Why would she want to use a place like this?"

"Not exactly a castle. A pretty impressive estate ..."

"She wasn't wearing stockings."

"What?"

"She wasn't wearing stockings."

"Really?"

"And what were all those clothes on the floor?"

"Clothes?"

"For heaven's sake, Oliver, don't tell me you didn't notice them?"

"Well, yes, I — no. Not actually."

"They looked like air force things," Guinevere said. And more than a touch of exasperation had entered her tones. Which were getting more distinct; coming nearer and nearer.

"What?"

"Well, go and see for yourself!" she said.

At which point in the dialogue I emerged insouciantly from the bedroom, faultlessly attired in my uniform, except possibly for the socks being inside out, and one length of the black tie being considerably longer than the other. But such déshabillé was not too obvious.

"Oh, hulloa, Guinevere. And Oliver," quoth I. "Didn't expect to see you here. Still, good to see you again. Well, I'll be on my way," I concluded, heading for the door with my greatcoat over my arm. "I'm in a bit of a rush, too, actually."

I was hoping to make an exit as casually as the baroness had managed it.

"Just a minute," said Gwinny, quite loudly. "Bartholomew. Stop right there."

I stopped right there, busily thrashing my way into the greatcoat.

"Bandy? What the devil are you doing here?" Chistelow said, sounding much more astonished than Guinevere.

"Isn't it obvious?" she said, slamming open the door to reveal the disordered bed. I'd never seen someone slamming a door open before.

"Look at that. Her and him. In there, in her — her foul, filthy den of iniquity," she cried, her voice so fricative with rage and disgust as to be in danger of seizing itself by the throat.

"Yes," I said. "Caught in the act, eh? Mea bloody culpa, eh, what?" Christ, stop. This was no time for my English accent. "Well, there you are," I continued, defying myself. "That's the way it is. Way things are, eh, what? Well, I did tell you we were through, Gwinny, but I just wouldn't listen, eh? That is, you wouldn't ... Er," I said, acknowledging that to Er was human.

"Anyway," I concluded, now busily brushing my epaulettes, "there you are. I've fallen for the baroness, in spite of the way she — Anyway, that's it, and I shall now take my leave as serenely as it's possible to do so, considering. Good afternoon, Gwinny. Good afternoon, Air Mice Varshal," I concluded.

And I actually managed to get halfway through the door before Guinevere supplied the 'considering' aspect by picking up the dusty bust of Leopold III and hurling it at the back of my head.

SHOT OF A SWANKPOT

THOUGH GENERAL VON RUNSTEDT'S sneaky attack through the Ardennes forest was still in progress, by the end of December it was petering out despite the favourable conditions, i.e., the poor weather. The rain and overcast was still keeping the allied air forces grounded.

On the final day of 1944, as the bad weather showed signs of lifting, the RAF held a celebratory bash in the biggest available hall at the Evere base, to which flight personnel of the allied air forces were invited, plus nearly enough Belgian dames to go around. Unfortunately, though I invited her, the baroness was not one of them. So I invited burly Harriet Hullborne instead.

The great space of the main drill hall had been quite imaginatively done up in military style, mostly by the ground staff of the Mosquito squadron that presently occupied the Brussels base. There were hosts of coloured lights, tinsel left over from the Christmas celebrations, the flags and squadron emblems of the various Allies, parts of a Junkers dive bomber displayed on one wall, and blow-ups of Betty Grable, among other fine sights. It presented a brilliant scene that quite overcame Major Hullborne's inclination to despise it all because it wasn't American.

As for me, I'd been hoping for an opportunity to swank about in the magnificently adorned and decorated senior officer's uniform. Unfortunately the promised promotion to group captain still hadn't come through. I wondered if it ever would. After all, I only had Philby's assurance that it was in the works. Why was it in the works, anyway? There was no reason for me to go to a three-power conference, and who was Philby? Just a spy, that's all. Besides, I didn't want to go to Russia. Stalin would have my guts for garters, according to what George Garanine had said, all those years ago. But then, what did he know? Stalin was a good guy. He was one of us now, in the fight against Hitler. Poor dead George's hint about Stalin still bearing a slight grudge, just because I'd discovered that he had worked for the Tsarists as well as the Communists, it was all nonsense. The Soviets and us, having fought the fascists together ever since 1941, were at the start of a new era of friendship and co-operation, right?

★

Though the party had not really begun until eleven o'clock, it was already a swinging success. Hundreds of swirling celebrants were gyrating on the dance floor or shouting joyfully from the surrounding tables, or jiggling about five deep at the bar at the far end of the cavernous drill hall. Just listening to the hot RAF band on the brightly draped platform, and regarding the swirls of blue uniforms below flushed faces, and the pretty frocks or the bright gowns of velvet and satin, made me feel quite stupendous.

On our way back to the long bar, the major bellowed, "Looks like I'm the only American here."

"Because you're so special, Harry," I said, gaily but meaninglessly; while Harriet insisted on looking for some significance in the remark, and demanded to know what was so special about her, and by the time I'd evaded further questions I was beginning to wish she'd stayed home with her farting bulldog.

"I mean, whatja mean, special?" she asked in her gruffest voice, but drawing herself even more to attention than she already was at.

Actually, I was quite enjoying her company, she was such a queer mixture of gruff naiveté and feigned aggressiveness. I felt she needed protecting from cynical old Europe. On the way here in her car — she had given me a lift in her bloated brown Ford V8 — we had had quite an argument about Yurrup, in the course of which I had tried to put her right on a number of issues, including her attitude to fighting. Although a dedicated member of the armed forces, she felt that war was a Bad Thing. She trotted out every one of the usual arguments to the effect that war is hell and oughtn't to be allowed. "We guys in the army, we know that's what we're for. To preserve peace and give our lives for our country if called upon to do so," she said, raising her chin aggressively, "but I tell ya, Bandy, there ain't hardly one of us, men or women, who deep down don't hate the whole idea of war. Surely you're just as ready any time to kill for peace, right?"

"Personally I love war."

"You do?"

"Sure. I couldn't wait to get into it, way back there in 1916. Only thing wrong with that particular war was it wasn't going anywhere. But I was ambitious, so I joined an outfit that was going somewhere, even if it was upward rather than forward. I've been fighting practically ever since, and enjoying every moment of it. I suppose being a woman, you're not aggressive in the way —"

"I'm as aggressive as you any day, mac," she said in her most belligerent tones. "I just hate 'n despise war, that's all I'm saying."

Shortly before midnight, and introduced by a blare of brass from the band, a portly squadron leader wearing USA threads on the top of his sleeve, who fancied himself in the public speaking role, told us all about the war. We were entering its final stage, he said. Peace was at hand. The German attack through the Ardennes was their last big effort, and it was already out of puff. The Jerries were on the ropes. The new year would see the end. The brown jobs — sorry, the Allied armies — would still have a li'l work to do, a li'l mopping up, but as far as the air war was concerned the worst of it was over. The Luftwaffe was finished. He himself was convinced of it. He was equally convinced of something else, whatever it was. But now, he intoned, if everybody would raise their glasses in a toast to the happy new year that was scheduled to arrive in a minute or so. He hoped that it would be on time and not late for the festivities, like our Air Officer Commanding, he added, beaming at Oliver Chistelow, who had just arrived. The squadron leader concluded his address with a hope that the AOC had remembered to bring in the new year. Which was now twenty seconds away. Ten. Nine. Eight.

The huge gathering joined in the counting, and every woman in the house received many great big hugs and kisses. And then it was 1945.

The long bar at the far end of the drill hall was so busy that I had managed to fight my way to all the lovely Scotch bottles only about three times in three hours. By three in the morning I was still nearly as sober as judgement day. Worse was to follow. By four in the morning the only booze left was Belgian grenadine. And Chistelow had still not managed to acknowledge me. Occasionally I had caught sight of him amidst his scrambled-egged and fruit-saladed companions and aides, but he had seemed determined not to see me, not even when on one occasion he'd slow-waltzed past just a couple of feet away. I guess he was too busy enveloping his partner, a dazzlingly pretty WAAF sergeant, in his arms, like a blue-clad Dracula.

"How does he always manage to snare the youngest and prettiest girls?" I demanded of Harriet Hullborne. "Huh."

"You're just jealous."

"I am. I fancied that one myself," I growled; though actually, I was more irritated by the way the old fatso was ignoring me.

"You fancied her? I thought you were in love with the baroness."

"Oh, God ...."

"What's up now, Doc?" Harriet asked, with a frivolous grin. The jollity heating the big hall was finally getting to her.

"John Oakley. He's headed this way."

I started to slide and hide behind the ample major, but the tall figure in the impeccable uniform decorated with the transverse purple bars of the DFC had already seen me. Towing a plain WAAF with a sulky expression behind him, Oakley was preceding deftly in my direction through swirls of dancers. He seemed to have acquired a coterie of fighter pilots. They were following him as he came up, his outstretched hand aimed straight at my *cojones*.

"Bartholomew," he yelled over the racket, spreading his arms wide as if expecting a loving and slavering dog to leap into them. However, observing a distinctly unwelcoming mien, he just reached forward to seize a lacklustre mitt and shake it cordially.

"Hey, real pleasure meeting you again, Bart," he said, with an enthusiasm jousting with his custard-smooth face and losing on points. "Bart indeed, eh?" he exclaimed, turning to his acolytes. They were looking at him with amazing, not to say sickening, respect. "Boys, this is none other than Sir Bartholomew Bandy, a genuine bart, believe it or not."*

The boys were just starting to transfer their expressions of respect to me. Oakley was quick to recover their attention and allegiance. "Let me tell you about this great man," he went on, gripping the arm of one of his sergeant pilots. "To start with, he ought to be back in Canada by now, receiving the plaudits and gratitude of the entire country for his magnificent accomplishments over so very many years," he cried, not only emphasizing the last few words, but repeating them, hoping, I suppose, that in the presence of so many young pilots this was likely to make me extra conscious of my age. "Very, very many years," he called out, very loudly indeed.

Next, turning to the WAAF he was escorting he added, "You know, Ethel, this man will go down in history. He really will, I tell you, for he's one of the greatest Canadians since the Reverend Sebastian R. Seedey, the hero of Pugsley's Creek in the war of 1847. You'll remember him, of course, from your history primer, back at the old Dunderhead High School or whatever it was called, right, Ethel?"

Ethel's expression changed from sullenness to uncertainty.

"No, but, Ethel," Oakley said in his kindest tones, "one day you'll

---

* Oakley, of course, is misinformed, confused, or once again deliberately spreading misinformation about Our Hero. So far as he has confessed in these Papers, Bandy, though a knight, is not a baronet ("bart."). — Ed.

be able to tell your children, if you manage to have any, that you once were in the presence of one of the country's greatest men. Right, boys?" he concluded, turning for confirmation from the rest of his blue-clad brood.

They all twitched appropriately with barely a glance at me, though the girl with the rather greasy black hair looked at me for a sceptical five seconds without much respect, possibly because I was clinging onto Harriet's arm as if to save myself from a cigarette, blindfold, and some last rites, while Oakley continued to extol my virtues in his own inimitable way. And now the bastard was assuring his listeners that I would probably end up as the Allied Ace of Aces when the tally of my successes in the air was finally computed.

"Ethel, my dear," he was saying, "I hope you appreciate the great honour accorded you, of meeting such a great man, if only briefly, before his unfortunate past catches up with him." Releasing the girl, he reached forward to gently touch Harriet's arm. "Oh, but I shouldn't spoil it for you, Major. It is major, isn't it, that star thing on your shoulder? The point is you mustn't believe everything you hear, no matter what people say."

"Why, what do they say?" the major asked, already upset at the demeaning way John had reacted to the badge on her shoulder — as if the golden emblem had been deposited by a clean, vegetarian, but incontinent squirrel.

"They say it was entirely unjustified anyways," Oakley added evasively. "The black mark."

"What black mark?" Harriet demanded.

"No, forget it, Major."

"What black mark?" Harriet demanded again, even more determinedly. "God damn it, I have a right to know — he uses my office."

"No, no, Major, it's too ..." And Oakley turned away, his face a mask of tragedy. And no matter how hard Harriet tried to get at the truth, John Oakley remained loyally reticent about the black mark and the appalling disgrace that it so obviously represented.

PART TWO

INTO THE VALLEY OF DEARTH

RUSSIANS, TO WHOSE COUNTRY I was now reluctantly bound, had been a problem for me for nearly three decades, thanks to people like George Garanine, and my 'wife', Darya Filipovna. But the less said about her the better.

Another bugbear was Rodominov, though I couldn't help liking him even after discovering that he was a Soviet agent. In a weak moment I had even enabled him to escape the British authorities toward the end of World War One. I met him again, a couple of years later, while I was trying to escape from *his* country. Accompanied by the above-mentioned Darya Filipovna — but I prefer not to mention her — I was scuttling through the Soviet Union, as described in ... I think it was in Vol. IV that I told of the journey south from Moscow, in which I described our dodging not only the Reds but the Whites, Greens, Cossacks, and marauding deserters as well. I managed to cheat, trick, and barge my way through the civil-war-torn countryside for a while before I was finally captured by the Red Cavalry.

That should have been the end of these Bandy Papers. The Red Cavalry had a terrible reputation, sparing neither men nor women, or even children, if they were not of the correct ideological hue. But just in time I was saved by a black-clad member of the cavalry unit, who turned out to be Comrade Rodominov. He also turned out to be a commissar. As such he outranked everybody, and so was in a position to help, by allowing me to flee. And Darya Filipovna as well, but the less said about her the better.

I liked Rodominov, and have often wondered what happened to him. I doubt he survived for very long in Stalinist Russia, especially as he was of noble birth., though he kept very quiet about his antecedents. He was actually born a prince. Mind you, princes were two per rouble in Russia in those days. Still, you weren't advised to put it in your CV.

Anyway, what with my military history, from the involvement in the Allied Intervention in 1918 right through to my experience twenty years later in the Spanish Civil War, where the Soviet Union had backed the Republicans against the Franco fascists, Russia had figured rather too prominently in my life. Now here I was, voluntarily returning to the country. At least, I think it was voluntary, though I didn't seem to be having much say in the matter.

A slightly complicating factor was that Stalin had once been quite keen on assassinating me; for a while, anyway, after the First World War. Which was where George Garanine came in. He was sent to Canada to dispose of me. You will find the whole sordid story in Volume ... whichever one it was — Good God, I really am falling to bits when such details escape me.*

Since then, I had become less and less convinced that anybody, other than a few close friends, could possibly want to kill me. Besides, I only had George Garanine's word for it that Stalin nurtured such dastardly intentions, and George was not the most trustworthy of sources.

It was all so long ago, anyway. Old Joe Stalin must have given up by now. After all, despite my travels from continent to continent, I must have been within range of his defective left arm at some time or another over the past twenty years; yet here I was, still alive and kicking, if somewhat disordered by love. It couldn't have been that Joe didn't have the means. For instance, during the civil war, when Spain was crawling with his agents, surely one of them could have seized the opportunity. Of course, it was possible that I had evaded them by accident, but I found that hard to believe. Surely, even my good luck couldn't have kept me out of his reach for twenty whole years if he was really in the mood.

No, no. By now, hardly a peppercorn of doubt could set my self-confidence a-sneezing. My awareness of how he had hunted down everyone who had ever disturbed so much as a minute of his Kremlin slumbers had grown dim. Even my experience with that spy in Leningrad, Serge Ossipov, failed to bring up the dimmer of doubt. Serge had brought the misfortune on himself — making the mistake of poking his nose into Stalin's GPU file, and discovering that Stalin had been a Tsarist informer whilst busily undermining the same Tsar through his other activities in the Communist party.

Nope. I refused to let it worry me that Serge's biting of the dust in the Lubianka had much to do with his reading of the dossier. Surely I was right not to concern myself with that particular cause and effect. I mean, let's face it. When Stalin had Serge bumped off, he wasn't yet aware that pages of his own dossier was missing and that Serge had them. Damn it all, Serge thoroughly deserved his fate for being so stupid as to let it be known that he had proof of Stalin's role as a GPU

---

* ... in Volume V, *Me Too*. - Ed.

stool pigeon.

As to what happened to the missing pages, I suppose that Serge had hoped to convert them into an insurance policy. Unhappily for him, he was bumped off before Stalin learned about such missing clauses. But, gee whiz, Joe must have been annoyed, eh? when he realized he'd liquidated old Serge a trifle prematurely.

Mind you, it's possible that the reader of this memoir, or readers, if there's more than one, might at this point consider the fate of the co-founder of the modern Russian state, Lev Davidovitch Trotsky. Old Trotsky was to pay a ghastly price simply for being an erstwhile colleague of Stalin's. Years after he had settled down for a nice quiet life in Mexico, munching salt and sipping tequila, he was ice-picked by one of Stalin's agents.

Actually, Trotsky's family was tracked down and obliterated as well, including his most distant relatives, and even casual acquaintances. But all that was deep in the past. Things had changed. Stalin had attained his heart desire. He was at the pinnacle of his career. He was just about to win the war and gain the enforced allegiance of half of Western Europe, at this very conference.

No, no, it was all nonsense, the threat from Stalin. Even if he knew I knew about the missing pages from the dossier, I couldn't believe he was still in a bad mood about it. Not really, not after all this time, surely. After all, none of my friends or family had been eliminated the way Trotsky's family were dealt with, and — anyway, Stalin was much too busy, what with countless millions of Russians still to slaughter or send to the gulag. Joe was hardly likely to have time for little old me, was he? Course not.

So here I was, on my way back to Russia by way of Malta and Egypt, experiencing no apprehensions whatsoever except for a mild concern for my health, because some quack had intimated that, mentally and physically, I was going downhill like a sled on Everest.

Admittedly, my nerves weren't quite as steely as they used to be, but let's not exaggerate. Really, my only concern was the state of my cranial cilia. My head of hair, after pausing for breath in late 1944, had resumed its war of independence. It was definitely getting scarce. Other than that, though, I had not a care in the world. After all, I was no Trotsky; I wasn't all that important, not really. Nor was I one to take myself too seriously, despite the occasional modest flashes of conceit.

So there.

It was on the second of February, 1945, that a converted Lancaster bomber, with a pack of junior diplomatic and military types, not excluding your neurotic hero (did I really categorize myself a neurotic just then? And if so, what nonsense!) banked over the hills and the white villages of the Crimea, and whacked down onto the heavily repaired runway at Simferopol.

We were to be allowed two days of freedom before the three power conference was due to start, and the servicemen and civilians who descended to the tarmac were in an excited mood, not entirely due to the quantities of booze they'd been absorbing en route. Even before masquerading water bottles were upended over parched thrapples, the atmosphere was one of optimism and good cheer. Though the war still had some weeks to run, the end was plainly in sight. After nearly six years of valour and vice, self-serving and sacrifice, boredom and bravado, dedication and default, the conflict was actually coming to an end. All that was needed now was for the three war leaders to start the world afresh, with the help of us high officers and some minor help from the queers and Arabists of the Foreign Office.

Despite the long and tedious delay that is so natural a part of any military activity, we chattered aboard the bus to Yalta with as much excitement as managed to sneak past our desire to behave with quiet dignity. Naturally we continued to think of ourselves as major players in this final act of the comedy of the war. We knew we were not quite as important as Winston, Joe, and Franklin D., but significant enough as associate designers of the next version of the world. To demonstrate our importance there could be no better example that that of Air Vice-Marshal Chistelow, when, a few days later, he would stand, proud and foursquare, not too far behind the Big Three while they had their photographs taken.

At this point in our narrative, however, Chistelow didn't quite share an objective view of my own vital importance re the future of civilization. When we all boarded the bus for Yalta, he used his bulk to jam me safely into the window seat, so he could keep both an ear and an eye on me. His aim was to ensure that nobody else could hear the rotten things I was likely to say about Russia, and that I would have to listen when he ordered me to behave.

First, it seemed that he needed to reassure himself that I was properly in control of myself. After one deep breath and two false starts, he humphed, "By the way, old man, are you feeling all right these days?"

"Course."

"Yes, I know you're coarse, but are you completely sound, mentally, do you think? You know, emotionally, and all that sort of stuff?"

"Absolutely."

"Oh, good," he said, looking relieved at not having to stray into filthy psychoanalysis. "Fine. Well, look here, Bandy I've been meaning to talk to you about your attitudes. I know you've not had the most thrilling experience of Russia in the past," he said. "But things are different now. They are now a great power. Damn it, man, there is much to be admired in their great accomplishments since the Revolution. For instance, they've done wonders in educating the peasants, I understand. And then there's the ballet, and their great hydroelectric projects, and ... and ... And all the other things. But most particularly, Group Captain,* I really must ask you to bear in mind that they are our allies, and have made the most sacrifices in this war."

"M'm."

"So I don't want any nonsense from you, Bandy. Understand?" he said, his tone sharpening as he realized that I was looking out the window and not paying much attention.

"No nonsense. Right," I replied, nodding.

"The thing is, you have a tendency to make the most of a bad situation. Stirring things up, and so forth," he said, lowering his voice in case he was overheard by the NKVD man. This was the Russian bruiser in the uniform with the green secret police tabs who had been corralling us from the moment we landed. At the moment he was seated at the front door, the bus's only escape route.

"Another thing, Bandy," the Air Vice-Marshal continued. "When we're in company, I'd appreciate it if you occasionally addressed me as sir."

"H'm? Oh — yes, sir."

With some sarcasm — in fact, quite a lot of it — he added, "Not all the time, of course. Couldn't expect that from you, Bandy. But just every now and then, to show I'm the one who's supposed to be in charge."

He ran a hand down his plump face as if to iron out a dispirited expression. "Though of course we both know that when you're around, nobody's in charge of anything," he muttered.

When there was no rejoinder, he glanced at me, uneasily, but I was

---

* Bandy's promotion back up to Group Captain occurred in an earlier draft and was deleted in Donald Jack's later revision of Part One (see Afterword); however, since throughout Part Two Bandy is consistently addressed as Group Captain, suggesting Jack had not entirely made up his mind yet, I left it as it was. After all, the promotion could have come through between New Year's Eve and leaving for Yalta. - Ed.

still busy looking out the window. As the bus groaned onward along the winding road, shuddering ever higher into the blue sky, I was becoming quite entranced by the bright green slopes and the splendid mountains through which we were passing, when I wasn't feeling scared that the bus would go over one of the many cliffs.

Passing through the few villages en route, I was quite surprised by how little damage they had suffered, considering that some heavy fighting had taken place in the peninsula during the previous year.

The weather was wonderful. It was amazingly mild for February, even for this subtropical zone. The sky was a splendid deep blue decorated with artful clouds that readied the scenery for a whole pack of picture postcards.

Scenically, the best moment of the journey came when the bus levelled out along one particular stretch of road to present a glorious sunlit view of the Black Sea. It wasn't black at all, either, but a valuable silver colour.

The sea view and the mountains and the occasional Cézanne of village fascinated the other passengers as well. They exclaimed at the sights, and rose to their feet to obtain a better view, until the NKVD man at the exit ordered everyone back. "You are to stay in seats," he said.

"Did you see that?" I whispered to old Chisters.

"What?"

"The NKVD man — making notes?"

"Making notes?"

"He was looking at the people with cameras. They'd better be careful."

"What are you talking about? He could have been making notes about anything. And what do you mean, NKVD man? He's just a bus company rep."

"Oh, I see," I said, my eyebrows looking terribly enlightened.

An hour or so later we dropped down into Yalta, which, by then, was a bit of a relief after the sometimes scary swoops and scoops of the old road.

Like some of the villages on the way here, Yalta seemed to have escaped without much war damage. In fact it seemed in quite good shape, almost welcoming, with its white houses and sunlit public buildings set against the green hills. But then, why wouldn't it look good? It owed little to the Soviet planners, having been created long before their time. Before 1917 it had been a fashionable resort for the other aristocracy, the real ones, not the ones with the socialist privileges. The worst the communists had done to the town was to indulge in their usual architectural brutality in the form of a few civic buildings and the sanatoria scattered along the coast through Livadia and beyond. Otherwise, as the bus trundled through Yalta toward the seafront, the damage done by kraut and commie was surprisingly muted. Some of the downtown houses were as lovely as the bright, white villas of Spain.

Upon reaching Lenin Square, which faced the waterfront and not unsurprisingly contained a statue of Lenin, the bus was boarded by several uniformed reds with green badges. They checked our names once, but counted us three times before the bus drove off again, to empty its contents into three different hotels.

The AVM and I were placed in the Yuzhnaya Hotel, which was just a couple of hundred yards further on from Lenin Square. After a quiet consultation between a uniform and a member of the staff I was given a really nice room on the top floor of the three storey hotel.

I had the large room all to myself, which was a pleasant surprise. Most of the other officers were having to share accommodation. The three army men in our party were considerably miffed to find themselves bunched up in one room.

"How the hell has he managed a room all to himself?" they muttered, practically in unison. They were certainly glaring at me in unison.

That evening we attended a meeting with assorted Soviet officials who had been detailed to acquaint us with the conference arrangements. In a sudden access of shyness, or perhaps it was my native reserve, I failed to ask any questions, not even about my own duties and responsibilities, though they would plainly be of some importance, judging by my accommodation.

It was only after the get-together ended that Chistelow saw the room. He had come up to the top floor mainly, I think, to remind me again to be on my best behaviour, but this obviously didn't apply to himself. When he stepped into the room he stopped dead, as if he'd run into an iceberg.

After a while: "Fine room they've given you, Bandy," he said faintly.

"Yes. Pretty good, isn't it?"

"Mine is on the ground floor, at the back of the hotel."

"Is it?"

"Yes. With a view of the rubbish bins," he said, looking out the window at *my* view. It encompassed several miles of waterfront property and a dazzling beach.

"Oh, dear."

The beach was undeniably handsome, though in parts as stony as Chistelow's face.

I watched him with interest as he visited several items of luxury, before halting at the alcove where the double bed preened and fanfaronade. He studied it with an increasingly bitter expression.

I might add that I also had a gold dressing table, an antique armchair probably looted from Nicholas and Alexandra's bedroom in the northwest wing of the Winter Palace, and a large, ornate mirror positioned so as to enable me to admire myself whilst propped languidly on the heap of silk pillows.

"Done you proud, haven't they," he said.

"No more than one deserves," I responded, with a smirk, cruelly unsuppressed.

"The honeymoon bloody suite."

"M'm," I replied.

He turned to bathe me in the warm magenta reflecting from his furiously flushing cheeks. "They must think that the four rings on your sleeve entitles you to all this," he grated. "Or — you didn't by any chance bribe somebody to switch rooms with me?"

"Oh, no, sir," I said, looking shocked. "Russians don't go in for that sort of bribery. It must be something to do with my air of overweening authority."

"Christ," he muttered, trying really hard to look as if he really despised decadent affluence. It wasn't easy, until he discovered that the accommodation included an oil painting in a very expensive frame. It showed the interior of a locomotive works, with a number of proletarians at work, building bogies and things. The workers all looked not only jolly but jolly good fellows as well.

Chistelow's face quite failed to reflect the pictorial contentment. However, a certain amount of relief became evident when he'd finished glaring at the elaborate work. "Don't think much of your picture," he grunted.

"A study of the nation's most highly favoured workers, I guess," I said.

"What?"

"Stakhanovites, I believe they're called."

"Yes."

"The best of the workers," I explained.

"Yes, I know."

"The elite of the proletariat."

"Yes, all right!"

"The aristocrats of the Russian working class, who —"

"I know! I know all about Stakhanovites!" he shouted. "I'm not entirely ignorant, Bandy!"

"Course not, sir," I said; but I must have said it in too sympathetic and understanding a tone, for his flushed cheeks burned almost like charcoal with fury.

He managed to put out most of the conflagration, however, before wrenching into a 180 degree turn and marching to the door. "Anyway, all I wanted to say was, don't show me up by being late for dinner," he said loudly, and walked out.

I suspect he would have slammed the door really hard, if it hadn't caught in one of my Persian carpets.

Dinner, however, was not for another hour or so. In the meantime I descended to the long, narrow bar just off the dining room. At least, I suppose it was the bar, though the counter was missing. You just ordered your drink from a chap in a grubby jacket.

Which of course I did, quite promptly; and he came back with not just a glass but a whole bottle of vodka, and a tattered cork mat to protect the surface of the small round table at which I made myself comfortable.

There were only two other tables. At one of them sat a blonde lady in a navy blue gown, who gave me a most charming smile. The trio of British army officers at the other table didn't.

"Hear you have a fine room all to yourself," the major said; and when I answered in the affirmative he refused to look at me for the rest of the evening.

The lady was much friendlier. When by accident I knocked over my glass of Stolichnaya, she was most sympathetic. "I think it is the unsteady condition," she said.

"I'm not unsteady," I responded. "It was only my third glass."

"I meant of the table," she said.

"Ah, of course. The table is definitely unsteady."

"Perhaps you would not mind sharing mine," she said. "It is not so unsteady, I think."

So I moved over, and within minutes was deep in conversation with the lady, whose name was Vera Lermontova.

"Lermontova, eh?" I cried. "Not related to the poet, by'n chance?"

"Ah!" she exclaimed back. "You know of our famous poet and writer? He, too, was an officer in the Guards. You are so distinguished, you are in Guards, too?"

"In the Air Forsh, Ma'm," quoth I.

"The air force? Then you are a flyer! But of course you are," she exclaimed, allowing me to share her perfume by leaning even closer to caress my wings. "Ah, to fly in the clouds, to be detached from this world. It must be truly wonderful. You must tell me all about it," she said, placing her wing-fingering hand gently over my bony mitt.

"But, please," she said, delicately withdrawing her hand after only a few seconds, "You must call me Vera. And I to call you Bartalamyeh? Yes?"

"Why, yes, that's my name, all right," I said, and soon I was placing my hand on hers just as intimately. By Jove, she looked lovely in her dark blue dress, even if it was a trifle worn, as if it had had an intimate affair with the local laundry.

It was clean, though, her dress. Scrupulously clean. And before you knew where you were, you were talking to it intimately — to the lady inside it, that is. Mind you, I was no pushover for socialist wiles. She might be a spy. Just in case she was, I was careful not to provide her with any useful information. Name, rank, and number, that was it. And that I loved a Belgian baroness.

"And does she love you?" Vera asked with a concerned expression. To which I replied with a look, a complacent wink, and smirk of such profound sentimentality that any decent woman would have made a poor excuse and departed. However, I managed to distract her by adopting another look indicating that I was about to be sick. Filled with contingent vomit and apologies, I made my own excuses and fled.

Did I mention that a small bathroom came with the accommodation? Well, it did, and I got there just in time.

I fear I was too drunk even to feel conscious-stricken at my abrupt departure, though I could have summoned plenty of excuses, not the least of which was an exhausting day of travel made worse by my uneasiness at returning to the land of the Peter and Paul Fortress. A foolish concern, but there you are.

Vera was not in the restaurant next morning when I came down for breakfast. Chistelow was there, though, and he was stap full of condemnation. He had been told about my white-faced abandonment of the bar. After a hushed tirade he gave me to understand that he wasn't the only member of the deputation to be disgusted. "One of the army officers is threatening to make an official complaint about your behaviour in the bar last night," he said, with a sharpness to his voice that could have sawn a tank in half.

"Behaviour?" I croaked.

"Exactly. You don't even remember sending a bottle of vodka flying."

"Flying?"

"You're an utter disgrace to the air force, Bandy. You were blind drunk last night. What kind of example is that to our Russian hosts?"

Actually, Russians were world beaters in the excessive drinking stakes, but all I could croak was, "Sorry, sir."

"I damn well hope you mean that, Bandy," hissed Chisters. "Because if it happens again I shall take action as promised, and ask them to send you straight back home."

As we were entirely dependent on Russian transport I took this as a meaningless threat, to pay me back for being given a better hotel room than him. All the same, I was feeling so horrible this morning that if it had been possible, I'd have gone home like a blue-arsed fly to the nearest turd.

"All right. We'll say no more about it, Bandy," the AVM said. "But pull yourself together, will you? Lately you've been acting very strangely. Quite erratically, in my opinion."

Preparing to attack his breakfast , he added, "Too much time to yourself these days, that's your trouble. And too much publicity, since downing that Hun. Personally I don't see what all the fuss was about — though even the Russians here seem to know all about you."

I was too busy trying not to look at his breakfast to answer, so he continued to analyse me. "All this luxury isn't doing you any good," he went on. "Like that room you're in. I hear they even took out one of the double beds — to make even more space for you. I mean, what the devil's going on, when a simple group captain — I don't know," he ended, hunching over his glistening eggs.

Apart from the ghastly clatter from his knife and fork as he ate, he was silent for the next few minutes, until he noticed I wasn't eating. I was favouring a single cup of coffee that morning, but even that ambition died a premature death as he masticated yet another mouthful of egg, fried potato, and other items I prefer not to describe.

So when Chistelow informed me that I would not be needed until the get-together with our counterparts in the Soviet Air Force that afternoon I made my excuses gratefully, and lurched to the nearest exit.

After a whole morning of wandering around Yalta, I began to feel a little better, especially after the weak morning sun had dried out most of the sodden cotton wadded between my ears. By noon I even started to enjoy the walk, initially along the promenade, where a beating headache was soothed rather than jangled by the sea as it lapped and rattled on the rocky shore. There were a few citizens scattered along the shore, sitting on folded blankets while they read, or chatted, or gazed out to sea. Two small girls even wore bathing suits, though January was barely out of date.

In London the security wallahs had warned us not to take maps, or any sort of orienting material that might arouse the suspicions of their opposite numbers in Yalta, so I'd made do with some genning up in a London library. The source appeared to be right about the climate's being subtropical. So far the weather was so mild that there was no need for the Canadian longjohns I'd packed away in my luggage.

I'd also brushed up a little on the local history. It reminded me that in Tsarist days, Yalta had been a fashionable resort. The Russian aristocracy, encouraged by the climate, had poured oodles of roubles into the town's development. Quite a few handsome buildings had been flung up, not just here but all along this part of the coast, including the resort of Livadia, a couple of miles further on. Which was where the conference was due to start on the following day.

I thought of checking it out, but after a full morning's walk, I felt too feeble to make it. I hadn't been sleeping or eating very well lately. Still, I managed to find Anton Chekhov's house. It had been converted into a museum. It was closed.

Getting back to the hotel at one pip emma, I attempted to sneak up to my splendid bedroom for a nap; but Chistelow caught me.

"Ah, there you are, Bandy," he said. "Was wondering where you were. We're just off to the drill hall in Lenin Square. Come along."

For a ghastly moment I thought he was expecting me to practise my about-turns and quick marches. But apparently it was just a get-together with some of our opposite numbers in the Soviet Air Force.

We remained stuck at the drill hall for most of the afternoon, but though we had to listen to several speeches from our comrades in the Soviet Air Force, each speech ended with a glass of vodka, so it wasn't too bad; though I could have done without the Slavic nosh. The tables set up in the drill hall were creaking under the weight of caviar, which I was already getting tired of. Luckily a couple of dozen bottles of Stolichnaya kept the Beluga company, so I was quite satisfied, generally speaking, though I did have two minor criticisms to make. They had failed to supply the traditional fireplace into which I could fling my empty glass at the end of every speech, so I had to fling mine at a small electric stove over in the corner, much to the surprise of the Russian officers and the embarrassment of Air Vice-Marshal Chistelow; the other thing was that the Russian officers had more medals than me.

Bunch of show-offs, in my opinion. Still, as the festivities gulped down the hours, the speeches of welcome, solidarity, etc., began to sound more and more sincere, to such an extent that at one point I got up from my seat with the agility of a factory hoist, and, raising my glass, cried, "In return, we toast our brave Russian friends! Vazvrashashayas na rodeenoo, na, my khatelee by peredaht vamnah shee loochaheeye pazhelahaneeya!" Which was not particularly appropriate, as it indicated that we were leaving immediately, though the party still had a few hours to run. However, it also implied that we might come back again. Anyway, my awkward Russian revisited earned such a thunderous round of applause from a heap of generals that I realized that I had quite enjoyed the afternoon after all.

I had almost recovered from this get-together with our glorious Russian allies by dinner time, when I again encountered Vera Lermontova, in the foyer just outside the dining room. She was wearing the same navy blue gown. A collection of hints and appealing looks from her led to our sitting next to each other at dinner. By the second course — after caviar on toast, naturally — she was praising me to the very vaults of heaven on account of my distinguished appearance, my undoubted record for bravery judging by my rows of medals, not to mention all the other gold bits scattered about my person, all obviously mined from a distinguished career, and my brilliant grasp of the language.

She didn't actually say which language, but I knew at once that she was referring to my Russian. Also, she thought my uniform was beautiful. "It's lovely cloth," she said, reaching over to smooth a lapel with a careworn hand.

"Yes," I said. "Dish know that the Brish originally bought the blue air force material from the Russians, way back in 1917. True. Originally it was meant for the Russian calvary. Cavalry. Dish know that? Bright blue, it was."

"It is so interesting," she said in tones of such sorrow that I craned around for a gypsy violinist.

Now she was asking about my wife, and I was telling her. "My husband, too, died in the war," she said. "In nineteen forty-two. Ever since I am so lonely."

"Oh, dear," I said, reaching for her hand.

"You too must feel very ...?"

"Yes, I did, but I'm better now, thank you."

By the end of dinner she was mentioning ever so delicately that her room was on the middle floor. "Is next to bathroom," she said.

"Mine has its own bathroom," I said proudly.

"You are so lucky, Bartalamyeh," she whispered, gently stroking my hand.

"Oh, it's nothing, really," I said. "Actually the plug is missing."

"Pazhalsta?"

"The bath plug. There isn't one."

"No?" she said, looking at me a trifle uncertainly.

"But the bolster in the bedroom more than makes up for it," I said. "There's more than twice as much of that."

"What is a bolster, please?"

"A long, long, very long pillow for the bed sort of bolster," I confided, leaning over slightly too far.

The mention of the bedroom seemed to restore her spirits. As with her usual delicacy she rendered me upright again, she murmured, "I am so long since I shared such a room."

"Whaarroom," I began, as if illustrating a passing jet plane. I tried again. "To which room am I referring, Greta?" I enquired.

Again a touch of uncertainty. "Greta?" she asked.

"Actually it's Bartholomew."

"Yes, I know. You are Bartalamyeh. But I mean, who is Greta?"

"Greta?"

"You called me Greta."

"Did I? I wonder if I was thinking of Greta Garbo. I met her, you know, but she wanted to be alone."

Soon she was holding my hand all over again, bowing her head and stroking the hand in question affectionately. "So long," she whispered.

"Why? Where are you going? "

"Going?"

"You said so long."

She was beginning to look disoriented; nevertheless, she was still holding my hand against her chest. To compose her nerves, I felt. Composing them in A flat, I thought to myself, and snuffled with amusement over my own inspired thought processes. Which flat? My flat, of course.

However, I had to be careful not to lose track of her conversation, especially when she said, "It is so long since I had love."

Ah. Now I had it straightened out. "Oh, I see — you weren't saying ta-ta," I exclaimed, utterly enlightened. "I get it now. You were referring to my hand when you said 'so long'. I *see*," said I sagaciously, nodding in agreement with myself, and also simultaneously studying the hand in question as it lay flat on her chest — well, not exactly flat, but rounded. As it lay rounded on her chest. Besides, she hadn't got it right. My hand was wide enough, I suppose, but I didn't think it was particularly long. Not noticeably long, or even lengthy.

Ah, but wait! was it possible that though talking about the dimensions of my hand — *she meant something entirely different?* Woman often did that, you know.

A while later I knocked on the door of Chistelow's quarters, way down there on the ground floor of the hotel.

I was still puzzling over the conversation I'd had with Vera; but not for very long, for Chistelow answered very promptly indeed. "What the hell d'you think you're doing to my door — bashing in a six inch nail?" he shouted.

I stood and stared at him, uncomprehendingly.

"Well, what is it?" he demanded.

When I failed to answer, he stared for a moment, then: "Well, don't reel about — it's not a country dancing class. Come in, if you're coming in," he said.

Now I was staring at his narrow bed, which was cowering in a recess. The recess was much less capacious than my recess, I had to admit.

He was staring at me. He had even perched a pair of steel-rimmed glasses on his neat little nose so as to see me better. "Is there something wrong, Bandy?" he asked, almost concernedly. "Apart from being drunk again?"

There was indeed something wrong. I had left Vera a while back in order to visit a bathroom; but somehow, by the time I emerged, I had forgotten where I had left her. Which decided me to go to bed while I could still remember where it was.

On the way to accomplishing this, I started to feel really guilty about Greta. Or was it Vera I felt guilty about? Yes, Vera. The point was, she was a nice lady. That's what the point was. The point was, could I trust her to control her overwhelming feelings for me, from the moment she entered my bedroom? I didn't think it likely that the poor woman would have the strength of will to resist my body, such as it was, or wasn't. Besides, it belonged to Clemmy. I could not be untrue to her. I loved Clemence. It was important to remember that.

By the time I located Chistelow again a decision had been made. "Look here, sir," I said turning to face him all over again.

After rather a long silence: "Well?" he demanded.

"Look here, sir," I said stoutly through thin, determined lips, "I want you to have my room on the top floor."

"What?"

"I've decided, sir. It's not fair, me getting the accommodation up there which is practically a royal suite if one is even allowed to call it such a thing in Bolshevik Russia. It's definitely not fair, them sticking you, an Air Mice Varshal, in sush shordid accommodation as this. "

"What d'you mean, sordid?" he snapped, looking around. "It's not sordid at all. Just a bit plain, that's all."

I was not to be deterred from my noble theme. "No, I mean it, Airmiles Vice. You must have my room forthwith. I've given it a great deal of thought, sir, and that's the great deal of thought I've come to."

"You're drunk, Bandy. I can't take advantage of that."

"No. I really mean it, Vicemiles Chiselow."

"Don't be ridiculous, Bart. Go to bed."

Though I didn't have a mirror handy, I looked, I think, quite offended. "You don't believe I'm acting with unselfish generosity, Airspace Vassal?" I paused. "Sorry, Air Vice-Marshal, should have said. Sorry. Tongue running away. No, sir, let's face it I've decided that it's you who warrants that room on the top floor, sir, not me. No, sir, I've quite decided. No, no, sir, I insist, I utterly insist."

For a while he argued against my truly glorious offer. He even insisted on revisiting the room to make sure I hadn't made a mess on the carpet, or something. But in the end my sublime gesture prevailed.

"Are you quite sure about this, Bart?" he asked, as he collected his shaving gear from the grubby bathroom and his jammies from under the sordid pillow. "Some people might say that I was rather taking advantage of, well, not to put too fine point on it, a chap who was not entirely and completely ...?"

"No, no," I said, firm as anything. "No, no, no. No, siree bob, sir. You deserve it, not me. After all, lets face it: it was almost incometah –– incomprehen — prehensible why they would give me the best accommodation in the joint. Almost incomehencoop — prehensile — pre — etcetera; though I suppose the misunderstanding may have arisen because of my fame, which even the Russians seem to have heard about. You know, that air-type victory over that famous Jerry ace, whoever he was —"

"Yes, well, very good of you, Bart," mumbled the air vice-marshal, as he rushed out of the room with another armful of air force kit for the upstairs room.

"Quite all right, Airmice Varshal," I said, treading on his heels. "After all, your disgusting quarters were far below your needs. Admittedly not entirely suitable for me, either, but there you. After all, a senior officer like yourself — if it's possible to find a senior offisher who is like yourself — even remotely —"

"Bandy, you're treading on my heels. You're ruining my good shoes."

"After all, let's face it, sir, you deserve better than to rough it in those squalid quarters back there in the bowels, the bowels of the hotel, which you have been forced to endure —"

"Yes, yes," Chistelow said, panting after his increasingly rapid ascent to my room — his room, now, the lucky devil.

Lucky but tactful. As he looked around his splendid new accommodation, it was very tactful, the way he suggested that now was a good time for me to take my things downstairs, as he had an important meeting this evening with his opposite number in the Soviet Air Force. To prove it, he looked at his watch.

"Right. In that case, I'll leave you, sir."

"Good. Fine. Thank you very much, Band —"

"And enjoy my room, sir. And don't you lose any sleep, sir, dwelling on the accomodation I will have to endure down there in the basement. Right down in the depths of —"

"Yes, thank you, Bandy. Thank you."

"This splendid accommodation is what you deserved all along, and not for one minute must you dwell on the selfless sacrifice of your devoted assistant, in the —"

"Bandy, please. I really must go."

"I quite understand, and don't you worry one bit, Oliver, that pit down there will be quite good enough for the likes of me. Really it will," I said as he closed the door in my face, but quite gently, really, and not in an offensive way; not in the slightest.

Mind you, I rather regretted the wonderfully generous exchange of kips, on account of the clattering in the kitchen yard outside the ground floor window. There was also an intermittent thumping of feet on the hotel stairway, which seemed to be about two inches from my quivering tympanum as it tried to bury itself ever deeper in the bolster — which was several feet shorter than the one I had so generously and selflessly surrendered. It was long after midnight before I finally slumbered. Next morning I awoke with only a slight memory of a disturbance in the middle of the night of a somewhat more obtrusive nature than the thudding hooves. A banging sound, and loud voices, I think, but the memory, as I say, was indistinct, and I had been sound asleep again within minutes.

I didn't even think about it, as I was busy carrying out an inspection. Given my suspicious mind, I was hunting for microphones. I didn't see why I should share my snores with anyone except Clemence.

I didn't find anything unless the mikes were buried in the plaster, but the hunt soon confirmed that my new quarters weren't nearly as nice as the room at the top where I'd belonged. There was only one chair, for instance, so if I'd had visitors they'd have had to sit on the bed, or I would; and the white tiles in the separate bathroom weren't at all healthy. Some of them were cracked, and surrounded by discoloured grout. Also, the shade of the bedside lamp was missing. However, I discovered it on a shelf in the cupboard, along with some debris which went quite well with the fluff, dust, and old bent nails under the bed. The lampshade had been stuck in there, I suppose, because it was damaged, with only part of the shade still clinging to its wire frame.

After completing my morning ablutions in the rusty water, I lurched off for the dining room in as upright a manner as a whanging head would permit, hoping for a cup of coffee before they cleared all the tables. There I met one of the British army officers, who confirmed that there had indeed been a disturbance. On the top floor of the hotel, apparently.

"Top floor?" I croaked. My voice often sounded rusty, first thing in the morning.

"When I heard it was your room," the major grunted, "I understood right away." He opened his mouth to continue, but then stopped, and stared at me directly for the first time. "But I heard you'd been dragged away."

"What?"

"They didn't take you?"

"I'm sure nobody told me I'd been dragged away," I said, passing a collection of metacarpal bones over my brow, to see if I was still there. I wasn't even sure I could confirm it with my fingertips. "No, it's okay –– I'm still here."

"So I see," said the major, not looking particularly overjoyed about it. "Well, they took somebody."

"Who did?"

"I don't know. Whoever was making all that racket upstairs, I suppose," he said.

When two woman in kitchen whites and hairnets appeared in the kitchen doorway he started to move away, but curiosity overcame him.

"Hell of a racket," he said, looking at me suspiciously. "Thought it was you they were beating up," he went on, looking slightly more cheerful. "But you say it wasn't you?"

"Don't think so ..."

"Ah, well, there you are," the major said. He paused to see if I had anything to add. When it became obvious that my arithmetic was defective that morning: "Anyway, you'd better cut along," he said, glancing at his wrist watch. "Bus is due at nine-thirty, I understand."

I finally achieved ignition. "Wait a minute," I said. "Are you saying that the disturbance was in the vicinity of my room?"

"Not just in the vicinity, old man. Actually in it, far as we could tell."

"There was a kerfuffle in my room?"

"Can't have been your room, though, can it?" the major said, his eyes sharpening. "Because here you are."

"But I swapped rooms with my boss last night. He had my room."

The major's eyes were now honed to perfection. He stared at me for a moment, then: "H'm," he said. "Must have been him they took, then."

After a moment I turned and mounted the stairs as rapidly as my head would allow. When I got to the room I felt as if my innards had received a quicklime enema. The door was open. Inside, the bedclothes were tangled. One of the sheets was on the floor. So was a sprinkling of blood.

"Oh, Jesus," I croaked out loud. "It's him they wanted all along."

But it was all right. Chistelow was safely back at the hotel by nine o'clock that night, none the worse for wear except for a bruised face, a limp, and a stiff back. "Oh, there you are," I exclaimed with enormous relief as he limped into the lobby.

He failed to respond, that is, apart from a very long-lasting glare. Even the flight lieutenant accompanying him, who was a lawyer in civvy street, glanced at me in a distinctly unfriendly way before following the air vice-marshal to the noisy stairs.

Genuinely concerned, I started to follow. The flight looie got in the way.

"Perhaps you'd better give him a moment to himself, Group Captain," he said.

"No, I must see him. Find out what's going on."

He trod further up the stairs, actually barring my way. "I don't think he wants to see you at the moment, sir," he said. He essayed a friendly smile, but it didn't quite work. He had entered the hotel looking exceedingly worried, and the look hadn't had a chance to fade.

"But —"

But now the flight looie was too busy helping old Chisters, who was supporting his back with one hand and holding onto the rail with the other.

Within minutes he had managed to get almost half way up the stairs. Not more than two or three minutes later he reached the bend in the stairs. Now he had only two more flights to negotiate. Now he was out of sight.

I took two tentative steps, but then stopped, a bit reluctant to follow, because of the way he had looked at me. His expression seemed almost to suggest that whatever the reason for his misfortune I was partly to blame, somehow.

All the same, I knew where my duty lay. After thinking about it for a while I decided to take him a bottle of vodka. He looked to me as if he needed a snifter.

Reaching the third floor, I tapped at the door. Silence. I tapped again. Even more silence. Taking a deep breath I opened the door, and peered inside.

It was all right. The flight lieutenant must have left while I was in the bar. And the room had been tidied, including the bed, upon which the AVM was stretched, though not entirely in a straight line. He was lying under the quilt in his underwear. His trousers, hung up nearby were, I noticed, economically sprinkled with blood.

"Sir?" I said, as softly as possible, as, the moment I registered on his blacked eyes, he covered his face and moaned — though this action might have been inspired by a desire to protect it from the ceiling light which I had switched on, the better to inspect him.

"Sir?" I asked again. "Everything all right? "

The groan was slightly louder this time, though again, there was no answer.

I realized then that it would be up to me to keep the conversation going.

After another, longish pause, I went on — in the English accent into which I am inclined to descend at awkward or worrisome moments, "I say, they weren't rough with you, were they, sir? Didn't actually biff you in the boko, or anything like that, did they?"

He seemed to have remarkably little to say this evening. He was still covering his face.

"I've been quite worried about you, sir," I continued. "I mean, disappearing like that. Middle of the night, and all that, what? So I thought I'd better ..." I concluded, explaining everything with a gesture that spoke volumes.

He finally opened a volume himself. To my relief he didn't seem too bitter about anything. I'd experienced a faint concern that he might have been inclined to blame me for something or other, but it seemed to be all right.

"I'll give you a brief explanation," he said from behind his hands, so that his voice was a little muffled. "And then I expect you to get out of my sight. That woman friend of yours, what's her name?"

"Clemence d'Aspremont de Forget?"

A faint moan escaped his fingers. He appeared very fatigued, as if he'd had a hard day. "Oh God, do I have to go on talking?" he said faintly. Apparently deciding that he did, he went on, "The lady whose hand you were cuddling in the restaurant."

"Oh, her."

"She came into my room in the middle of the night. She crept up to the bed. But apparently I wasn't the one she was expecting. When she saw me, she screamed."

"Oh?"

"Immediately," continued the air vice-marshal, "three thugs in glistening raincoats burst into the room, hauled me out of bed, beat me, then dragged me downstairs, down all three flights of stairs, I might add, and threw me into a car."

"Oh."

"I've been answering their questions all day. They seemed to think I was you."

"Good Lord."

"People kept coming to look at me. Finally, they let me go. Without a word of apology, or even an explanation."

"I see," I said, not seeing a thing.

Finally he unclamped his hands from his battered face. "Now, get out, Bandy, if you don't mind, and let me rest," he said. "And then we'll be having a word with a few people, not excluding you, over the treatment I've had to put up with."

"But sir —"

"Bandy. And turn out that damned light, please."

I opened my mouth to continue. Instead, something about the way he had spoken, sort of quietly but in a really deep sort of way, caused me to reach for the light switch; and so I left as quietly as I had entered.

ME ON RELIEF

ALTHOUGH WE WERE SUPPOSED to have been attending the Yalta conference for several days, as far as I was concerned, nothing was happening. I wasn't even being invited to the palace. Only those members of the British and American delegations whose names were read out each morning were allowed to board the bus for Livadia.

The selection was made by a large Russian in an even larger suit. When I asked him when I was likely to be called he just shrugged and repeated that my name was not on the List.

Even my air vice-marshal wasn't being invited to the conference, and he was blaming me. "It's your fault," he said angrily at the end of our fourth day of hanging around the L-shaped Yuzhnaya Hotel — with bugger-all to do, as he put it. "Until the misunderstanding over that woman, I was down for the second level advisory group," he shouted, "conferring with our Russian friends over certain decisions worked out at the conference. I was due to take a significant part in the last stage of the British bombing campaign. Then they suddenly cancelled my part in it. And we damn well know why, don't we."

"Uh ..."

"Damn right we know. Because of you! If you hadn't insisted on giving me your room it would never have happened. Bloody humiliating, it is. I've never been treated like that in my life. And I think you did it on purpose!"

I was genuinely shocked. "How can you think such a thing, sir," I exclaimed.

"It's all too damn easy to think it, where you're involved! You still haven't explained why you suddenly decided to give up your room."

"Far as I remember, it was unadulterated generosity, sir."

"Very convenient, wasn't it? Saving you the ordeal that I went through," he muttered.

The funny thing was that, despite all that had happened to him, he still believed in the Western liberal certainties about the Soviet Union. He actually excused the thugs only a couple of days later — only now they were security advisors. Nothing to make a fuss about, really. Being biffed by NKVD or MGB goons, it was just a misunderstanding.

When our gallant allies were amalgamated properly into the civilized European mainstream after the war, they would pull themselves together and start behaving decently. You know, like British bobbies, what? He remained as blinded to the reality as all the other Western propagandists, sympathizers, and fellow travellers.

Chistelow was just not in the right frame of mind for sensible rejoinders, so I made do with asking for his thoughts on the refusal by the authorities to admit us to the conference.

He wasn't susceptible on that front either. In fact, he seemed to think that that, too, was my fault. Worse, his faith in the Russians was thoroughly restored when they finally admitted that a mistake had been made; that the lady in question had admitted that, however beefy the occupant of the bed seemed, she'd had no cause to scream.

"I should think not," I said supportively. "You're definitely not all that unprepossessing, sir."

"Anyway, the fact is, they did apologize in the end. As for the treatment I was subjected to, it was perfectly understandable, in the circumstances — when you get right down to it," Chistelow said, after he'd given me another of his looks. "Anyway, it's perfectly obvious what it was all about," he continued. "She screamed because she was expecting you."

"Run that by me again, sir?"

"She screamed because you weren't in bed," he said impatiently.

"I admit — under duress — that people might just possibly scream when I'm in bed; but when I'm not even there — "

"Anyway, the point is, you could have made things extremely difficult for the Allied cause if I hadn't been prepared to overlook it," he shouted, glaring at me for the umpteenth time; and he strode away before I had a chance to ask him if he had any thoughts on the promptitude with which the police had barged into the bedroom after the scream.

I'd been hoping to learn the answer to that question from the lady herself, but she had left the hotel, and nobody had seen her since.

I tried questioning the doorman, the evening and daytime desk clerks, and two or three others, but nobody could or would tell me anything about Vera and in fact none of them seemed to know her. Such was my frame of mind by the sixth of February I couldn't decide whether the irruption was a cause for alarm or otherwise. Certainly the incident had not made me feel any more welcome in the USSR. As for the decision by the authorities to deny us our places at the conference, I must say I was disappointed in the British authorities for not making more of a fuss about it.

"It's just a temporary hiatus," a middle-ranking FO type said apologetically to Chistelow, "until they sort things out. The Russkies aren't terribly efficient, you know," he explained, as he attempted to phone London to ask them to send on the aide-mémoires that his minister had forgotten to bring.

They soothed the AVM readily enough. However, they didn't make much of an effort to soothe me or insinuate me into the conference, although I pointed out that I was a translator, a vital spoke in the machine. "How will people know what they're saying unless I'm there?" I asked everybody, including the Russian in the big suit, the one whose job it was to check everybody in the bus each morning.

"You are not on list," he said for the umpteenth time.

"But I'm needed. I'm a translator."

"You are so good translator, why you not talking to me in Russian? Why you are talking in English?" he asked.

"Because you're talking English, that's why," I responded in a forthright way. "I'm merely being polite, that's all. If you were talking Russian, in that case I would —"

He interrupted with a rapid speech in Russian. Then: "You see," he said triumphantly, "you are not translating."

"Give me half a chance, if you don't mind," I said tartly. "I was busily composing my reply." But by then he was slamming the bus door in my face.

Finally, everything got sorted it out, and word came that both Chistelow and I were to be allowed to join the three-power conference. Maybe it had just been another cock-up. All the same, by then almost a full week had gone by since our arrival — and not one word of the Russian language had I translated, except for the notice in the restaurant about spitting being prohibited.

This prohibition didn't apply to the weather, though. It had suddenly turned wet and chilly, and it was raining non-stop by the eighth of February when Chisters and I finally reached the Livadia Palace.

I like to think that it was my forthright demeanour and native determination that finally assured us our rightful place among the heads of State of the three allied powers, but I suppose one has to tell the truth now and then, which was that while Chistelow went straight to work with his opposite numbers in the Russian army air force, they seemed strangely disinclined to allow me to do much translating. In fact, to do any at all. After all that hard work I'd done back there in 1919, too: learning all sorts of new constructions, memorizing heaps of phrases, and familiarizing myself with the exotic pronunciations of the Russian language — like the letter r, to be pronounced as if it were a g, the funny-looking H being pronounced as if it were e, P being pronounced r, and R pronounced yah when written backward, and so forth.

Admittedly, they might have had some slight justification for their reluctance to let me translate their secret pacts, and other items of political skulduggery. I admit that I wasn't *completely* fluent in Russian, even though I had a perfectly good excuse, as I hadn't indulged in the language on a regular basis since my retreat from Moscow as described in Volume IV of my journals .... Or was it Volume V?* Nor, I suppose, was I entirely to be trusted to keep silent about such things as the betrayal of the millions of poor devils, the USSR's own soldiers, whose only crime was that they had been overrun by the German Army, but who would end up in the prison camps as a result, if they weren't executed first.

The town of Livadia turned out to be well worth the visit. I had anticipated more examples of the brutal state architecture of Soviet Russia. The palace was quite beautiful, a fine, shining city of graceful walkways, patios, and gardens surrounded by luxurious buildings in the early Renaissance style that had once made St. Petersburg — Petrograd — Leningrad — whatever — such a dazzling city.

Livadia Palace was quite a size. In its day it was capable of accommodating hundreds of visitors, courtiers, hangers-on, which was hardly surprising as it was once the summer residence of the Tsar and his family. If I hadn't been feeling a shade unsettled ever since Kim Philby had arranged this important and interesting job, which I had yet to start doing, I would have been thrilled to bits by the visual splendour of Livadia.

However, not wanting to upset myself by discovering why I was so unsettled, I tried to concentrate on improving my education, i.e., by making mental notes, in case the West ever managed to pull themselves together from their worship of the USSR and become ready for a spot of espionage. The British left wingers certainly wouldn't want to learn the truth, but I didn't think it would take the Yanks long to start feeling about the Commie bastards the way I did.

As part of my praiseworthy efforts to educate the Western World, and because the surly apparatchiks didn't seem to want my help, I attempted to get to know ordinary members of the public, if there were

---

* Volume IV: *Me Bandy, You Cissie* - Ed.

any left. While strolling through the pine grove that led to the former Tsarina's dacha, I approached a girl who looked sixteen years old but, like so many lovely Russian women, was probably twenty-six. Actually she approached me, to practise her English. She had taken the English course at university, she said, but until now had never had the chance to actually try it out on a decadent bourgeois capitalist hyena.

Her educational endeavours didn't last long, though. She must have been advised to avoid me, for on the following day she scuttled away in alarm the moment I raised my eyebrows.

I wasn't surprised, of course. That was the Russia I knew. Shame, though. She was a very pretty girl.

Oliver Chistelow's endeavours weren't any more successful than mine. "I tried to get you involved today," he said on our way to yet another vodka party, this one to be held in the International Sailors' Club just across from our hotel near the waterfront. "I told them that, whatever your shortcomings, you're a true leader, and could contribute quite a lot to the discussion. But they didn't —"

"Whatjamean, shortcomings?" I interrupted.

"But they just looked at each other, and that was it. Not another word."

"They're not short at all," I mumbled. "In fact —"

"Look here, Bandy," he snapped, "what I want to know is, what's it all about? I know you're difficult, but ... But why are they so against you?"

"Who knows, sir? But, sir, coming back to the subject of shortcomings. Of course, it doesn't bother me in the slightest that you should categorize me in such terms," I said, smiling in a particularly reasonable sort of way, with barely a smidgeon of resentment over his description, "I mean, it's water off a duck's back as far as I'm concerned, but just as a matter of intellectual curiosity," I continued, continuing our deep discussion on his totally unjustified characterization, and continued it for some time, until I realized that the air vice-marshal was looking at me in a very queer way indeed.

"Bandy," he said. "Are you all right?"

"Sir?"

"You're behaving very strangely, you know — even more than usual."

Now I was strange, as well as having shortcomings. I glared.

"So what is it, old chap?" he said gently. "Why are you behaving so oddly, these days?"

"Oddly? Me?" I laughed again.

"They said you were cracking up, back at the squadron. I didn't believe it, at first, but ... We're all getting a bit worried about you, Bandy. You know that, don't you ...?"

* * * * * I have decided to omit the rest of the conversation.

Anyway, I have something much more important to talk about. Next morning, I saw George Garanine. At least, I thought it was him. But maybe it wasn't. It might have been. It couldn't have been. Maybe Chisters was right after all, that I really was cracking up.

But to change the subject: at this stage in the proceedings, the allied leaders had been holding their meetings in the main part of the palace. I'd tried a couple of times to get a little closer to the conference hall, to allow old Winston to see me, and thus imprint upon his mind the definite fact that I was here; if I disappeared, a frequent occurrence in Russia, he might remember me and do something about it.

Of course, nothing was going to happen to me. Still, there was no harm in taking out a small insurance policy with the great man, who had known me since 1917 — oh, alright. Whom I had *met* in 1917.

At one point I ventured onto the alameda, and managed to get within a hundred feet of the fine bronze doors that guarded the inner sanctum, before I was turned away by the picket of unusually smart Soviet troops, of the slick sort that has to march up and down in front of Lenin's tomb for years on end. There were quite a few Western guards as well, the American soldiers looking almost as clean-cut as the Russians as long as you didn't see them marching.

The Soviets were the first to move me on. I told them in my best Russian that Churchill was an old pal of mine and that I just wanted to say hello, when he had a spare moment from the deliberations. The dolts wouldn't even listen. During a second attempt to get through, an American major made a note of my name. He wrote it down quite deliberately in his little notebook. Even the Russians hadn't bothered to do that. Maybe they already knew my name. For a moment I couldn't decide which offended me most: being made a note of, or not being made a note of.

It was during my retreat from that second foray along the Roman-arched colonnade that I again hallucinated George Garanine, in a thicket of Bolshies.

A psychic-type operator would claim that the vision had probably been brought on by suppressed anxiety. This was nonsense. I mean, apart from anything else, George had been missing for too many years. He couldn't possibly look that good after all this time, including a decade in the Siberian camps, and after experiencing the ferocious Eastern Front? It was a young man I saw, over there. After all this time he should have looked as old as me. Older, in fact, because he was ... well, older. Ach, nein, the man was obviously a doppelganger, or a favourite cousin from the Omsk or Tomsk oblast. Forget it. It couldn't have been him. What about all the putsches and purges that Stalin had imposed on millions of totally innocent people since 1934? Mind you, George might have escaped the worst of the gulag, being a particularly charming and loveable fellow. Everybody said so. True, he used to get on my nerves, until I had felt like liquidating him myself, sometimes. But this could not possibly be him. Besides, it might affect Clemence's love for me if the handsome bugger turned out to be alive. This must not be allowed. So to make sure he was defunct, I ran after the spectre, racing round the entire central building of the palace. It took one and half minutes at a speed calculated to cause a hundred protective tommy guns to be trained on my slithering, panting form, before the ghostly vision disappeared into a side garden.

Panting to a halt at the hedge around the garden, I obtained a view of the group of Russian officers who had been pacing up and down just to the north of the conference building.

And there he was, standing next to a stone sundial, and eating agitatedly from a bag of sweeties. He was dressed snugly in a greatcoat which looked brownish grey in the wet midmorning overcast, or the colour of a rusting hulk.

Damn him. He certainly didn't look like he was rusting. And I could deny it no longer. My memory had gone 'snap'. It was George, so recognizable now by the greedy way he was snatching nice things to eat out of his paper bag. Candies, perhaps, or the sunflower seeds he used to jam his cavities with. Except the bastard never had cavities. He always had such perfect, shining white teeth, the bastard. Ten to one even they had survived the gulag.

Wait. There was hope, yet. A more penetrating look suggested that he wasn't entirely cheerful. More like he'd just received a shock, such as glimpsing somebody who might possibly make life just a shade more difficult for him? He was acting nervous, no doubt about it, nervously nibbling — sunflower seeds, judging by the pinching of the fingertips.

At practically any other time in my life I would have sprung from the dank shrubbery and faced him with a hearty hulloa, in order to discomfit him. Something restrained me. Was it a nervous breakdown, or was it maturity, at last? Was I finally getting over this urge to unsettle the world? More likely my stagnation in the vegetation was the result of an inertness that had been creeping over me from the moment we had landed in Simferopol. Fear of Stalin? Absurd, of course. Good old Joe had long forgotten all about me. After all these years, for Chrissake. Besides, they wouldn't dare touch me even if they wanted to. That air battle with the German ace had turned me into a Charles Lindbergh, and that was saying something, when you consider the events and incidents of my life, from running a White Russian army in Northern Russia to that sojourn in the Peter and Paul Fortress, and my spell as a politician and rum-runner; not to mention my acquaintanceship with famous people from Sir Thomas Beecham to whatsisname; you know – – the Prime Minister of Canada? The one who hated me the most.

It was funny, the way that air battle last fall seemed to have eclipsed all my other achievements, at least as far as longer-lasting notoriety went. In fact, the fame had spread as far as the Crimean peninsula, judging by the way various Russians kept staring at me and then looking away. Admiring looks, of course, but ....

My concern, if that's what it was, restrained me from challenging George there and then, and by the time I had unfrozen, he had disappeared. But he must have been based somewhere in Yalta, for I saw him again that very evening. He was turning into the clubhouse of the Proletarian Fishery Collective Farm, in the company of three other smartly-turned-out officers. Funnily enough, this was just where I was headed. I'd been informed that this was the only drinking place within walking distance of the palace.

After the quartet of officers, all looking quite elegant in their brown uniforms and polished boots, had settled at a long table in the main hall of the club, they called raucously but good-naturedly for service. Fairly soon, a bottle was plonked onto their table by a lady peasant who looked like an overfilled laundry basket. When she failed to return promptly with mixers, snacks, or even glasses, the officers uncomplainingly made do by swigging from the bottle in turn, passing it around and uttering a toast with every transfer.

As the hall was otherwise empty, except for a chap with a long white beard, a brown blouse, and off-white trousers tucked into the longest pair of boots I'd ever seen, I located myself behind a pillar, which was advertising a field of wheat. I gestured to the old chap with the boots, but it was quite a while before he decided to serve me. However, this was a good thing, because by then the officers at the far end were making enough of a racket that there was little danger of their attention being drawn to the pillar with the picture of the collective farm.

"Dobre vecher," I murmured to the bearded one. "Napeetak pazhahlsta — vodka."

He stared at me so fixedly that I feared I might have ordered a chamber pot. Trying to sound even more friendly in hopes that he wouldn't report me to the secret police on account of poor pronunciation, I smeared on as friendly an expression as could be summoned, and murmured, "Do you know, Comrade, you look just like Tolstoy." And when he didn't answer: "You know, with the saintly beard, was against everything modern? And quite rightly, too, eh, comrade?"

He was less impressed than ever, though he did finally come back with a bottle of a clear liquid which I hoped was vodka. At least it was accompanied by a glass, though a ridiculously small one that looked as if it had not been cleaned since the Battle of Stalingrad. So, like the officers at the other end of the cavernous club, I drank straight from the bottle.

Sagaciously sipping, I settled down to wait, occasionally edging an eyeball around the pillar to keep the officers in sight. I was not too worried about being spotted, as George and company were definitely not in an observant mood by now. If they had noticed my friend Tolstoy listening attentively to a pillar at the far end of the hall, it failed to distract them from their own increasingly boisterous confabulation.

As they were obviously in no hurry to leave, I settled down for a long wait. In the meantime, I attempted to clean the shot glass by repeatedly pouring vodka into it, but either the vodka did not possess its usual scouring ability, or it was the surface of the glass that was scoured, but the container's appearance remained distinctly impaired. Still, I persisted in my efforts, and in time I think I managed to restore at least a semblance of pristinity to its former self, though it required it to be filled and emptied a good many times before the restoration was achieved.

After a while I focussed on my watch. Good Lord, was that the time? The bus was due to leave very, very soon. I was in danger of missing it. But George and his friends were still racketing, gleefully slapping each other's backs or their boots. Either Tolstoy or the laundry basket lady had brought them another bottle or two. So I read the poster again, the one on the pillar. It featured a field of wheat, and two happy kulaks, a man and a woman. They looked pretty old but extremely healthy and utterly content as they lifted 250 pound bales onto a farm cart.

Ah! They were leaving, at last, the officers, that is. Actually they had gone. Trouble was, George had gone with them. He had been sitting over there quite contentedly with his friends until just a moment ago. I knew it was just a moment ago because it was when I had ordered another bottle of Tolstoy from old Comrade Vodka. I distinctly remember requesting the real stuff this time, say a Zubrovka, rather than the Proletarian Paintstripper.

Yes, I remember, now, catching sight of George as he hurried out after his friends so unsteadily that he brushed against a table, causing its legs to grind very unpleasantly over the concrete floor.

Though as George had lurched out of the hall he had stopped to stare straight — well, more or less straight — at my pillar, and at me who was supposed to have been safely concealed behind it. He appeared to have observed me after all.

To give the lad time to get some distance ahead of me in the darkness — good Lord, was it that late already? — I poured the last of the alleged Zubrovka into the shot glass, hardly spilling a drop in the process. It was at that point that my failure to turn up for the bus created a diversion in the form of a chap wearing a uniform with green flashes. Entering as casually as if he didn't expect to see anything of interest, his gulaging eyes froze when he espied the chap in the blue uniform who was busily raising a tiny glass to toast a propaganda poster pasted to a pillar.

After trying, convicting, and sentencing me on the spot, he turned and marched out again. A moment later he was back with two more NKVD types.

All three of them glared at me malevolently while they stood there deciding what to do. After a heated a discussion all three of them came over, to inform me in a distinctly hostile way that the bus to my hotel had departed. "The bus has gone," one of them said in English.

"Oh, dear."

"You have missed bus," he said, in tones suggesting that I was now condemned to wander the earth to eternity.

"I suppose I'll have to walk back."

"You will not walk back. It is forbidden."

"You'll just have to give me a lift, then, won't you, Comrades," quoth I.

It seems they'd already had that splendid idea. I could tell, because they grabbed me one to each arm, and frog-marched me out of the hall, through the lurid darkness to a shuddering Pobeda. There they helped me into the back seat of the car.

"There's no need to shove," I said, as they slammed the door. Well, they had no need for it — the way they heaved me onto the back seat in that uncouth manner. After all, I was quite ready to accept a lift back to the hotel.

But was it a lift back to the hotel? I must admit that, even under the affluence of inkohol, a slight stirring of concern could be detected, bosom-wise. These ill-tempered gentlemen were certainly not behaving like tourist officials, in my opinion. Had they been dangling stethoscopes I'd have taken them for the kind who reorganized the minds of dissidents in hospitals dedicated to that purpose.

The car, though, was behaving decently enough. It rattled but was scrupulously clean. But then, in Russia, both of you were in trouble if you didn't keep your car nice and clean.

As it turned out, my fears proved groundless. They really did take me back to the hotel, and even opened the car door for me when I had trouble operating the lever thing. Maybe I'd been misjudging the Russians all these years. The three men in the uniforms with the green flashes might not be quite up to the standard of the uniformed doorman of the Ritz, but apart from the abrupt manner with which I was taken back to the Yuzhnaya, at least they had not beaten me up. So I rewarded them with a speech of thanks, beginning with, "Ya tsenyoo vahshe vneemahneeye ..." But my palate got mixed up by a plethora of e's, so the result was not quite as impressive as I'd intended. Nevertheless, as I turned away from the car, aimed carefully for the front door of the Yuzhnaya, and set sail, I considered that I had been handling the language unusually well this evening, apart from all the e's.

As for George, I finally decided that if he didn't wish to be seen in my company, that was his lookout. I certainly wasn't going to force him to be sociable.

Mind you, if we ever met I would certainly tell him off. I was certainly going to ask him why he had treated my darling Clemence so badly, the way he had pretended to be dead, and all the time he was alive. It was disgraceful. If I ever saw him again I would give him a piece of my mind, you bet; if I had any left over.

I understand that I went to bed quite early that evening. This was just as well, as I received a visitor quite early next morning. In fact, it was a little before five a.m., and the visitor was George Garanine.

★

The sight of George in a wet greatcoat did not make me feel much better, even though I'd spent most of the previous day trying to speak to him privately.

I'd experienced quite a few hangovers lately, but this morning's took the biscuit. Even before I opened the pair of putrid shellfish that were my eye sockets and saw George fumbling through the backyard door, my head felt as if it were being used as a pile driver.

I think he had been trying to get in for several minutes, judging by a dim memory of a tapping sound and a voice that I thought was part of a train disaster. He had finally forced the door open, and now stood shivering in front of the curtain, which, mindful of the blackout, he had carefully drawn behind him.

Previously I'd never seen him act other than with the placidity of a sponge pudding. Now his already rumpled face was pale with anxiety. Not that I cared whether he were anticipating the death of a thousand cuts, or an investiture at St. Basil's. I didn't even feel surprised to see him. All I could manage was, "Christ, what're you doing here?"

"My dear Bartalamyeh, how delighted I am to see you," he whispered, feeling his way through the gloom. Almost immediately he added, "But please go away. You are like apparition in Macbeth — Banquet's ghost, yes? For days, everywhere I look, there you are. It is dreadful. I cannot stand it any longer. Please, please go away."

"You're stealing my lines," I croaked. "That's what I want to say. You go away. For pity's sake."

He came closer, looking all hunched up, like a stand-in for Quasimodo. "Much as I appreciate your interest in me, dear Bartalamyeh," he whispered, "please stop trying to see me. It is very dangerous for me."

"All right, I'll stop, I will. Just leave me to die in peace."

Instead, he sat on the bed, distractedly removing the great army cap that Soviet Russia issued to all of its officers, which was sodden with rain. He shook it abstractedly. Great fat raindrops sprayed into my face.

If he thought that was likely to revive me he had another think coming.

"George, for God's sake," I moaned, trying to work out what time it was. Light seemed to be seeping around the window curtain. I think it was just malfunctioning eyesight.

"You have been trying to see me for days," he said, and when I tried to speak out of a mouth that had gone missing in the Gobi Desert, he repeated it.

"Yesterday was the first time I saw you," I parched, wiping the rainwater from my face and licking my fingers, desperate for moisture.

"I saw you days ago. I am here because there is nowhere left for me to hide from you," George whined.

"I'll stop. I promise. Just don't whisper so loudly."

"I am becoming a wreck, Bartalamyeh. Is all over if I am seen talking to you."

"So goodbye," I croaked, jacking up one eyelid, but only to confirm that it was not permanently glued down.

George was now lighting a cigarette, afterwards using the flame to warm his hands. The crude cigarette tube had hardly the strength to contain the black strands of tobacco. Not that there was much of that. The cigarette was mostly filter.

As my other eye became unglued, he struck another match, which, unfortunately, illuminated his face. I'd presumed it would look as bad as I felt, but no such luck. Close up, the face I had not seen for twenty years looked as handsome as ever, and worse still, almost as placid. If my molten brain had allowed it I would have felt thoroughly indignant at the failure of his face to learn from experience.

Though perhaps my bleary eyes were being too hasty. In the brief flare of matchlight, I thought I detected a spot of feeling, preferably one of distress. Not real distress, of course. That was all mine, especially when he switched on the bedlight and I discovered that he really did look twenty years younger than me, though he was almost the same age.

The absolute bastard. His brow was quite unlined. Not that that had any significance whatsoever. It had so rarely ever been clouded with thought.

"God's sake, George ..." I said. It was now my turn to whine. "Whajawant, anyway?"

"I am appealing to you, Bartalamyeh. I know you are the kindest, most decent man in the whole world — and so will listen to my appeal," George said, somewhat erratically as, seated on my bed, he covered his legs as best he could with my quilt. "Please do not make things difficult for me. It has taken me all this time even to earn a little of their trust. It would be such a shame, beloved Bartalamyeh, if they discovered that you were my dearest friend — and had been for an entire quarter of a century. It would ruin me entirely."

Moving very slowly indeed, I racked myself backward so that the headboard could take some responsibility for my weight. My head was no longer a demolition ball. Now it was the material being demolished.

"When you came here from Belgium, you actually rejoined the army?" I enquired in a kindly sort of way — kindly because anything other than such a tone would have hurt too much. "Leaving Clemence thinking you were dead?" I said, shading my eyes from the dim bedroom light and wishing that I was talking about myself.

"You know Clemence?" he asked eagerly, forgetting to keep his voice down. "You have met my dear wife?"

"She was quite worried about you," I hissed, adding, "for a while. Sort of. Anyway, the point is, what happened to you?"

"I was in Siberia, most of the time. In the camps."

"You were actually released?"

"Only because of the war. They were so desperate for experienced men. It is why they let out so many Red Army officers. I also was let out."

"Well I never ..."

"But since I was back in the army in 1941 — not once, not once, Bartalamyeh, did I ever get a chance to go back to her," George said, now wearing an expression just visible on his down-turned face that not even I in my most slanderous moments could deny was one of profound sadness. "I was observed all the time. I could not even send a letter. I would not dare go near any foreign source," he said tonelessly, hanging his head.

"Of course, Clemence has pretty much forgotten all about you," I said, also hanging my head, possibly for another reason.

"I am so glad," he said simply. "I could not bear to think that she still cared for me after all these years."

"She loves me now, as a matter of fact," I said, shamelessly.

Sitting beside me, he reached for my cold hands and clutched them to his breast. "You know her well?" he whispered urgently. "Tell me how you met her. Tell me everything."

"Shhh!" I shushed, trying to wrench free.

"She is all right? She is happy? Oh, please tell me everything!" he whispered, and to my further embarrassment and shame he actually raised my hands to his face, as if I were some haggard substitute for the woman he still pretended to love.

Pretended? No. He wasn't pretending to love her at all. I could see he really did. He still cared about the Baroness de Forget. The bastard. He still loved her.

SHOT OF GEORGE GARANINE

OVER THE NEXT COUPLE OF HOURS, through a filter of enfeebled comprehension further distorted by intermittent headaches, sensory deprivation in the fingertips and taste buds, plus shudders and vibrations from a variety of muscles, I learned far more than I ever wanted to know about George Garanine's life.

"Oh, Christ, I'm not up to this," I moaned to my pillow.

I thought I had seen the last of George Garanine way back there in the mid-twenties, when I saw him off from Gallop, Ontario, after he had wasted months trying and failing to assassinate the Honourable Mr. B. W. Bandy, MP, on the orders of the far from honourable Mr. Josef Stalin.

The orders had been inspired by Stalin's suspicion that the peripatetic Canadian had heard rather too much of the truth about the crude Georgian's early life. Stalin's instrument, George Garanine, however, failed to oblige. Hoping to save his relatives from the dictator's vengeance, George promptly departed for Russia to give himself up. It was characteristic of my friend that he would change his mind en route. Concluding that Stalin was no more likely to spare the lives of his relatives than those of a few million other victims, he travelled no further than Paris. Instead of sacrificing himself for others, George became a taxi driver.

He discovered quite a few other Slavs in that occupation, including members of the nobility, who, having lost everything in the Revolution, were reduced to taking whatever jobs they could land in the French capital. A remarkable number of them became cab drivers. George felt quite at home among them. He believed that he himself was an aristocrat. He had certainly been brought up in a rich and noble family. Actually he was the illegitimate son of a household servant, but the family were so taken with the boy's strikingly good looks and agreeable personality that they adopted him, pensioning off his mama in the process.

From then on, the little fellow was so cosseted, mollified and mollycoddled that his self-reliance diminished to the point where he would have had difficulty competing against an Australian XXX.* Still, good luck, good connections, and a dazzling smile enabled him not merely to survive the Revolution but even to feel quite at home in the resulting disorder. Trotsky even made him a Red Army captain.

In Paris, these qualities were soon working splendidly for him, when he met the young Belgian baroness, Clemence d'Aspremont de Forget, who for some reason fell so profoundly in love with him that not even her genuinely aristocratic family could detach her from the handsome and stalwart taxi driver. Not that their concerns survived his charm and his affectionate personality for very long.

Now read on, as they say, with him bringing me as much up-to-date as I could stand.

"I see," said I, in a croak dredged from the bottom of a Cyclopean cesspit. "In Paris you conned and flannelled one and all. Including Clemence."

Garanine laughed at me fondly. "Oh, Bartalamyeh," he chuckled. "You are as wonderfully rude as ever. All the same, I am so relieved to hear, my dearest Bartushka," he continued, wetting me all over with his liquid gaze, "that she is happy. You say she has forgotten me. That is good. I am so happy to hear it, Bartushka. I would find it unbearable if I thought that my beloved Clemence had suffered because I was not able to come back to her; to comfort her. And I am so happy," he said, shivering, and drawing a little more of the quilt over his knees, "that she has fallen in love with such a wonderful man as you, my dear friend."

"Bollocks," I mumbled.

By then I was on my third jug of water, in an attempt to drown the animalcules cavorting in my mouth. I was having to drink from the jug because the hotel had failed to supply the room with drinking glasses.

"Well, go on, go on with your story," I said irritably.

Which he did, in his soft, dreamy drone. It appeared that, shortly after he married Clemence round about 1930, he came to the attention of the SDECE. The French secret service had been looking for someone to carry out a surreptitious but not particularly delicate errand in

---

* This is cryptic. We assume Jack doesn't mean a member of the Australian XXX division, which acquitted itself quite well against the Japanese in New Britain in 1945. It's possible "XXX" is merely marking a place he meant to come back to, in order to insert a word that temporarily eluded him, since I did find one similar row of X's inarguably filling in for something that was never inserted. In the later draft, the sentence ends flatly at "diminished". If anyone knows what an Australian XXX might be, let the Bandy website know! - Ed.

Russia. One of its agents, a distant relative of Clemence's, met George at Longchamps racetrack, and decided that he was perfect for the job. It was a simple enough task. It involved the collection of some unspecified papers from a contact in Moscow. When George was offered an expense account and a few hundred francs, he agreed to do the job, especially when he heard that he could travel part of the way on the Orient Express. That was an ambition of his: to travel on the Orient Express, even second class.

Actually, I'd heard this part of the story from Clemence. He had been too susceptible to the French approach, she felt, on account of feeling guilty at the way he was losing her money on the nags. She had tried to reassure and dissuade him. She'd had an intuition, she told me, that the errand would not be as simple as George seemed to think.

For once her efforts were in vain. George admired the French, and wanted to contribute something to the country which had done so much for him, like letting him drive the taxi into which his beloved Clemence had strayed one day. He insisted on going to Russia. It was only a visit, anyway, and he had promised to undertake the mission, he said. Clemence, whose father had once been quite seriously considered for the post of ambassador to a small African country, had tried to convince her husband that even honourable men were allowed to have second thoughts now and then.

"I tried so hard to convince him," Clemence had said, "that I didn't mind if he lost a little money at Longchamps. Actually, Bart'olomew," she said with a soft smile, "he was even more fun when he lost. When he did, he could look so downcast and guilty it made me love him all the more. But for once he wouldn't listen."

In Yalta, as there was room on my face for a mean look, I made way for it. "Yes, Clemence told me all about you being so honourable," I said. I assayed a contemptuous chuckle followed by a spiteful simper. However, it can't have come out right because my fraudulent reaction didn't affect him in the slightest.

"This material you had to collect in Moscow, why couldn't it go in the diplomatic pouch?" I asked sullenly, as I positioned my head very carefully on the long bolster, determining not to move it again until the Crimean conference was over in three days time.

"I wondered about that myself," George said, in that soft, naive way of his. "But the Quai d'Orsay explained it all very satisfactorily. Something to do with the fact that I wasn't French. I was Belgian, you see."

"Belgian?"

"Yes. When I married Clemence, I changed my name to hers," he said, "and they did me great honour of making me a Belgian."

"You changed your name to hers? So you were Clemence d'Aspremont de Forget as well?"

"No, Bartalamyeh. It —"

"I mean, wouldn't it be a bit confusing, you having the same name as hers? People wouldn't know who they were talking to, you or her."

"Of course they would, Bartalamyeh. It would be obvious who I was."

"Yes, of course. You'd be the one sponging off her — hanging about outside the ladies' toilet, perhaps."

"I don't quite see what the ladies' toilet has to do with it," George said, looking quite puzzled. "Besides, I only took her last name."

"You took her last name? Then all she'd have been left with was Clemence d'Aspremont? So you had become a thief as well as a Belgian," I slurred, becoming, I think, a trifle light-headed, "taking her name away from her."

"Goodness, you are stranger than ever, Bartalamyeh," George said with a slight frown. "I'm just telling you that my new name was Georges de Forget, that's all."

"Oh."

Drawing the quilt more closely around himself, he murmured on, "Actuellement, I loved the sound of my new name. Georges de Forget. Beautiful, isn't it? Surely it belongs in a golden treasury, don't you agree?"

"M'm. Look, I still haven't understood why you agreed to go to Russia," I said.

"Well, they praised me so much, you see, the French. I was so flattered. So proud to be of help to a Republic that had welcomed me with open arms. Besides, they offered a lot of money. Several hundred francs, you know, for just a few days' work. It was very good, don't you think?"

"But you were married to a rich woman. You didn't need the money."

"I was contributing so little to the marriage, Bartalamyeh, you see, apart from my keen brain and my understanding of life," he said, tugging at the bed quilt so that it started to slide away from me. "Also I needed the money to buy something beautiful for Clemence."

I tossed my head jealously .... I will say no more about this other than to say it was a grave mistake.

"Anyway," said George, or Georges, or both of them, "I went to

Russia, and I was caught, and sent to Siberia, that's all there is to it."

"Yes, and that's another thing," I croaked. "Why the hell would you do it, with Stalin ready to use your guts for garters?"

"Oh, he'd forgotten all about me, by then," George said with a simple smile.

I was just about to issue a series of pshaws, until I remembered that that was how I perceived my own circumstances: that Uncle Joe had forgotten about me, too.

"Anyway," he continued, "they found the foreign material on me. I think it was because my Russian was out of date. As for the papers, I believe it was just family stuff, letters and so forth, nothing very important." He shrugged. "All the same, they sentenced me to ten years. Also for having a false name."

"They gave you ten years for being Belgian? Yes, people do say ... Anyway, surely your employers the French kicked up a fuss on your behalf?"

"No. But to be fair, they did warn me not to expect any help if I was caught."

I closed my eyes in despair at the man's idiocy. "And Stalin never found out about you?"

"He can't have done, can he, because I'm still here," George said with a smile.

"Imagine him not finding out that you were back in Russia," I mused, feeling rather relieved to hear this, and by no means just on George's behalf.

"Even he cannot know everything, I suppose," George said with a twitch of sympathy for Stalin's bad luck in not being properly informed. "As we say in Russia, *There has to be a time when you stop treading on the garden rake.* Anyway, to the people at Dzerzhinsky Square I was not important — just one more enemy of the people to be dealt with, I suppose."

"So the French abandoned you, and you were sent to Siberia. Then what?" I mumbled, and tried to keep my napper as stationary as my eyes as I listened, and as he shrugged away his years in the prison camps.

As far as I could gather, the circumstances were not unlike those that had established his childhood progress from want to want for nothing. No doubt his qualities of being nice, charming, and helpful had helped over the next dozen years in the camps. Probably even brutish guards would ultimately make things just a trifle easier for a sweetie pie like Georgy Porgy. His simple survival proved that he was spared the worst of the Gulag.

He was even released a few months before his time was up. Which came about when the Great Patriotic War started, and Stalin realized that he had left the Red Army critically short of experienced officers. So many colonels and generals had been liquidated during the great purges of the 1930s, or dispersed to the camps, that some divisions were barely able to function.

As George described how he had had the great good fortune to be among hundreds of military men to have their former ranks restored, I'm afraid my attention wandered a bit. In fact his soft-toned reminiscences slowly sank into a delicious lullaby, compelling sleep rather than rapt attention. Next thing I knew was that a line of light was showing through the windows, and I was shivering with cold.

At least the headache had diminished merely to a jungle thudding, so I was able to sit up, albeit very slowly, and feel around for the quilt, intending to draw it more closely around my spindle-shanks. Except it wouldn't draw.

I tugged, but it was held fast. I hauled on it, but managed to gain only an inch. It was only when I'd pried my eyes open that I found that George, sound asleep, was also stretched out on the bed, and had wrapped almost the whole of the quilt around himself.

I propped myself up on one elbow and stared at him in outrage, reminded all over again of what George was like. Now I remembered! Now I remembered the beastly way he always managed to ensure that, however poor the conditions, he was the one to make himself the most comfortable, the most serene, and the most certain to ensure that however sincere his heartfelt concern for the wellbeing of friends and relatives, his situation was invariably the most favourable.

And presently, his comfort was entirely at my expense. There he was, sound asleep beside me in my bed — wrapped in my quilt.

Bathing him in the glow from my crimson eyes, I reached over to shake him viciously.

"Wake up! You get out, right now," I croaked, and added a few other choice expressions which would have sent him crashing to the floor had he awoken in time to hear them.

"What? What is it, Bartalamyeh?" he muttered, sounding as if he'd been asleep for hours.

Using the light from the window I squinted at my watch and found that it was after eight o'clock. The bastard *had* been asleep for hours. And he hadn't even taken off his boots. I could see them sticking out of my quilt. He had been sleeping in my bed for over two hours.

"Do you know what bloody time it is?" I squawked.

When I told him, his response was slightly better than his usual phlegmatic gawp. Actually it was wide-eyed shock. He started to thrash his way out of my quilt as if suddenly surrounded by the League of Decency.

"Oh, mon Dieu," he said, and, fighting his way free, he lurched to the window. "It's daylight!" he cried. "Oh, mon Dieu! I was supposed to be on parade at seven!"

"Over an hour ago," I said, feeling a little better now that I had bad news to impart.

Thrashing back the curtains, he wrenched open the glass door, rushed out, and fell over the garbage cans.

Simultaneously, slowly penetrating the sounds jam-sessioning in my head, came a knocking at the bedroom door, a percussion that had been going on for at least a couple of minutes. And the thumping was getting terribly impatient. So was the voice: Air Vice-Marshal Chistelow's. And not just his voice, but his fist. It was busily rattling the door knob, and twisting it irritably.

Now he was inside the room, glaring at my propped up body in the unruly bedstead. "The bus will be going soon — and you aren't even dressed," he said — terribly loudly. As if that wasn't enough he was also saying, "Though I'm not surprised, after your disgraceful display last night."

"Why, what happened?"

"What happened? What happened? You rolled in last night practically paralysed! I've never seen anyone so drunk before. Utterly disgraceful, Bandy! Reeking of drink."

"Vodka doesn't reek," I whispered shamefully, and at much lower volume in the hope that it would set him a good example.

It didn't. "An utterly immoral demonstration it was. Reeling like a fairground wheel," he bellowed. Normally he was too much the gentlemen to bellow, but not today.

"Sorry," I whispered again.

"Sorry isn't nearly good enough, Bandy," he continued, though at least he reduced the clamour to a mere hubbub. "From the moment you joined the delegation your behaviour has been quite unforgivable. What the devil is the matter with you, Bandy? You never were much of a symbol of an upright, dignified senior officer, but over the past few weeks you seem to have degenerated even further, until last night's lurching around, shaming and humiliating us all in front of the Russians — with you owlish looks and your calls for some woman, Vera, as if you thought you were in some Egyptian bordello. Or was it a chap called Vito or Vitale, or something? No, it was George, someone called George you were going on about. I mean, what the hell did you think you were doing?" And he continued along these lines for a while, as I tried not to remember a single thing about last night.

At which point, George Garanine walked back into the room, somewhat dishevelled and distinctly decadent-looking after his collision with the victuals, his tunic still unbuttoned after his night in my quilt.

"I am so sorry, dear Bartalamyeh," he said huskily, standing on one leg to shake a cabbage leaf off his starboard boot. "I cannot get out, this way."

Air Vice-Marshal Oliver C. Chistelow stood frozen, staring at him.

"There is no way out this way, darling Bartalamyeh," George said, smiling apologetically, and ever so lovingly. "People are watching."

At that point he noticed the rigid Briton.

"Oh, hullo," he said, sounding almost girlish in his disoriented condition, and otherwise as handsome as ever. Spectacularly, almost invitingly lovely.

Chistelow slowly turned back to me as I lay there looking almost as dishevelled as George. It was only then that I realized that I hadn't entirely completed the task of undressing the previous night. I'd removed my trousers, and the underpants were missing, but for some reason not my air force shirt and black tie. They were still in place. As was one of my socks. The other was dangling from one naked pedal extremity. There was a hint of underpants, too, in the disordered bedclothes.

Slowly, as if the feeble motion might escape Chistelow's shocked and blistering gaze, I withdrew the feet under cover of what few bedclothes George had left me.

Almost as slowly, the air vice-marshal's gaze roamed over the disordered bed itself, just as George, always so helpful on such occasions, said, "We should not have slept in so long, Bartalamyeh. Now I am late for my parade."

He shrugged, and gave his boot a last wiggle to dislodge the cabbage before setting off for the door, adding, "Oh, well, dearest Bartalamyeh, it can't be helped."

At the door he turned a beautiful smile on the still frozen air vice-marshal. "As our Russian proverb has it, *A fly cannot land on the ceiling the right way up.*"

"What?"

George smiled even more affectionately as he translated the proverb into English for Chistelow's benefit. Until that moment, a simpering and smirking George had addressed the air vice-marshal in Russian. In that language he couldn't have sounded more pally and seductive if he had accompanied himself with a spot of Tchaikovsky. Bowing politely to the goggling air vice-marshal, he squeezed past him and hurried out. A moment later he returned to search through the disordered bedclothes, exclaim with satisfaction as he found his damp and pulverized cap, and again smile and squeeze past Chistelow, hurrying off on whatever business was required of him.

At least the performance seemed to have suppressed Chistelow's incipient outrage. The air vice-marshal was now looking strangely uneasy and apologetic, not to mention nervous and apprehensive, as he stood rooted near the door. He looked as if he was the one who had been caught indulging in vile practices, as he began backing slowly out of the bedroom, even before I had a chance to explain how George had come to be late for his morning parade.

CURTAINS FOR BANDY?

THAT SAME MORNING I DECIDED to forego the charms of the Palace; you'd have thought I had turned down some glorious inheritance. When I failed to turn up at Lenin Square for the bus ride, the guardian angel in charge of the foreign *krestyanski* came pounding over to the Yuzhnaya Hotel, steaming like a choo-choo.

You'd have thought I'd done something unforgivable, like a tearing pages out of *Das Kapital*. Directed by a frightened hotelier, the guide in his green insignia'd uniform came stomping into the so-called bar where, just to prove I was not ripe for the AA, I was having a nice cup of tea. Anyway, it was only about nine o'clock. There he informed me that such a refusal was not acceptable. My name was on the list. I would have to go.

"Won't."

"Come. This minute, you understand."

"No."

"It is against the rules."

"Fuck the rules."

He stood at the entrance, glaring at me as I sat there, sipping from a cup of milkless, sugarless tea as insouciantly as my stiff upper lip would allow. "But you are not allowed to refuse," said he, a little less confidently.

"Too bad. I'm having a day off," I said, and drew out my tobacco pouch before conceding that it had been deprived of tobacco since the previous Fall. Mind you, lately I'd been thinking of reviving its fortunes, to soothe the old nerves. I'd always found pipe tobacco useful as an aid to impressing people with my unnatural calm.

My day off caused trouble and resentment from hosts and visitors alike. The busload of fuming officers, the fumingest of the lot being Chistelow, were held up for forty minutes, while practically everyone in uniform for miles around attempted to overcome my mulish resistance. But I had decided, well, the hell with them. If they weren't going to give me a proper job, why should I got through the motions, especially when I wasn't familiar with the choreography?

So instead of looking like a spare mentule at the old nuptials, as vulgar schoolboys used to say, I wandered around town, looking haunted but managing to identify none of the Slav gumshoes who were, I believed, following me. I was certain they were there, slinking behind me from door to doorway .... Unless my apprehension was unfounded, and was just another symptom of quivering trepidation.

Actually, upsetting the guardians proved to be almost worth it. Only half the chill morning, with its seaside odours garnished with drowned dogs and salt seaweed, had gone by before I caught sight of their Miss Lermontova.

My heart raced when I saw her coming out of a bakery, but the acceleration had no connection whatsoever with either love or loaves. For once the store, named Food Shop No. 2, wasn't symbolizing the Russian famines of the 1920s and 30s, but actually had something to sell, as proved when I saw Vera emerging from the queue of head-scarved women with a loaf of bread in a string bag.

At which point , half way through my agitated perambulations and thoroughly supplementing the morning's paranoia — I did nothing about it. With despairing face, I just stood and watched as she walked on. Even when she turned right at a shell-splintered palm tree and disappeared from sight, I failed to act.

What was the matter with me? It was all the worse because it was in hopes of finding her that I had taken the day off.

That evening in the hotel I missed dinner, so as to appreciate more thoroughly the architectural features of the bar-less bar. After I'd done justice to a bottle of Zubrovka, or possibly Pertsovka — unless it was Polish Ostrova — I sauntered out, intent on a mission, which was to have a word with my air vice-marshal. For once he had failed to make an appearance. In case he had been beaten up again, I went along to his room, to console him.

I found him seated shirt-sleeved on his splendid bed, polishing his brass buttons. "Shame you couldn't bring your Jeeves, eh Wooster," I said recklessly.

"Oh, hello Bandy," he replied tonelessly, without looking up. Either he had given up on me completely, or maybe this time *he* had a hangover.

I gazed over his equipment. He was using a full complement of tins, polishes, dusters, brown plastic button holders, and so forth, all neatly laid out on the bedside table, next to his beautiful leather button-polishing hold-all.

"Surprised they wouldn't let you bring your servant, Oliver," I persisted, in the hope that he would put me on a charge and send me home.

I strolled over to the far wall and pretended to straighten the perfectly straight picture of the happy Stakhanovites.

Chistelow really was pissed-off with me. He actually smiled. "We had a good meeting at Livadia," he said. "Pity you missed it, Bandy. Quite a good do, it was."

"Lots to drink, was there?" I slurred, remembering that some sort of planning meeting had been, you know, planned, for today.

"Don't be cheeky," he said, though soon forgetting to stand on his dignity, he went on to say that there was to be a major gathering of the troops in a couple of day. "On the final day," he said. It was to mark the success of the Yalta conference. "One of the Russian generals made a speech, saying it had already proved highly successful," he said, happily polishing. "Claimed it would come to be known as the most successful of all the war conferences."

"From which I gather that Uncle Joe has got everything he wanted," I replied.

"What the devil d'you mean?" he demanded.

"You know — he's managed to establish his dictatorshit — sorry, 'tatorship — over even more of Europe."

Chisters frowned. "You know, Bandy, that's just the sort of cynical remark that's causing you to stand out at this conference," he said, as cuttingly as he could muster. And he continued to lecture me to the effect that I had better be careful, or my fame, or should he say notoriety, in the West, would start to go downhill even more rapidly.

I suddenly found myself making a fresh appraisal of the amply proportioned senior officer with the dinky nose. Though he had spoken as censoriously as he usually did when addressing me, the usual feeling behind it had greatly subsided. He was not growing mellow, but the way he now glanced at me, with more than a hint of ... concern, was it? Whatever it was, I felt once again that there might be a bit more to him than ire and pomposity.

Quite affected by this new understanding of my old pal Oliver, I started to lean toward him, prepared to dangle an arm round his plentiful shoulders and squeeze them ever so encouragingly.

Uh ... better not. He'd probably put me on a charge for dumb insolence. Or mimed insolence? All the same, I had the feeling that he was slightly more of a friend than his exhortations and censures had previously indicated. Maybe now was the time to ask for a promotion.

He suppressed a hiccup. "This colonel I was talking to," he said, pausing from his work to thump his chest, "seemed to know all about you."

It took an effort to concentrate. "Eh?" I said.

"This Russian colonel chap. Seemed to know quite a lot about you."

"Oh crumbs."

"You and your friend with the big boots," he went on, polishing away, and frowning at himself when a hiccup wobbled his cheeks.

Instinctively, I lowered my voice. "What? Who? Captain Garanine? What about him?"

"That his name? Yes, the colonel and I, we had a good laugh about it. He was most interested." He hiccupped again. "Damn. Must have been the purple veggies we had for dinner. Did you know what on earth they were, Bandy, the purple veggies? Oh, no, you weren't there. It's not exactly improving your appearance, you know, Bandy, you not eating properly. Where was I? Anyhow, the point is, my dear Bandy ... What was your point, Bandy old chap?"

Chisters was a good deal drunker than I'd thought. I said quietly, "I wish you hadn't mentioned him, Oliver, to the Russians."

"Was that his name, Oliver?"

"No. I meant —"

"Same name as me, you know. My name is Oliver too. I don't mean Oliver number two, I mean ... Well, well. Anyway, Bandy old chap, — by the way, I have a certain amount of admiration for you."

"Oh, yeah?"

"Not much, but more than some people have. Where was I?"

"George Garanine. The Russian interest in him."

"Oh, yes. I didn't say who he was, 'zactly. I just described this chap who was up to no good in your room. All I said was your good friend was a handsome fellow in beautiful boots, who didn't seem to have got on too well in the army as he was still only a captain."

"Christ."

Chistelow looked a me owlishly. "What d'you mean, Christ?"

"Why didn't you just give him his fare to the gulag."

"The what?"

"Siberia," I said; and when he continued to look uncomprehending: "Their prison system."

"Nonsense."

"What else did you tell him at this meeting, Oliver?"

"They had all us Allied officers at this meeting today, that's all I was saying," he said, now looking offended. "Except you, naturally. They had us all in for drinks, you know. In this really beautiful ballroom in the palace, and after we'd toasted our respective leaders a few times, they advised us to doll ourselves up in our best tuck and bibber for the grand finale, day after tomorrow," Chistelow said, finally completing his latest bout of polishing, and picking up his No. 2 Buffing Duster.

"What grand finale?"

"The grand finale, of course. You know, when it comes time to celebrate the triumphant occlusion of the conference in two days time. Did I say occlusion? What on earth did I mean? Never mind. Anyway, So I want you to be on your very best Bandy old man, right?"

He paused, realizing he hadn't quite got it right. This time he spoke more carefully, "On your best behaviour, Bandy," he amended, authoritatively, and with great dignity. "Understand?"

By good or bad luck I saw Vera Lermontova again, the following afternoon. It was nearly dark but it was her, all right. She was standing among a group of people on the far side of Lenin Square. There was a suitcase at her feet.

That morning I had finally admitted that I was in a funk, and in no mood to play truant again. I was the very first to report to the bus to Livadia Palace, half an hour before it was due to leave. I'd even taken the trouble to learn the bruiser's name, in order to placate him.

"You have been removed from the list," said M. G. Arteniev.

He had been pretending to scrutinize his bloody list of *nyemski*, but the performance was unconvincing. If he'd owned a face that could express anything but stolid resistance to contentment, you could have told right away that he was imparting the best bit of news since the Battle of Stalingrad.

"What?"

"You are not on list."

"I've changed my mind," I said. "I've decided I'm badly needed at Livadia."

"You are not on list. You are stroked out."

"Let me see."

His hands, which looked like chunks of iron ore hewn from the Karaganda region, clenched his paperwork more firmly. "You will take my word for it."

"No, I won't."

"You will. "

"Won't. Let me see." I snatched for the papers, but he held on to them, looking as if schadenfreude had just been invented.

"Give up, Bandy," said Air Vice-Marshal Chistelow wearily. He was standing with one hand clapped to the bus, looking as if he were trying to stop it falling over. "You know you can't win."

"I want to go to Livadia," I shrilled, very nearly stamping my foot. "I've a perfect right to go, if I want."

"Oh, Christ," said one of our army officers. "We'll be a day late this time."

After quite a long glaring contest with Arteniev, I turned away, looking defeated.

As his triumphant face finally dipped into the bumph in order to check another name on his list, I moved away, but then suddenly turned, dived through the mob, and, and using it as a buffer, nipped aboard the bus. Five seconds later I was seated comfortably in the nearest vacant seat, arms folded over my proud blue greatcoat, which I was wearing because it was chillier than ever this morning.

And there I sat, smirking at M.G. Arteniev as he stomped aboard in a stony NKVD temper, of the type where the face remains expressionless but the skin takes on a sulphurous hue. And would you believe it — he actually had the impertinence to reach over and seize me by the starboard lapel!

However, even a brute like that had more sense than to make too much of an issue of it. His crude behaviour might have been all right when dealing with a communist flunky, but to a foreign guest who was quite obviously a chap of considerable importance, judging by his smooth, bland, and maddening but distinguished visage ... I mean, really.

Anyway, that's how I got the rejoin the others at Livadia. Yet despite my triumph over that brute, Arteniev, I kept expecting something awful to happen. Moreover, I was filled with anxiety at failing to spot George anywhere near the Palace. Or was it relief rather than concern for his safety? I was in such a state by then that I couldn't tell the difference.

However, the day ended with nothing more serious happening than a glimpse of two of the Big Three as they emerged from what seemed to be a pally inspection of the Tsarina's dacha, up the hill. Though held back by an excess of guards who looked to me like dangerous Mongols, I obtained my best view yet of Winston Churchill, who was in RAF uniform. Unfortunately, Stalin was with him, attired in a tunic that, in its modesty, trumpeted a power that needed no badges of rank. On their way back to the palace proper they were followed by a gold-braided shower of awed admirals and generals. Roosevelt wasn't with them, perhaps because his wheelchair couldn't cope with the steepness of the garden, but more likely it was because of his health. When I glimpsed him later on, he was looking drawn, wan, and depressed. Very understandable, in my opinion — after having to deal with Stalin's demands for days on end. Actually, I heard that it was Roosevelt's depression that had led to his agreeing to surrender a large part of eastern Europe to the Soviets, despite Churchill's strenuous objections. The poor old chap just didn't care any more. A couple of weeks later, he was dead.

Churchill failed to notice me. Thank God, so did Stalin, mainly because I was hiding behind a hemlock.

When I got off the bus on its return to Yalta, I was still thoroughly paranoid, worried, jittery, or feeling just a touch anxious — call it what you will. I was wondering for the hundredth time why I had agreed to join the conference, and if that chap in the Secret Intelligence Service had manoeuvred me into the Soviet Union to give him some advantage or other; but of course, that was nonsense. Philby had better things to do than move me around like a paranoid pawn.

Anyway, as I had not been snaffled by the NKVD, and today was very nearly their last chance, everything was okay, or so I told myself several times. I was feeling a bit better by the time the bus ground and shuddered into Lenin Square that eleventh of February, 1945.

Yet as I got off the bus, I was still busily reassuring myself. I mean, come on, face it, lad, I was saying really reassuringly: Stalin has a war to run. He's long since given up on me. Are you going to tell me that a mere group captain who, twenty years ago, had heard the merest tittle of gossip about the great leader's past, could possibly pose a threat? Or that a posh person like Philby could possibly provide a poor, pale, palsied pilot for these political proceedings for any perfidious purpose? Pah!

Anyway, as I was saying: there was me on that chill, dark evening, cosily bundled in greatcoat and grand illusions, stepping off the bus for the second-last time, treating that brute, Arteniev, to a triumphant smirk that was already well-lubricated with vodka, just about to follow the other officers as they dispersed to the warmth and comfort of their various hotels, when I caught sight of Vera.

As already stated, she was waiting on the far side of the square among a shuffle of travellers, mostly young girls and older women, who were patiently waiting for the long-distance bus to take them home after a holiday in the Crimea.

To buy time, I bent over to tie my shoelace. I kept on tying it until the other Allied officers had dispersed, most of them still talking excited about the conference's semi-climax. As the sun sank behind Bear Mountain, I sidled across the square, and as deftly as a considerable distillation of rye or wheat or perhaps potato would permit, picked up the popsy's portmanteau — Lord, I must stop these alliterations, they were hurting my lips — and gently but firmly led her behind the blasted trees that crowded that side of the square.

I had taken her so much by surprise that her only resistance was a passive glance to confirm that I had a face. As I drew her into the broken, wintry trees she remained quite passive, as if she had been waiting for something like this to happen, since Doomsday or the Revolution.

Temporarily out of sight of any followers, I placed the suitcase at her feet, then looked at her with a face moulded from several question marks. Anaesthetized by fear and booze, I was feeling nothing. Well, maybe a touch of sorrow for the poor woman and regret that I had to do it this way. She had enough to fear from her employers, assuming they were government people. She was still wearing her blue dress, under a black coat that had seen better centuries. Without make-up she looked years older than when she had so briefly but delicately placed her hand over mine in the hotel bar.

"Please," she said, looking palely down at the tatty suitcase. "I will lose my place in the queue. I have to wait all night. I must not miss the bus tomorrow morning."

"You have to wait all night for a bus?"

"It is nothing."

"Where would it be going, Vera? Police headquarters?"

"Oh, no. In the end, just back to Moskva. I have all the papers," she said, reaching into a coat pocket, and showing me just the top few inches or so of the official documentation that would allow her to travel. "I am not of the police, at least, not normally. With you, this was a special job. Though I am sure I have not heard the last of it, for ruining their plan."

"What plan, Vera?" I asked. When she remained silent: "An excuse to collar me?"

"I suppose so," she said. Then, with a shrug, "Yes, of course."

"Do you know why, Vera?"

"Of course I don't. They don't tell you that sort of thing."

"You've worked for them before? Yes?"

"No. Yes. Once or twice. Please, Comrade Bandy. I will lose my place in the queue," Vera said tonelessly. "I can tell you nothing. I don't know what it is about. They just told me what to do. I don't know anything else. I swear that is the truth."

After a moment I started to walk away, but then turned back, fumbling at myself. When we entered the country we had been allowed to exchange pounds for just a handful of roubles, but most of what I had left I offered her.

"Oh, no, Comrade. No, please."

She stared at the brand new roubles. I took her hand and pressed the thin sheaf into her palm. "I'd have to hand it back tomorrow anyway," I said, looking around in case there were any spies or militiamen in the shrubbery.

When there was no immediate reply, I turned to go. But I received her thanks in another form when she suddenly snatched at my arm, and stared fixedly, meaningfully. "They were very angry at the mistake," she whispered. "Very angry." After which, clutching the suitcase as if it were a cardboard lifeline, she hurried off in the direction of the square.

So now I knew. They were determined to get me.

I went for a walk along the sea shore until it was completely dark, and then back to the hotel. Everybody seemed aware of it when I walked in, but nobody looked at me.

I checked the restaurant. It was empty, but dinner was due to start in just a few minutes. I was starving. Walking through to my room, I tried to remember the last time I had eaten. Actually it was only a few hours ago, at Livadia. But before that it was at least two days.

I could hardly wait to wash and brush up and nosh on the surprisingly tasty food they were offering in the restaurant. First, though, I thought I'd better do the usual search of the room in case they'd planted something dastardly, like photos of the naval base at Sevastopol, or a copy of *Men Only*, before scuttling back to the restaurant. As I peeked into all the usual places I wondered why I hadn't veered into the bar. Maybe it was because I'd given away most of the cash. I wondered why I had done that. I didn't owe Vera anything ... or maybe I did. The warning had been written all too plainly in her eyes.

A moment later I found something. Standing on the room's one and only chair to check the water tank above the toilet, my fingers brushed against something which I first took to be flaking paint. There were careless specks of it on the floor, though the rest of the bathroom was unusually clean. I repositioned the chair for a better view behind the white enamel water tank, and climbed up again. Almost immediately I found that the thing previously encountered by my fingers was a tiny corner of folded material that they hadn't quite managed to force into a crevice. It felt like cloth, jammed into a small gap between the plumbing and the wall in order to make the tank sit more firmly, but on wiggling the material between thumb and forefinger a little more of it got drawn out, and it became evident that it wasn't made of cloth, but thick cottony sort of material, a sort of stout blue paper.

By borrowing the scissors from my toilet bag and using the points to pry the toilet bowl away from the wall a quarter of an inch, it became possible to draw out the whole of the folded material, which was a blueprint.

Bringing it into the bedroom, I unfolded it on my bed and stared uncomprehendingly at an elaborate drawing, mostly curvilinear, of something that could have represented a new sewage plant for all I knew. There were many official numbers and abbreviations, though, in Cyrillic handwriting. I had no idea what it was a drawing of, but it sure looked elaborate, and terribly official, and secret.

Obviously, the first thing to do was get rid of it before a squadron of M.G. Arteniev look-alikes burst in, found it, and gave me a good talking-to, or a thorough drubbing and a bullet in the back of the neck, Dzerzhinsky Square style. Turning off the lights, I crept out through the curtain and into the kitchen yard, and prepared to ditch the blueprint. This proved to be a hopeless idea, as the garbage bins out there were empty. They had been overflowing with kitchen waste, cockroaches, stained mattresses, sago, rice, and tapioca, just the day before, but I seemed to have picked the local council's bi-annual collection day.

I scuttled back inside, and jittered back and forth, about two paces to each point of the compass, looking everywhere, but couldn't think of a single place where a determined search would not find the bloody thing. Eat it? Much too difficult to swallow. I could feel my eyes flicking everywhere with increasingly demented energy. I tried and failed to make sense of the warped thinking of the bastards, which required them to hide an incriminating document in the tiniest hidey-hole, rather than simply digging it out of their raincoats and planting it in the cupboard or under the carpet when I wasn't looking, and then accusing me.

The cupboard. I rushed to it, remembering that there was a hole in the wall, partly hidden by the aforementioned damaged bedside lampshade, but, oh, for Christ's sake, a hole in the wall? I would have been better off leaving a trail of breadcrumbs and an arrow saying, *This way, Hansel.* Or was it Gretel?

I finally found a place, but it was only a very temporary location, a place to conceal the heavy, folded material just long enough for me to find a way of killing myself that wouldn't hurt too much. The idea came only because all the hotel lamps I'd seen, including the ones in my original room and in this one, were identical products from the same manufacturer, whose designer — if they had designers in Russia, other than apparatchiks with ambition — favoured the same blue-grey, semi-abstract pattern for all the lampshades. The idea may have been to match the bluish wallpaper in the lobby and various other rooms, including the bedroom upstairs which should have been mine, had it not been for my overweening generosity and utter selflessness in surrendering it to Chisters.

★

In the restaurant that evening, I decided to eat as much as I could in anticipation of — if I was lucky — a long spell of starvation. Accordingly I tucked into everything they had to offer, starting with the traditional black and white breads with dollops of caviar on top, and proceeding with belt-creaking dedication right through to a dish of locally grown *cherneeka*, some ice cream, and two cups of cool coffee.

Unlike the hotel staff who remained resolute in their determination to avert their eyes, old Chisters kept staring at me from the other side of the room. For once he looked as if he'd have preferred my company to that of the other senior officers on his side of the restaurant. I wondered if it was because I was looking so lovely.

I certainly felt wonderful. The anxiety had drained away into the sump. I think it was the result of Vera Lermontova and her confirmation that they really were out to get me, one way or another. More even than her words, her very tone and the intensity of her stare had told me how close to the shores of doom I sailed.

After she had scuttled back to the bus queue, I had walked to the Black Sea, as far as the promenade along the stony seaside would allow, before the barbed wire metallically flowered. When I turned back, I had found myself released from the fear and uncertainty that had trailed me from the moment I stepped onto Djugashvili's patch. Now I knew. There was nothing more to worry about. They were bound to get me in the end, or perhaps less painfully in the back of the head.

The beginning of this strange euphoria, which had somehow been sensed from across the restaurant by Chistelow, was a belated consequence of the Normandy episode. The air battle had undoubtedly made me famous. Newspapers, journals, film and radio people had been going on about it almost ad nauseum. Not content with such previous epics in my life as my honeymoon night in Scotland and my hundred yards swimming certificate, a magazine writer had even awarded me a medical degree. Bart W. Bandy, KCSI, CBE, DSO, MC, DFC, and so forth — and MD, supposedly derived from the University of Toronto's accelerated medical course undergone during the First World War. Dr. Bandy? I wish. Actually I had quit before graduating, being in a hurry to join the most criminal war in history before it ended without me. Now books were to be written about me before I even had a chance to distort, exaggerate, or amplify any of it.*

On the other hand, the air battle that had roused the hurrahs had also permanently damaged, it seemed, the nerve that had fuelled the derring-do. As a man of action, I had finally been paid off, wound up, expired: curtains for Bandy, eh?

---

* Ed.'s note: The earlier ending of this paragraph was less elegant and polished than Jack's revision of it, but makes an interesting digression and seemed worth including, in part for the mention of the Spanish Civil War adventure, which Jack would have liked to write, but never did. In 1999, while writing to us about the first version of *Stalin*, abandoned because of poor sales for *Hitler*, he observed, "All the same I rather miss old Bandy, and would have loved to involve him in the tumultuous Thirties, including the Spanish Civil War ...".

They are now celebrating my other world war, as well. I'm being credited even by some quite distinguished sources as being the top-scoring fighter pilot on the Allied side, but counting in my WWI total. On top of that, they're dragging in all the other adventures as well, from my downhill movie career to my uphill struggles in command of an independent air force in India, in defence of the Empire, and the way I had saved the tatters of Democracy from its shame on the plains in Spain. Unfortunately they were also delivering [poss. delving?] *into the time when I was a rum runner and Member of Parliament, the sources treating this part of my career as a moral lapse, but forgivable, really, at least in Canada, whose citizens heartily approved of rum runners so long as the rum was only running into the United States. And so on, and so forth, with books about me being planned on both sides of the Atlantic, and in one case actually being written before I had a chance to exaggerate any of it.*

Where was I? For a moment my face fell into one of the empty dishes as I realized I had forgotten what I was thinking. Maybe father had been right, that I had destroyed too much of my brain with liquor. Oh, no, it wasn't father, it was the family doctor, way back there in Beamington, Ontario. What was his name again? "Damages your brain," he'd warned me. "Makes you forget. Mark my words, lad: every drink, ever single dram means one more brain cell gone. Three drinks, poof! Three brain cells gone. Ten drink, ten cells. Before you know it - bang! A whole segment of your brain gone." That was what he told me. What was his name again? Oh, you know! The family doctor! Well, bugger it. Look it up in Vol. 1. While you're doing that I'll fish my hopeful expression from the sugar bowl.

After dinner, I wandered right past the bar, and continued to my small room at the back of the hotel. I even smiled at one of the army men route. The brigadier recoiled, dropping his swagger stick.

In the room I sat on the bed, and just for something to think about, without any real hope, I dwelt on various methods of getting out of the country. I reckoned that there wasn't much time, as in a few hours they would be driving everybody home after the end of the conference. Hide in the luggage compartment for forty-eight hours? Not a chance. Course not. Anything else? Well, if there'd been an airfield nearby I might have tried stealing an aircraft, but the nearest airfield was at Simferopol, over the hills and far away. Walk out? It would take weeks, with not the slightest possibility of help. I'd managed it once before, but that was in 1921 or thereabouts, when the Soviets hadn't got their various repressions properly organized.

By sea? That might be worth thinking about. Turkey was just the other side of the Black Sea. But on the trip to Livadia I had not seen a single small boat, either in the water or drawn up on shore — not even a fishing boat. Last Wednesday I had observed one ship on the horizon. Judging by its low silhouette, it was a naval vessel. So, no chance of escape by sea, either.

I was still sitting on the side of the bed when my air vice-marshal knocked and entered, belching. "No room for you in the bar, was there?" he asked. "Too crowded, eh?"

"M'm."

"Looks as if there's going to be quite a celebration in the dining room later on," he continued. "Then the ceremonies tomorrow — triumphant end of the conference, and all that. They say Uncle Joe has got everything he wanted." He looked at me. "You've had an easy trip, haven't you? Not a stroke of work for nearly two weeks."

"M'm."

After a moment: "What are you looking so happy about, all of a sudden?" he said.

"I guess I've gotten over the jitters," I said.

"I thought you were looking better this evening." He did a quick survey of my face. "Not that that was saying much. You were looking as if you were cracking up. What was it all about, anyway?"

"Me looking a trifle harassed? I guess I was trying not to believe it."

"H'm?" He belched, and thumped his chest again. "Believe what?"

"Among other things, that Uncle Joe was out to get me "

"Ah, yes. Well, now you know it was all nonsense," Chisters said, giving up on his indigestion and wedging his bum into the room's only chair. "About Stalin being any sort of danger."

I nodded, for no particular reason, while Chisters went on to praise Uncle Joe to the skies. But he was nothing if not fair. To balance things properly he criticized Churchill severely. The PM was said to have been extremely difficult during the Crimean conference and had argued quite mulishly about Stalin's demand for the return of Russian soldiers and civilians who had been taken by the enemy. "Apparently old Winnie seemed to think there was something suspicious about Joe's demands. Such nonsense," Chistelow snorted. "As if Stalin would, or even could, take it out on millions of men and women, just because they'd been captured or overrun. It would be like chastising the British army for having to be brought back from Dunkirk." And the air vice-marshal went on for some time about Winnie's shocking abundance of mistrust.

Puffing through his juicy lips, his outstretched shoes wrinkling the threadbare carpet, Chistelow finally showed signs of running down, whereupon I broke in. "By the way, Oliver," I said, "I wonder if you'd do something for me."

"What?" he asked, turning suspicious all over again.

"After they've trumped up an excuse for holding me, you won't let London and Ottawa forget me, will you? At least, not for a while."

He was busy suppressing another gastric uprising, so the words didn't register immediately.

"What do you mean, holding you?" he asked, his features rearranging themselves into an impatient smile as he thumped his chest. "Good Lord, Bandy, I thought you said you'd got over the collywobbles. Holding you, indeed. That's nonsense."

When I didn't immediately respond, he snorted and heaved himself out of the chair. "For God's sake, Bandy, pull yourself together," he almost shouted. "You've gone all fuzzy again, damn you." Then, even more angrily: "Look, I've had just about enough of this!" he said, and stomped to the exit. "I'll talk to you later about this poor spirit of yours, Bandy. Damn it, these last few months — been damn close to a lack of moral fibre. You've been a great disappointment, as far as I'm concerned. A great let-down, as my advisor and assistant for one thing — not least because you haven't once assisted me or given me one word of advice since you arrived."

Turning in the doorway, he added, only slightly less truculently, "We'll talk things over later, when you've had a drink and managed to pull yourself together. See you in the bar? All right?"

I wondered vaguely if there might be some slight inconsistency between his criticism of my boozing and the exhortation to proceed to the bar, but soon forgot it when I received another visit from George Garanine.

Once again he stole over the back wall of the hotel and into my quarters. This time he came somewhat earlier than five in the morning, thank God. It was about one a.m. when he rattled his nails on the window and almost immediately nipped into the room, hurriedly closing the curtains after him.

I had not gone to bed, having so many things to think about that night. As booze was not the problem, I was able to see him quite clearly. And just as clearly, he was in trouble. Usually as spic and span as a butler, he looked as dishevelled as if he'd been spun in a centrifuge. His greatcoat wasn't even properly buttoned, though admittedly there were enough buttons for a Mayday parade, two long columns of them speeding down from a disconsolate collar.

"Hello, George," I said.

Despite the cold air flowing through the man-sized window — the temperature had fallen steadily since the start of the Yalta conference –– his brow was embroidered with what looked like beads of mercury and might have been raindrops, though I suppose it was just sweat, and he was breathing heavily. "Bartushka," he said, but then stopped, and felt his way into the visitor's chair.

"Trouble at mill?" I enquired, in what I thought might be a Lancashire accent.

"You have spoiled everything, Bartushka," he moaned.

"Oh? How?"

"Please? Why did you have to come?"

"I've asked myself the same question."

"Though of course it is my own fault, truly it is, Bartalamyeh. Being so scared that you would compromise me," he muttered, withdrawing deeper into his greatcoat like a despondent tortoise. "As we say in Russia, *A peppery cook is likely to produce peppery dishes*. When I heard you were here I should have ..."

"Sneezed, George?"

"Now I am to be arrested, just for knowing you."

"Arrested?"

"I suppose they are already searching for me."

"I'm sorry, George."

He took a deep breath in an attempt to steady his breathing.

In saying sorry, I meant it, for once. Until now I had never discerned anything in George's expression other than love, contentment, and deepest sympathy. No wonder I had often detested the very sight of him. Now he looked shattered, as if his handsome face had been bathed in caustic soda, and the soft tissue remoulded to form a spaniel.

Though plainly exhausted, he got up and paced the available floor, but soon fatigue persuaded him to sit again. "I just don't understand it, Bartushka," he whimpered. "Unless I am to be punished just because I know you." He leaned over and covered his face in his hands, just a shade theatrically, I thought.

"Maybe it's because they've been looking for an excuse to nab me," I suggested.

Removing his nicely manicured hands from his face, he answered quite unexpectedly with a shrug. "Yes, I suppose so," he muttered.

I stared. "You know about it, George?"

"Of course. Because you know about the Great Leader. That he was reporting to the Tsarists while he was with the Bolsheviks."

He suddenly realized that he had answered at normal volume. He clapped his hand over his mouth, and winced under it. "You told me years ago, in Canada," he whispered dully.

"So I did," I muttered back, and very nearly amplified the answer, but decided not to tell him the rest of it. Once he was interrogated, as he surely would be, he would not be able to keep any secrets.

As he now demonstrated. "Anyway, Bartushka, that is why I have come."

He paused, and for a moment I thought I could have told him what he was going to say: that he had come to warn me of my great peril, and that I must escape forthwith.

Not a bit of it. He wanted *me* to help *him* escape. "You must conceal me among your Western friends," he said, his eyes boiling over with entreaty. "You have a spare uniform, yes?"

Glancing at my watch to see how long we had, I muttered, "I would gladly offer it, George, but you wouldn't have a chance. You know the way they check everybody."

He slumped, already knowing this to be true.

"In that case, I will tell you the truth, Bartushka, for the first time," he said.

"Good show, old bean."

Again he rose, to pace as much floor as the bedroom would permit. He had managed a good two or three feet before he stopped and turned. "I have not told you everything — when the French send me to Russia, all those years ago," he said, his voice turning husky under the strain he was suffering. "When they send me to fetch papers —" he shrugged to indicate that those particular papers were of little interest to him — "I hope to have opportunity to collect something more important." Agitation was causing his English to deteriorate markedly. It also reduced his voice to a whisper. "So I could collect the Ossipov papers, so I could blackmail Koba, and make fortune."

Try as I might to subdue an excitement which was certain to be rendered pointless, my heart started to thump like billyho.

The Ossipov acquisition. He was talking about the actual written material which would establish that, before the Revolution of 1917, Stalin had been giving information to the Tsarists about his Bolshevik colleagues.

There was burst of band music from a distant radio. Just as abruptly it was turned off.

"You're talking about the stuff Serge Ossipov swiped — part of the Okhranka file on Stalin?"

"You know about this?" George asked distractedly.

"Course. I got it direct from Ossipov."

George sank back into the chair, staring and sweating.

"At first I just thought it was crap," I continued, "until you indicated that Stalin had taken it seriously, after he'd liquidated Ossipov but before he learned that I was also in the know, and might even have the material Ossipov took from the Tsarist file."

"Yes, pages," George said dully, now sounding so hopeless that he even forgot to whisper again. "That is why I was so keen to go back to Russia. I knew where Ossipov had hidden the papers. "

I glanced at my Swiss watch — a Christmas present from George's wife, actually — to see how much time we had left.

"Think of the value," George went on, his eyes lighting up for as long as it would take to light a Russian cigarette. "Seven original pages from an Okhranka file about the Great Leader, with Tsarist stamps and signatures and references. Think how much they would have been worth. When I got them home to Belgium, I was to put them in the bank, only to be opened if Koba dared to liquidate me." His blue eyes had suddenly lit up like bomber flares. "Think of the value, Bartushka! Surely Stalin would pay millions. Millions!"

Nicely balancing his brightly optimistic eyes, mine had been dunked in ditchwater. "Why would you bother?" I asked. "You were married to a rich woman ..."

"It was pride, you see, my dear. After so long with no money, and having to hold out my hand like a schoolboy ... I have my pride, you know."

"You have? Well, I never."

Clearly interpreting my expression for once, he smiled sadly and said, "You are right, of course. I have no pride. Perhaps this is why I have always loved you, Bart'olomew Fyodorevitch: because you don't have any pride, either. We are the same."

"Oh, Christ."

"But I think now it is the end of the dream. Also for you. Because you know something that is not to the advantage of the Great Leader. That is enough to ..."

Unwilling to upset me, he mimed the missing words by spreading his hands to the approximate width of death. "And I, too, am doomed, simply because I visit you at five in the morning — surreptitious — surreptitiously, is that the word? "

"Bloody hell, George," I said, but then stopped. I mean, what could you say to such an idiot? To have given up a life of ease and the love of a woman like Clemence for the sake of a few pages from a dossier which could take so long to authenticate that George might be dead of old age long before Stalin got to him.

There was a clattering from the kitchen around the corner, on the far side of the yard outside, in the other part of the L-shaped hotel. George spun around so fast that the sweat sprayed from his brow, as if miming a lawn sprinkler for a nice game of charades. He positively quivered with terror.

"They're working late in the kitchen ... All of us guests leaving early tomorrow ... today," I said, surprised to hear the tension in my voice. And here was me thinking I was calm as custard.

"Where are the seven pages, anyway?" I added, just as we heard footsteps in the corridor outside.

George froze still further, if it were possible to descend below absolute zero.

He didn't have to freeze for long. There was a suspenseful pause while the potential visitors, no doubt a force of Byelorussians, Khanates, Muscovites, Cossacks, and an assortment of Siberians, checked to make sure they had the right room. Not that a wrong room was likely to save any innocent occupants. The very fact of being talked to by the NKVD was enough to put anyone under suspicion.

In this case they had the correct address; and so came the dread, inevitable pounding on the door.

ME IN SHIRT SLEEVES

INSTEAD OF THE ANTICIPATED HOST of Soviet thugs, there were only three, and as they traipsed into my room in the Yuzhnaya Hotel, they looked quite presentable .... No, I take that back. I wouldn't care to present one of them to my bank manager. Still, two out of three wasn't bad.

The principal spokesman was a Mr. Soultanov. A bulky man with coarse, greying hair and an authoritative manner, he appeared to be a civilian, judging by his apparel. Though somewhat old-fashioned, with wide lapels stretching from nipple to nipple, his three-piece was sufficiently well-cut to suggest that it had been tailored, pre-war, in a civilized part of Europe rather than in Russia.

Once he had finished flicking his eyes around the room to make sure there were no other decadent bourgeois formalists to be dealt with, he even treated me to a polite smile as, in an oddly Anglicised way of talking, he introduced one of his two companions, a Mr. Chvedov.

"How d'you do?" quoth I.

"How do I do vot?" Mr. Chvedov growled. He didn't look nearly as couth as Soultanov. I immediately revised my arithmetic that two out of three wasn't bad.

As if to make up for his associate's bad manners, Mr. Soultanov continued to smile. "By Jove, it's an honour to meet you, Comrade Bandy," said he. "I've heard so much about you."

"Well, now you can hear my side of it," I said, then winced, realizing that I had overdone that response on too many other occasions. Not that Mr. Soultanov was paying much attention. He was still looking around and lacerating the faded blue wallpaper with his honed optics.

Turning to Comrade Chvedov, he murmured, still in English, "Captain Bandy is a fighter pilot, don't you know, famous throughout the West."

Chvedov didn't seem the least impressed, perhaps because I looked twenty years out of date as a fighter pilot. Personally I preferred to believe that he wasn't too familiar with the English language. He looked rather more Oriental than European, with a yellowish face and squashed sort of eyes, as if he'd knuckled them too often. He also looked dangerous. I made a mental note that if I ever had to pronounce his sibilant moniker I had better be careful not to insult him with saliva.

Like his boss, he was in civilian dress — if the Russian suit he was wearing with its great padded shoulders could be categorized as anything other than Frankensteinian.

The third visitor wore a brown uniform with a wide shiny belt, and what looked like a Greek symbol at the bottom of his sleeve. He had not been introduced, but I already knew him. It was none other than Comrade Arteniev, the bruiser in charge of the busload of capitalist hyenas. I couldn't tell what rank he held. His uniform had little in the way of decoration other than the gold symbol on his left sleeve. It looked like the Greek letter pi, which was certainly not short for pious, judging by the way he was gazing at me.

Still looking around interestedly, Mr. Soultanov continued to address me in the most fluent English I'd yet heard in Russia — of the sort familiar to readers of Mr. P.G. Wodehouse. He seemed to have all the silly English expressions off pat: I say, old bean, don't you know, jolly good show, and so forth. I learned later from a chatty Mr. Arteniev that he had been taught in the Okhrannoye language class by an English turncoat of the sort who used such expressions.

Apart from the nincompoopery, sometimes delivered in an upper-class accent that I sincerely hoped was satiric, Soultanov's English was perfect. Even George's version was not as free, despite his years in the West. Incidentally, I noticed that from the moment the polite Russian walked in, George had taken up a particularly respectful posture.

So far, Soultanov had totally ignored him. Now he suddenly turned to the rigid captain and said curtly, though still in English, "You are a good friend of Captain Bandy?"

By now, George's English was starting to desert him completely. "Oh, no," he said, his consonants clicking like castanets because of a bone-dry mouth, "I don't think of myself as good. Just average, Comrade Commissar."

Soultanov — because his sixty-year-old face was somewhat brown and wrinkled I was beginning to think of him as Comrade Sultana — stared at George with little of the feigned respect so far aimed at me. He tried again. "I asked if you were a good friend of Captain Bandy. Yes?"

George's lower lip quivered. Obviously he would have loved to deny he knew me at all — that he had just dropped into my bedroom after midnight to change the sheets. "I met him slightly in year nineteen-nineteen, Comrade Commissar," he said.

"You also knew him in the West, isn't that the case?" Soultanov asked sharply.

George took so long trying to work out whether it was safer to agree or disagree, that the commissar waved his hand dismissively. "In a moment you will be taken out and searched," he said, in his remarkable English. "But first ..."

Turning back to me, he reaffixed the smile. "You also must be searched, I'm afraid, Comrade. Bad show, of course. Just a precaution, what?" he said, "in case you are in possession of anything you might have removed from this room. As we jolly well say in Russia, *When a duck waggles its behind, it doesn't necessarily mean something*."

"Like most of your sayings," I began, but he overrode the reply with his next words.

"It's just that, according to an informant — she will prove to be as misinformed as most of our sources, I have no doubt — you might be in possession of an item that is of some importance as regards the safety and security of our country." He paused to run over the English sentence in his mind. Deciding that it had emerged unharmed, he continued. "I am sure you will wish to clear up such an unjust — avowal? Is that a proper use of the word?" he asked, as respectful as ever.

"Oh, yes. Avowels and consonants should always be cleared up."

As if I had merely hummed a bar or two from 'O'Flanagan's Nightshirt', Soultanov concluded with, "Would that be all right with you, Captain Bandy? A search of your person?"

"As I am on a diplomatic mission, searching me will not go down at all well with the Canadian government," I said, in tones of utmost gravity.

Actually I didn't think Ottawa would care a fig. They had still not forgiven me since World War One, when they were compelled to award me a senior officer's pension because they had forgotten to demote me in time.

"But I'm sure you'll do it anyway," I added, deciding at that precise moment that I was doomed anyway, so I could be as cheeky as I liked. It didn't matter another fig.

"Mission, shmission," Soultanov replied with a cold smile. "We know that you are not diplomatically accredited, old boy." He signalled to Arteniev. With the light of battle in his eye, the bruiser and bus conductor lumbered forward. With a gesture that I considered to be exceedingly crude though all too readily understood, he ordered me to strip.

"I say," I said, in my own version of the jolly old lingo — though there was more than a touch in uneasiness in my use of it, at least, "you expect me strip in front of all these people?"

But when Arteniev stepped closer still and raised a fist the size of a bunch of bananas braced with reinforcing rods, I decided to humour him; though just to show that I would not be bulled or cowed, I took my time about it, unbuttoning my shirt with care, laying my woollen vest neatly aside, folding the slacks and looking around for a hanger. Mind you, I speeded up a bit when he used the banana trick even more meaningfully.

When I protested about removing my underwear and socks as well, his patience snapped like the elastic of the underpants. He clouted me on the side of the head, knocking me down, and would have followed it up with another blow had Mr. Soultanov not restrained him with a sharp word.

Comrade Sultana wanted me unmarked — for the time being, at least.

Picking myself up, head ringing like a loco approaching a crossing, I glared at the brutish guard as soon as I managed to find him in the mist. Falling against the bedstead had really hurt, not to mention the cranial reverberations.

The clothing was then searched as carefully by Comrade Chvedov as if he were looking for fleas, before the individual items were tossed dismissively in my direction.

While I was putting them on again, I glanced in George's direction. He was staring at the floor.

For him, there was worse to come. The bus conductor was now studying him with anticipation. After receiving murmured instructions from Soultanov, who had recovered amazingly fast from his tut-tutting at the way Arteniev had treated me, the brute turned on George, driving his fist into the side of my friend's neck. While George was still trying to regain his balance, Arteniev directed him to the exit with a kick.

Ordered to open the door, George fumbled for the handle, and managed with difficulty to get it open. He was then sent staggering with another kick, straight into the far from welcoming arms of several uniformed men who had been waiting patiently in the corridor. Arteniev followed him out, and slammed the door behind him.

While this was going on, Comrade Soultanov had been staring at me, as if hoping I would crack under the terrible strain of somebody else being slugged — unless that was a look of relief he was wearing, now that he didn't have to admire my naked form any longer.

He gestured at Comrade Chvedov without taking his eyes off me. "Searching your room is just a precaution, what?" he said, as I rehearsed the quickest way to beg for mercy. After all, they would be finding the blueprint of ... whatever it was a blueprint of ... any moment, now.

Not just yet, though.

With hardly more than a perfunctory glance at the rest of the hotel room, Comrade Chvedov clumped straight into the bathroom, getting ready to look surprised at what he'd found, behaving with as much subtlety as a starving hyena espying a dead relative. He was obviously in on the plant.

Still shivering, though fully dressed again — in fact, I'd also donned the tunic, hoping to get warm, and to see if the decor of wings, rings, and ribbons would stay the brutish hands by sheer bedazzlement. I anticipated quite a shower of the kicks and blows when they discovered that the plant had withered. The thought greatly interfered with the conviction that I'd been in worse situations than this. The self-reassurance wasn't working too well at the moment, judging by the state of my legs, which had already succumbed to funk. I was sure that Soultanov's piercing gaze — why couldn't he have a nice civilized English look to match the accent? — had registered my apprehension as I faltered onto the bed.

I felt I had to say something. Some quick thinking finally resulted in, "Weather seems to be deteriorating a bit, doesn't it?" as I idly rubbed my leg where it had previously whacked the ironwork.

This inspired comment did not elicit a response, though, possibly because Soultanov was beginning to look a trifle distracted by Chvedov's failure to come rushing out of the bathroom, triumphantly waving the evidence.

There seemed to have been a delay. Soultanov had even managed to drag his eyes away from me, so that he could listen more attentively to the sounds emanating from Chvedov in the loo, or bog.

A minute or so later, Chvedov returned from the bathroom, but only to grab the chair, and take it back with him, presumably so that he could better grapple with the toilet tank. In passing, he muttered something to Soultanov, who stiffened, and started to follow him in there. Halfway to the bathroom he changed his mind, walked to the bedroom door, and shouted for Arteniev. In less than a minute, Arteniev was back, rubbing his knuckles and looking enquiringly at Soultanov.

"Keep an eye on him," Soultanov said, gesturing at the bed, and disappeared into the bathroom.

Arteniev turned in the middle of the room, and, hands on hips, looked at me yearningly.

We waited, listening to the activity in there. I could feel my face growing hot with tension. How the devil had they missed the glaringly obvious blueprint? Were they taunting me? Ready to spring? That was nonsense, surely. How could they not see it? Arteniev's clenched face was pointing almost straight at it.

Trying desperately to steady my breathing, I looked at the ceiling, then at the floor, finally at the bus conductor. "They needed a pee," I said, jerking a thumb toward the bathroom, and amazed that I had the control to keep the words on an even keel, so to speak. "I suppose it's the cool weather we're having."

Arteniev just looked at me.

Another clump of time passed. All kinds of noises were coming from the bathroom. The clatter of chair legs against floor tiles. A booming sound, perhaps from a thump against the overhead tank. A scraping sound. A faint screech of metal, resulting in a muttered but heartfelt curse.

After an hour or a minute, Soultanov came out. "Well, now," he said, but then stopped, not least because he was breathing hard, as if he'd actually done some work in there, instead of just supervising.

Chvedov followed him out of the bathroom. He hadn't bothered to wash his hands. They were filthy. He, too, was looking more than a trifle put-out. His face was red, which, on top of his yellowish skin, was producing a distinctly unpleasant hue. He started to say something to the boss, but Soultanov cut him short with a grating mutter in Russian. I didn't catch what was said.

Chvedov seemed to have gotten dust in his eyes, presumably from the grubby plasterwork. He kept rubbing his eyes, making matters worse, and sticking one pinkie in the corners of his starboard eye socket while he blinked around the room.

The mutter from the boss must have been an order to search the rest of the hotel room, for that's what now engaged Chvedov, though he rather gave the impression of not being at all confident that he would find anything, since he had failed in the toilet.

I didn't want to think, in case my face stepped forward to volunteer the slightest hint of what it was feeling. Aware of how keenly Soultanov was studying my reactions, I tried desperately not even to glance at the searcher as he fumbled and thrashed around the room.

I kept trying to divert myself with other thoughts. Now they were searching my bag. Surprising that they hadn't checked it before. Chvedov was shaking it, emptying the contents onto the floor. There was a bar of chocolate in the valise, my reserve bar of Cadbury's. I'd started munching chocolate while flying Sopwith Camels in the First World War, and had only curtailed the habit when oxygen masks became necessary. Not that they weren't needed in WWI as well — we just didn't know any better than to fly at 20,000 feet without an oxygen supply. The bar was hidden in a little pocket. Would Chvedov find it? Bartalamyeh Fyodorevitch Bandyeh, you are charged that on the twelfth of February, 1945, you did illicitly and with malice aforethought import a foreign sweetmeat in order to rouse the people of the Soviet Union into a frenzy of capitalist chocoholism. I'd be found out. Ruined. Yes, he'd discovered it. After a careful inspection, he was tearing the wrapper off. Now he was snapping it apart. How could he treat a precious bar of chocolate in that fashion? Didn't he realize that decent chocolate was almost as scarce in the RAF as it was in Velikiluki? They probably hadn't seen chocolate in Russia since 1941.

Amazing. He failed to pocket it. He just threw it aside. Not content with ruining the bar of chocolate I'd been saving for the journey home, now he was tearing the bed apart, upending the mattress. I tried to distract myself by feeling indignant at the way he had pitched my candy bar into the dust. Instead, here I was concentrating on the 'she' mentioned by our Mr. Soultanov. He had referred to 'an informant'. Was he referring to Vera? She had veered a thousandth of an emotional inch from the party line through her hint that they were determined to get me. Why hadn't the blasted woman veered another fraction and mentioned that she had planted something incriminating in the room, and given me more time to get rid of it? No, no, no, for God's sake, don't think about that, don't think about anything except chocolate.

While we waited in silence, apart from Chvedov's loud breathing, he completed the search, then started all over again. Again, it didn't take long, as the room was so small, so Spartan, almost featureless, only one cupboard, one chair, one lamp — stop thinking, don't think about that! — that the second search took no longer than the first. However, it was much more violent, resulting in some terrible damage, including the fracture of my fountain pen, the disembowelment of my shaving foam, and the ripping to shreds of my copy of *Fanny Hill* — even its camouflage, the colourful cover of *Letters of Edward Gibbon 1896*, ended up torn to bits.

★

The search had ended. The three of them had fallen utterly silent.

To describe them as looking flummoxed would have been an understatement worthy of Pliny the Elder.

Now they were exchanging glances. Where else to look. What to do now. How to get out of it now.

Where to look? It was so blindingly obvious! Why weren't they seeing it? What if it were some other sort of trap? For a second I thought it was, when Soultanov, pretending to look distracted by the ugly shadows the overturned lamp was casting, actually set it straight again.

Any moment now, "Ha-ha! February Fool! We knew all along! We just wanted to make you suffer!"

But nothing at all was being said. A genuinely distracted Soultanov was genuinely replacing the lamp on the bedside table, and then turning away, his hand to his forehead, as if he'd had a sudden attack of migraine.

Back on the bed's overturned mattress, I was very close to fainting. Fortunately, being already hunched over, nobody noticed. Seems they had more important things to think about. Like when I heard Soultanov ask Chvedov in a grating Slav growl that was indiscreetly loud as well as sounding totally different from his delicate English, "Find the officer who delivered — whatever material it was! And the woman! Quick, before she leaves. Go, go!"

Chvedov hurried thankfully from the room, while Commissar Soultanov paced the few available square feet of uncluttered floor space. He no longer looked friendly and benign. Still, he seemed to be making an effort, however painful it must have been to treat an anti-Soviet *nyemski* with such consideration, merely because this arrogant swine, who had lately been so prominently featured in the gutter press, had checkmated the lot of them.

When he finally turned, his face was a picture of rage heavily coated with a metaphorical assortment of rouges, powders, lipsticks, and a dreadful smile. "I say," he said, loosening his knuckles when he realized that they were threatening to burst from the ever-tightening skin, "it seems we have disturbed you unjustifiably, Captain. It seems we are victims of an unforgivable error — no doubt from one of those unreliable sources already mentioned — who shall be punished," he added, in tones so dire that even the bus conductor's breathing paused for a moment.

After clearing my throat once or twice, I responded, perhaps a little shakily, and definitely with more than a hint of *lapsus linguae*, "I shall, of course, be reporting this proper incident to the disgraceful authorities. I've never been so insulted in all my life," I said indignantly.

The latter sentence was, even in a transformed version, of course, a blatant fib. In the past I had been subjected to far worse insults than this middle-of-the-night example. However, that was another story. The most interesting part of this one was not only that the object of their search had been staring them in the face all along, in the form of a brilliantly illuminated bedside lampshade made out of a blueprint, but that they had not even known what they were looking for, judging by what Soultanov had said.

They had only been told where to look.

Presumably because the job had been done in too much of a rush following the failure of the first attempt to frame me, with the blueprint planted by a lady who was now on her way to Tashkent.

Oh, God, it was so good, so good, to discover that the Soviets could be just as inefficient as us Westerners.

BACK IN MOSCOW

I REACHED THE SOVIET CAPITAL in the latter part of February, after a long and circuitous trip because of the dislocations of war. Upon arrival, I found that they had not greatly improved the city since I was there as a prisoner-of-war in 1919. They had stuck up a number of apartment blocks and government edifices, which were in the customary brutalist style, though the architects preferred to call it Constructivism. The new buildings, regrettably, had largely escaped the bombs and shells. It was mostly the workers' houses that had been hit, on the outskirts of the city.

By the end of February I was still there, comfortably installed in the Lubianka, the dread edifice a short drag from the Kremlin. Muscovites invariably averted their eyes from the prison, if they absolutely had to cross the square in front of it. It was as if merely glancing at the Lubianka could get you into trouble.

Strangely enough, the folks there were making life quite comfortable for me. They just didn't want to lose sight of their distinguished guest.

Assuming that reality was something you had to face up to, I was fairly sure I was facing up to it. I'd already had to acknowledge the truth during the incredible disorganization of the journey from the Crimea, by air, road, and rail, which was that escape was impossible. It would have been difficult enough in peacetime. In 1945, a prevalence of alert citizenry, from clumping soldiery to partisans on skis, would have made it impossible to cross so much as a frozen field unreported. Hell, it was hard enough for a loyal Soviet citizen to get out of their official district, let alone a suspect foreigner out of the country. The general public was almost as dangerous as the *khvost*. Probably, after four years of war, many of them weren't too sure who was worse, the enemy or their own apparat. Anyway, you needed documents. Without them you had as much chance as asterisk in *Fanny Hill*.

For that and the above reasons, I'd no intention of skedaddling, for the nonce, anyway, especially as they had settled me in some quite nice rooms in the prison. These included two bedrooms, a living room, kitchen, bathroom, and a door, which was kept locked except when my staff needed to go outside. The suite, normally used to accommodate visiting bigwigs, was on the top floor at the front of the building and provided a fine view of Dzerzhinsky Square, or might have done had the windows not been rendered a shining opaque by ice.

Naturally I did not have the accommodation all to myself. That would have been unheard of in Russia. Sharing the rooms with me was the sixty year-old commissar, Addourahman Soultanov, and Comrade M.G. Arteniev, bus conductor and brute-beast. There was also a young Ukrainian soldier who frequently received a kick from Arteniev.

As for the yellow-faced one who had tramped into my room in Yalta, he had been left behind in Kiev. "Been liquidated, has he?" I asked Arteniev.

Comrade Soultanov had made the position entirely clear even before we set off from Yalta. "Of course you are not under arrest," he said. "We would not dream of treating so celebrated an ally in that fashion, what, what? We are looking after you, that's all, until we can get to the bottom, so to speak."

"Whose bottom?"

"Of the situation, old boy."

"But what situation? Nobody's told me what the situation is."

Still, by the time we reached Moscow they had their stories straight. They had been searching for a document that had gone missing from the yards at Sevastopol. "That was why we had the rooms searched, including yours, don't you know. We did not think you would mind," quoth the merry commissar with a sly wink, "so you would not to feel left out of things, what?"

"Good Lord, no. I like people fumbling through my personal effects," I said, "not to mention being biffed on the boko."

Soultanov thought for a moment, apparently to make a mental note of this out-of-date phrase before continuing. "But of course, until it is all sorted out, we must behave strictly in accordance with Soviet law," he said, with another of those smiles that was starting to get on my wick.

As he spoke, he was strolling around the living room, which had a picture of Stalin on the wall, and a very large radiogram and even a few records, Tchaikovsky's music, mostly. "Meanwhile, you need not worry too much about the investigations in Yalta — though if you are guilty," he said, wagging a playful finger at me, "it could possibly result in a jolly long stay in the salt mines." He essayed another playful smirk. "As for your failure to catch the flight home, you must not worry about that, either, Bartholomew, old chap." God, he could even pronounce the English *th*. "An explanation has been passed to your authorities."

"Gee, that's a relief," I said, aware that the Soviets could do wonders with the truth. Still, they usually avoided the fibs that could be too readily disproved. Their excuses to the West even included a little visual support. As soon as we arrived in Moscow, a woman photographer with a camera even larger than her bosom had turned up to take pictures of me for the Western media. This was in response to some of the things Air Vice-Marshal Chistelow was saying. Apparently he had given an interview about me to the press.

"Chistelow?" I queried. "The bastard — what's he been saying?"

"He is expressing concern for your safety."

"Splendid chap, old Chistelow."

"As you see, we are taking pictures, to show you in your very comfortable circumstances," he said, and proceeded to encourage the bulky snapper to arrange things so that it looked as if I was in the lap of luxury.

Damn it all, when she aimed the big, old-fashioned camera, I should have stimulated some extra Western sympathy by looking cowed, beaten, and starved. Unfortunately, before I could pull myself together, she caught me looking cosy as a cooing pigeon. The bitch even recorded something on my face that could easily have been interpreted as a smile. By the time a decent sort of famished mistrust had reasserted itself it was too late. The two nicest pictures of me in my comfortable quarters had gone west. I believe that no prisoner of the Bolshies had ever looked happier than me, when I featured in the Western newspapers.

Since then I had heard no more from the West — not a word, for instance, from the British or Canadian embassies had been allowed through.

By early March, as the ice in Dzerzhinsky Square began to melt, I sensed that another element had been inserted into ... whatever the equation was. From the first, Soultanov had behaved quite reasonably, apart from his ghastly English expressions. There was the occasional threat, but usually it was delivered as if it were a joke which I was invited to share. I assumed that the commissar could afford to be so untypically tolerant, even respectful. But the respect didn't last long, once he got to know me.

By then, I had come to realize that he was a Soviet official with a lot more clout than your everyday, common-or-garden commissar. On one occasion he bragged about his friendship with the state security chief, Lavrenti Beria. But as time dragged on, something caused Commissar Soultanov to become a touch edgy. Maybe he had a time limit for getting the goods on me. The smiles were melting faster than the icicles on Dzerzhinsky's statue, down there in the square. Or maybe it was on account of my determined, alcohol-free serenity. I was so bloody calm, as he put it, that it began to get him down.

Increasingly, hoping to disturb my tranquillity, he would turn up late at night, with such ejaculations as, "I've had some bad news, old chap. I'm sorry to tell you this, but ...." And then he would pause, and wait for me to start gibbering, blubbing, or cowering.

When my jawbone quivered, as I tried to suppress a yawn, his own face hardened. "It doesn't look good, Captain Bandy," he said sharply. "The authorities are close to establishing your guilt." Raising his voice, which was usually soothing, he outlined the case for the prosecution. This was now nearing completion, he warned, starting with the way I had deliberately refused to do any honest work at Livadia. It had given rise to the suspicion that I had intended to sabotage the conference by pure inactivity. He also dwelt on Vera Lermontova's part in my incipient downfall. He said that though she had been temporarily misplaced, somewhere between Novye Kazanka and Oktjabrsk, when found she would undoubtedly confirm that I had made an attempt to lure her into my bedroom. The Soviet Union frowned upon that sort of immoral behaviour, he said. It was only pure chance that had saved the lady from a night of unbridled lust and debauchery.

However, if I agreed to sign a confession deeply regretting my hostile attitude and conduct towards the Soviet Union, his friend and colleague, the Prosecutor-General, Comrade Andrei Vishinsky, might be persuaded to take a reasonably sympathetic interest in the case.

When I didn't answer immediately, he spoke in tones that were quite harsh for him. "You will save yourself much discomfort if you confess," he said.

I looked up, startled. "What, what?" I asked. "Ooh, I'm sorry, Addourahman, old chap, I wasn't listening. Really sorry about that. Busy combing what remains of my hair. Have to be very careful with it these days, don't you know. It can be such a problem trying to hide an acre of barish pate, what, what. Anyway, what was it you were saying, Addourahman?" (By now we were on a first name basis, don't you know.)

The next day, feeling that I needed taking down a peg or two, he threw in a tour of the downstairs departments. In the past I'd spent time in three other Soviet prisons, including the Kresty prison, Number Two Gorohovaya Oulitsa, and the Peter and Paul Fortress, Petrograd. By comparison, the Lubianka was quite acceptable, and astonishingly extensive when you counted the levels below ground. I was even allowed to inspect some cells occupied by men with faces so sunken as to render the eyes invisible.

The tour ended with a short walk along an underground corridor, where those who were not suitable for a public confession or who were simply not worth it, received a surprise bullet in the back of the head. "I imagine that is how you will end up, Mr. Bandy," Soultanov confided.

"I say, old boy, that's a bit harsh," I said, and at that precise moment decided that I would never again treat myself to an English accent. I'd been trying to imitate it for thirty years, but Addourahman had quite spoiled it all for me. No, from now on — pure Canadian, eh?

Apart from inventing things to say when my time came to confess to everything from incest to overeating, I was still trying to decide what had changed Soultanov all of a sudden. At first, I think he had enjoyed tormenting me with Russian humour and phrases from his English language course. (At one point I wondered if I could get his English instructor liquidated, by convincing Soultanov that the man had got the English phrases all wrong?) But then, suddenly, the burly commissar with the unfashionable lapels stopped seeming to care whether he got anything on me or not. Now, why not? There could be only one answer. With Stalin behind it all, I was doomed anyway.

Still, I continued to hope that some lovely decadent Western influence might come to my aid, preferably in plenty of time. I mean, damn it all, I was a hero, wasn't I? Umpteen papers and magazines had said so, right? They couldn't just leave me to whatever fate Uncle Joe had in mind. So as I say, I decided not to think about it, except to hope that they cared enough about Western opinion long enough for me to fool them. Say, by adopting a fresh identity and living in the wilds of Toronto, maybe with a face lift and a wig. A wig with curly hair. I'd always fancied having curly hair.

Though mind you, this was communist Russia, and even if there was a fuss it would eventually die down ....

No. There was no point in thinking about that, either.

One frozen day in the middle of March, with ice still inches thick on the sidewalks, it happened. I was to be released from the Lubianka.

"We're taking you to new accommodation in the Kremlin, old chap," Soultanov said, though, true to the Soviet tradition of keeping you guessing until you'd reached retirement age, I wasn't told until I was actually being led out into Dzerzhinsky Square, complete with my trusty valise.

Renewed hope springing eternal, like a bouncy toy from the Canadian National Exhibition, I said, "Gee, just when I was getting comfortable up there," trying to work out why they had given up the sensible idea of just moving me straight downstairs to the cells.

I didn't even have a proper escort, just the commissar himself and a couple of plain soldiers.

It didn't make sense. Unless I really was as important as they seemed to think I was, and they were being extra careful.

Waiting for me to make a run for it, straight up Kutuzov Prospekt? That was it! Then, BANG, followed by a close-up of a twitching hand in the dirt between the cobbles. You know, like in a Russian film?

Apparently not. One of the soldiers had even been deputized to carry my valise.

"There you are," quoth Comrade Soultanov. "You see how fair we can be? You can't say we don't look after you," he said with a suddenly regained smile and a gratis wink.

And so, pretty much unencumbered by restraints of any kind, we emerged from the unostentatious Lubianka entrance, and took the shortest possible journey to the city of golden domes and silver spires and leaden bells.

The escort had even been told to look natural. They looked unusually smart, almost as dapper as the ones whose job it was to goose-step so perfectly in front of Lenin's dried-blood-coloured tomb. Admittedly they walked behind us somewhat self-consciously, because they were being photographed. Perhaps the previous snaps hadn't quite convinced the West that I was having such a good time, so they were taking pictures of me again, looking free as a bird in the ever so friendly company of a beaming Soultanov in his smart overcoat and fur hat. For one photo he even linked arms with me.

Would they caption it, 'Wish you were here', I wondered.

They had a perfect day for the outing, too, as we crossed the Dzerzinskaja and along the Marx Prospekt. Though still icy cold, the sky was sublimely blue, and the women were doing a good job of cleaning the streets, or at least diminishing the packed snow with sharp shovels; that is, when they weren't staring at *the handsome gentleman in the blue coat with the subdued gold braid, and the face of a haughty god* — as, with due impartiality, I described myself in one of my notebooks.

I must admit I felt more than ever glad to be alive when a few minutes later we emerged into the great space in front of the Kremlin, especially as the sun came out, right on cue, as if it had all been arranged specially for me; unless the lighting was for the gorgeous cathedral that dominated the square a good deal more colourfully than Lenin's dried-blood hangout on the other side.

Though we had not arrived in a sweep of Stolypins, or Zils, or Zuks, or whatever the new motor cars were called, the guards at the entrance seemed to have been expecting us. They treated Soultanov to a rigid salute as we strolled through the entrance and turned right toward the building on that side.

"It is where you are staying, for the time being," said Soultanov, gesturing at the long, sand-coloured facade.

"Me and Stalin, eh? I take it this is where he lives?"

At first Mr. Sultana looked profoundly irritated, but then, restraining himself, he muttered, "Our great leader is at his dacha, I believe. And this is not his building."

I soon guessed whose building it was: the Ministry of the Interior's, probably the Department of State Protection's principal administrative base in the Kremlin. An innocent looking building, part of the set for the charade that, however horribly some people were being treated in the Soviet Union, Koba knew nothing about it. Which is what many Russians believed: that Stalin would be shocked once he learned what had been done in his name over the past thirty years.

Inside the building there were a few uniformed types in evidence, but most of the occupants seemed to be apparatchiks. You could tell who they were by the way they were all holding fistfuls of papers as they marched purposefully from office to office.

I was still trying to work out the reason for my transfer, as Commissar Soultanov, who was looking more and more senior with every stiffening of limb in the vicinity, ushered me along the left-hand corridor to an elevator. It was actually working, and quite smoothly, too. And once again, I found myself ensconced on the top floor. My new apartment, though, looked less like real living quarters and more like a theatre set where the stage manager has not had time to add the homey touches — a book here, a coal scuttle there, a spy camera somewhere else. Nor was the 'apartment' as spacious as the last one. There was a living room with two chairs, a hasty table, the inevitable photo of Stalin, and not much else. It was also the bedroom, as it contained a steel bed, which had obviously not had a good night, as it was lying on its side. The floor of the room was of poorly polished wood, discoloured in places, as if the windows had developed a habit of letting in the rain. And there was an adjoining kitchen, just capacious enough to boil an egg, though not to scramble it if you were too vigorous with the whisk.

"Where's the facilities? Toilet and so forth?"

"H'm?" Soultanov looked around vaguely. "Ah ... There you are." He pointed to the fittings in a walled-off tiled space next to the kitchen. He opened a cupboard door, revealing shelves with sheets, blankets, and some mouse droppings. "And there is radiator," he added, his English slipping ever so slightly, "so you will be quite warm."

I looked around, and there it was below the window, a massive iron contraption spewing hot calories. In fact, the place was so warm that it had melted most of the ice from the double windows. "I am sure you will be more comfortable here, my dear Bandorschina," he added, almost roguishly.

Bandorschina? Didn't that form of my name suggest that I was a difficult sort of person, a real terror? Bloody cheek.

"I trust you won't mind the damage," he added.

"It could be worse," I muttered, looking around.

"I was referring to the bomb damage," he said, gesturing at the window. It was only then that I noticed the scaffolding that was blocking most of the view.

I took a deep breath, and turned to him determinedly. "Look, Soultanov, do you mind telling me what it's all about? You keep telling me I'm free, but you've been stopping me from going home for weeks. What am I doing here?"

"My dear Bandorschina," he said, using the word again, "you are our honoured guest, until we have finished our enquiries, don't you know? We're jolly well looking after you, old chap, and doing so," said, his face darkening, "jolly well, in my opinion. Now, as to the meal arrangements," he continued, "as with your privileged position in the Lubianka, all your meals will be brought to you directly from the kitchen. In this case, from our canteen ..." He hesitated, as if he wasn't quite sure where the canteen was. "Downstairs, somewhere. As this is a privileged building, I think you will find the food quite adequate. With plenty of drink," he added, both his head and his words adopting an interrogative angle. "Vodka? Georgian wine? Scotch whisky, even? No? You persist in this astonishing onslaught of temperance, Captain Bandy?"

"Just gone off booze a bit, Addourahman, that's all. But, look here —"

But he was starting to leave. "Now I must leave, Captain Bandy, if that's all right with you —"

"It's not all right. I just want to know what's happening, what you have in mind," I began, but he was already out in the corridor, busily reassuring me that I would be quite comfortable here, until it was all sorted out. It was only a matter of time before the difficulty was cleared up.

"Yes, but what difficulty? What —"

"By the way, you will be seeing less of me from now on, old boy," he said.

"Oh? What — who —"

"Duty calls, don't you know. But don't worry, old boy, other people will be along very shortly, to take care of you. What, what?" he concluded, as he entered the elevator.

A moment later the elevator door slid shut, but not quite soon enough to shut off his expression, as it changed from the usual, mocking camaraderie that I had quite gotten used to over the past month, to one of ice cold hostility that was as close to hatred as superficially civilized features could manage.

Meanwhile my escort, the two smart soldiers in blue uniforms, had settled into the room next to mine. What bothered me quite a bit was the glimpse I caught of the interior of their room, before they gestured in rather an ugly fashion for me to return to mine. Their room was completely empty.

★

By then, my state of mind had been rendered only a little more bearable by the composure I had forced on myself from the moment I realized that I was done for, unless I kept my head, and any other parts that were worth keeping. In case the danger was directly connected with the synthetic-looking apartment, I looked around it carefully, but there was nothing of exceptional interest, except for the view. Because of the heat, the windows had been mostly cleared of ice, and I was able to see quite a lot of the city. The thought actually crossed my mind that the hard work being done by the ugly great radiator was part of the plot. The heat was melting the ice so I could see ... what?

Come on, man. Radiators in Russia tended to get exceptionally hot. Last time I was in Moscow, even the old-fashioned tiled stoves so familiar from nineteenth-century Russian literature had invariably been hot as hell, even when George Garanine was supposed to be feeding them.

I turned to the windows. All that ironmongery out there, was that suspicious? It could hardly have been set up specially for little old me, now, could it? Opening a window, without much difficulty because of the heat of the apartment, and looking out, I saw it had been erected along about a hundred feet of the building, right up to the left-hand corner. It was genuine scaffolding, set up to repair the damaged fabric of the building, presumably from the bomb blast mentioned by Mr. Sultana. So that was sensible enough, wasn't it? Though from here I couldn't see any damage.

Continuing my researches, I leaned further out, looking down past the scaffolding planks, and noted with interest that the structure was based in a snow-drenched side garden which ran along the whole of this side of the building. Later I learned that it was called the Alexander Garden.

My window was several floors up from the garden, but it didn't look as if it would be difficult to climb down there, because of the scaffolding. Now, what did that mean? That they were encouraging me to escape? And then what?

Also arousing some curiosity about my new quarters was the way they had cleaned it up. They had painted all the walls, though for some reason they hadn't bothered with the floor, which was in poor shape, badly marked — by the former office furniture? So formerly, this was an office.

Feeling exhausted after such a terribly strenuous walk of fifteen whole minutes from the Lubianka, and after all, it was nearly afternoon, I sorted out the bed and made it up with the blankets from the cupboard, then lay down. Of course, this was just for a spot of cogitation, though it was all too puzzling to permit any sort of coherent thought. Perhaps it was because I was hungry. Was that what it was all about? Did they intend starving me to death? Oh God, this was getting more ridiculous with every passing minute. Still, I would have welcomed a snack if there'd been anything to eat, but there was nothing in the kitchen. I would have to make do with the brought-up meals that Soultanov had promised. Poisoned meals? Was that how they were going to do it? Some nice hot palmeni, with delicious pork in a boiled container of dough and seasoned with prussic acid? Oh, for God's sake, Bandy, pull yourself together. All the same, poison would be easier to explain to the West than a simple disappearance.

I looked at my watch. It was still early afternoon. I got up again, and decided to go for a walk around the building to see what happened. I didn't believe for one moment that this would be possible. In fact I got all the way to the ground floor by the stairways rather than the amazingly functional elevator without challenge, unless one counted the curious stares from the travelling apparatchiks.

Though I didn't really feel like talking, I attempted to strike up a conversation with some of them to see what happened. Nothing happened. Nobody would talk except to mutter excuses and glance furtively at the rows of unfamiliar ribbons on my chest, and the rest of the decor.

I thought of leaving the building, just to see what happened if I strode confidently toward the guards at the walkway into the Kremlin. At the last moment I decided to put it off for a while. It was too cold. After all, I'd been shivering like a vibrator within minutes of leaving the Lubianka. If I was to run for it I would need something more substantial than an RAF greatcoat. In the end I walked back to the pseudo apartment, lay down and was asleep in half an hour, worn out by all that thinking that had got me nowhere.

It was getting dark when I awoke with a start. Flailing out of bed, I looked around wildly, trying to remember where I was. Then I remembered. I'd been sharing a pale, pink pillow with Clemence. No wonder my heart was thudding like a pile driver.

A moment later, there came a loud, impatient rapping at the door, and when I opened it, there was George. Bloody George, smiling as happily as if he'd won at Longchamps.

I must have been less in control than I'd thought. I sank into one of the available chairs, feeling as if I'd been tenderized by a Siberian knout.

Immediately, he began marching about the half-dark living room as confidently as if he had a lease on the place. "My dear Bartalamyeh, were you sitting here in the gloom?" he said loudly. "What are you thinking about, my friend? We do have electricity in Moscow, you know. All you have to do is turn on the switch. See?"

And he turned on the switch, plunging the room into lightness.

I was still staring at him, amazed that once again he had escaped the secret police.

"I thought you'd be in the salt and pepper mines by now," I husked. My usual irritation soon followed, as it invariably did whenever George was in a particularly good mood. "You woke me from a wonderful dream," I growled.

He looked interested. "What was it about?" he asked.

"Whajamean, what was it about?" I shouted. Then, to teach him a lesson: "As a matter of fact, it was about your wife! A really intimate dream about your wife!"

Reaching one of the two chairs, he leaned on it, looking ever so sympathetic. "You love her, don't you, Bartalamyeh Fyodorevitch?"

"What?"

"I quite understand. I love her, too," he said, quite cheerfully. "But I don't suppose either of us will ever see her again."

I opened my mouth to mount a barrage of mixed insults and incredulous gasps at his astonishing insensitivity, but he was off again. "Anyway, that is all in the past. We must look to the future, my friend, when I, perhaps, will be old and useless, but you undoubtedly will develop into the hero of many a book in various foreign languages." He started to move around once more, but again halted at the curtains, which he indicated with a grand, Thespian sweep of his arm. "But consider, my dear Bartalamyeh," he cried, "that now is no longer a need to draw the blackout curtains. Isn't that wonderful? The war is almost over, do you know that — apart from the last, ferocious fighting in Berlin, from which the Red Army is about to emerge victorious. One can only thank our great leader for the way this great country of ours has managed to survive the onslaught of the Hun, and not only that but is emerging victorious." He seized the curtains, and closed his eyes in ecstasy as he held the dusty material to his face as if clutching a cloth of gold in the field of Mars. "And best of all, to think that, I, I, Georgi Garanine, have been allowed at last into our glorious capital to witness to the triumphant climax of the Great Patriotic War!"

In a rather less ecstatic manner he released the window curtain and emphasized again that this was his first visit to Mockba since being spared the climax of his thoroughly well-deserved ten-year sentence in the camps by the gloriously forgiving nature of the Great Leader.

I just gaped at him. I couldn't even think of a decent insult.

Now his tones were more stirring than ever. "Ah, Bartalamyeh," he said, placing a noble hand on my shoulder. "You have no idea what a pleasure it has been to add my insignificant but truly sincere efforts on behalf of our glorious Union of Socialist Republics to this great moment in history ...." And so on, and on, and on. The bugger seemed intent on proceeding in this fashion for several days, striving for nice things to say about the country, the authorities, the Great Leader — about every bleeding element of Soviet society. In fact, he only ended when he became too choked with emotion to continue into the next millennium.

Christ, I could have painted a landscape, washed my undies in the sink, and made and devoured a four-course dinner during his final peroration alone. "What the hell's the matter with you, Garanine," I managed at last. "What on earth —" But before I had a chance to run to the guards next door and borrow a Degtyaryova machine pistol, or at least a Nagan revolver with which to pepper Comrade Garanine, he was off again, this time to reminisce dreamily about the good old days following my release from the fortress in Leningrad into his care in Moscow. "It was the great Stalin himself," he said dreamily, "who gave me the job of guiding you, Bartalamyeh Fyodorevitch, through the intricacies of the glorious dawn of socialism in the hope that you, too, would see the light. The —"

"For Christsake, George," I managed at last, and then added, with a really mean expression on my face, "And anyway, it wasn't Stalin, it was Trotsky." But he managed to override my exasperation rather hurriedly, by raising his own voice in one last hosanna to the glorious dawn of Soviet Communism.

"It is hot in here, isn't it?" he said suddenly, drawing a wrist along his undoubtedly overheated brow. Just as suddenly, he drew back the window curtain to its full extent, and prepared to open the window. "Let's go outside for some fresh air, shall we, Bartalamyeh?"

I couldn't take much more of this, other than to gape in a hypnotised sort of way, especially when he heaved up the window and threw a muscular leg over the sill. "My goodness, they really heat these government buildings, don't they," he gasped as dark, cold air billowed into the room.

Now the other superbly polished boot was sliding outside. He was following it. Wait. His trousers had caught on a nail. It forced him to slow down from his almost frantic efforts to get out into the freezing cold; not quite frantic enough to risk tearing his fine trousers. He managed to free himself, though he slowed to a stop when he realized that I was making no effort to follow him.

Wide-eyed below a pair of greying eyebrows, he stared back into the room, saying almost desperately, "Well, aren't you coming, Bartalamyeh? Some fresh air, perhaps? It is so wonderful and cool out here."

I continued to stare at him. Actually I could have done with some fresh air, if it wasn't too extreme. I had been clammy with perspiration from the moment I awoke from the dream. That is, assuming I had actually awakened from it. It seemed to me there was considerable doubt about that. My disinclination to actually climb out onto what could easily be a shaky structure of clamped-together iron poles, into forty or fifty degrees of frost in the dead of night or its premature equivalent — was that a natural resistance to a stupid idea, or part of the dream?

"Well, aren't you coming out, Bartalamyeh?" George asked, as if inviting me out on a date.

Convinced that he had gone mad, I thought I had better play it cool — though preferable not quite as cool as the frigid molecules that were now marching into the room in columns of three.

"Uh, no George. Not just at the, uh, you know, moment. It's too dark."

"Oh, come on. It's not so bad."

"It's too cold."

"Oh, don't be so silly. Please, Bartalamyeh. You can get a beautiful view out here."

"No. Sorry."

"Oh, come on."

"No. I'm not going out there," I said angrily, moving even further away, in case the madman actually tried to drag me out for a walk along the dim scaffolding. I mean, what the hell did he think he was playing at?

George was now looking quite desperately from me to the wooden runway and pipes, and out into the vast space beyond all the pipes. No lights were glimmering across the across the city, but the starlit sky was more than making up for it.

"I am really disappointed," he said. Actually he seemed more despairing than disappointed. "But I suppose you are right. Now it is too dark," he ended, and reluctantly drew his big polished boots back into the room, ramming the window down with a crash.

A few minutes later, muttering that it was time for him to go back to his own room, he departed, but not before he had taken out a pencil stub and defaced the newly plastered wall with a few words, licking his fingers and rubbing the words out again.

It didn't entirely restore my confidence in George's sanity. The message on the wall read, *Will write and slip under door*. And out he went.

After that, I went back to bed; or rather, I sat on the cheap structure of frame and one or two springs, holding my head safely in place as I gazed down at the black marks on the semi-polished floor, wondering how George was going to manage it. Slipping under the door was not going to be easy, as there was only a one or two inch gap there, after the Soviet carpenters had finished the building work. After all, George was a fine figure of a man, broad-shouldered, handsome, and stalwart; he wasn't going to slip under any door all that easily, despite a steady diet in the camps of greasy water masquerading as soup, and years in the army noshing on black bread and the like ....

Strange the way he had managed to keep most of his teeth, I

thought, yawning. I hadn't been in jail nearly as long as he had, but I had really looked after the old molars ever since, apart from the one dragged out by a Parisian dentist.

Which caused me to think of food. They had promised to bring up the meals on a tray, but I had received nothing at all. I'd knocked next door to see if my guardians could help, but they refused to address a single word to me. I though of going down to the kitchen, if it really existed .... A moment later it was hours later. I had been dreaming again. I dreamed I was sliding past the sentries and drifting into the city, until someone shouted at me to go home. I awoke, a little worried that it was crazy I was going, not home.

It was five in the morning before the note finally slithered under the door. It read: *Eat this note.*

How typical of George. Eat this note. Nothing else. Good God.

Admittedly, that wouldn't be difficult as it was an exceptionally small note, a shred of paper torn from the corner of a newspaper. It wouldn't be too hard to digest. Or was the teeny bit of surviving newsprint part of the message? No, all it said was, *eta lekahrstva ne pamaglo.*

A medicine not being any good? No, that wasn't likely to be part of his message.

When I happened to glance at the other side of the shred, though, I realized that the instruction to eat the paper was the end of the message. The beginning of it read: *Will explain all. Be ready to escape daylight.*

ON THE METPO MOCKBA

IT WAS UNDOUBTEDLY DAYLIGHT by the time George reappeared. It was twelve noon. Noon, apparently, was being 'ready to escape daylight'. Unless, by escaping daylight, he was talking about the middle of the night. But then, why turn up in daylight? I mean. No wonder he looked haunted, as if he had been refused a visa by the archangel Gabriel.

He was carrying his army duffle bag, as if he really believed in the possibility of escape. He was behaving strangely in other ways, too. Normally as imperturbable as a cabbage, he had launched immediately into a torrent of chat and gossip, as if picking up an entirely fictitious conversation interrupted only minutes ago. However, his haggard face and desperate looks had great difficulty in maintaining the pretence. He looked terrible. He looked as if he had aged twenty years overnight.

Luckily, he had plenty of other things to do, distractions — like snatching a message, presumably from Garcia, from the top pocket of his epauletted uniform. His hand was quivering so much when he proffered the note that I thought he was offering to fan me, on account of the room's unnaturally high temperature. The radiator at the window was positively crackling with the heat.

At least he had brought a more detailed communication this time, even if it was written on a ragged piece of cardboard. For God's sake, didn't he have any decent writing paper, I wondered, as I squinted at the soggy scribbles.

Mikes everywhere, it read, in decidedly shaky script. As if I didn't know that. *Great danger. You must agree follow me out window with luggage.*

I'd hardly absorbed the message before he snatched it back, tore it into tiny pieces, and looked around for somewhere to dispose of them. The cardboard must have been picked from some rubbish heap, judging by its soggy condition, yet he was desperate enough, finally, to stuff the pieces in him mouth and munch them dedicatedly, until a convulsive swallow defied his digestive system.

Now he was acting like a flustered manservant: gathering all my effects together from the shelf at the kitchen sink, but doing so as silently as possible, while continuing to gasp, chortle, and talk loudly for the benefit of the microphones.

Not knowing what to say, I said it. "Weather's a bit better today, George," I alleged.

As if this was at least a portion of the response he'd been hoping for, there was a small decrease in his quivering anxiety. It was not much of an improvement. His face was still a disorderly mess, as if he'd breakfasted on Mill's bombs.

It was a shame, really. He had been so handsome, once. Not as far as I was concerned, of course, but maybe to a misguided woman, or a racehorse. I'd seen horses wander up to him for a pat or caress. Though mind you, he had usually been offering some cube sugar as well as the syrup of his personality. There was no sweetness and light today, though.

"Yes, the weather is beautiful this morning," he said, gesturing violently for me to continue with the chitchat. Meanwhile, he snatched up my valise and looked around wildly for something to put in it.

It was true that though the weather was not beautiful, it had certainly improved. There had been something of a thaw during the night. The freezing cold had largely been replaced by a mist that must surely be wrapping the bright domes of the Kremlin like Easter presents.

George was starting to run out of silly things to say. I thought I'd better help. "Yes," I said. A lot milder."

"What?"

"The weather. Much better today."

"Oh. Yes, yes, that is true."

"I was going to go for a walk this morning," I said. "But they don't seem too keen to let me out of the Kremlin. I guess they love me so much they just can't bear to part with me."

"I'm sure they are just concerned for your welfare," George gasped. He was trying to suppress a panting sound while packing my bag as soundlessly as possible. I half expected him to pass out from hyperventilation, or overwork; he was stuffing everything in sight into my valise, including, for some reason, an ashtray, though I'm sure I'd mentioned that I'd given up smoking.

"Though it's true that a fellow does need exercise now and then," he panted, and gabbled on for at least another two or three minutes before suddenly blurting out, as if he'd suddenly thought of it, "I know! Why don't you go for a walk out of the window?"

I had been feeling a little better this morning. Not much, but just a shade better, even after a night of hideous dreams. But by now I was inclined to go back to bed. He really was as crazy as he looked — almost as if he believed that there was the slightest chance of escape from the very middle of Mockba.

Still, having nothing better to do, I replied, "What, walk out the window? But, George, I would fall to the ground. It's a long way down you know."

"No, no, Bartalamyeh, I meant walk on the, what did you call it, the scaffolding?"

"Why George," I replied, "what a good idea. As you say, it is very hot in here, and I would definitely appreciate a bit of fresh air."

"Yes, it is true, it is terrible hot in here, is it not, Bartalamyeh Fyodorevitch?" George said, making desperate gathering motions as if the consequent manual pressure would blow me a little faster toward the window.

"No, I wouldn't mind a spot of fresh air, out there on the scaffolding, which has been erected outside this very window," I said, getting into the spirit of it.

George had already darted over there, to take hold of the catches and raise the window to its fullest extent. Because of the thaw it went up quite easily. George then rushed back, to grab my arm and rush me to the opening, which was already admitting plenty of the fresh, damp air we were both apparently so keen on.

Because he was basically an indolent fellow concealed within a graceful form — or at least that was the case, until a few years of starvation and a hard war had created a few extra hollows and angles — I had forgotten how strong George was. He had me halfway out the window, causing me to bang my knee quite painfully, before I had a chance even to say 'ouch'.

"My greatcoat — I can't go out without a coat!" I managed at last. At which, George stared at me for a moment in horror, his mouth opening and shutting as if it were being operated from within by a disorganized quadrate muscle, until he realized that I had not entirely compromised him.

"Yes, of course," he cried, rushing to the bed over which I had folded the greatcoat. "You are right, the weather may have improved but it is still quite chilly. You must of course have your greatcoat, as it is, as we say, still quite chilly, despite the ..." Running out of suitable nonsense, he thrust the coat into my arms, and resumed squeezing me out the window. After which he shoved his green duffle bag through into the chill, before clambering onto the scaffolding himself. Then, looking as if another profoundly good idea had just occurred to him, he stuck his head back into the building and called out very loudly indeed, "But of course, I must not be late getting back, for I have an important engagement this afternoon at the ...." The creative impulse faltered at that point, and he ended with, "at the — at some place or other."

So far, feeling that any sort of action was better than just hanging about in an office masquerading as accommodation for a renowned western visitor, I had gone along with George's little farce. I didn't expect anything to come of it, but at least I would have a few minutes of fresh air and a few yards of exercise. So, shrugging into the greatcoat, then gripping the valise as if I really meant to go somewhere, I turned left along the duckboards. Turning right would have taken us past the room inhabited by the militiamen.

George, clutching his duffel bag to his chest, caught up just as I was passing the only other window between us and the corner of the building. And naturally, somebody was looking out: an elderly lady wearing glasses and a head of hair like the floor of a barber shop.

She was seated at a desk, speaking on the telephone. Catching her eye, I smiled, nodded casually as if traipsing high up along the side of a government building with all my worldly possessions in a bag was a regular part of my duties. For no reason whatsoever I started to whistle sibilantly through nervously pursed lips, a recent ditty about oats-eating equine quadrupeds and little lambs munching ivy, wondering when the woman would raise the window and give the alarm. Surely it would be any second now, unless of course she had been issued with the regulation Nagan revolver and took a few pot shots at the suspicious characters in their heavy coats, who were carrying their luggage in case they had to put up for the night out there. Instead, it seemed that, (a) she was too busy on the phone to solve the mystery of a couple of men shuffling past her office window fifty feet up, or, (b) she was too short-sighted to take us in, or, (c) recognizing the green state security badge on George's coat, she concluded that asking questions might not be a good idea. George mentioned later that she was still on the phone as he went by.

It was only another few steps to the corner of the building, and I was already trying to decide how to climb down to ground level when George spoke up. "By the way," he told the back of my neck, "they've laid a booby trap somewhere along here."

I stopped so suddenly that his duffle bag ran into me. The sounds of the city suddenly became a lot clearer: the clang of a streetcar on Kalinenprospekt, the exertions of an aircraft climbing into a chill wind that brooked no good, the loud quarrelling of two of your typically discontented Moscovians, the scrape of a shovel wielded by a 200-pound lady street cleaner, the bells of a basilica summoning the devout to prayer, the clop of a troika as it ... No, that wasn't right. I was straying too far into the previous century.

"Did you say a booby trap?" I enquired.

"That was the whole idea, you see. That is why we are here. I was to encourage you to escape down here, and to make sure you failed ..."

"I see," I said, ever so calmly. "I was supposed to fall to my death."

"Also, there was talk of a booby trap."

Slowly I turned and looked at him. He shuffled a bit, and after a moment, looked away. While I looked down at my feet, wondering if the last yard of duckboard, before it reached fifty feet of open space, had been sawn nearly in two.

He must have felt that my look required an amplification of some sort. "I've forgotten where exactly they've sabotaged the, you know, the structure along here," he said after clearing his throat.

I remained deathly still.

"No, wait, I remember now," he exclaimed. "It is at a pipe connection. Let me see ... Yes, here, where you would have had to climb down. Yes, there — see? Where they have loosened the connection —" he rattled it, just in case I had not observed the exceedingly loose pair of bolts, "— so the moment you started to climb down it would disconnect, and you would be hurled bodily to the ground."

I closed my eyes, gripping my valise and the ironwork harder than ever, particularly disturbed by that word 'bodily'.

"But once past this danger, Bartalamyeh, there is nothing more to worry about. And I am sure I would have remembered all the details, before the accident happened."

I nodded, eyes still shut, holding the icy-cold piping harder than ever.

Then it was my turn to clear my throat. "You will let me know if you remember anything else of importance, won't you, George?" I said. "You know, before we both plunge to our deaths."

"Oh no, I wasn't supposed to go down with you," he said.

"You weren't?"

"No. All I was supposed to do was check to make sure you were dead, before I called for help."

After a while, I managed to let go the scaffolding. My hand freed itself without too much difficulty, as the pipe was not as cold as it would have been on the previous day, when my hand would have stuck to the frozen metal. However, given the increase in temperature, which would have obviated the — obviate has always been one of my favourite words, actually, ever since I discovered it lying unattended one day on an aerodrome in France sometime in 1917. I had been arguing with a fellow scout pilot, I remember. He had sneaked a childish contraption into my bunk bed which emitted an exceedingly vulgar sound whenever — he'd had it made in the maintenance Bessenau hangar, I remember. Anyway, the point is, I insisted on finding my own way down to avoid the sabotaged pipe connection. Suspecting that George might have got it wrong, I chose another route, starting with a tightening of the almost disconnected bolts, this despite George saying that we should just leave them. Somehow I felt that if the connection was not fixed it might affect the entire structure all the way back to my room, and therefore the entire geometry of pipes and connections and bits of duckboard would collapse and sent me plunging helplessly to the — but enough of that.

Five minutes later, climbing down by an alternative route, we reached ground level, in the deep snow of the Alexander Garden.

That was when I was finally able to look at George without thinking of clubbing him unmercifully. (I'd often thought that way about George.) It was as if I'd set off fifty or sixty feet up with a trembling, haunted, terrified officer and reached the ground with another person entirely.

I actually did a double take — first time it had happened to my head since I used to do it on purpose in the silent films, way back there in the 'twenties. It was astounding, absolutely amazing, the way George had changed in just a few minutes, from a trembling wreck right back to the handsome captain I had first met as my POW guardian in 1920.

"We have succeeded, Bartalamyeh," he said, filled with so much emotion that it was overflowing from his eyes. "We have escaped. We are free."

In fact, we were about as free as a cat in a sack in a river, but for the moment that didn't distract me from a bit of wonderment at the sight of him. I swear that even his skin had cheered up. From a shivering grey it was now almost golden with the light of relief, the brightness of joy. I swear that in the space of a quarter hour he had come to look at least twenty years younger, and, it seemed, to have reverted to the glorious optimism he had so often displayed even in the sordid quarters we had shared in the run-down house off the Petrovka Ulitsa, lo, those many, many years ago, and back to the happiness and good humour that had so frequently pissed me off in those far-off days.

Frankly, I was amazed. His very figure seemed elated. The stoop of hopeless fear had straightened up as if the scaffolding had been his drill sergeant. His eyes, which had grown dull with terror, had regained their vivid blue. He had never been a proud man in the sense of insisting on his dignity, though it had occurred to me in the past that the resulting simplicity gave him more dignity than I had observed in many a self-important acquaintance. And if he would still always manage to keep the warmest seat by the fire, he quite genuinely cared that everybody else should share as many calories as possible.

Long ago I had come to recognize that his love for his friends was genuine and immutable. For that reason he always forgave people for their worst reactions to his good fortune; he never seemed to have the slightest reservations about their vices and foibles. Hell, he even loved me, even when the foolish man thought I was being particularly envious, resentful, rude, or difficult.

"If I live to be as much as sixty years old, I shall never forget how much you have done for me, Bartushka," he said in an almost tear-stained voice. He actually seized my free hand and started to bring it to his lips, before I wrenched it away. "You have saved my life."

"Don't know what you're talking about," I said, loud enough to dislodge snow from a nearby Norway spruce. "We're just out for a walk, that's all."

"Oh, Bartushka," he said with an ever-so-fond smile, and against reaching for my thoroughly clenched fist.

"Gerroff!"

He smiled even more affectionately. "But you are right," he said, brisk as a sudden gust of wind at Portage and Main. "We must away before they realize we have made our escape."

"For God's sake," I snapped. "Made our escape? We're a thousand godamn miles from civilization, here."

"Yes, we must be on our way," he said, taking my arm, and refusing to take note of my resistance, he initiated a fast flounder through the snow toward the nearest exit from the Alexander Garden.

"On our way where?" I panted. "I told you, we're stuck in bloody Russia, not late for lunch on Sparks Street!" George knew Sparks Street well. He used to pick up girls there in Ottawa.

"It is all planned," George said as we floundered down a steep slope and onto a deep, front line trench on the Mane-Znaja Ulitsa. "First we must find the Metro. And then we take the train to the airport."

I gaped, or would have done had he let go, but he was still rushing me away from the Kremlin as if our lives depended on it. Which they did, of course, but all the same — I hadn't even adjusted yet to the idea of escaping from my room, let alone the entire country.

"Wait a minute. Wait a *minute!* What's this about an airport?"

"It's all right, Bartalamyeh, I have reconnoitred already. The Metro train goes right there, you know. Or fairly close. One mustn't exaggerate. Once we change trains at Belorusskaja, it is only two stops, but a careful walk then we must take."

Totally bewildered for perhaps only the hundredth time in my life, I would have forced him to stop right there in the middle of the crowded street — we were in the process of crossing it, toward an open space populated mainly by museums — except that I skidded on the polished ice and had to rely even further on George's urgent humerus and radius.

I was still breathing hard with perplexity masquerading as exasperation as he paused on the other side and murmured to himself in Russian — from which I gathered that he had forgotten the way to the Metro. Finally, making up his mind without any help from me, he strode off again, with an officer's bag in one hand and me in the other.

For want of a decent-enough excuse to return to the comfortable accommodation in the Kremlin, I allowed myself to be urged along the boulevard. It was one I had noted from my bedroom window. A wonderful bedroom it had been, really warm, and quite comfortable once I'd sorted out one of the coil springs in the bed which had been spiralling slowly into the middle gluteal muscle, necessitating a distinct anticlockwise withdrawal. After that I had slept quite comfortably, and very warmly because of the lovely heat. Yes, quite a cosy bedroom, really.

Until I remembered their filthy, dirty trick. I still couldn't really believe it, that they would have the nerve to get rid of me, a chap who had been so prominently in the news, lately. However, I wasn't going to think about that right now. I would rely on George, until he proved utterly unreliable.

For the time being, he had actually managed to find one of the country's surviving cathedrals, alias the gorgeous if now rather shabby Metro station. I very nearly congratulated him, until I remembered to keep my voice down. We were surrounded by foreign eyes and ears. Also elbows, every one of which was being rudely used like sculls in a rowing boat, to steer the owners into the lower depths.

Once aboard the free train, and over the general racket of coughing citizens and buffeting tunnels, George said, "By the way, if you had survived the fall, the Comrade Commissar said I was to kill you, Bartalamyeh. And then I was to inform the British Embassy."

"What for ?"

"So they could see it was an accident. They would even be allowed to take your body home, if they wished. Apparently Stalin had no wish for it."

"Huh."

"All of this assumes that I had not made a mess of polishing you off," he added with a high smile but a low voice as he became aware of how much interest other passengers were taking in us. We could hardly fail to be noteworthy, considering that one of us was wearing a foreign greatcoat and a cap with oodles of gold, and the other was wearing the dreaded green insignia. NKVD officers didn't usually travel in the metro with the common herd.

For once, though, the public reaction to such uncommon sights was muted, almost tolerant. There seemed to be an atmosphere of excitement in the city. I wondered if it was to do with *Maslenitsa*, the festival during which Muscovites bade farewell to the bad spirits of winter. No, it was surely more than that. Even as more and more kulaks, bureaucrats, grey women in even darker clothes, etc., crowded onto the platform, threatening either to crush the other passengers against the sumptuously coloured tiles or to shove them off the edge of the platform, the excitement seemed to remain, positive enough even to restrain the Muscovites from pushing George in front of an oncoming train, assuming they had the nerve to treat a chap in a secret policeman's uniform in that way.

We had been standing compressed on the platform for a several minutes when the public address system coughed, cleared its throat, and dropped several heavy goolies onto a thin sheet of aluminum. This introduction was followed by a loud, grating, incomprehensible Tannoysky announcement.

Noting the subdued dismay around us, I asked George if he'd understood. "Some difficulty further up the line," he frowned, taking my wrist in order to see what time it was. He had sold his own watch to pay for his escape, he told me.

I glanced at the same wrist, and was surprised to see that it was already mid-afternoon, past three o'clock.

Now the crowd, though still incomprehensibly good-natured, began to rustle, jostle, or wrestle back to the exit. George plucked at his lower lip, for the first time looking a little anxious. I wasn't sure if this was an improvement over his previously happy expression or not. With difficulty, because of the crush, he managed to drag a Metro map out of his army bag. He studied it intently for quite a while before bellowing over the noise to the effect that we had better take another route, as there wasn't much time left. So saying, he rammed the map into his breast pocket, took my arm once more, and steered me back the way we had come; though even that took so long that it was four o'clock before we were finally free of the mob.

Back on the street he set off at a surprisingly urgent pace for an alternative Metro line.

"We have to be there at six," he said, breathing heavily.

I managed to slow down a bit, mainly because he'd finally let go of my arm. "We have to be where at six?" I enquired.

"The airport, of course. Come along, Bartalamyeh," he said, now sounding quite anxious.

"You don't expect to get a flight, do you?" I asked incredulously.

"Don't be such a slowcoach, Bandyeh. No, of course not. Not a regular flight."

"Whajamean, not a regular flight? What else kind of flight is there, for God's sake?"

"The problem with the Metro is very good news, Bartalamyeh," he said. "Now, instead of changing at Belorusskaja we shall be able to go straight through on the Vodnyj line. That is really a very good change of plan, you know."

"If it's that good, why didn't we take it in the first place?"

George laughed a little breathlessly. "Oh, Bartushka," he tittered, as if I'd said something really amusing; and before I could make any more points, he had snatched my free arm once more and was rushing me yet again through the crowd.

Now we were back at the Marx Prospekt, and trying to find the right line. George had only very recently learned how to cope with the Metro, and it took another increasingly tense rush through all the brilliant tile work of the system to find the correct colour code.

We were just in time for a train to Aeroport, and actually managed to get a seat, but by then it was five o'clock, and even George was evidencing a shade of concern at the lateness of the hour. Observing this, I finally forced him to tell me exactly what was happening.

"But I thought you understood," he said with a patient, though still somewhat breathless smile. "We are to fly from the airport. The airplane leaves at six o'clock."

I now felt that calmness and infinite patience might do the trick. So calmly and patiently I repeated my definite conviction that, unless he was thinking of stowing us in the undercarriage space where we would soon be dead anyway, there was not the slightest chance of getting on any plane at all except the type that flew round in circles at a funfair.

"Oh, didn't I tell you?" he replied, not entirely looking me in the eye. "It is perfectly true, Bartalamyeh Fyodorevitch, that we would have no chance of leaving exactly in accordance with an airline schedule. No, what I had in mind was the weekly clandestine service to Finland, which, of course, is next door to Sweden."

Becoming animated again, he twisted round to face me so that I could see the enthusiasm and conviction on his face the more clearly. "I say clandestine," he explained, ever so kindly, "but only in the sense that the aeroplane is delivering material for onward transmission to other Western destinations, without actually specifying what exactly the material is. Otherwise the flight is perfectly regular, you know, with all the proper paperwork, and so on." He took my hand, and patted it, ever so fondly, and said, "Are you with me so far, Bartalamyeh?"

"I ... I suppose so ..."

"I learned this at headquarters, Okhrannoye Otdyelyenye — Ministry of the Interior, you know?"

"Yes ...?"

"Anyway, that is what I have planned," George said, releasing my hand and clapping his own together with a look of profound satisfaction over the entire planning procedure.

Except that he still hadn't mentioned what the plan was, until I pressed him, my eye filled with apprehension, if not utter foreboding.

"The plane, as I said, leaves exactly at six every Sunday." He paused to check the name of the station into which we had just shuddered. "You are to fly it, Bartalamyeh. To fly us both to safety, in order to restore me to the bosom of our beloved Clemence."

LOOKING EXTREMELY THOUGHTFUL

NATURALLY, THE METRO STATION named Aeroport was nowhere near its namesake, or if it was, George soon turned the wrong way. Less than half an hour before his alleged plane was due to leave, we were completely lost.

He had made a reconnaissance three days previously, but only to the extent of locating the passenger terminal, and making a visual check on the alleged hangar on the far side of the airport. He claimed that a weekly flight took place from there at 1800 hours every Sunday. Today was Sunday.

A drunken friend of his had named the enterprise based at the hangar as Operation Sanitarniye Pyelyonkee, and had even told George how to reach the hangar, provided he didn't mind getting arrested.

Naturally, our endeavours under George's leadership in finding even the way into the airport, let alone the hangar itself, had us completely lost within half an hour of leaving the Aeroport metro station. The openness of the land on this side of the airport had disoriented him. Twenty minutes before the plane was scheduled to take off — according to him — we were still lost in the mist. Yet all that George seemed worried about was our luggage. He claimed that the bags, much admired by the Metro crowds, wouldn't look right if we staggered with them across country from snowdrift to snowgully. We ought to abandon them.

I refused. I didn't care about his duffle, but an expensive leather toilet bag was part of my equipment — a Christmas gift from the baroness, as a matter of fact. I wasn't going to dump that, no siree bob. Quite apart from the fact that I wasn't at all confident that George could get us within miles of the aircraft. Even if we did, what then? The idiot seemed to believe that I was capable of stealing a plane from under the noses of the entire Soviet Union — half of which must be looking for us at this very moment, while the other half were getting their knouts and knuckle-dusters ready for when we finally were apprehended. My confidence, not terribly high to start with, sank even faster as he took what he thought might be a short cut across a ravine, leaving a straggly white trench to make it even easier for the ravenous killer dogs to follow us. As we floundered out the other side, my shiny shoes were soaked, my socks were saturated, and my tootsies were nearly as cold as the looks I was now giving him.

When we finally reached the lane he was short-cutting to, he seemed to have lost his sense of direction entirely. Admittedly the mist, which had persisted all day, didn't help, but still, the damn fool had been planning his escape from the moment he arrived in Moscow. No wonder he had failed to rise above the rank of captain in an entire quarter century. Hell, he hadn't even brought a compass.

"We'll get there," George said, withdrawing his head into his collar like a tortoise. "I know we will. You will succeed, Bartalamyeh. You can do anything."

"Eh, shaddup."

"I am sure this is right way to hangar. Note that this road we have reached, it has been snow-ploughed. Obviously it must lead somewhere important. They wouldn't have ploughed a road for ordinary people."

I was too pissed off to respond. So on and on we plodded through the snowy wastes, with me melting my way through by means of a hot-faced silence. Actually I was astounded that we had even got this far.

"I'm sure it will be just over the next rise, Bartalamyeh," he said placatingly.

Yeah. If any man had a right to be placating it was him. Him and his demented thought processes, which seemed to devolve as follows: a plane was due to take off on Sunday. Bandy was a pilot. Therefore Bandy would take off on Sunday. Christ!

Still, I made another bleeding effort to bloody-well look on the effing bright side. Though the Bolshies were probably preparing another 'accident' for us right at this moment, they hadn't caught up with us yet. After all, one must keep trying, eh? However hopeless the situation. Just so long as we were not caught out here in these infinite white fields by gulag thugs in cars busily thrashing the ground with the tire chains that would soon encircle our bleeding ankles. Assuming, of course, that we didn't freeze to death first, or I didn't mercifully obviate George, and contentedly mutilate his body.

I mean, Christ, why did I keep on trying? When you got right down to it, I had as much chance of surviving now, as of sampling a church supper in Nova Scotia tomorrow. What chance now of catching sight of the hugger-mugger hangar in the growing gloom, the furtive dark, and even if we did, it was a military installation, surreptitiously engaged, according to *him* over there, in a crafty operation against the

West — so much for Allied solidarity, eh? Even if we found it, it would be as strongly guarded as Stalin with his personal bodyguard, which was said to number 202 choice troops, the number of the devil.

But: "You'll think of something," George said encouragingly. "You did it once before, when you stole that German plane in the First World War. That's what gave me the idea, actually."

"Oh, belt up."

"You remember? When the pilot landed to claim you as a prisoner of war, but you fooled him, didn't you, Bartalamyeh. You jumped in and flew it back to your own lines. Don't you remember? When you –"

"Just shut up, George. Please."

"You told me all about it one day in Ottawa. You remember? It was one of the times in the last war when you became famous. It was when —"

"It only succeeded because the Jerry pilot climbed out of his machine for a few seconds! Because he — Oh, forget it!"

After a moment, George put a hand on my shoulder and squeezed it. "I know we will get there, Bartalamyeh," he said simply. "I believe in you."

"Oh, Gawd ...."

We trudged on, again in silence, except for the crunch of inadequate footgear in the snow. On and on we lurched along the darkening, snow-ploughed lane. And just as that fool George Garanine had promised, upon reaching the top of a slight rise in the ground, the hangar appeared, quite discernible despite the mist. It stood next to another building, just a few hundred paces beyond a perimeter fence.

"Good Lord," quoth I.

"See?" said George with a smirk like Woolworth's glue. "Told you so."

Naturally, the scenery came complete with a checkpoint at the bottom of the slight slope of the road. It comprised a guard house overlooking a red and white guard pole which was lowered across the road, and a floodlight mounted on a pole, the ensemble interrupting furlongs of neglected though unscaleable fencing.

As far as we could see in the mist, there was plenty of space in front of the hangar, but nothing to fill it with. By now it was well past six p.m., but there was no sign of an aircraft. Of course, that would have been too much to expect. George couldn't possibly have got that right, too.

Although we were not likely to be observed in the mist and under a darkening sky, we crouched down to study the terrain. At first there was little air activity, no sound or discernible movement even over on the busy side of the airport. But after a while, an aircraft was heard, droning softly in the distance. Suddenly it appeared, coming in from the far side of the field, lights twinkling at its wingtips. The poorly synchronized splutter of its engines hardly registered on the ear before the pilot throttled back. Its already indistinct outline disappeared behind a snowbank that was guarding the runway.

Could it be coming this way, to the clandestine hangar? It reappeared a mile closer. Now the pilot was increasing power for travel over the snow-packed runway. But after two right turns he headed toward the main terminal, somewhere on the far side of the field.

We flicked our eyes to the spot where our road entered the airfield. There was little activity down there; despite which, my heart put on revs. The authorities were bound to have sent out a general alert by now, surely, after I had failed to co-operate properly by falling down dead; yet there was no indication that this post, at least, was on the lookout for a decadent Western formalist. Which was the best news yet, in a day not noted for items of good cheer.

We waited, hunched down and shivering, until the sky grew quite dark. After a whispered consultation we crept forward through the mist for a closer look at whatever wasn't happening along there. We were about a hundred feet from the back of the guard house before the sound of creaking woodwork froze us. For a moment we looked like a pair of Quasimodos, misshapen by fright, before we sank with perfect synchronization behind the nearest heap of snow.

The door of the splintery guard house was opening. One of the sentries — there were bound to be at least two of them, I reckoned — was emerging, clutching his coat tighter about his throat.

Now he was looking around. Now he was attempting to increase his height, the vain fellow, by adjusting his extra-large fur cap, size ninety-nine and a half. The cap didn't seem to sit too happily on his noggin. He kept pushing it from one position to another without evident satisfaction.

Lights blazed. All of a sudden. Oh, God, we'd been seen — caught, crouching in the snow as if doing our number twos.

My heart rate increased. Instinctively I picked up a two-foot stanchion left over from a recent repair to the perimeter fence. Now I was ready to give my all for King and Country, though I was still not entirely certain which country to give my all for. Anyway, I was not going into captivity, Russian style, that was for sure.

Luckily, sacrifice was not required. Not right away, anyway. The lights — two shielded bulbs for the convenience of the sentries, and the one high up on the pole that illuminated a small area all around the guard post — had not quite reached as far as our respective blue and brown uniforms. And the sentry hadn't looked around fast enough to catch us. In fact, now he was re-entering his quarters. He'd had enough of all the open air, now faintly tainted with a drift of gasoline from the recently landed plane.

Still agitated, I continued to swish the metal bar nervously as I studied the building next to the hangar. It was tantalizingly close to the perimeter fence: a bunkhouse, perhaps, accommodation for a few men. As with the hangar, which looked unused rather than the starting point for some clandestine operation, it was blacked-out.

"Do you think we are too late — the aeroplane has left?" George asked, but my thoughts were too busy competing with the darkening sky to permit a reply.

We waited for something to happen. Nothing did, except that after a while, both guards reappeared outside their hut. They seemed to be watching out for something, looking carefully up the road, as if expecting traffic. The other guard, incidentally, was having no difficulty whatsoever with his hat.

After having no difficulty with his hat for several minutes, he and his pal went back inside, presumably to resume their watch on the road through the largish window that faced the pole and the entrance. No chance of sneaking past, then. The striped guard pole must be under constant observation.

Meanwhile the misty sky was going down fast on dimmer. Long past seven o'clock. Almost dark everywhere, except in the bright white circle around the guard post.

I threw away the stanchion, but George picked it up, and swung it to see if it would make a satisfying whooosh. After that, we kept watch, hoping for something more interesting to happen: an invasion from Mars, perhaps, a few fairies to appear and play ball with an assortment of sugar plums, a flamethrower to scorch over the snow and provide us with a few badly needed calories of heat. No such luck. Over on the right, way beyond the fence, two or three chaps could be heard clamouring outside their quarters in the building next to the hangar. They were talking loudly, and laughing. One of them sounded as if he were being sick.

Somebody pointed a flashlight. It illuminated another somebody who was taking a leak. He seemed to be attempting to create a nice design in the snow. Then they all went back inside. Still nothing whatsoever was happening near the hangar.

Over the next half hour I did a quick shufti along the fence. By eight o'clock I had confirmed that it was unscaleable.

"That's that, then," I said when I returned, feeling colder than ever, with a stomach that had been remoulded in lead.

"They said there was a flight every week," George muttered.

"M'm."

"Quite routine, even if it was ... Uh ... What word am I thinking of?" George said, his voice juddering with cold.

"We might as well turn back, George, old bean," I said leadenly, to keep my stomach company. "No point freezing out here."

"There must be way."

"Not without shooting our way in."

"I couldn't do that, Bartalamyeh," George said. "I could never do that. In my whole life I have never hurt a soul."

"And you a NKVD man?"

"I was just a clerk, Bartalamyeh. When they found out that I was no good, they gave me the job of delivering lectures to the men on dialectical materialism."

Though the temperature had risen since the previous day, we were likely to freeze to death if we stayed in the open for much longer. Clutching the greatcoat closer to my throat, I said, "George, let's be thoroughly absurd for a moment and assume there actually is an aircraft in that hangar."

"There must be. Because it takes off from here every Sunday," George said, his bright blue eyes weeping in the cold.

"Yes, so you said. So I guess they're just singing 'Yo Heave Ho' in there, right? Or practising their Cossack dancing." George opened his mouth to protest, but I ploughed on. "Anyway, let's say you're right. The question is how are we to get in there to find out? Is there any way to get past that guard post? Say by going round it, from the main airport building?"

"Oh, no, Bartalamyeh. You must think of something else. You know very well that they are always on the lookout for people who are not behaving properly, like trespassing, or committing rape. Besides, there is the mist. If we did not freeze to death, we would get lost out there."

I gazed into a darkness surrounded by bright lights on a striped pole and wraiths of mist. I was sure he was right; we would probably stand little chance of getting onto the airfield from anywhere else, or crossing it unobserved. However, I did not wish to be sensible, especially with George; so, adopting a mulish expression, I argued.

To make things even worse, George responded quite reasonably, though his common sense ended as usual with several contradictions. "You would die of exhaustion, out there, Bartalamyeh," he said. "Of course, as a Canadian, you are used to even worse conditions than these. Still, it is not such a bad idea, when you consider what the Leader has in store for you if you fail to die of cold. Of course, Stalin would much prefer to see you shot, bludgeoned, poisoned, disembowelled, or looked after in hospital."

"Looked after in hospital?"

"You know, in our special hospitals, where they give you all sorts of medicines to protect you from harmful, anti-social thoughts, or any thoughts at all."

"I don't wish to hear any more about that, George, if you don't mind."

He attempted to laugh into the charcoal mist, but his frozen features refused to accommodate him. "But I am sure you will think of some other way to help us escape, dear Bartalamyeh, when you have finally pulled yourself together."

I was just about to turn him to stone, Gorgonwise, when a suddenly flurry of activity attracted my attention.

"Look! Look!" I hissed.

Beyond the unkempt but breachless fence, an aircraft, momentarily illuminated by lights from the hangar, was being trundled onto its hardstanding.

"Good Lord, George, you were right," I faltered. "There really was an aeroplane in there ..."

"See? Did I not tell you?" he said excitedly, "I told you there was a plane!"

We were able to see the aircraft quite clearly, because of the light illegally flooding from the hangar. Most of the illumination was switched off when the figures around the aircraft realized they were defying the blackout. Still, it took them a good two minutes to do something about it, affording us a misty view of the activity.

One or two of the aircraft pushers and shovers were staggering. Not too much — maybe just a few ounces of vodka worth. But at least, now we knew what they'd been doing in there: boozing, and possibly getting the machine ready at the same time.

Not that the Ivans were making it any easier for us. The situation had not improved in the slightest. Short of shooting our way in, we were not likely to get past that striped pole over the road. Anyway, I had no weapon and, typically, George had packed his Soviet issue revolver at the bottom of his kit bag just when he might need it most.

The appearance of the aircraft had further unsettled George. "You are not trying hard enough, Bartalamyeh Fyodorevitch," he hissed into the darkness. Actually the dark was soupily glowing, now that a Slav moon was peeping over the horizon. "You are supposed to be so clever, why have you not thought of anything yet? After all, consider what I have done for you. I have saved your life. I could easily have curried favour with the authorities, you know, by pushing you off the scaffolding, as arranged. Comrade Addourahman Soultanov will be very displeased with me," he muttered agitatedly, thumping his boots together to dislodge cakes of snow.

I stared back at him in a way that made him more unsettled than ever. "As we say in Russia," he continued agitatedly, "*A citizen has a good chance of being listened to by an apparatchik on crutches.*"

I was becoming so agitated myself by then, that I actually took a moment to think about his Russian proverb, and even repeated it in my mind, before snorting, and getting ready to kick him in the coccyx.

Before I could do so he said, "It is Clemence, isn't it?"

"What?"

"It is to do with Clemence," he said, teeth chattering like castanets.

"What's to do with Clemence?" I asked, quite deflated with flummox. "What the hell are you talking about now?"

"The way you are being so angry with me."

"I'm not angry with you."

"Yes, you are. You have been angry from the moment we met."

"I'm not in the least angry with you," I spoke, ever so calmly into the mist-flavoured moonlight. "Disgusted, perhaps, scornful as usual, contemptuous, derisive, disdainful, perhaps. And maybe just a shade reproachful, mocking, and so forth, fifth, and sixth. But angry? Angry, George? Well, perhaps that, too."

"What a vocabulary you have, Bartalamyeh," said George, his admiration temporarily overcoming his agitation.

"I know. And I haven't even used my favourite word yet — obviate. Which I sure feel like applying to you at this moment. Godamn it, George —"

"You love Clemence, don't you, Bartalamyeh," he said gently. "That is why you are so angry with me."

"Oh, for God's sake."

"And you want her for yourself."

"I ... I ..."

"But there is no need to feel guilty," he went on. "As for myself, I love her, I have never stopped loving her, even in the camps ...." He considered his words for a moment, apparently found them suitable, and nodded. "Yes, even in the camps, I thought of her with all my heart."

At which point he covered my mitt with his own and squeezed gently, causing the ice on it to crackle. "But if she wants you, my dearest comrade, and I am sure she does, I will gladly give her up, I will step aside ...." He swallowed, and looked away.

"Provided I can get you out of here," I put in sourly. After which it was my turn to look away, with, in my case, a different sort of emotion, namely faint shame.

Well, at least it had warmed me up. My face was now quite comfortably warm.

"It is not only that, Bartalamyeh," said George. "It is because I love you, even when you are most difficult."

"Me? Difficult?"

"I am just trying to say —"

"Yes, yes," I snorted "Anyway, what are we going to do?" I added wildly, hoping that a brilliant idea might occur to George. It certainly wouldn't come from me, now that my brain matched my stomach.

"Clandestine," George said suddenly.

"What?"

"It is that word I was trying to think of."

We stood there like children's snowmen for what seemed like a couple of decades, though I was almost certain that it was only a day or two before we faced up to it — or at least I did. Unless we started moving, if only backwards, we were in danger of freezing to death.

There was nothing more we could do, now — not that we'd accomplished anything anyway. The point was, there was no escape. We were hundreds of miles from civilization as we knew it — or at least as I knew it. The pain had been in vain. We were too chilled even to think straight, especially me in my inadequate Western uniform and stupid blue greatcoat. Even straightening up physically was almost beyond me.

My only consolation was that freezing to death was not a bad alternative to being despatched by Generalissimo Stalin.

Unless ...

Unless I could get him to listen to reason.

Yes! Right! Surely Uncle Joe would think twice about obviating someone as important as me. Anyway, he wasn't all that much of an ogre, was he? Course not. Old Stalin was quite a civilized sort of chap, right? To the West he was a great hero. And anyway, he wouldn't dare. After all, I was really well-known, now. Mind you, I'd been famous in the past, and it hadn't lasted much beyond a quarter of an hour. All the same, I'd never been as well-known as I was now. Sure I was good for twenty-nine minutes? After all, let's face it again — he wouldn't dare. Not right away, anyway. I mean. Look how long it had taken him to obviate old Trotsky. Maybe I had years to live.

"We should have gone to the Embassy while we had a chance," I muttered.

"Your embassy? I told you, Bartalamyeh, they would seize me if I tried to enter. And they would find some way to stop you, my dear, there is no doubt about that."

I felt really annoyed at him for suddenly being so sensible. "Maybe we should just give ourselves up," I said sullenly.

"What?"

"At the guard post." I tried to point to it, in case he'd forgotten where it was, but my arm was too feeble. "They've probably got a nice fire in there."

"Are you mad, Bartalamyeh?" he whispered.

"Well, we can't stop here," I snorted though a pair of iron lips. "Or we'll freeze to death." And with frozen face suddenly overcome with mulish, not to say vicious determination, I creaked round 180 degrees, and started to retreat back up the road, with George plucking ineffectively at my sleeve.

"Can you not think of anything, Bartalamyeh?" he pleaded. He was beginning to sound a bit disenchanted with me.

More enraged than ever at my own helplessness, I spoke as nastily, cuttingly, and contemptuously as I could manage. "In case you hadn't noticed, Prince Myshkin," I said, knowing he would recognize the reference to Dostoievsky's feeble, useless, epileptic idiot, "the guards down there have been on a special lookout for hours on end — for us!" Which was undoubtedly true. Over the past hour alone and on at least three occasions, one or both of the guards had emerged from their hut to gaze up the road, quite plainly watching out for two escaped enemies of the people.

Still in the same filthy, consuming, comforting rage, I wrenched free from his hesitant fingertips, and started up the slight rise in the road but, affected by cold and fatigue, I lurched and started to lose my balance; naturally, in attempting to stabilize me, George made it worse. We both ended up tottering toward the nearest snow bank.

Which instability saved us from being run over by a fast-moving vehicle, since we didn't hear it until it was almost upon us.

Perhaps it was fatigue rather than ear wax, or cerumen impaction, as we medical men might have called it on particularly pompous occasions, that affected our hearing. After all, the huge car was roaring angrily enough, as it breasted the rise and bore down on us with its electric, slitty eyes.

The driver, travelling at urgent speed over the shiny, snowpacked surface, saw us only as he came over the rise. He wrenched so sharply at the wheel that the vehicle slid wildly, but luckily in such a way as to swing the huge automobile away from us at the right angle. Shooting past our own slithering figures as we attempted to remain upright, it continued along the road for another few feet, sliding sideways, before crunching heavily into the piled snow at the side of the road. Both passengers were flung forward and then back again, quite violently.

If there was one person in this world who could act fast in an emergency, it was me — except when hiding from a woman, a brass-hat, a senior politician, or a canvasser for a good cause. As the front seat occupants sagged or groaned, and the passenger in the back seat enriched my Russian vocabulary with several swear words, my first thought was to make myself scarce. This amounted to little more than a slight twitch to starboard. I was too chilled to dive for cover. George, however, more than made up for my inactivity. The bloody fool went over to help, with concern scrawled like graffiti all over his Hollywood face.

The army chauffeur appeared to have been knocked out. I suspected that he would wake up in time with two black eyes, a loose tooth, and a stiff neck. The chap beside him seemed much the worse for wear. He was mumbling in an incoherent way. However, the one in the back seat was in much better shape, obviously. It was a woman, and in response to George's solicitous enquiries as to whether she was all right, she replied in a rough and furious voice that of course she was not all right. She had been thrown about as if in a concrete mixer. And it was his fault, she shouted, pointing at George. It was plainly his fault for getting in the way. They had an urgent appointment at the airfield, she bellowed, thrashing out of the back seat. And now look what he'd done, him and the stupid driver between them. They would be late. They had already been delayed for more than two hours because of the drunkenness of this fellow, she bellowed, viciously prodding the lolling young man in the leather coat, who was slumped against the driver as if they were two old pals together.

She didn't seem to care that the boy was barely conscious. In fact, a moment later she was trying to shake him awake, and quite roughly, too.

When George leaned over to help the chap, she turned on him as well. "Never mind him," she shouted, and went on to repeat what she'd just said, that they had to get to the aerodrome, not waste time reviving the one who had got them into this difficulty in the first place.

Though the moon was half-drowned in the mist by now, its light, plus the glow from the checkpoint at the bottom of the slope, showed the lady to be amplifying a fine fur coat, which she now wrenched open, in order, I think, to give her muscles something to do — like hitting poor, defenceless, frozen army officers like George. Under the coat a plain army uniform with one medal ribbon appeared. It was otherwise an unadorned green or perhaps something darker. It was also without epaulettes, and had been cut as well as anything could be tailored in the USSR, despite the bulkiness of her body.

Despite the modesty of her attire, probably inspired by the Great Leader, I assumed from her authoritative and hectoring manner that she was somebody with clout, an authority capable of overriding that of many a senior officer; in other words, a commissar type, as I whispered warningly to George.

He seemed to know better. "GRU," he whispered back. Army intelligence.

As for the front seat passenger, he was wearing a leather coat that made me think aircrew. He had a good-looking but inexperienced sort of face. Even his fair hair was inexperienced, being rather long, and quite curly, in defiance of Article 406A of Tsar's Regulations as amended 011/11/1917.

He had lost his cap and he was holding his head, groaning a bit. Seeing no possibility of fleeing, I drew closer, to note a trickle of blood down his forehead. It didn't look too bad, though I thought he looked a bit concussed, until I realized that like so many Russian chaps I'd seen this day, he was more than a little the worse for wear, booze-wise. I hoped to God he wasn't flying, if he was aircrew.

While the awful woman was raving on about being late for something or other, George was trying to question the young man in a surreptitious sort of way. Feigning interest in the concussion, he was actually asking such questions as, what did the young man do for a living in the army, and where was he bound. Unfortunately, after a good thump on the noggin, the young officer was not responding very well to all these busybody questions. All he wanted to do was put his head down and go to sleep.

No, it was not a desire for sleep. He was pawing around, trying to find his fur-trimmed leather hat, but all he succeeded in doing was to smudge the trickle of blood all over his forehead. The blood looked black in the diffuse light, but I couldn't discern much damage to his scalp.

George kept talking to him, quite sensibly for once, despite being constantly interrupted by the scornful woman. She had started to snap at George most of all, apparently deciding that he would be a pushover. The more respectful he sounded, the more she went after him, in tones stropped on her leather tongue. She was telling him more and more forcefully with every passing minute that there was nothing wrong with the boy except that he'd had too much to drink. *And that he was supposed to be flying a plane.*

A crack on the head wasn't going to do him any harm, she maintained, but it would badly interfere with her plans.

By now she was out of the car, and establishing that she was even shorter than her temper. She was almost as wide as she was tall, in fact — five feet and a bit of ferocity. I felt sure she was on leave from running a few thousand square miles of gulag territory.

Christ, was she ever in a temper. Even George was beginning to look a trifle displeased with her. Especially when she slapped the young pilot in the front seat because he had started to groan again.

I was following the altercation with difficulty. I could understand George, but little of the woman's coarse speech, which didn't sound much like the upper class pronunciation that George had learned from his private tutors and passed on to me, back there in 1919. However, I understood enough to appreciate that she was not the sort of person I should tangle with.

To my surprise, the reverse was true with George. When she punched his shoulder with her huge, horrid hand and told him to straighten up and take over the driving, it turned out that he was the one who should not have been tangled with.

Over the past few hours, George, still believing in ultimate escape, had become much more forthright, even authoritative. After she had finished belabouring him with her bellowing voice, he tried one more time to convince her that the young pilot, who had apparently gotten side-tracked into a boozy party to celebrate Spring and the Red Army's final onslaught on Berlin, was in no fit state to fly. He even dared to tell her that she had no right to treat the boy in this fashion.

"He is hurt. You are making him even more confused," he said.

To which the woman's response was to bellow louder than ever. Near the end, she actually drew back her fist and treated George to an uppercut. It would have been a straight left, except that she was several inches too short, so that the blow had to be reoriented in a way suggesting that she was delivering a particularly aggressive communist salute.

After which she suddenly turned on me, and I gathered she said something like, "And after the pilot is arrested for dereliction of duty, there is the matter of the emergency news bulletin about a foul Hun spy in an Allied uniform," in so loud a voice that I feared it alone would bring the rest of the barrack soldiers running, the better to hear her suspicions that she had found a beastly Jerry spy.

Luckily, I was distracted from dying of fright. George had apparently decided that his ten years in the gulag had been quite enough to be going on with, thank you. Buoyed by his foolish belief that he was close to breaking free from the USSR, and realizing that he had had enough of bowing, scraping, saluting, or kissing the authoritarian ass, he hit the bitch on the head with the stanchion.

In what I believe was his first ever outbreak of temper, he bonked her on the boko hard enough that even her stout fur cap with the ear flaps was not proof against the blow. The lady toppled like a hairy, oversized target in a coconut shy.

Simultaneously, the young officer, who should have flown out at 1800 hours, leaned out of the great plutocratic Russian vehicle, which was a copy, I think, of the American Packard of the late 'thirties, and was sick on its lovely clean running board. "That's better," he said, leaning back blearily on the imitation-leather front seat, leaving the door open, and he immediately went back to sleep.

After George and I had surveyed the collection of bodies in silence for a while, I stirred, still quivering as if I was the one who'd been clobbered.

I was also the first to speak up. "Now you've done it," I said.

George took another few moments to think about it. He looked remarkably calm, considering he had clubbed someone who was probably quite high up in the hierarchy, and was a defenceless woman to boot — well, perhaps not entirely defenceless, given those whacking great fists of hers, which had already reduced George's face to a far less beauteous state than hitherto.

When he finally answered, it was in tones quite a bit more resolute than his previous haverings.

"This is a spot of good fortune, Bartalamyeh," he said.

"Eh?"

"Quick, take off her clothes."

"What?"

"Put on her uniform. I know these people. Commissars are not required to show anything other than their GRU passes. We can use hers."

I thought about it, at far less than my usual lightning speed. "I'm not taking off her clothes," I said in a shaking voice.

"Bartalamyeh," hissed he, urgently. "They will not let you through, otherwise. It is the only way."

"I don't care. I'm not touching her."

"You must."

"No."

"Bartalamyeh —!"

"Won't. Anyway, they wouldn't fit. She's several feet shorter than me, and yards wider. It's a ridiculous idea."

"It is only way to get us through," George said, suddenly sounding so commanding that I turned a face toward him that was almost as shocked at his decisiveness as inflamed with embarrassment at the very idea of having to remove even so much as the lady's ear-flaps.

"Come on," he said, hauling the woman onto the car's running board with a surprising surge of strength. Holding her upright with one knee, he started to wrench at her fur coat, first off one shoulder, and then the other.

I continued to protest, but George had taken command, so suffused was he with a power moulded from desperation mixed with urgency. I wasn't aware at that moment that the urgency would provide him, if all went well, with permanent protection from Comrade Stalin.

Hating every second of it, and muttering vicious protests, I found myself going along with the stupidest, most hopeless, most ridiculous scheme that even a Wodehouse would have rejected in a trice. I mean, Christ. It was bad enough helping him to divest the woman of her outer garments and provide the shrinking eye with a view of skin that was like something shrugged out of by a heartily relieved python — but the odour! Even in the icy air she stank to the heavens of sweat, borscht, Bessarabian brandy, shit-crackling fibres, and drifts and whiffs of Kremlin debauchery, or at the very least an effluvium from the depths of Muscovite squalor.

Naturally the blasted garments didn't begin to fit me properly. The trousers barely reached to kneecap level, and the waist would have suited an entire chorus line. As for the tunic, it bulged in the chest region to an extent that could have supplied the foundations for a new skyscraper — stop. Enough. I cannot bring myself to dwell on the garments for one moment longer. Good God, even the fur coat — no, stop, I say. I mean it, now. No more.

In the end I solved the difference in scale by leaving my uniform on, and dragging her garments over the top, but I drew the line at unsnapping her garters and putting them on as well, complete with stockings. Instead, I rolled my blue trousers above my knees and secured them with the elastic from her voluminous knickers. The astonishing thing was that we actually got away with all the flam-paradiddle, though not before I was forced to redress the ghastly woman in a sweater and one or two other items from my valise, so that she wouldn't recover consciousness to discover that she had died of cold. Oh, God. Dressing her was almost as dreadful as the previous unteasing strip. I had to practically tread all over her bosoms to get them and other fatty deposits to stay put under the air force wool.

Well, at least she wasn't getting any of my glorious rows of wings, rings, ribbons, wound stripes, stars, and garters. Many of the gongs would have been impossible to replace, as they had been awarded by countries that no longer existed, or by regimes that had been overthrown.

Meanwhile, George was busy making the driver of the pseudo-Packard comfortable on the floor under a blanket, after which we both heaved the woman into the trunk, with my nice sweater and other RAF items getting all crunched up and rendered permanently malodorous where I'd had to force her adipose tissue into places where limbs, bulges, and projections were never meant to go.

The second most important thing I had to worry about came when we drew up at the gate. Could even the most doltish guard be taken in by the woman's warrant card and her laisser-passer when they were proffered by G. Garanine, on behalf of someone who looked like a degenerate from a Roman orgy?

I owed much to George. I hoped I would remember that, when the time came for me to betray him with Clemence. He handled it all brilliantly, by a mixture of bored indifference to everyone except the unspeaking if not unspeakable personage sitting alone in the back seat of the car, who was busily reforming his face in the hope of matching it up with the GRU warrant; though naturally, I would never admit that my superior and aristocratic visage might bear the slightest resemblance to the woman's mug, which was quite hateful in its brutal intolerance. And that's enough words for one sentence.

We made it mainly because we were more than expected. We were damned late, and it was urgent that we be passed through without further delay. Still, the guards seemed a trifle dubious about something; incredibly, not so much about the strange figure in the back seat of the big posh car, who seemed to be made up mostly from folds of flesh and uniform, as about the young chap who was supposed to be flying the aircraft whose engine had been kept warmed up and ready to go. This was where George again demonstrated a mental vigour that I never knew he possessed. Leaning over from his position behind the wheel of the car, and talking impatiently and in a long-suffering fashion to both the guards and the barely-conscious aviator, he fished through the latter's pockets and brought forth the appropriate paperwork. The men at the gate, still overawed by or suffering from a fear of the GRU, accepted the credentials and some other genuine paperwork on behalf of the far from genuine stiff on the back seat, but nevertheless continued to look askance at the lolling pilot. I watched one of the guards wrench his eyes off the high-flying low flyer to gape at the aircraft waiting a hundred years away on the white hardstanding, then back to the young feller-me-lad who was supposed to fly it but who was mumbling incoherently from shock and vodka. A smidgeon of doubt definitely crossed the guards' faces at this point. You could read the result on one of the faces quite easily. He was asking himself if the officer was in quite the right shape for flying even into a temper, let alone for a journey of many versts. Surely not; but then, of course, these fly-boys seemed to be able to get away with anything nowadays, even being spifflicated.

Let us return to the important one in the back seat of the tremendously important car. She was in danger of vanishing so deeply into the mounds of clothing that surely she might never be found again. The slightest twitch was causing her to sink ever deeper into the malodorous garments. Luckily there had been no call for her to stir. You could hardly expect an agent with such important credentials to be ordered out of the car, as was the custom. So for the time being, at least, they had not yet discovered that the important man in there was an important woman — or rather, that the woman in there in the disjunctive state wasn't, but that in fact she, or rather, he, was a ....

I was interrupted by another frightful moment, when one of the guards finally dared to ask what seemed to be a challenging question of lordly Captain Garanine of the NKVD, Department Z (Ultimatums Division). The guard's query was delivered in an accent that I was in no condition to fathom, but George somehow handled it, though without entirely allaying the guard's suspicions. I tried not to stare at George in wonder. Somehow he had become completely transformed from the kind, decent, honest, loveable gentleman I used to know and for whom I felt such affection, when I was not hating him. Now he had become this seemingly unassailable prince — who remained calm and authoritative, somehow, even when we heard a thumping sound from the trunk of the car.

The commissar-type woman was trying to get out.

HOPEFUL AS EVER

AS THE COMMISSAR-TYPE BINT thumped feebly from inside the trunk of the Russian car, I decided to stop breathing.

My life flashed before me. For some reason it started in 1916, with the shooting of a darting starling. The Ottawa river. The flick of memory included even the remembered guilt, suppressed because it was too late to halt the instinctive movement of sports rifle to right shoulder. But the life review quickly ended only a millionth of a second later with me being shot somewhere beneath the surface of Dzerzhinsky Square.

God, it was good, being dead. No further need to worry about what was to happen next. No more cold fear, or concern about money – – I'd come back from India a rich man, with a bountiful wife, bounteous optimism. But the glorious lucre had disappeared — crash of '29 — though happiness managed to survive, right up to the Spanish Civil War, when disgust over the behaviour of the West ensured that the ghastly slaughters of World War One would remain a permanent debit, and spirit would be mangled as effectively as the political poltroonery did for my darling Sigridur.

Until I realized I wasn't dead, damn it. Just done for. The feeling that I could not possibly escape, not again, not this time, returned, stranded by absconding hope. How could George, George who'd suffered infinitely worse than me for ten whole years in camps that were almost as dreadful as the German ones that were now being properly revealed, how could he be so suffused with the certainty that we would get through? Where did this ridiculous strength spring from, after the experience he'd been through? We were facing impossible odds from the Soviets, defying a million souls stained by Comrade Marx, and there was the maniacal vengeance of Stalin still to come.

So if things were so hopeless, why had my heart given a little hop, skip, and jump? Just because the thumping sound in the posh trunk was being obscured by the changing of the guard?

A non-commissioned type, in the inevitable cap that made him look like a beaten-up bunny, was coming across the snow with another two members of his bullied estate. They had been approaching so silently that already they were just a few yards away. Obviously intent on approaching us without warning.

Unless it was just the effect of the snow, which was soft and slippering enough that one of the new guards was having difficulty keeping his balance. He even hiccupped, once, to be rewarded by a cuff from his NCO.

Now they were only five yards away. They had been warned that a spy was on the loose, that was it. We were done for. Four yards, now, and then they would have us. The guards at the gate were turning towards the new arrivals. They were coming to attention, though casually enough. Probably because of the slidey surface. Their faces brightened somewhat. Prospect of obtaining additional help in beating us up.

Two yards. The new arrivals crunching to a halt. Surely it couldn't be just the changing of the guard after a duty roster of six snaffled hours? And anyway, there was still the thumping on the trunk lid, and George suddenly discovering a frog in his throat. He was coughing like a diseased lion.

The newly-arrived NCO was speaking through the hum in my ears. For some reason he was punching one of the men, shouting at him. Simultaneously one of the original guards was turning on George. Ah, yes, this would be the clobbering move, before they dragged us away for good, for evil. Another customary beating before being safely imprisoned, for the time being, below Dzerzhinsky Square.

George was talking, the second he'd finished coughing. He was even holding out his hand rather impatiently, wiggling a set of four fingers. A demand for something. Some of the papers he had handed over. And he was actually receiving them. He was getting them back, minus the documents that were meant to be surrendered. He was still talking. He had been coughing and talking nonstop from the moment the lady started the flam-paradiddle on the car trunk lid.

He was actually turning away, George was, turning back to the car. He was adjusting the young pilot, as if he were a dummy — helping him to sit up a little straighter in the front seat. Now the still handsome, though careworn, gulag-battered captain — he hadn't earned much promotion since 1920, eh? — was walking around to the driver's door, still behaving impatiently, as if he felt that they had held him up quite long enough, even for a Russian bureaucracy. He was in the car. Now he was reviving the motor. It had not been turned off since we arrived. The motor had been beating unsteadily. Now it was roaring. George was pressing the accelerator too hard as he clunked into gear.

The wheels skidded wildly for a moment, before settling down, and the car moved off, quite circumspectly, now.

The red and white striped pole had actually been raised. It was up, up and away.

The car was crunching, still quite casually, over the snow. I started to believe in George Garanine all over again. The Packard-type was following a crude, cleared stretch of ground. In no time at all, or too much of it, it was onto the hardstanding beyond the guard barracks. And then it stopped opposite the aircraft waiting under the fuzzy moon.

I never did remember exactly what happened between the leaving of the gloriously raised barrier and the wait beside the aircraft. There was no memory at all of my shaky climb from the car onto the hard-standing, and the subsequent wait for George to finish chatting in a dignified but nicely democratic fashion to the two or three mechanics who had emerged from their shelter inside the hangar the moment we drew up near the Lavochkin fighter, a single-engined two-seater laden with drop tanks. Well, perhaps a smudge of memory, of me climbing, terribly stiffly, out of the car. I must have removed the lady commissar's fur coat for some reason, perhaps because it was such a poor fit. Luckily I didn't leave it behind. It was colder than ever, by now.

Later, trying to connect the dots of memory into a comprehensible whole, I felt that one of the original men on the gate had not been at all eager to let us through. Had he heard the noise from the trunk of the car? No, said George. He thought the sound was too feeble, and that it had grown weaker.

Reminded about the cooped-up commissar, George thought he had better check on the lady while the mechanics were busy elsewhere. He peeked in. The trunk may have been reasonably well insulated. The woman had lost consciousness. Concerned, he left the trunk a few millimetres open, to make sure she didn't suffocate. "I couldn't let that to happen," he said.

Again, later, I could only assume that the gate guards had been distracted by the relief, or that George's impatient chatter had somehow degraded their curiosity, even about the strange-looking VIP in the back of the car, the one in the fur coat which was so ample that a couple of smugglers could have hidden in each of its hairy arms.

I was still in a daze when I finally climbed over the awkward coaming and into the pilot's seat, to be followed a lot more elegantly by our Captain Garanine. Though addressed by them more than once, I was careful not to answer the ground staff. I must have seemed very stand-offish. What the hell had he to be stand-offish about, eh, comrades — him looking like the carcass of a reindeer eaten away by rats. Some Kremlin bigwig, eh, comrades, him and his great blank mug.

Now I was looking over the assortment of economy dials and switches, still trying to decide between a haze and a daze. There was no urgency whatsoever in my actions as I wiggled things and tried to make sense of the crude layout of instruments. I suppose that even now, on the very threshold of liberty, I was convinced it was a trick, the equivalent of the reassuring walk down there in the Lubianka just before they shoot you in the back of the head. It just wasn't possible to escape, that's all there was to it. Twenty years ago, even in the chaos of the Revolution, it had taken me months, through battlefields, privations, and outlaw bands, to reach safety. And all I had now was George's mad confidence, his utter certainty, that we were somehow already free.

One of the mechanics was shouting up at the open canopy. "They are asking if you want something," George whispered, from behind. "A starter, whatever that is?"

"What?"

"To start the engine, they say?"

Despite my dreamlike state, I must have already taken in at least a few small details of the Lavochkin. I suppose it helped that I'd read an article on Russian aircraft, one idle day in the RAF library, and I even remembered a little of the information about the machine with the big, bulbous radial that looked not unlike a Hawker Tempest, or rather, a Focke Wulf — the type that had almost got me last year and made me wish that I had given up combat flying while I still had a reasonably tight sphincter.

I must even have noticed the telltale aperture in the big, fat airscrew hub. This was surely for a Hucks-type starter. "Yes. Tell them to connect it," I said, so huskily that I had to repeat the words.

At least it encouraged me to concentrate a little better on understanding the instruments, of which there was no great variety. Amazingly, no artificial horizon was in view, the compass was pretty rudimentary, and the gunsight was a wide lens rather than the usual transparent plate, but I was not prepared to shoot anybody. After all, the Russians had done more than anybody to defeat the fascists, even if their own ruby, damask, or vermilion versions of fascism were now certain to prevail, God help us.

Unfortunately, scanning the instruments failed to wake me up properly. I needed a good slap in the face, but George was not the sort of person to administer it, not normally, anyway. So I continued to absorb meagre amounts of information through a pair of glass eyes. The most important parts of the gen were in kilos, metres, and kilometres.

Lemmee see, you had to divide something into metres in order to produce miles per hour and poods, right? No, wait — poods were large quantities of something in Russian, weren't they? Well, anyway, I'd find out what everything meant when the time came to crash on take-off.

Hullo? Was I actually starting to believe in taking-off?

Good Lord, I was getting quite serious about it. I was really starting to believe. I was half-converted. Our father which art in galleries, hallowed by thy nemesis.

Here was a clock in the cockpit. Last thing I'd have expected in a Russian aircraft was a clock, but was it actually working? What's this? Twenty-one something hours? Was that all it was?

Manifold pressure gauge. Pitot-head heating. This one must be propeller pitch. But what's this lever? Don't know. And this one? Ditto. Ah. Fuel. I knew that one, all right. And it was full.

"You don't think we should leave, Bandushka?" enquired George, ever so softly into my port lug. Yes, I knew what that was for. For hearing. And this must be a compass deviation card? Yes, I would certainly need that, assuming ....

At least the prop was ready to turn. I seem to have called out "Switch off," with George, shouting through the open canopy, translating it, and whispering at me about my not calling out in English, if that was all right with me.

I seemed to be doing everything automatic pilot-wise. A Heath Robinson device in front of the aircraft was straining and turning the propeller. In seconds the engine was firing. Though it was a while since they'd given up keeping it warm, the motor started straight away, and they were hauling the ugly apparatus aside.

In this dreamy state of mine, or was it somebody else's dream, I found myself asking George after the proper pilot of the Lavochkin. How was he getting on? I was enquiring. But George could no longer hear me over the thunderous noise of the engine. At least the noise was starting to wake me up.

High bloody time, too, as they say in the theatre. Especially when George shook me hard by the shoulder, really digging his fingers into me. When he did it again, even more urgently, and I looked around, he was making stabbing motions to his left.

At first, disoriented even by the mild glow from the instrument panel, I saw nothing, until his forefinger waxed more insistently than ever, which is when I saw the car coming over the slight rise in the road outside the airfield, urgently flashing its lights. It was heading toward the airfield gate.

Now here was another vehicle. And another. And a tank.

A tank, so easily recognizable: the star of the Red Army, the T34. And ... my land, it was followed by two, three, four other vehicles, half-tracks. And another tank, another T34, bringing up the rear.

At last, I was ready to snap out of a dreary, draggy, dribbling dream. One moment I was Dan Dreary, brother to the Queen of May; next moment I was Captain Brice Carruthers, come to save the Universe from the dreaded Drools.

It was as if I'd activated an electric lavatory brush mistakenly connected to the comfy seat beneath. I jumped, and not merely into action. In a trice as fast as Brice I snapped on practically every switch and toggle in the cockpit except the one to raise the undercart, and that only because it wouldn't work if the aircraft was still on the ground, at least I hoped not, what?

Seconds later, the heel of my hand was rejecting the throttle, jamming it forward just enough to start the machine trundling over the ice, fast enough to get away in time, but easy enough so as not to cause the two-seater to slide sideways into the nearest snowbank, of which there were many available.

The Lavochkin pushed forward, but it was having trouble. Something in the way. While I was shoving on more pressure I looked to the left again. Not only was the mechanized unit halfway to the gate, but soldiers were appearing at the entrance to the barracks, as if they, also, had been alerted, along with the outside world. The soldiers were only a hundred yards away, clawing themselves into ensembles of khaki and fur. And in the meantime starting in our direction. With rifles and those stubby Russian machine-guns.

The big, bulbous-nosed fighter-special, with its drop tanks and taped gunports, was not moving forward. Not an inch. Why wasn't it moving? Go, move! The convoy was almost at the gates. The guards weren't skittering in agitation. Then the striped bar was rising.

The landing wheels must be jammed behind the chocks. I hauled back the throttle, searching for a gadget to alter the airscrew pitch so I could give full power for a few seconds while I shoved the throttle forward again. The beast tried quite hard to climb the five-inch slope. It bellowed, pawed the snow, strained, jolted, but refused to gallop. It was revving up for a full power take-off. No go. I had to pull back on the throttle again, wishing I could ask the mechanics for advice.

Wait! They seemed quite ready to help. Good Lord — they seemed quite prepared to help the beastly spy get away. Unless they had not yet seen the tanks and half-tracks. Yet they were hesitating. Why? 'Course: fearful that I might jam on power again, and chop off their heads with the propeller. I waved, ever so reassuringly. They ran forward — rendered the wheels chockless — and waved back. Bless them. Hope their local commissar didn't hear about it.

On with the power. This time the Lavochkin moved. It was shuddering free.

But going where? I could see nothing beyond the great nose and the spinning three-blade prop. I had to rely on the bluntest edge of memory of the look of the hardstanding. It opened onto the field — naturally. Bound to be a taxiway to the nearest runway — assuming they bothered with a runway, and didn't use a tractor and a train of rollers to beat down the snow in whichever direction took their fancy.

Increasing speed slightly, I started to swing the nose from one side to the other, leaning forward, quite superfluously, in the seat. Seat belts not yet fastened, by the way. Must remember to do something about that.

We'd lost sight of the new arrivals, but the tanks and the half-tracks must be through by now, and heading toward the hardstanding – – unless they could get ahead, onto the airfield? I would definitely be disappointed if they did. However, I had enough to worry about, with trying to distinguish white taxiway from white field under the misty white moon. But I was beginning to feel exhilarated. That was a bad sign. It tended to make me foolish and reckless. Stop it. This minute. And you still haven't found out what that row of knobs is for. Something to do with the cannon? Forget it.

Trying to subdue the foolish lightness of spirit, I put on just a shade more power, assuming that a Russian plane based in their sort of countryside would almost certainly have tires at fairly low pressure — in my case, helping a little to brake the aircraft before it rammed too deeply into a snowdrift. Meanwhile, thank God for the moonlight, however fuzzy. Until it was time for the bastards to shoot at me.

The old brainbox was working quite efficiently by now. It contained a picture of the aircraft that had landed here soon after our arrival, which was providing, I hoped, quite a good idea of the orientation of the runway.

George was squeezing my shoulder again, and shouting. It was impossible to hear him over the rhythmic beating of the engine, but I could sense the motion of his hand, jerking — pointing at something, probably. I could guess at what: the armoured vehicles coming up behind.

Risking a collision with frozen snow, I increased power — mind filled with inconsequential thoughts — like, damn it, I should have the fuel at full rich — unless they were using zero octane or something. Probably were. But I had not the slightest clue where the knob for it was. Or the tap, or the lever, or whatever. In the meantime I continued to jig and swing the plane from side to side as if rehearsing for a hoe-down, treading hard on each rudder pedal to keep the brute averaging a forward progress in what I most sincerely hoped was the best direction to go in, along the grey route into the dark.

I started violently. A stream of orange tracer was whipping past.

The fiery bullets were wavering like water from a hose. I felt my spine getting ready to receive a few of them. I suspected that there was a lot of wood in the aircraft, probably very thin wood. The tracer would be burning through in a second.

It seemed no. Seconds before they had the range of the plane, the shooting stopped. Stoppage?

Worse. One of the T34s had appeared, crunching over the airfield. Now veering towards us. The others had stopped firing as if to leave the fun to the tank.

The huge gun of the T34 was already swinging in our direction. And there was nowhere to turn. The snow had been shovelled up on both sides of the taxiway. Not high enough to hide us, either — no chance of that. And to make things easier for them, I was heading straight across the aiming point of that whacking great gun.

Perhaps we were too close. The tank stopped and hesitated. One of those devastating shells could knock out a German Tiger; imagine what it would do to an aeroplane. I kept going. What else was there to do, anyway, without burrowing into the snow like a gopher, hoping the predators would just go away and leave us in peace.

The runway — it might not be as far as I'd thought. It was hard to see in the dark but it might be off at right angles to the space ahead, which must have been cleared to enable aircraft to change direction after they'd landed. I risked a little more power, though that was pretty foolish, given the visual conditions, but I had this ridiculous impulse to see where I was going. The increasingly wild swings from side to side were threatening to lurch the machine into frozen, cutting snow. All the same, this was not the right time to slow down, with a bloody great gun aiming at you.

It was still there, as was established a second later. There was a yellow flash that lit up a good half acre of snow. Even over the noise from the engine I heard the shell go whoosh. Which suggested that it had come rather close. I even wiggled the rudder, to see if I still had a rudder.

They must have fired again, only a few seconds later. That seemed to be a damn quick-firing gun on the Soviet tank. This time I was privileged to see the result, a visible flick of light, a thud that shook the aircraft, and a big cloud of smoke that rose to comfort the moon.

Land sakes, that was close. They were certain to hit us next time – – unless I could get to the right angle turn ahead, an area of snow that had been brushed, swept, bulldozed, or tractored almost down to the tarmac. It suggested a stretch into which one might turn onto a runaway — though what did I know? What did I know of Russian aerodrome practice?

Only a few seconds to the turn. Another stream of orange tracer from behind, wavering through the dark air like the piss of the gods. Just after I'd jammed on right rudder to make the turn, a shell exploded on the left, shaking the whole aircraft. It was so close that I felt a great buffeting on the fuselage. Damn them, didn't they realize they were damaging one of their own aircraft, what was wrong with them?

With all my heart, not to mention a liver, pair of kidneys, cooked spleen, et cetera, I prayed that the shell had not torn anything else that was needed to keep the Lavochkin going. Resisting the considerable temptation to go even faster, I actually went slower. The tail was jauntily skipping on its tail wheel — too much speed. I could tell because the bulky radial snout was bowing as if to a king.

The nose rose up again, and swung, back and forth. Christ, the speed I'd been travelling at, it was a miracle I hadn't dug into a snowbank with no way to back out.

The runway appeared! Oh, God yes! Though a sheet of ice, polished by landing wheels, a glossy grey surface was fading into the silvery dark as if demonstrating the laws of perspective. It was the runway, trimmed at the edges, reassuringly straight. Nearly there, if the T34 wasn't so rude as to intervene.

Hard on the rudder, more throttle. The nose bowed again — dropped sufficiently to permit a full forward view of the runway. Oh, god, I hoped the engine had had time to warm up. Forget about it, forget the temp gauge. Ready — steady — wheels actually skidding sideways in their ungraceful, disgraceful haste. Go! Throttle palmed forward — restrain from shoving too hard and threatening God knows what in this utterly unfamiliar aircraft — wiggling the pedals to keep straight — the flash of a parting explosion in the snow — and then an amazing acceleration down the runway. By Jove, by Jehosephat, by

Saint Jiminy, this was a bloody fast machine, they must have pinched the design from the Brits or the Yanks. Then the glorious tightening of the joystick, the lessening pressure that said it was time to fly.

So I flew.

I managed to suppress my exhilaration long enough to prompt George to close the canopy so that we didn't freeze to death prematurely, and to ensure that he had his safety harness sorted out. Then I could let go, and feel that once again I had sort of triumphed. We weren't there yet, not by a long shot. There were still a hundred problems in the offing, not least finding the tap that would lean the fuel enough to get us out of Soviet airspace in time. But there were enough good things to keep me going. I was almost bursting with pride, with beatitude, with gratitude to the God I had banished from the trenches of the First World War. I had survived once more, for a while anyway. And I didn't think I had left too much unhappiness behind me, apart, of course, from the one who deserved it, whose initials were JS.

George seemed to share the elation. He couldn't stop talking, though he hadn't found a leather helmet with connections that could keep us in touch. Burning with coincident joy, he kept rubbing my shoulder. I believe he would have kissed the side of my neck if he had been able to reach it, but the safety harness held him back, *spaseebo*!

I didn't mind not being able to hear a word over the racket from the engine. Like Greta, I vanted to be alone, in aerial ecstasy. I wanted to be immune to any sensation other than the enfeebling satisfaction following the adrenaline rush.

The pedal vibration saved me. It was not until I realized that my feet were shaking so violently that they might kick a hole in the fuselage, that I regained at least a modicum of sense. The aircraft might already be full of holes anyway.

George kept talking, on and on, though it was obvious that he could not be heard over the engine noise. He seemed desperate to tell me something, to give me some wonderfully good news, apparently, but as I regained my senses, pure self-interest reasserted itself. After shuddering in the cold for hours, all I cared about was warmth. I couldn't find any heating controls anywhere in the cockpit, and we were flying high. I throttled back while pottering with the gadgets — I'd finally worked out the fuel-emaciating procedure — and headed downward into a more temperate zone. I believe Soviet pilots mostly worked at lower altitudes, to make themselves available for their first priority, army co-operation; but it was still too chilly for me.

Soon the elation vanished in inverse proportion to the discomfort. As I'd been reminding myself from the moment I landed in Normandy last year, I was too old for this racket. I would say so to the Great Leader, if ever I got a chance, stap me vitals if I didn't. I would try to convince him that from now on, he had nothing to fear from poor old Bandy. Maybe then he would give up on me.

Of course, that might not be so easy. He must be hopping mad by now, to have so narrowly missed us at the airport, on top of his failure at the scaffolding. Even now, he must surely be sending squadrons of fighters after us; though even the Brits with their advanced radar would have trouble finding us in the dark. Almost as much trouble, I suspected, as George and I would have, in getting out of it.

The rest is just technical stuff, of consuming interest to cryogenic specialists and met men, navigators, and manufacturers of drop tanks. Once I'd decided that Scandinavia should be our destination — unfortunately, given that warm Turkey was out of reach — I settled the fighter roughly in the right direction and at a rate of fuel consumption from the five fuel tanks that might take us about 900 miles north-west. After that, there was nothing more to worried about, until it was time to crash.

As it turned out, four hours later, we were too low, fuel-and-moralewise, to get past an island in the Baltic Sea. Praying that it was somewhere beyond the reach of the Soviet Union — and not many countries would be beyond its influence, I reckoned, now that Roosevelt had proved at Yalta that he was too weary to resist Stalin any longer — we managed to put down in a white, starlit field, though the plane defied a beautiful touch-down by leaping like a kangaroo, and probably damaging the undercarriage as a result. But what did I care. It wasn't my plane.

Two mornings later we were escorted by boat to Stockholm — for Sweden was the country that the island belonged to. Normally we should have been interned, but now that the war was nearly over, the Swedes felt it was safe to post us on, though I had to fight to keep them from returning George to the Soviets.

"But the Allies have agreed to send every Russian back to his homeland," they protested, while George argued that he was not a Russian. He had taken Belgian citizenship, and would be able to prove it as soon as they allowed him to go home.

The formal Swedes proved unable to resist the Garanine charm that had, incredibly, survived a decade of vile treatment, not to mention four years of having to tell new recruits to the Red Army about dialectical materialism; they agreed to let him accompany me to England.

They were even a little impressed with me, when word came from the British embassy that the RAF would be sending a flying boat for me as soon as possible. For some reason, though, it did not arrive for nearly ten days. I was a trifle miffed about that, and of course the embassy was extremely apologetic about the delay, though not nearly as regretful as when they got our hotel bill.

It was while we were waiting in his hotel room in Stockholm that George told me what he had been trying so hard to tell me just after the take-off from Moscow. At the time, I gained the impression that whatever he wanted to say was even more important than the escape itself.

Now, for no apparent reason, he seemed to have lost interest.

"What were you trying to tell me, anyway?" I asked.

"Oh, it was nothing."

"Come on: give."

"Well ... I was going to tell you about the dossier," he said, mumbling and shrugging as if we had better things to talk about.

"Dossier?"

"You know, about Stalin being a Tsarist informer."

"What about it?"

"Why I was so very happy, Bartushka," he said gloomily, "when they finally allowed me to visit Moscow. You remember — so that I could help you fall to your death."

"Yes, yes, go on."

"Coming to Moscow was first opportunity I had in years, to collect the material."

"What material?"

"The material we are talking about, dearest Bandyeh," he said, impatiently. "The pages from the dossier about Djugashvili, as he was then. The pages that poor Sergei Ossipov got hold of."

"M'oh, yes. Serge couldn't get to them in time, before he was executed."

"Anyway, when I was sent to Moscow I was finally able to retrieve the missing pages," George said, looking gloomier than ever. "I had known for years where they were."

"Well, I never ...."

"And I left a letter for Stalin, to let him know that I had them."

I stared, open-mouthed. "*What?*"

He smirked. Fortunately the smirk didn't linger for more than a few seconds.

"You told Stalin you had them? My God ... What did you tell him? *When* did you tell him?"

He turned away with a shrug. I felt like biffing him on the boko, which was so familiar a reaction as to be almost comforting. "But George?" I cried. "You must actually have told him before we skipped town. Before we were actually free. I mean ... Before we actually got away, for God's sake!"

"Of course," he said, with another impatient shrug, as if we were discussing a railway timetable rather than a flight from certain death.

When I continued to gape, he sighed heavily, while continuing to look slightly irritable. "What's wrong with that, Bartushka?"

After a while I said, "This billy doo to Uncle Joe? It's really true? You actually blackmailed him?"

"Well, naturally, he had to know that I would be putting the pages from the dossier in safe hands," he said, in a long-suffering sort of tone, "and if anything ever happened to you or me, all would be revealed, and he would be exposed."

After a shocked silence I said, "My God ... How could you have taken such a risk ... You're incredible, George ...." I sank onto the nearest chair, shaking my head wonderingly. Then, looking up again: "So why all the discontent?" My voice rose, "Damn it, don't you see? If he's actually read the letter, you have the world's greatest life insurance policy," I exclaimed. "We both have!"

In reply, he walked over to his suitcase. Naturally, he had managed to bring the contents all the way from Moscow. Fumbling somewhere under the lining, he drew out several sheets of paper. They were curved, crinkley, crushed and deformed. But then, after all, they were thirty years old. Actually, they looked as if they had been rescued from a steam bath.

Silently, he handed them over.

I shuffled the few pages uncomprehendingly. "What are these?"

"Is the material, of course, proving Stalin was Okhranka agent."

"But there's nothing here. They're nearly all blank. Washed out."

"Yes. I kept them in my underpants for too long, I'm afraid," George said morosely. "Perhaps I should have changed my underwear more often, but, you know, you get into bad habits in the army. All the unnecessary activity, damn it, and the sweat. As you see, it has wiped away nearly all the words, except some that are no use — and the rubber stamps. You can make out the official stamps, but as you see, that's all that's left."

WESTWARD, LOOK ...

IN ANTICIPATION OF A HOMECOMING fit for one of the war's greatest heroes and his princely oppo, I expected to be transported back to Blighty in the handsomest aerial carriage available. At the very least I expected a magnificent, four-engined Short Sunderland to come out of the West, pompous and ceremonious, to slosh down in the glittering, ice-rimmed water where Malar joins Saltsjon, the island-clustered inlet of the Baltic Sea. It was a bit disappointing to find that they had supplied only a Mosquito, and it landed miles away up north, and even then not without controversy. The Mossie was only a two-seater, so there was quite a quarrel with the pilot as to whether he should allow George on board. He had been told to collect only one person, said the young pilot — Ted, his name was. He pointed out that anyway, the de Havilland was a two-seater, and therefore there was no room for anyone else, unless he stuck George in the bomb bay. In the end, I pulled rank. Unfortunately, I suffered most from this admirable generosity. It meant that I had to seat George in my lap, because Ted, the young whipper-snapper, refused to give up the pilot's seat, despite the fact that I had more than one and a half hours in Mossies, and it hadn't really been my fault when it crashed in France that time.

Anyway, we managed to sort it all out in the end, and off we flew, with cries of farewell from the good people of Sweden ringing in our ears. They had come to see us off: two foresters and a herdsman, not to mention several reindeer.

We thumped down at Croydon only two or three hours later.

"There'll be a brass band, I expect," I warned George, to prepare him for a sample of the fame that had very nearly overwhelmed even me when I set off for Yalta almost three months previously. "Thought I'd better give you plenty of warning, George, old boy. I'm pretty well known over here, you know. There'll be a band, don't you worry, complete with horns, tuba and top brass, you mark my words."

In the shagged-out taxi, I explained to George that there must have been some sort of snafu. "First the inexplicable delay in picking us up from Stockholm," I said, "and then the embassy people behaving in such a miserly fashion to a national hero, and only lending me a fiver. And now this: no band, no welcoming committee, nothing ...."

"I am sure it is just a misunderstanding, my dearest Bartalamyeh," George said placatingly, as he looked with interest at the bombed buildings and even more bombed expressions of a war-weary populace.

At the Air Ministry, we were left waiting for nearly an hour. This was after a visit to Lincoln's Inn Fields, HQ of the RCAF, and if we were not kept waiting there it was only because the offices were closed. Admittedly, it was after four in the afternoon, but all the same. Somebody said the HQ must have been shut down now that the war was over, practically, but I'm almost certain I saw a Canadian officer peering at me from behind a curtain. In fact I'm sure it was the same one who had tried not to welcome me into the war in 1940. Lord, that was a long time ago .... Mind you, it was only three ranks ago, which was pretty unimpressive promotional history, so far as I was concerned, when you compared it with the First World War, when I had risen through half a dozen ranks — except, of course, for the occasion when I was demoted, because I'd stirred up so much trouble at this very Air Ministry.

Even when somebody finally came to attend to us, they turned out to be SIB men. They'd had a call from Croydon and wished to take George away for questioning.

I protested, but to no avail. The interview would not take too long — assuming it was true, they said, that George really was a Belgian, and that fine Russian uniform of his — on his way to a fancy dress party, is he, sir?

"And while we're at it, sir, may I see your warrant card?" the senior one asked, turning to me and looking as if he thought that I was the one who ought to be investigated.

I'd had all the bumf taken from me by Comrade Soultanov, including my identification, but I was able to show them the letter from the third secretary of His Britannic Majesty's Chancery on Strandvagen, which explained just enough of my alleged circumstances, sans-prejudice, to ensure that the Air Force policemen merely took a note of my name and a few other details, instead of putting me in an arm lock and marching me straight to the glasshouse.

"Wait," said George, just before we were wrenched apart — permanently, I hoped. He huddled close, holding my arm, and whispered, "Are you absolutely sure, Bartalamyeh, that it will work?"

I knew what he was on about. I'd already spent hours convincing him that the Reds were unlikely to touch either of us. They would never know that the proof had gone bad, that the excerpts from the Djugashvili dossier, which were now in my possession, had deteriorated to the point that they were now unreadable.

"Stop worrying, George," I hissed. "They won't dare touch either of us."

"But are you sure, Bartalamyeh, are you quite sure?"

"Yes, George," I said, ever so patiently. "So long as you don't tell them who is safe-keeping the material for us."

"By the way," I added cheerfully, "in case anybody tries torture on you — you know, pulls out your nails, amputates certain external organs, or worst of all, forces you to read Karl Marx — I'll make it even easier for you. I won't even tell *you* which lawyer has possession of the pages. I'll keep it a secret forever."

George clasped my hand, overcome with sheer admiration. "You are wonderful, dearest Bartushka," he said huskily. "Just wonderful."

So wonderful, that the minute he was led away, I determined to see his wife as soon as possible, and prepare her for the terrible truth about her hubby: that he was thoroughly lost on the Steppes of Central Asia, or better still, thoroughly dead.

After which, I would hold out my unbelievably sensitive arms and embrace my beloved, and comfort her. Yes, good, splendid. Or maybe I would pass the word to the authorities — some word or other, details to follow — ensuring that George spent another decade or two in jail. I felt that this was a generous compromise. After all, a British prison would surely be better than the Siberian camps. Think how much pain I would be sparing him.

I had only another few minutes to wait in the gloomy Air Ministry corridor, before a lady sergeant appeared, to escort me to another floor of the Air Ministry.

Last time I was here, the corridors were thronged with personnel, from despatch riders with urgent OA signals, to WAAFs with harried stockings. There had been air marshals galore in the various offices, looking worried that the war might end before they had ordered their new uniforms. This afternoon the place was a lot thinner, population-wise, and waistbandwise as well, the few people around looking a lot hungrier and wearier than they had in 1940.

Actually, I had been feeling increasingly fretful during the long wait, considering that I had particularly asked to see good old Oliver Chistelow. I had expected to be welcomed to his office with pipes and drums long ere this. After all, we had become, not exactly pals, but at least sharers of quite a bonding experience.

Even before I was shown into his office I was beginning to wonder what else was going on. So far, there had not been a single bouquet of flowers or request for an interview with the great Group Captain Bandy, KCSI, etc. And why wasn't I an air vice-marshal by now? Good Lord, surely they hadn't decided that I was getting too big for my boots, or something, and it was time to bring me down a peg or two.

I'd only been chatting with Oliver for a few minutes before I recognized that things really had changed. It appeared that I was no longer their blue-eyed boy, and not just because my eyes were brown, not even as far as Chistelow was concerned. After an apparently genuine burst of welcome, during which he listened to my recent history with every appearance of genuine fascination, he suddenly seemed to pull himself together. He retreated behind the barricade of his desk, coupled his hands together, placed them on the blotter, and said, "Sorry to have kept you waiting so long, Bart. I'm doing the work of about three men at the moment. So many officers are opting to leave the service early, to avoid being reduced too far down in rank." He paused for a moment, gazing at me with a really warm smile on his well-upholstered face. "I know of course that you won't want to stay on in the Air Force," he said. "Do you have any plans for the future, Bart? With your background and experience I have no doubt that you will not want for lucrative offers."

I suppose that if I'd been sophisticated, I would have disguised my feelings in a civilized way. Instead, I looked back at him in a thoroughly affronted fashion.

"Whatjamean, won't want to stay on?" quoth I. "You expect me to leave, just as I'm about to be loaded with even more awards and a promotion to at least air vice-marshal?"

So it was his turn to hide his feelings. "What? But, but," he stammered. "We assumed ... your age, and so forth."

Quickly recovering, he went on, "And may I remind you that you didn't add greatly to the prestige of the Royal Air Force in Yalta, either, did you, Bandy, when you get right down to it."

For a moment I was inclined to riposte that officially I wasn't really part of his outfit, so he knew what he could do with the RAF. But then I decided, the hell with it. I'd been upsetting my superiors for half a century. It was high time I settled down, and tried to get along with people for a change, instead of infuriating everybody from colonels to air marshals, the way I'd been doing since I first joined up in Toronto, way, way back there in '16 or whatever the hell century it was.

So I just shrugged my shoulders, and mumbled, "Yes, well ... incidentally, what happened to the brass bands, Ollie? Am I suddenly persona non-grateful?"

The AVM frowned at the familiar use of his name, but let it pass for the time being, i.e., half a second. "Well, of course you are — *Barty*," he said. "We had several days of extremely agitated communications from our Russian allies about you, demands that you and what they called your traitor friend, Garanine, be handed over forthwith, to face the gravest possible charges."

I stared at him. My heart missed enough beats to bring a Broadway musical to a numbing halt. We'd failed, then? Or somehow they'd discovered that our damning evidence was not worth a pinch of pixie dust?

Until he added, "Though it all ended suddenly, after a few days. Now, apart from demanding the return of the aircraft that you, um, 'borrowed', they seem to have lost interest in you entirely."

He tilted his plump, speculative phiz to starboard, and murmured, "Actually, we had the impression that the order to stop making a fuss came right from the top. Any comments?"

"I guess they realized they were just being fussy. Which reminds me, Ollie — Oliver: when am I going to get paid? I haven't received one penny of pay since last Christmas."

After Chistelow had paused for a moment to work out what the Bolshies had to do with my back pay, he suddenly brightened. "By Jove, yes, you're right, Bart. Why, that's right: it's the RCAF who are to blame — I mean, who are responsible for you, not us. I forgot all about that. Yes! What luck. The Canadians took you on; it's up to them to decide what on earth to do, now that nobody wants to know you any more." He reached eagerly for the telephone. "And they have lots of money, too, Bart," he added encouragingly. "I'll get onto them right away."

"Just a goldarn minute there, buster," I said, but it was too late. He must have found out where the Canadian Air Force was concealed, for he was onto them only a minute later.

There was one other difficulty to be solved before I rushed back to the continent to see my beloved, and that was the one concerning the King.

As was well known, His Royal Highness had enormous respect for me, as evidenced by his flattering determination that I should represent the Royal Family in recovering his brother's ill-advised communications with the Nazis. It was thought inadvisable that Edward VIII's letters and the diplomatic notes of his sympathetic conversations with the German foreign office should continue to exist in their present form, i.e., unburned. At least they should be hidden away in the royal archives. To this end, His Majesty had charged me with visiting Deutschland the moment the war ended — only a month away by now — to ensure that the material fell into the right hands — definitely mine and not those of any nosy historian, journalist, or American.

However, I had considerable difficulty in contacting His Majesty, despite all the help that came from friends in the Foreign Office before they were brought up to speed on who was 'in' these days, and who was to be treated with polite smiles. The FO managed to obtain an appointment for me, for the end of April, but that was several days away, and I was desperate to see Clemence before they released my dear old friend, her husband.

Bastards. They restored George to me before I could get away. I was forced to book him a seat beside me, on the Brussels Dakota.

Cable and telephonic communication with the continent had still not been re-established on a regular and consistent basis, and neither of us had managed to speak to the baroness by the time we landed at Evere.

We reached downtown by early afternoon, George attired in a new grey suit contributed by a Russian refugee organization, and me in my best blue. While George frittered and loitered outside the phone booth, apparently taking no interest in the proceedings, I telephoned my darling, in so shudderingly eager but confused a fashion, that when one of her servants answered I very nearly called *him* darling.

With regret, he informed me that the baroness was out, but was expected back by early evening. Rejoining George, I suggested that in the meantime we nip along to the Rue Neuve for a drink. "If you have any money," I added.

George turned out to have plenty of money. More than me, actually. I hadn't been paid for nearly four months and had had to borrow a fiver from the air vice-marshal, while George had been lent fifty bloody quid from an organization which thought he was Polish.

"Of course, my dear fellow," he answered, looking worried sick, which was proof that he was, as he had promised, resigned to losing Clemence. So. However starved my wallet, I was quids-in as regards the d'Aspremont de Forget stakes.

Mind you, I'd been a mite worried on the flight over. From the moment we had rendez-voused at the airfield, he had spoken hardly a word, not even the usual bunches of compliments and unbridled praise thrown like bouquets from his silvery tongue. But now, as we settled in the very same cafe that I had visited some months or centuries ago, he was fidgeting like an uncomfy cat. I was suddenly apprehensive that he had changed his mind, and had decided to fight for Clemence.

By late afternoon, he had become quite agitated, clasping and unclasping his beautifully manicured hands (what had the RAF police done to him? Taken him to a beauty parlour?) with deep lines of tension scoring his face. He kept glancing at me and looking away, presumably so as not to expel shuddering breaths all over me.

I failed to react, so as not to give him the slightest excuse to open up and ask for some favour or other — like reclaiming his wife. I feared he would protest that he still loved her, that he would beg me to withdraw from the contest. I paid no attention to his trembling agitation. I just kept on talking about this and that, commenting on the smart scene and on the obvious prosperity of the Belgians, especially when compared with the thin, exhausted Brits. I also told him that this was not one of my favourite restaurants because it was where a fellow called Kim Philby had somehow and in spite of my reluctance, fixed up my trip to the USSR. "You'd almost think he was on their side," said I.

"Bartalamyeh," he said suddenly, his voice trembling.

Oh Christ, I thought. Here it comes. Well, if he thinks I'm going to give up Clemence, he'd better think again. After once again escaping death by a hairsbreadth, I loved her more than ever, more even than flying, even more than life itself, surely. I loved her more than George could ever love anybody. He would always manage to put himself first, even if that was never his intention. Him with his stupid, loving manner and his glorious face (had they worked on his face as well as his nails at the beauty parlour?) and his kindness (except when clubbing women commissars), and his godamn decency. Pah!

"I want you to have Clemence," he burst out suddenly.

I turned and looked at him blankly.

"I mean it. You must have Clemence. I insist," he said, swallowing.

Another silence. Then: "Wot?"

"It is obvious that you love her very much, my Bandushka. Far more than I could ever love her — after all this time, all these years. Is ridiculous," he said, his voice shaking, his face pale as a flounder.

Having exhausted my vocabulary for the time being, I just stared.

"I don't deserve her, Bartalamyeh. She is for you. She is bound to love you, very much. I know it, I am sure of it," he said, smiling in a ghastly way, eyelids flickering, polishing the windows of his eyes. "How could I still love her after ten years, it's such nonsense, Bartalamyeh."

"Nearly fifteen years," said I, faintly.

"Yes, of course, my dearest Bartalamyeh, you are right, as always — nearly fifteen years. It is such nonsense." He laughed wildly. "I hardly think about her. Anyway, it is only right. You have always done so much for me, while I have done nothing for you. I do not deserve her. I am such a useless person compared with you."

He turned away, and it was just like that other time, in Moscow: one moment old and incoherent at the thought of having his escape plans stymied; the next, young again, and smiling like the god Optimus. Only this time it was the other way round, joining me in almost equal turmoil.

I just didn't know what to say. My lips flapped like a matching flounder.

All of a sudden the agitation left him. He turned again to me with an achingly sad smile, and reached for my hand, and said, "It is for you, Bartalamyeh. Because I love you. You saved my life."

"Nonsense," I managed at last. "You saved mine."

"No, you saved mine."

"No, you did. Anyway, what now, George?"

"We go to her house, and then I will leave you. I will leave you both," he said, somehow managing to smile and look simultaneously drowned.

The day was still brilliantly lighted at six o'clock when we both turned up at Clemence's mansion near the Arcade de Cinquentenaire.

We had not spoken a word for nearly half an hour when we reached the front door.

The fellow who answered the door was the same Albert who had served the champagne during my first visit to the Baroness de Forget's front room last year, the chamber with the giant portraits on the yellow silk walls. He recognized me just as promptly, presumably because I was so brilliantly spotlighted now by joy, despite an attempt to camouflage it for George's sake. But oh, the prospect of mating with the woman whom I loved to such an absurd extent that I would even give up flying, if she nailed me to the parquetry and insisted upon it.

We were informed that the lady had not yet returned, though she was expected back within the next few minutes. Would the gentlemen care to wait in the Waterloo suite? But while I agreed, George asserted that he would prefer not to enter the house, but just to say goodbye on the doorstep. In fact, right now, if that was all right with you, Bartholomew. He just didn't want to see Clemence, and that was all there was to it. He would say goodbye now. He still had to book into a hotel. Perhaps we could meet again, some time in the future, if I was not too busy. Oh, don't be so absurd, George, I said, and told him that I was quite fond of him, you know, in spite of his good looks and his charming manner, and I was quite ready to help, you know, help him to settle down in the West and all that, and all that. You know.

I was still rising up and down on my polished heels and looking tremendously sympathetic when an old Citroën came crunching onto the circular driveway and stopped short of the front door. George and I were still standing in the elaborate entrance, George determinedly shrinking back into the April shadows, and me making a last ditch attempt to persuade him to at least wait and shake hands with the lady before going off into the sunset.

We fell breathlessly silent as we heard Clemence's voice giving instructions to the chauffeur, both of us too frozen to step out of the cover of the fancy overhang, so that she didn't see me until she was on the first step to the front door.

When she saw me her whole face lit up with the most beautiful smile, and she opened her mouth to exclaim, but faltered when she became aware that somebody else was standing there, a chap in a superbly cut grey suit, no hat, but a new dark overcoat draped over his arm.

It might have been fifteen years, but even I could not deny that I was witnessing yet another of his ridiculous changes, like the one in the Kremlin when his even more ridiculous faith in me had transformed him from haggard middle age straight back to carefree youth in one emotional bound. Again, his face sagged into repose. It flowed back two ages, like a Dali watch melting into a fresh dimension. The overcoat, which he had been carrying so proudly, as if it were a symbol of his new life, slipped from his arm onto the wooden decking.

If he looked suddenly on the point of collapse, the change in Clemence was even more marked.

"George?" she faltered. "It's you, truly?"

Her face, too, was faltering, growing soft, softer with every second, her eyes growing huge, her breath accelerating. The thin frame that I had dreamed of protecting from the world's uncertainties and angers seemed to dissolve. Another observer might have wondered how the bright spring coat could even manage to keep its upright shape. She seemed so near to collapse that the chauffeur, following behind, reached anxiously forward as if catch her, as her single item of shopping, something in shining gold wrapping, fell from her hand.

And then she was moving forward as if in a dream. And George was taking her in his arms, and silently weeping.

★

I arrived back in London in plenty of time for the appointment with another George. This time it was an occasion considerably more formal, to be held in the front part of Buckingham Palace rather than in the posh bits to the rear where the glorious drawing rooms overlooked swathes of manicured parkland. I was admitted almost inconspicuously through an entrance to the extreme right of the facade, and invited to follow a pair of striped trousers along the ground floor. Ultimately we ended up in what proved to be the anteroom to a large, functional office, apparently the King's idea of an ideal place for an official discussion with the senior officer he hoped to send to Germany, the moment that country had pulled itself together and fallen apart.

While waiting in the anteroom, I busied myself chewing the interior of my cheeks, already imagining the affronted reaction when I told His Majesty that I did not wish to go to Germany; that I had decided that rescuing brother David from the slight embarrassment he had heaped, or rather teaspooned, onto the Royal Family, was one more adventure I did not wish to pursue. On the way back from Brussels I had decided that it was time I went home.

Since marching off to war nearly thirty years ago, as eager as were millions of other lads in their search for excitement and adventure, I had returned home on only a few brief occasions, apart from those three and a half years in the early 'twenties when I had hoped to design and build aircraft for the peace to end all peaces; though even those short months had been further shortened by the Ottawa government, when they steeled, or rather, buttered themselves, to have me arrested for ....

Well, anyway, I'd hardly been back since.

But now, Canada was the only place I wanted to be. I'd hoped to return rich and famous enough to attract a few glorious offers, but, over the years, my pecuniary fortunes had risen and fallen like ducks in a heavy swell, ending with the Wall Street waterfall. At the moment my finances were the subject of some quite acrimonious correspondence with Coutts and Company, but still, I remained optimistic that the slack would soon be taken up when I had finally, at long last, replaced aerial adventure with unmitigated selfishness, avarice, and commerce. Anyway, who needed flying any more? Governments were already plastering up every chink of independence that had escaped the attention of the aerial lawmakers.

I'd had enough, that was all that mattered; and enough of singing other ballads, not least those of people who thought they had a perfect right to ask a fellow to do their little chores for them, to clean up the skitter of their family affairs. What did I care what the King-Emperor said when I told him what I really thought of brother David's little indiscretions? I was going home, that was all that mattered.

Even so, I was feeling as tense as an alarm clock by the time a secretary emerged from the inner office and led me into the Presence; to be exact, into the stiffbacked seat facing the King at his desk. The vast desk was bare except for two telephones, a clock, presumably for telling His Majesty that it was time to throw me into one of his lakes when he learned what I had to tell him, and a broken seventeenth-century pot-pourri vase in blue, green, and gold, and a container of glue. Apparently the King had been busy mending it when I came in.

I was still determined to turn him down, despite my sympathy for King George number six. He had never wanted to be King. It was David's behaviour that had jammed the crown imperial on his napper; David, the elder brother, whose brief association with Hitler & Co. had led this chap, old before his time, to seek my help in regaining the embarrassing material resulting from that flirtation.

You were not supposed to speak first in the presence of the King, but I'd broken that convention so often in my dealings with various majesties that it seemed pointless to start now.

I was beaten just in time. The King spoke first, though in a distinctly nervous style. "Ah, Bandy," he said. "It is a great pleasure to meet you again."

"M'kew."

"You are l-looking quite," he continued, though with difficulty. His stutter seemed to have gotten worse.

"So are you, sir," I replied, also fibbing like mad. His Majesty looked worn out, for his age, as crumpled and weary as the rest of his victorious subjects.

"I have called you in," he continued, looking almost desperately, it seemed to me, to the secretary. Only now did I realize that the secretary was making notes of the conversation.

"Yes, Your Majesty," I said. It was definite, then. I would have to cast him still deeper into the pit of despair. He had called me in to prepare me for another bloody adventure, and in a minute would have to know that I wasn't going. "It's just that I wanted to tell you, sir, that I can't —"

"Please don't interrupt, Group Captain. It is quite difficult enough as it is," he managed.

"Sorry, sir. But, you see —"

"We have regretfully decided that you are not the right p-per, right p-pers, not the right one to carry out the errand in Germany," he managed at last, as he picked up and shook the bottle of glue, as if hoping to produce a few interesting bubbles.

Desperate, but determined to be heard, I opened my mouth again; but just like the glue, no bubbles appeared.

All I could manage was, "Wot?" Causing the secretary to look up sharply from his notepad.

"We recognize your great contribution to the war effort over the years, Group Captain. However, there have been worries concerning your visit to our ally, the Soviet Union, that make it inadvisable at the present time ..." He stopped, and looked a little desperately at the secretary.

Who paused for a moment to examine his propelling pencil before smoothly murmuring, "His Majesty regretfully considers that in light of the feelings being expressed by the Soviets, admittedly in as quiet and diplomatic a fashion as possible so as not to disturb the friendship so arduously built up between our peoples, it has been decided that Group Captain Bandy should not be involved in any activity in which Your Royal Highness is even remotely involved," the secretary said, concluding his remarks by clicking his propelling pencil — not once, but *twice*.

And then they both turned, and looked at me.

Who, after taking a deep breath, and metaphorically marching round the office once or twice with flags waving, and bunting waving as well, said gravely, "Naturally one is greatly disappointed at not being able to serve Your Majesty in this regard and to the fullest extent of the aforementioned regard."

"I'm terribly sorry, Bandy, really," George VI murmured, looking longingly at the glue.

"Is there no chance that you'll change your mind, sir?" I asked.

"I'm afraid not."

"Oh, dear," I said, and was still hanging my head, the very picture of disgrace, until I was well clear of the palace, having been shown out via a side entrance. I had reached a stretch of bright green grass before I raised both arms in the air and broke into a hornpipe, kicking my shoes in dainty lateral steps, and ending with a somersault, which turned out to be a bit of a mistake, as, not being quite as lithe as I used to be, I landed on my back with a thump, made all the worse by the fact that the grass was still pretty hard after a pretty hard winter.

A very hard winter.

Editor's Afterword

I WAS AROUND TWELVE OR THIRTEEN YEARS OLD when I first discovered Bandy in the local library. I was going through a phase of reading biographies and memoirs of First and Second World War pilots, and I picked up one of the first three books off the paperback shelf on the adult side of the library. Although I very quickly realized that despite the promising cover, with its planes going down in smoke, this was not in fact a biography, but a work of fiction, I read it anyway. Devoured it, in fact, and quickly found the other two as well. Bandy was the funniest thing I'd read since *Jennings and Darbishire*. And it had dogfights, too. As with *Jennings*, I frequently got scowled at by teachers and sniggered at by classmates for my insufficiently-muffled snorts of laughter as I read and reread Bandy during what was called "sustained silent reading" period. I introduced Bandy to my father, and although attempts to read the best bits out loud to my eight-year-old sister weren't quite such a success, she did appreciate the "turn left at the French dunghill" scene. Rather later, I introduced it to my husband as well.

Which is how we all come to be here, now, with the long-awaited *Stalin versus Me* in our collective hands. Following Donald Jack's too-early passing, when the market decided Jack's publishers, McClelland and Stewart, against publishing it, our admittedly very tiny publishing company leapt eagerly into the breach, spurred on by the numerous emails our Bandy website was receiving from fans demanding to know when *Stalin* was coming out. We approached Jack's daughters with an offer of publication and in surprisingly short order, and with the eager support of Douglas Gibson of McClelland and Stewart, were in possession of two versions of the *Stalin versus Me* manuscript. One, which appears to be a somewhat earlier version, was incomplete. The other is a revision of it, containing new elements, new characters, and several new chapters, but a revision which was not yet final — incidents which had been moved to a later point in the story had not yet been fully integrated into their new location, it contradicts itself in places, and some elements end abruptly rather than playing out to a dramatically satisfying conclusion. And that is what this afterword is actually about.

Stalin versus Me is something on which Donald Jack worked intermittently for a number of years. It was, on occasion, abandoned, archived, restarted, and revised. It seemed to us that there were two possibilities for publication. We could put a out a scholarly version, containing one or both manuscripts exactly as they stood, with extensive notes and "scholarly apparatus" tracking the changes between the two, as Christopher Tolkien has done with all the many versions of the *Silmarillion* material and the early drafts of *The Lord of the Rings* in the twelve volume (plus separate two-volume index) *History of Middle-earth*, or we could present people with the story. We decided that, at this time, the story was what most would want. Accordingly, I took the paper manuscript I had, the later version, as the version we would publish. I have, however, edited, since because of the changes Jack had made to that later draft which were not yet fully incorporated, the story contained contradictions and passages of time that occurred twice. For several chapters before the fiasco in the apartment on the Rue Leopold, people commiserate with Bandy on the baroness having dumped him, for example, since in the earlier draft, that incident happens at an earlier point and appears to have caused a rupture in their relationship. I've excised such minor contradictory comments, without altering the flow of the story around them. Again because of the incomplete nature of the revised second manuscript, with its additional episodes, August and December of 1944 seemed to go for about six weeks each; since the commencing date of the Battle of the Bulge cannot be changed, "it was weeks" has become "it was days" to keep the Rue Leopold incident where it belongs, sometime between 17 December 1944 (the day after the commencement of "the German onslaught through the Ardennes") and New Year's Eve. I also retained the wording of the earlier draft in passages where we both found that earlier version superior, and removed repetitions of words and phrases that were the sort of thing one, as an author, catches only in the final draft (leaving, of course, those obviously there for comic effect).

I have not, it is vital to emphasize, rewritten anything. (Hence the various contradictions, not resolvable by alteration of a few words, which remain.) Readers may notice that both the despicable Oakley and the likeable Harriet Hullborne disappear abruptly at the end of Part One, with neither story seeming finished — both belong to the later draft, which contains major changes mostly confined to Part One, aside from the final few chapters that don't exist in the earlier of our two manuscripts. Much as we, and everyone else, might want to allow Bandy the last word with Oakley, and to see how his relationship with Major Hullborne develops, that is not our business, but Donald Jack's, and any speculation on it must remain forever in the imaginations of the readers. Bandy's change in rank, from Wing Commander back to Group Captain again, which happens unremarked between Parts One and Two, is left alone, as is the discontinuity between the King's apparent decision that Bandy is not the man for his mission in Part One, and the assumption in Part Two, by both Bandy and George VI, that it has previously been agreed that Bandy will undertake the retrieval of the Duke of Windsor's incriminating correspondence. And since Jack, as the "editor" of the *Bandy Papers,* often inserted footnotes, this is a good place to point out that footnotes attributed "Ed." are ours, added to clarify some point, while unattributed ones are Jack's own.

We hope Donald Jack's many readers will enjoy this, the final volume of the *Bandy Papers*. We hope Jack would have approved of it. We thank the Estate of Donald Jack for granting us the honour of publishing it, Douglas Gibson for graciously sending us his copies of the manuscript drafts, and Jaren Kohlis for so kindly allowing us to use his photograph of the Lavochkin La-9 for our cover.

Of course, it was really all just an excuse to get to read it ourselves.

K.V. Johansen, July 2005

Glossary of Terms

As a twelve-year-old reading Bandy, I was often baffled by the assorted military acronyms and slang, letting them flow over me as part of the atmosphere, but never really sure what they actually meant. Many of the historical references, as well, were my first encounter with those aspects of modern history – – in truth, Bandy is *very* educational on many matters so far as a twelve-year-old is concerned, not unlike *The Boy's Own Paper*. We decided to add a glossary to *Stalin vs. Me*, for the benefit of whatever next generation of twelve-year-olds might be encountering this era for the first time here.

ack-ack — *anti-aircraft guns; anti-aircraft shells*
AFC — *Air Force Cross*
APC — *armoured personnel carrier*
Arbeitschlosenunterstutsungsgeld — *unemployment insurance money (Ger.)*
ATS — *Auxilary Territorial Service; the "Land Girls".*
AWOL — *absent without leave*
Bart. — *Baronet. (Essentially, a hereditary knight.) Which, however, Bandy is not. He's a mere knight (see KCSI), Oakley's attempt at a pun notwithstanding.*
bitte? — *"Please?" (Ger.)*
bocage — *old, tangled hedgerows (Fr.)*
buckshee — *extra, over and above standard*
caserne —*barracks (Fr.)*
CBE — *Commander of the Most Excellent Order of the British Empire. The middle of five ranks in the Order of the British Empire, and not quite high enough to grant the title "Sir".*
Cheka — *Short for Vecheka. The first Soviet secret police. Also known as "The All-Russian Extraordinary Commission to Combat Counter-Revolution, Profiteering and Power Abuse". Headed by Felix Dzerzhinsky. In 1922 they became the GPU (Gosudarstvennoye Politicheskoye Upravlenie), meaning "State Political Directorate", a section of the NKVD.*
cherneeka (chernika) — *blueberries (Russ.)*
Crazy Gang — *A group of six comedians popular from the 1930s-50s.*
Croix de Guerre — *A decoration awarded by France and Belgium to individuals or units for acts of heroism in combat.*
DFC — *Distinguished Flying Cross. A British Empire honour for "an act or acts of valour, courage or devotion to duty whilst flying in active operations against the enemy," such as standing up in your cockpit at 10,000 feet to pound on your machine guns with a hammer, while wearing a fox fur and dribbling chocolate.*
Djugashvili — *The original surname of Joseph Stalin, variously spelt Dzhugashvili or Jughashvili. First name sometimes given as Iosef, Iosif, Ioseb, etc., due to the fact that his name was transliterated from Geor-*

gian to Russian, and then to English, with various alphabetical confusion along the way. However, the "Stalin" part he made up on his own.

DRO — *daily routine orders*

DSO — *Distinguished Service Order. A British Empire honour for officers guilty of distinguished service during wartime (usually performed in combat, rather than at Headquarters behind the lines). Generally awarded only to officers of Major rank or higher.*

Dzerzhinsky Square — *Another name for Lubianka (or Lubyanka) Square, home of the KGB and the infamous Lubianka prison.*

e.a. — *enemy aircraft*

empressment — *literally, eagerness (Fr.) We leave any further interpretation to the imagination.*

erk — *aircraftman*

estaminet — *pub, wine-shop (Fr.)*

flam-paradiddle — *A type of drumming pattern. Also an alternate title for the radio play* Grave Tidings *written by Donald Jack around 1970. The first time it appears in* Stalin, *when Bandy is swapping uniforms before the aeroport checkpoint, Jack may be playing on the meaning of "flam" as a deceptive story or sham. The second time, when the Russian is pounding on the trunk, it's definitely drum-related.*

Garcia — *A reference to "A Message to Garcia", an essay written in 1899 during the Spanish-American War. It has been used as a business parable intended to instil employees with an urge to shut up and do what they're told.*

gen — *RAF slang: information. Derived from "... for the general information of all ranks ...".*

"Gone for a Burton" — *RAF slang: dead or missing, from "gone for a beer", referring to the brewing town of Burton-on-Trent.*

Heath Robinson device — *What Americans would call a Rube Goldberg device; that is, any sort of fanciful and unlikely contraption. Named for the British cartoonist who drew them.*

Hucks starter — *An old method of starting an aero-engine. It was a type of truck with an elevated boom that looked a bit like a spindly cannon. This stuck out in front of the truck and connected to the propeller-hub. The truck's engine power was communicated to the propellor by the spinning boom, and this got the aircraft engine to start.*

I/O — *Intelligence Officer; "the squadron spy".*

Ivor Novello — *Stage name of David Ivor Davies, a Welsh entertainer who was the same age as Bandy. The reference "... hadn't seen real cream cakes since Ivor Novello's* The Dancing Years *..." in the chapter "Rue Montover" refers to pre-war days;* The Dancing Years *was a 1939 musical. Novello is probably better remembered for his song "Keep the Home Fires Burning", than for his illegal procurement of rationed petrol to burn in his Rolls-Royce.*

jankers — *punishment duty*

KCSI — *Knight Commander in The Most Exalted Order of the Star of India (defunct since the independence of India & Pakistan in 1947). Membership of this honour mostly consisted of Indian potentates and long-serving bureaucrats in the imperial administration, but Bandy received it for saving India in* Me So Far, *entitling him to be called "Sir Bart".*

khvost — *Literally a tail or queue, also apparently used to mean a gang or group. Also "khvostism", a word used by Lenin to mean "reform-ism", conceding to social democracy, and "khvostists". (Russ.)*

Koba — *Another pseudonym assumed by Stalin; originally the name of a Robin Hood-like folk-hero in Georgia.*

krestyanski — *peasants (?);* ***kulaks*** *were the prosperous peasants, a class sent into internal exile or executed under Stalin. (Russ.)*

LAC — *Leading Aircraftman*

Legion of Honour — *The Légion d'honneur is a French order of chivalry, created by Napoléon I, equivalent to a knighthood.*

Mae West — *life vest (after a busty American actress; rhyming slang)*

MC — *Military Cross. A British Empire honour awarded for meritorious service. Originally given to officers of the rank of Captain or below, and Warrant Officers.*

met men — *meteorologists*

MGB — *A transitional name for an organization which split from the NKVD, to become the KGB in 1946.*

MO — *Medical Officer*

NKVD — *Narodnyi Komissariat Vnutrennikh Del, or "People's Commissariat for Internal Affairs". A branch of the Soviet government responsible for various functions such as overseeing the police, intelligence agencies, secret police, gulags, genocides, and other activities considered vital to state security.*

nyemski — *We at Sybertooth claim less fluency in Russian than Bandy. The best suggestion our research can come up with for "nyemski" is that possibly what was intended was the adjective* Nyemnetsky, *meaning "German", from the noun* Nyemets, *"a German". Although we can't find any evidence for our theory, given the long history of German-Russian conflict dating back to the Middle Ages, it might imply any European foreigner (like "Franks" in the medieval and even modern Middle East).*

Okhranka — *The Okhrannoje Otdelenie, also known as Okhrana. The imperial secret police in the time of the Tsar. Frequently used agent provocateurs to ensnare revolutionaries.*

oppo — *Naval slang for "opposite number", i.e. someone who did your job on another ship or shift. It came to mean a pal or chum.*

OTU — *Operational Training Unit*

Osler ("According to Osler ...") — *Sir William Osler, a famous Canadian physician; for more about him, read Donald Jack's* Rogues, Rebels, and Geniuses: The Story of Canadian Medicine *(Toronto: Doubleday, 1981).*

PFC — *Private First Class, US Army*

Portage and Main — *For non-Canadians: intersection in Winnipeg, Manitoba, reputed to be Canada's coldest and windiest meeting of streets; it has even been suggested that the corner be redesigned to include wind turbines for the generation of electricity.*

Quai d'Orsay — *a nickname for the French Ministry of Foreign Affairs, from its location.*

radiogram — *a combination radio and gramophone.*

Robertson Hare — *A film comedian of about Bandy's age, similarly bald.*

RT *(or **R/T**)* — *radio transmission*

Schadenfreude — *lit. "harmful joy"; malicious joy, gloating (Ger.)*

SDECE — *The Service de Documentation Extérieure et de Contre-Espionnage, the French external intelligence organization, which existed from 1947 until 1981. It would thus be not SDECE, but one of its predecessors, probably the Deuxième bureau, which sent Garanine to Russia in the 'thirties. The Deuxième bureau (an organ of the French General Staff) absorbed the Service de Renseignement — French foreign intelligence — after the Dreyfus Affair; domestic counter-intelligence was left to the Sûreté Générale. It seems that both of these essentially persisted under the Vichy regime, and the Free French introduced their own agencies, which came to be called the SDECE by the end of the war. Jack's historical research was usually thorough; he would undoubtedly have caught this, given time.*

SHAEF — *Supreme Headquarters, Allied Expeditionary Force*

SIB — *Special Investigation Branch, the detective service of the military police.*

SIS — *Secret Intelligence Service; after the War became MI6.*

SP — *Service Police*

Stanford Tucks and Johnny Johnsons — *Robert Roland Stanford Tuck (1916-1987). An RAF Ace, he briefly toured the USA in 1941 for promotional purposes before returning to combat. Captured in January 1942, he escaped near the end of the war and fought as an infantry officer with the Russian army until making his way to the British Embassy in Moscow. James E. "Johnny" Johnson (1916-2001) was Britain's leading ace, with 38 victories.*

SWO — *Station Warrant Officer*

TAF — *Tactical Air Force*

time-ex — *time-expired, period of service ended; seems to be used interchangeably with "tourex" here, although they don't appear to mean exactly the same thing.*

tourex — *tour-expired, tour of combat duty over.*

WAAF — *Women's Auxiliary Air Force. A British military organization, started in 1939.*

wingco — *Wing Commander; rank between Group Captain and Squadron Leader.*

WREN — *Women's Royal Naval Service*

About the Author

DONALD LAMONT JACK WAS BORN IN RADCLIFFE, ENGLAND, on December 6, 1924. He attended Bury Grammar School in Lancashire, and later Marr College, Troon (from which he was briefly evicted after writing an injudicious letter to the editor). From 1943 to 1947 he served in the Royal Air Force as an AC, or aircraftsman, working in radio communications. During his military service Jack was stationed in a variety of locales, though he concentrated on places beginning with the letter 'B': Belgium, Berlin, and Bahrain. After demobbing, he participated in amateur dramatics with The Ellis Players, and worked for several years in Britain, but he had by then grown weary of 'B'-countries and decided to move on to the 'C's. Thus, in 1951, Jack emigrated to Canada.

In his new land he found employment as a script writer for Crawley Films Ltd. of Ottawa, and as a freelance writer of stage, television, and radio plays, as well as documentary scripts, until his boss decided that Jack would never be any good as a writer. It was not long afterwards that Jack left Crawley Films to pursue a career as a full-time freelancer, which obviously suited him better as he went on to write many successful scripts and other works. His short story "Where Did Rafe Madison Go?" was published in *Maclean's Magazine* in 1958 and, re-titled as *Breakthrough*, was televised in Canada and the USA on *General Motors Presents*, becoming the first Canadian television play simultaneously broadcast to both countries. His stage play *The Canvas Barricade* — about an artist who lives in a tent because he refuses to compromise with materialism — was the first original Canadian play to be performed at the Stratford Festival, in 1961. In 1962 he published his first novel, *Three Cheers for Me*, which proved to be the beginning of a series of nine volumes about Canadian First World War air-ace Bartholomew Wolfe Bandy. *Three Cheers for Me* won the Leacock Medal for Humour in 1963, but additional volumes did not appear until a decade later when a revised version of the book was published, along with a second volume, *That's Me in the Middle*, which won Jack a second Leacock Medal in 1974. He received a third award in 1980 for *Me Bandy, You Cissie*.

His other works include dozens of television, radio, and documentary scripts, as well as two non-fiction books, *Sinc, Betty and the Morning Man*, the story of radio station CFRB, and *Rogues, Rebels, and Geniuses*, a highly amusing and enlightening history of Canadian medicine. Jack returned to live in England in 1986, where he continued to work on additional volumes in the Bandy series. He died June 2, 2003. His final novel, *Stalin vs. Me*, was published posthumously in 2005.

The Lavochkin La-9
Cover Photo by Jaren Kohlis

PURISTS MAY WISH TO NOTE that although the aeroplane on the cover is a Lavochkin, like the one Bandy flies in Part II of *Stalin vs. Me*, it's actually a slightly later model. The Lavochkin La-9 was first flown in 1946, and so was a little too late to be Bandy's plane. While it doesn't say in *Stalin vs. Me* which Lavochkin Bandy was flying, it may have been the La-7, which was similar in size and power to the La-9, though to be strictly accurate, neither of those planes were two-seaters; for George Garanine to have had a seat behind Bandy's their plane must have actually been something like the two-seater La-7UTI trainer. But rather than hold out until we could find an La-7, or an La-7UTI, we decided that Jaren's photo was too perfect for the cover to pass up, and luckily for us he was kind enough to grant permission to use it.

The Lavochkins are named for Russian aircraft designer Semyon Alekseyevich Lavochkin (1900-1960), who headed Soviet design bureau OKB-301 from 1937 until his death. During WWII, his team produced numerous successful planes, including the La-7 flown by the Soviets' leading ace, Ivan Nikitovich Kozhedub, who downed 62 enemy aircraft during the course of the war. Unfortunately, he was forced to shoot down a couple of American P-51 Mustangs as well, when they attacked him thinking his plane was a German FW-190. Such is the confusion of air combat. Perhaps the most surprising victory in an La-7 was Kozhedub's destruction of an Me-262, a jet capable of a speed nearly 200 km/h faster than the La-7. Kozhedub modestly attributed this to a mistake on the part of the German pilot — the Messerschmitt tried to out-turn the Lavochkin, something it simply couldn't do, despite its speed advantage. After the war, Semyon Lavochkin's efforts in jet design failed to live up to the fame of his earlier work, and OKB-301 changed its focus to creating new missiles instead. With Lavochkin's death in 1960, and the cancellation of the Burya intercontinental cruise missile (which Lavochkin had hoped to develop into a re-usable space shuttle), OKB-301 found itself lacking a clear purpose. But it was re-tasked in 1965 under Georgi Nikolayevich Babakin as a bureau for the design of space probes, which were sent to the moon, Mars, and Venus. The Lavochkin name is now carried by the Lavochkin Research and Production Association of Russia, which continues to produce spacecraft, including the Cosmos 1 solar sail launched in 2005 by the Planetary Society.

The particular La-9 shown on the cover served in the People's Republic of China air force during the Korean War, before being retired to a Chinese museum in the late fifties. It was purchased by the Old Flying Machine Company, England, (www.ofmc.co.uk) in 1996 and restored by Pioneer Aero Restorations of New Zealand (www.pioneeraero.co.nz). The engine was overhauled by W-Motor Service of Bubovice in the Czech Republic, and the propeller was made by Avia, also of the Czech Republic. The plane now resides at the Old Flying Machine Company at Duxford, UK.

Also from Sybertooth Inc.
www.sybertooth.ca/publishing

QUESTS AND KINGDOMS
A Grown-Up's Guide to Children's Fantasy Literature

K.V. Johansen

FANTASY HAS BECOME AN INCREASINGLY POPULAR GENRE of children's literature in recent years; *Quests and Kingdoms* provides a basis from which an adult unfamiliar with the genre of children's fantasy literature may explore it. *Quests* is an historical survey for the interested general reader, which will be of great practical value to library and education professionals as well. Though the aim is to give adults concerned with bringing children (or teens) and books together a familiarity with the children's fantasy genre and its history, for those who already know and love the classics of children's fantasy *Quests* will be an introduction to works and authors they may have missed.

Taking a chronological approach, *Quests* begins with the fairy-tale collections of d'Aulnoy, Perrault, and the Grimms and works its way up to the novels of J.K. Rowling and Garth Nix, covering over three centuries of fantasy read by children. The lives of 95 authors are looked at and placed in historical context, while their works are introduced through both synopses and analysis. *Quests* also includes chapters on Tolkien, retellings of traditional stories, and King Arthur and Robin Hood. More than 500 works are discussed, and the thorough index makes the book a practical reference resource as well as a history and an introduction to the best in the genre.

'HERE IS A MAGICAL THING, a reference book with a heart and soul. Brimming over with ideas, as well as facts and figures, the writing is elegant and the author's enthusiasm contagious. Here, too, a noble defence of fantasy and its literary value.'

O.R.Melling
***author of* The Golden Book of Faerie**

'JOHANSEN BRINGS A SCHOLAR'S ERUDITION and a child's delight to the field of children's fantasy. Her thoughtful survey elevates fantasy from guilty pleasure to moral education, and reveals it to be not a recent marketing-driven fad, but an ancient and unbreakable strand of human creativity. If you know nothing about the genre, this book will turn you into an aficionado; if you think you've read everything, you'll find new gems here, and old ones glowing with a new light. For teachers, parents, anyone who wants to uncover the wonder of reading,* Quests and Kingdoms *is a pirate's treasure map.'

Tristanne J. Connolly, St. Jerome's University

K.V. JOHANSEN has Master's Degrees in Medieval Studies (Toronto) and English (McMaster). The author of a number of children's books, she held the 2001 Eileen Wallace Research Fellowship in Children's Literature from the Eileen Wallace Collection at the University of New Brunswick. She also received the 2004 Frances E. Russell Award for research in children's literature from the Canadian section of IBBY, the International Board on Books for Young People.

462pp • $30.00 (US) • £20.00 (UK) • ISBN 0-9688024-4-3 • Trade paperback

CPSIA information can be obtained
at www.ICGtesting.com
Printed in the USA
LVHW041606200920
666586LV00002BA/199

9 780968 802472